MARVEL-VERSE
SPIDER-WOMAN

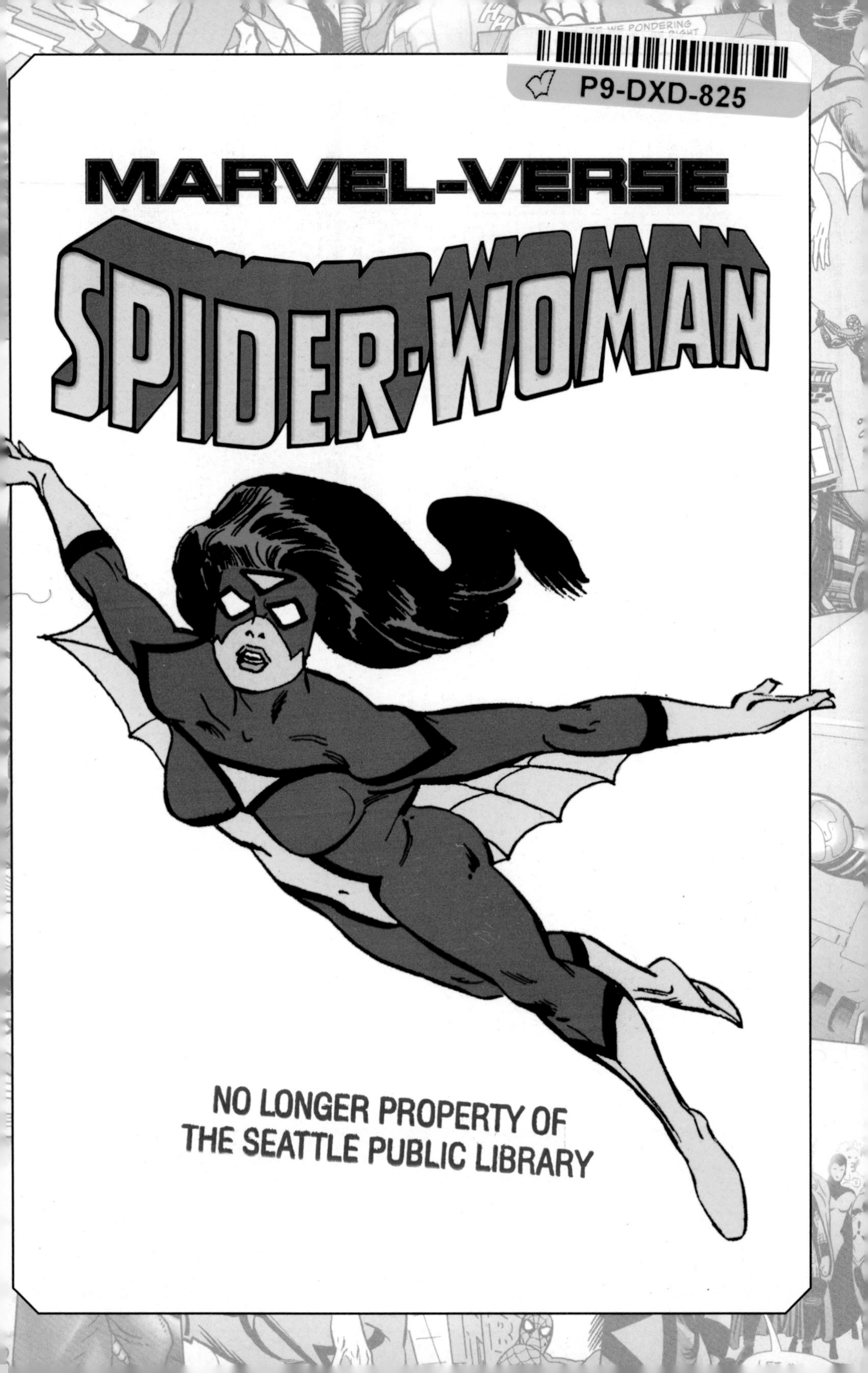

MARVEL-VERSE
SPIDER-WOMAN

SPIDER-WOMAN #1

WRITER: **MARV WOLFMAN**

PENCILER: **CARMINE INFANTINO**

INKER: **TONY DeZUNIGA**

COLORIST: **GLYNIS OLIVER**

LETTERER: **JOE ROSEN**

EDITOR: **MARV WOLFMAN**

SPIDER-WOMAN #20

WRITER: **MARK GRUENWALD**

CO-PLOTTER: **STEVEN GRANT**

PENCILER: **FRANK SPRINGER**

INKER: **MIKE ESPOSITO**

COLORIST: **NEL YOMTOV**

LETTERER: **JOHN COSTANZA**

EDITOR: **JIM SHOOTER**

MARVEL-VERSE: SPIDER-WOMAN. Contains material originally published in magazine form as SPIDER-WOMAN (1978) #1 and #20, A+X (2012) #8, and AVENGERS ASSEMBLE (2012) #18-19. First printing 2023. ISBN 978-1-302-95203-7. Published by MARVEL WORLDWIDE, INC., a subsidiary of MARVEL ENTERTAINMENT, LLC. OFFICE OF PUBLICATION: 1290 Avenue of the Americas, New York, NY 10104. © 2023 MARVEL No similarity between any of the names, characters, persons, and/or institutions in this book with those of any living or dead person or institution is intended, and any such similarity which may exist is purely coincidental. **Printed in Canada.** KEVIN FEIGE, Chief Creative Officer; DAN BUCKLEY, President, Marvel Entertainment; DAVID BOGART, Associate Publisher & SVP of Talent Affairs; TOM BREVOORT, VP, Executive Editor; NICK LOWE, Executive Editor, VP of Content, Digital Publishing; DAVID GABRIEL, VP of Print & Digital Publishing; SVEN LARSEN, VP of Licensed Publishing; MARK ANNUNZIATO, VP of Planning & Forecasting; JEFF YOUNGQUIST, VP of Production & Special Projects; ALEX MORALES, Director of Publishing Operations; DAN EDINGTON, Director of Editorial Operations; RICKEY PURDIN, Director of Talent Relations; JENNIFER GRÜNWALD, Director of Production & Special Projects; SUSAN CRESPI, Production Manager; STAN LEE, Chairman Emeritus. For information regarding advertising in Marvel Comics or on Marvel.com, please contact Vit DeBellis, Custom Solutions & Integrated Advertising Manager, at vdebellis@marvel.com. For Marvel subscription inquiries, please call 888-511-5480. **Manufactured between 4/28/2023 and 5/30/2023 by SOLISCO PRINTERS, SCOTT, QC, CANADA.**

10 9 8 7 6 5 4 3 2 1

A + X #8

WRITER: **GERRY DUGGAN**

PENCILER: **SALVADOR LARROCA**

COLORIST: **DAVID OCAMPO**

LETTERER: VC's **CLAYTON COWLES**

COVER ART: **SALVADOR LARROCA** & **DAVID OCAMPO**

ASSOCIATE EDITOR: **JORDAN D. WHITE**

EDITOR: **NICK LOWE**

AVENGERS ASSEMBLE #18-19

WRITERS: **KELLY SUE DeCONNICK** WITH **JEN VAN METER** (#19)

PENCILER: **BARRY KITSON**

INKERS: **BARRY KITSON** WITH **GARY ERSKINE** (#18) AND **RICK MAGYAR, JAY LEISTEN** & **DREW GERACI** (#19)

COLORISTS: **NOLAN WOODARD** WITH **JAY DAVID RAMOS** (#18)

LETTERER: VC's **CLAYTON COWLES**

COVER ART: **JORGE MOLINA**

ASSISTANT EDITOR: **JAKE THOMAS**

EDITOR: **LAUREN SANKOVITCH**

EXECUTIVE EDITOR: **TOM BREVOORT**

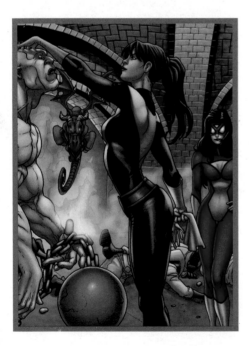

COLLECTION EDITOR: **DANIEL KIRCHHOFFER** ASSISTANT MANAGING EDITOR: **MAIA LOY**
ASSOCIATE MANAGER, TALENT RELATIONS: **LISA MONTALBANO** DIRECTOR, PRODUCTION & SPECIAL PROJECTS: **JENNIFER GRÜNWALD**
ASSOCIATE MANAGER, DIGITAL ASSETS: **JOE HOCHSTEIN** MASTERWORKS EDITOR: **CORY SEDLMEIER**
VP PRODUCTION & SPECIAL PROJECTS: **JEFF YOUNGQUIST** RESEARCH: **JESS HARROLD**
BOOK DESIGNER: **STACIE ZUCKER** MANAGER & SENIOR DESIGNER: **ADAM DEL RE** LEAD DESIGNER: **JAY BOWEN**
SVP PRINT, SALES & MARKETING: **DAVID GABRIEL** EDITOR IN CHIEF: **C.B. CEBULSKI**

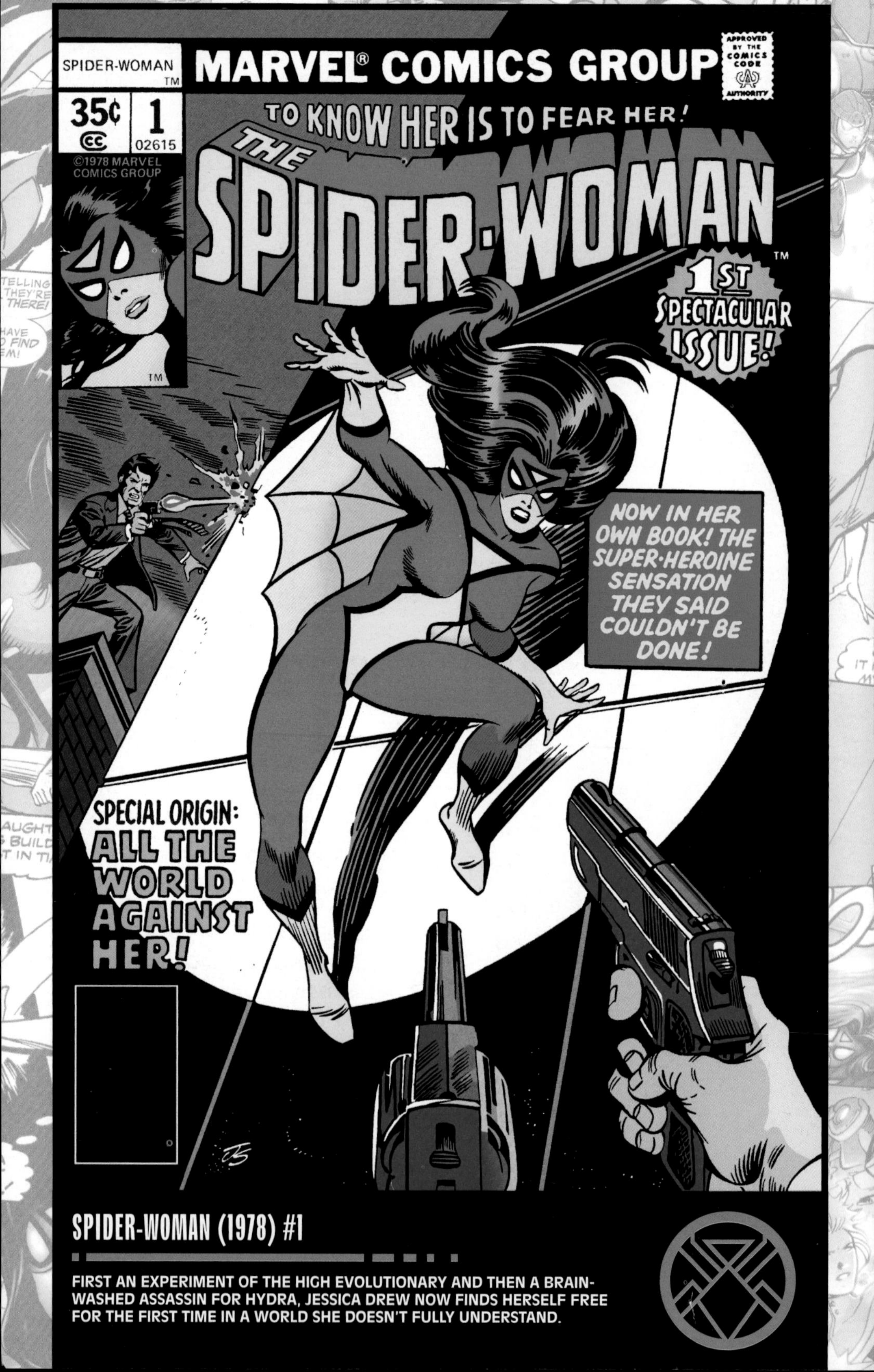
SPIDER-WOMAN
TM
MARVEL® COMICS GROUP
APPROVED BY THE COMICS CODE AUTHORITY
35¢
1
02615
©1978 MARVEL COMICS GROUP
TO KNOW HER IS TO FEAR HER!
THE SPIDER-WOMAN
TM
1ST SPECTACULAR ISSUE!
NOW IN HER OWN BOOK! THE SUPER-HEROINE SENSATION THEY SAID COULDN'T BE DONE!
SPECIAL ORIGIN:
ALL THE WORLD AGAINST HER!

SPIDER-WOMAN (1978) #1

FIRST AN EXPERIMENT OF THE HIGH EVOLUTIONARY AND THEN A BRAIN-WASHED ASSASSIN FOR HYDRA, JESSICA DREW NOW FINDS HERSELF FREE FOR THE FIRST TIME IN A WORLD SHE DOESN'T FULLY UNDERSTAND.

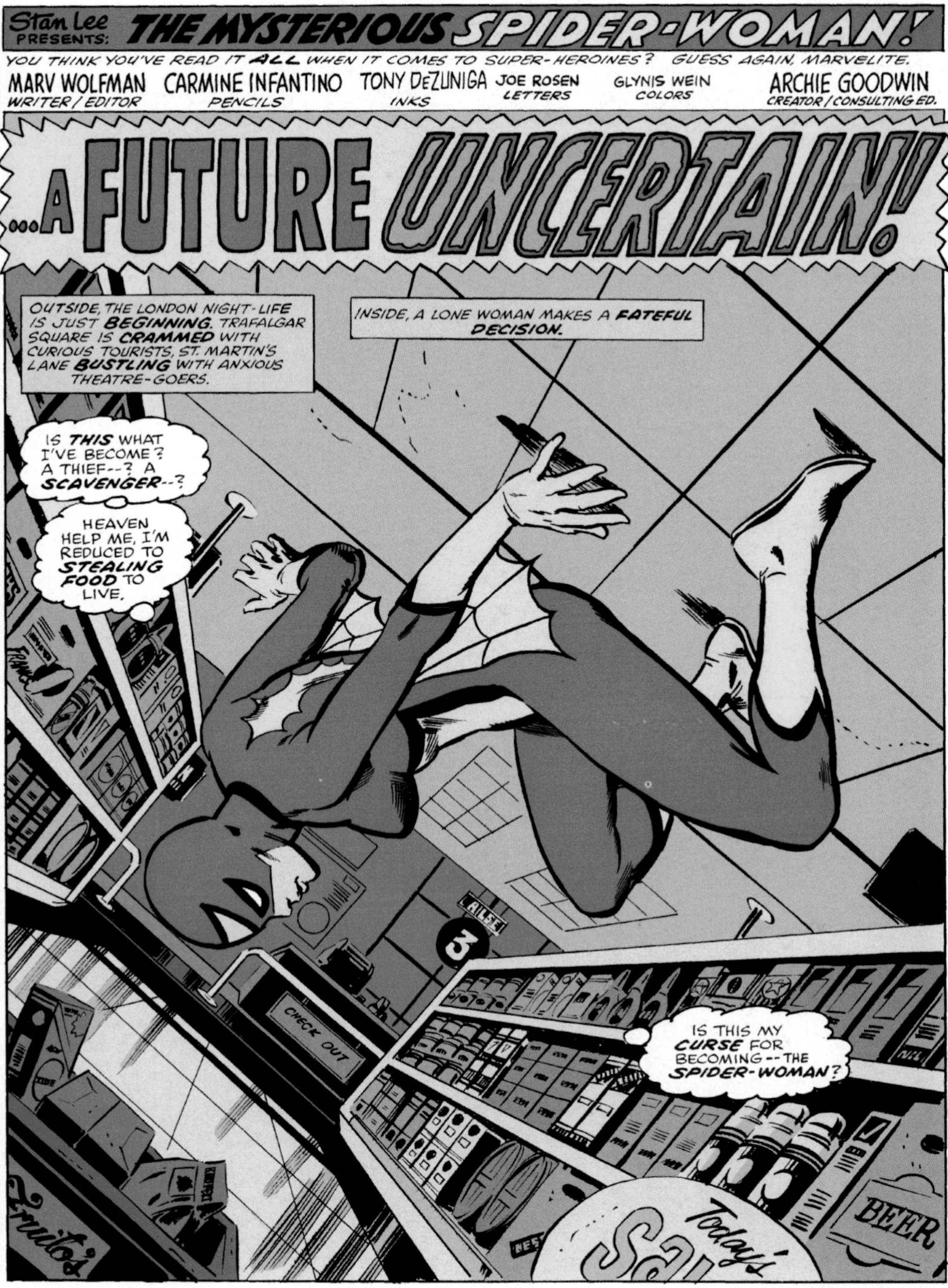

Stan Lee PRESENTS: THE MYSTERIOUS SPIDER-WOMAN!
YOU THINK YOU'VE READ IT ALL WHEN IT COMES TO SUPER-HEROINES? GUESS AGAIN, MARVELITE.
MARV WOLFMAN WRITER / EDITOR
CARMINE INFANTINO PENCILS
TONY DeZUNIGA INKS
JOE ROSEN LETTERS
GLYNIS WEIN COLORS
ARCHIE GOODWIN CREATOR / CONSULTING ED.
...A FUTURE UNCERTAIN!
OUTSIDE, THE LONDON NIGHT-LIFE IS JUST BEGINNING. TRAFALGAR SQUARE IS CRAMMED WITH CURIOUS TOURISTS, ST. MARTIN'S LANE BUSTLING WITH ANXIOUS THEATRE-GOERS.
INSIDE, A LONE WOMAN MAKES A FATEFUL DECISION.
IS THIS WHAT I'VE BECOME? A THIEF--? A SCAVENGER--?
HEAVEN HELP ME, I'M REDUCED TO STEALING FOOD TO LIVE.
AISLE 3
CHECK OUT
IS THIS MY CURSE FOR BECOMING--THE SPIDER-WOMAN?
BEER
Today's

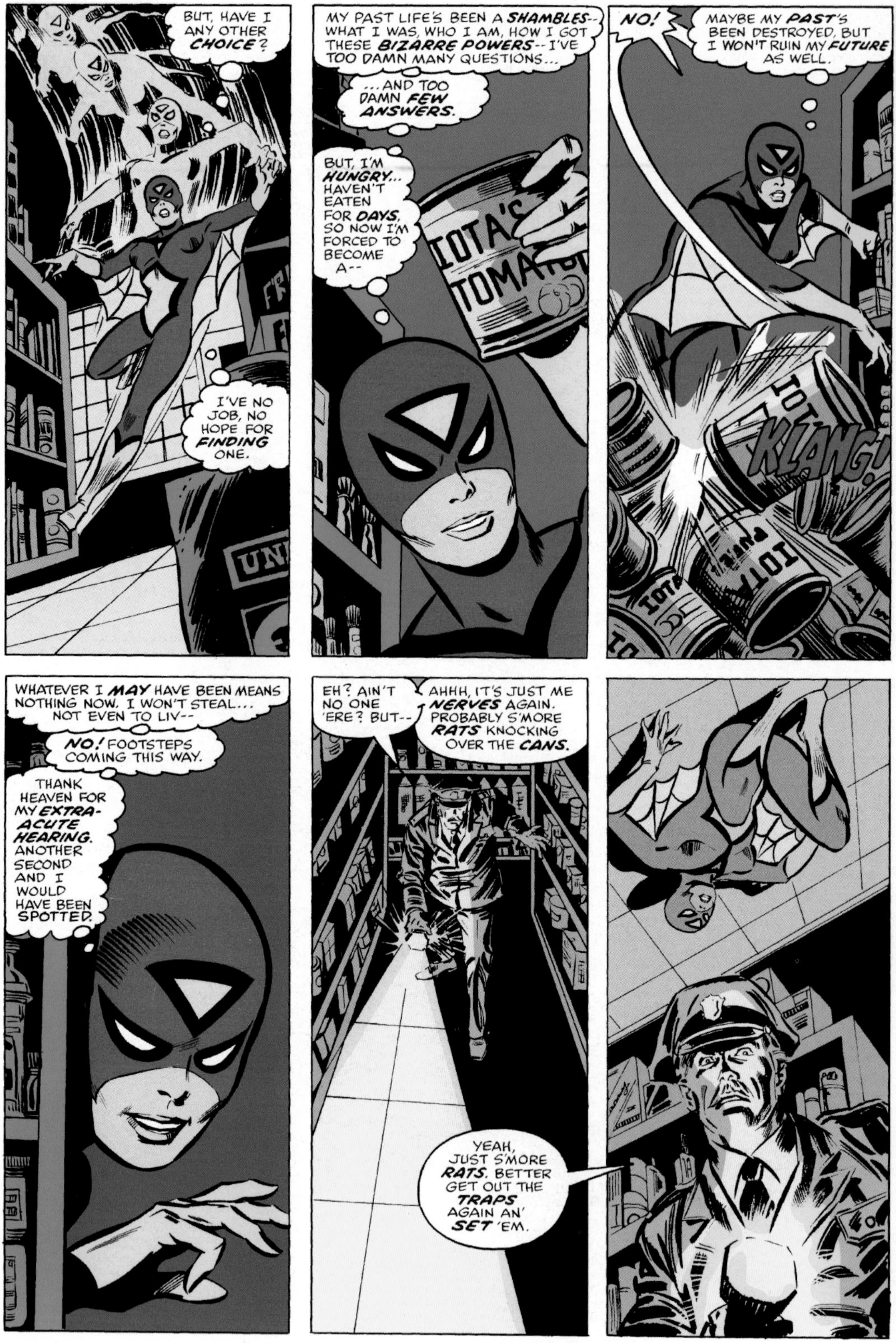
BUT, HAVE I ANY OTHER CHOICE?
I'VE NO JOB, NO HOPE FOR FINDING ONE.
MY PAST LIFE'S BEEN A SHAMBLES-- WHAT I WAS, WHO I AM, HOW I GOT THESE BIZARRE POWERS-- I'VE TOO DAMN MANY QUESTIONS...
...AND TOO DAMN FEW ANSWERS.
BUT, I'M HUNGRY... HAVEN'T EATEN FOR DAYS, SO NOW I'M FORCED TO BECOME A--
IOTA'S TOMA
NO!
MAYBE MY PAST'S BEEN DESTROYED, BUT I WON'T RUIN MY FUTURE AS WELL.
KLANG!
WHATEVER I MAY HAVE BEEN MEANS NOTHING NOW. I WON'T STEAL... NOT EVEN TO LIV--
NO! FOOTSTEPS COMING THIS WAY.
THANK HEAVEN FOR MY EXTRA-ACUTE HEARING. ANOTHER SECOND AND I WOULD HAVE BEEN SPOTTED.
EH? AIN'T NO ONE 'ERE? BUT--
AHHH, IT'S JUST ME NERVES AGAIN. PROBABLY S'MORE RATS KNOCKING OVER THE CANS.
YEAH, JUST S'MORE RATS. BETTER GET OUT THE TRAPS AGAIN AN' SET 'EM.

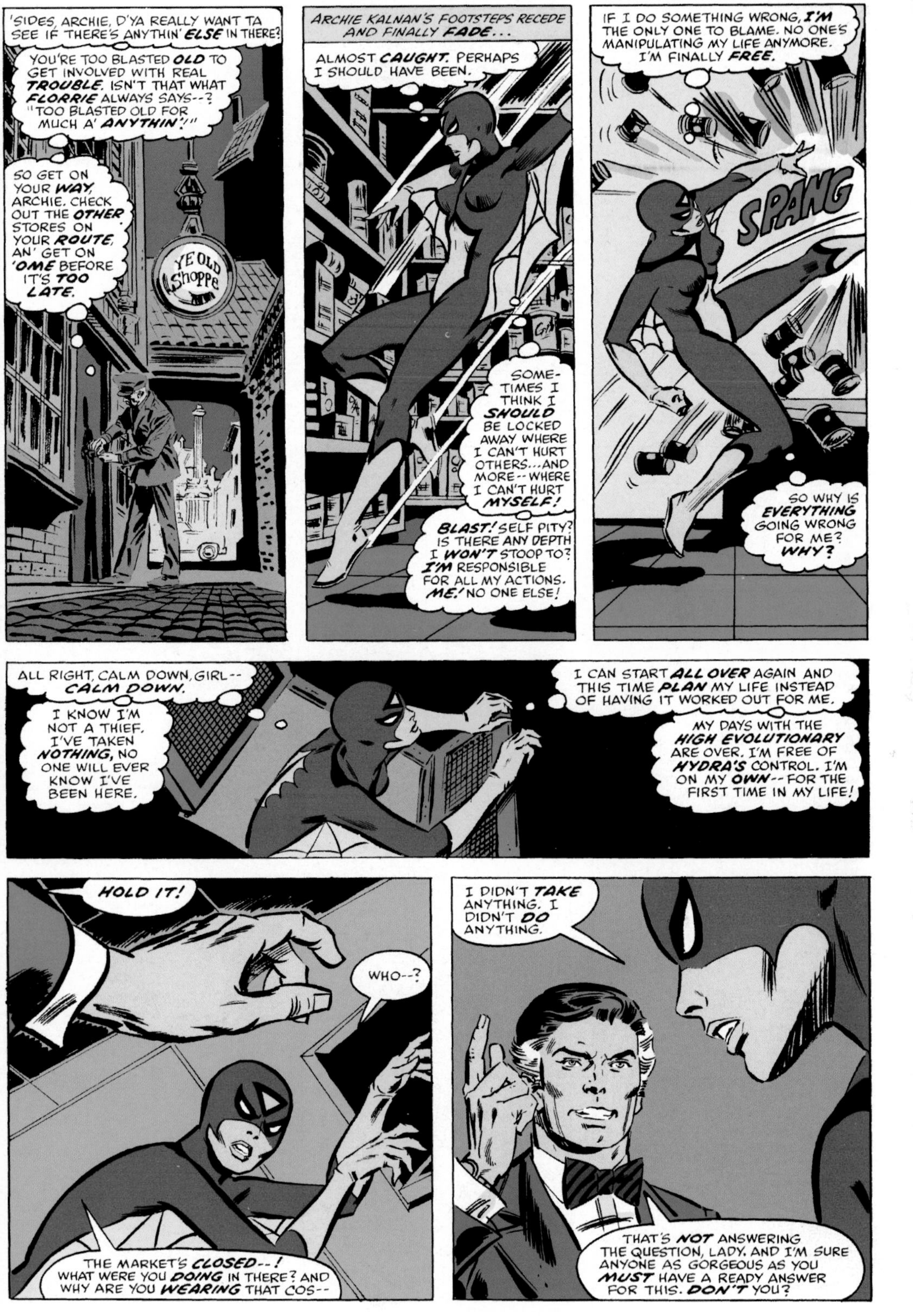
'SIDES, ARCHIE, D'YA REALLY WANT TA SEE IF THERE'S ANYTHIN' ELSE IN THERE?
YOU'RE TOO BLASTED OLD TO GET INVOLVED WITH REAL TROUBLE. ISN'T THAT WHAT FLORRIE ALWAYS SAYS--? "TOO BLASTED OLD FOR MUCH A' ANYTHIN'!"
SO GET ON YOUR WAY, ARCHIE. CHECK OUT THE OTHER STORES ON YOUR ROUTE, AN' GET ON 'OME BEFORE IT'S TOO LATE.
YE OLD Shoppe
ARCHIE KALNAN'S FOOTSTEPS RECEDE AND FINALLY FADE...
ALMOST CAUGHT. PERHAPS I SHOULD HAVE BEEN.
SOMETIMES I THINK I SHOULD BE LOCKED AWAY WHERE I CAN'T HURT OTHERS...AND MORE--WHERE I CAN'T HURT MYSELF!
BLAST! SELF PITY? IS THERE ANY DEPTH I WON'T STOOP TO? I'M RESPONSIBLE FOR ALL MY ACTIONS. ME! NO ONE ELSE!
IF I DO SOMETHING WRONG, I'M THE ONLY ONE TO BLAME. NO ONE'S MANIPULATING MY LIFE ANYMORE. I'M FINALLY FREE.
SPANG
SO WHY IS EVERYTHING GOING WRONG FOR ME? WHY?
ALL RIGHT, CALM DOWN, GIRL-- CALM DOWN.
I KNOW I'M NOT A THIEF. I'VE TAKEN NOTHING, NO ONE WILL EVER KNOW I'VE BEEN HERE.
I CAN START ALL OVER AGAIN AND THIS TIME PLAN MY LIFE INSTEAD OF HAVING IT WORKED OUT FOR ME.
MY DAYS WITH THE HIGH EVOLUTIONARY ARE OVER. I'M FREE OF HYDRA'S CONTROL. I'M ON MY OWN--FOR THE FIRST TIME IN MY LIFE!
HOLD IT!
WHO--?
THE MARKET'S CLOSED--! WHAT WERE YOU DOING IN THERE? AND WHY ARE YOU WEARING THAT COS--
I DIDN'T TAKE ANYTHING. I DIDN'T DO ANYTHING.
THAT'S NOT ANSWERING THE QUESTION, LADY. AND I'M SURE ANYONE AS GORGEOUS AS YOU MUST HAVE A READY ANSWER FOR THIS. DON'T YOU?

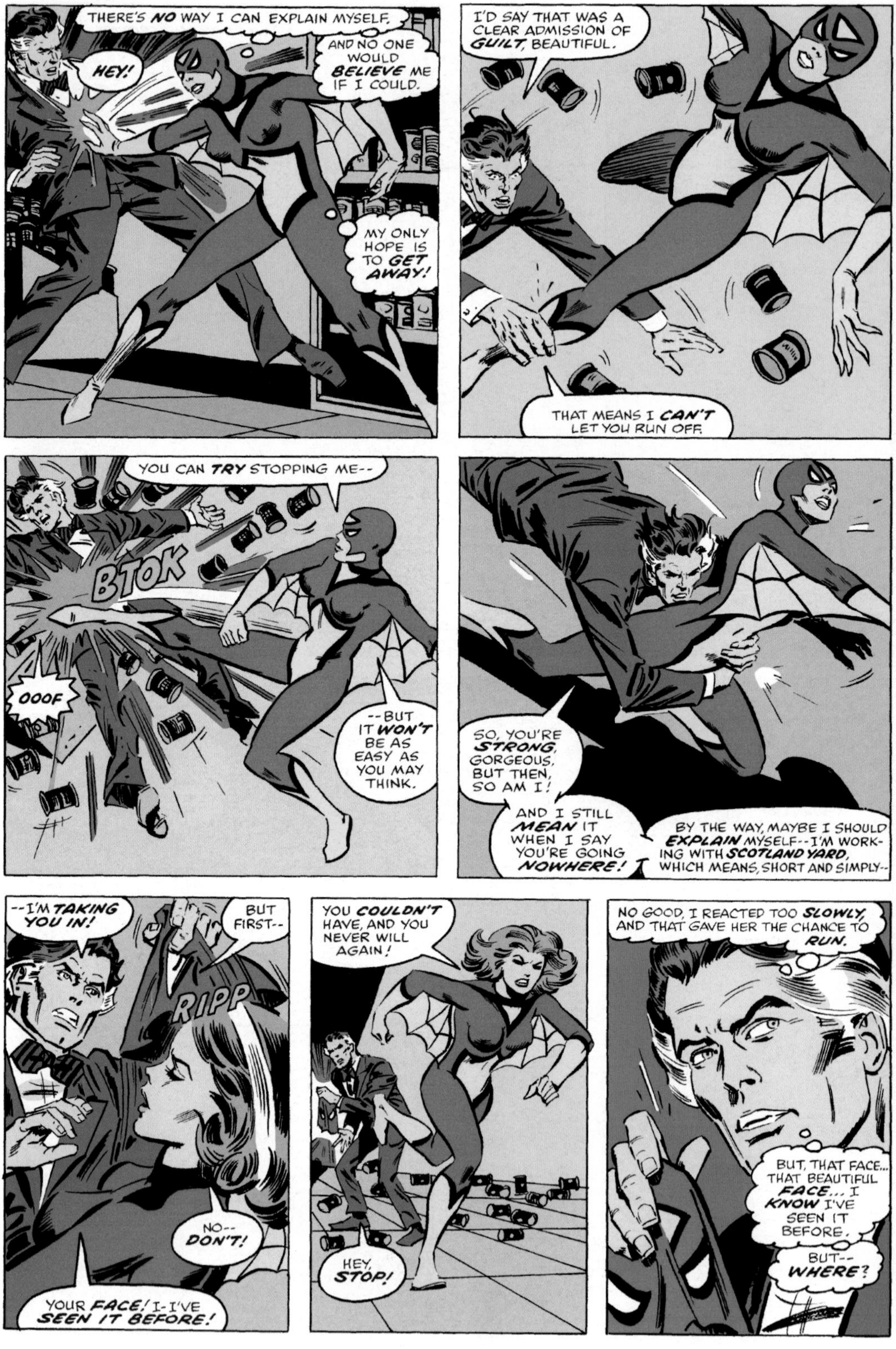

THERE'S NO WAY I CAN EXPLAIN MYSELF.
HEY!
AND NO ONE WOULD BELIEVE ME IF I COULD.
MY ONLY HOPE IS TO GET AWAY!
I'D SAY THAT WAS A CLEAR ADMISSION OF GUILT, BEAUTIFUL.
THAT MEANS I CAN'T LET YOU RUN OFF.
YOU CAN TRY STOPPING ME--
BTOK
OOOF
--BUT IT WON'T BE AS EASY AS YOU MAY THINK.
SO, YOU'RE STRONG, GORGEOUS, BUT THEN, SO AM I!
AND I STILL MEAN IT WHEN I SAY YOU'RE GOING NOWHERE!
BY THE WAY, MAYBE I SHOULD EXPLAIN MYSELF--I'M WORKING WITH SCOTLAND YARD, WHICH MEANS, SHORT AND SIMPLY--
--I'M TAKING YOU IN!
BUT FIRST--
RIPP
NO-- DON'T!
YOUR FACE! I-I'VE SEEN IT BEFORE!
YOU COULDN'T HAVE, AND YOU NEVER WILL AGAIN!
HEY, STOP!
NO GOOD, I REACTED TOO SLOWLY, AND THAT GAVE HER THE CHANCE TO RUN.
BUT, THAT FACE... THAT BEAUTIFUL FACE... I KNOW I'VE SEEN IT BEFORE.
BUT-- WHERE?

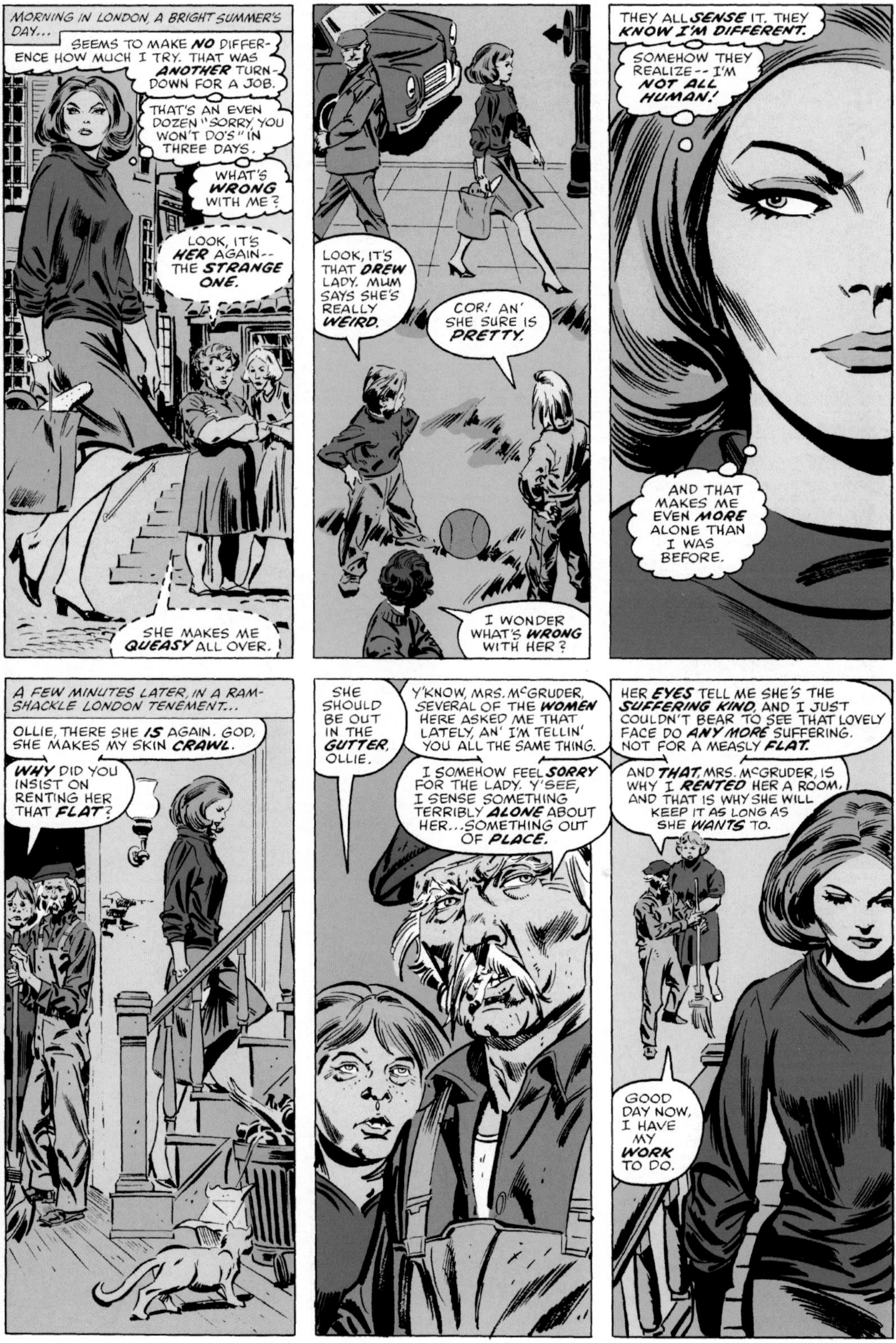
MORNING IN LONDON, A BRIGHT SUMMER'S DAY...
SEEMS TO MAKE NO DIFFERENCE HOW MUCH I TRY. THAT WAS ANOTHER TURN-DOWN FOR A JOB.
THAT'S AN EVEN DOZEN "SORRY, YOU WON'T DO'S" IN THREE DAYS.
WHAT'S WRONG WITH ME?
LOOK, IT'S HER AGAIN-- THE STRANGE ONE.
SHE MAKES ME QUEASY ALL OVER.
LOOK, IT'S THAT DREW LADY. MUM SAYS SHE'S REALLY WEIRD.
COR! AN' SHE SURE IS PRETTY.
I WONDER WHAT'S WRONG WITH HER?
THEY ALL SENSE IT. THEY KNOW I'M DIFFERENT.
SOMEHOW THEY REALIZE-- I'M NOT ALL HUMAN!
AND THAT MAKES ME EVEN MORE ALONE THAN I WAS BEFORE.
A FEW MINUTES LATER, IN A RAMSHACKLE LONDON TENEMENT...
OLLIE, THERE SHE IS AGAIN. GOD, SHE MAKES MY SKIN CRAWL.
WHY DID YOU INSIST ON RENTING HER THAT FLAT?
SHE SHOULD BE OUT IN THE GUTTER, OLLIE.
Y'KNOW, MRS. McGRUDER, SEVERAL OF THE WOMEN HERE ASKED ME THAT LATELY, AN' I'M TELLIN' YOU ALL THE SAME THING.
I SOMEHOW FEEL SORRY FOR THE LADY. Y'SEE, I SENSE SOMETHING TERRIBLY ALONE ABOUT HER...SOMETHING OUT OF PLACE.
HER EYES TELL ME SHE'S THE SUFFERING KIND, AND I JUST COULDN'T BEAR TO SEE THAT LOVELY FACE DO ANY MORE SUFFERING. NOT FOR A MEASLY FLAT.
AND THAT, MRS. McGRUDER, IS WHY I RENTED HER A ROOM, AND THAT IS WHY SHE WILL KEEP IT AS LONG AS SHE WANTS TO.
GOOD DAY NOW, I HAVE MY WORK TO DO.

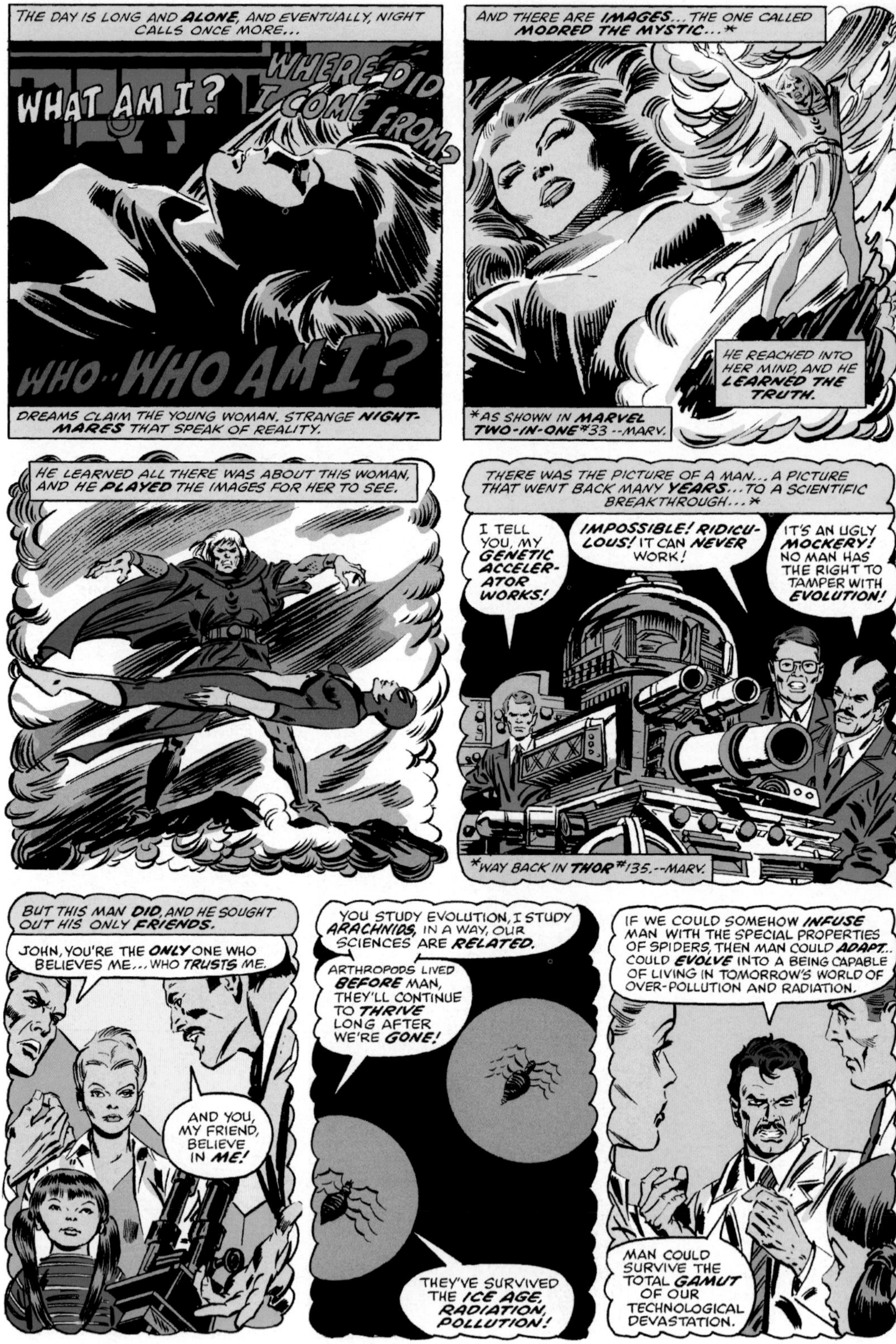

THE DAY IS LONG AND ALONE, AND EVENTUALLY, NIGHT CALLS ONCE MORE...
WHAT AM I?
WHERE DID I COME FROM?
WHO.. WHO AM I?
DREAMS CLAIM THE YOUNG WOMAN. STRANGE NIGHT-MARES THAT SPEAK OF REALITY.
AND THERE ARE IMAGES... THE ONE CALLED MODRED THE MYSTIC...*
HE REACHED INTO HER MIND, AND HE LEARNED THE TRUTH.
*AS SHOWN IN MARVEL TWO-IN-ONE #33 --MARV.
HE LEARNED ALL THERE WAS ABOUT THIS WOMAN, AND HE PLAYED THE IMAGES FOR HER TO SEE.
THERE WAS THE PICTURE OF A MAN... A PICTURE THAT WENT BACK MANY YEARS... TO A SCIENTIFIC BREAKTHROUGH...*
I TELL YOU, MY GENETIC ACCELER-ATOR WORKS!
IMPOSSIBLE! RIDICU-LOUS! IT CAN NEVER WORK!
IT'S AN UGLY MOCKERY! NO MAN HAS THE RIGHT TO TAMPER WITH EVOLUTION!
*WAY BACK IN THOR #135.--MARV.
BUT THIS MAN DID, AND HE SOUGHT OUT HIS ONLY FRIENDS.
JOHN, YOU'RE THE ONLY ONE WHO BELIEVES ME... WHO TRUSTS ME.
AND YOU, MY FRIEND, BELIEVE IN ME!
YOU STUDY EVOLUTION, I STUDY ARACHNIDS, IN A WAY, OUR SCIENCES ARE RELATED.
ARTHROPODS LIVED BEFORE MAN, THEY'LL CONTINUE TO THRIVE LONG AFTER WE'RE GONE!
THEY'VE SURVIVED THE ICE AGE, RADIATION, POLLUTION!
IF WE COULD SOMEHOW INFUSE MAN WITH THE SPECIAL PROPERTIES OF SPIDERS, THEN MAN COULD ADAPT... COULD EVOLVE INTO A BEING CAPABLE OF LIVING IN TOMORROW'S WORLD OF OVER-POLLUTION AND RADIATION.
MAN COULD SURVIVE THE TOTAL GAMUT OF OUR TECHNOLOGICAL DEVASTATION.

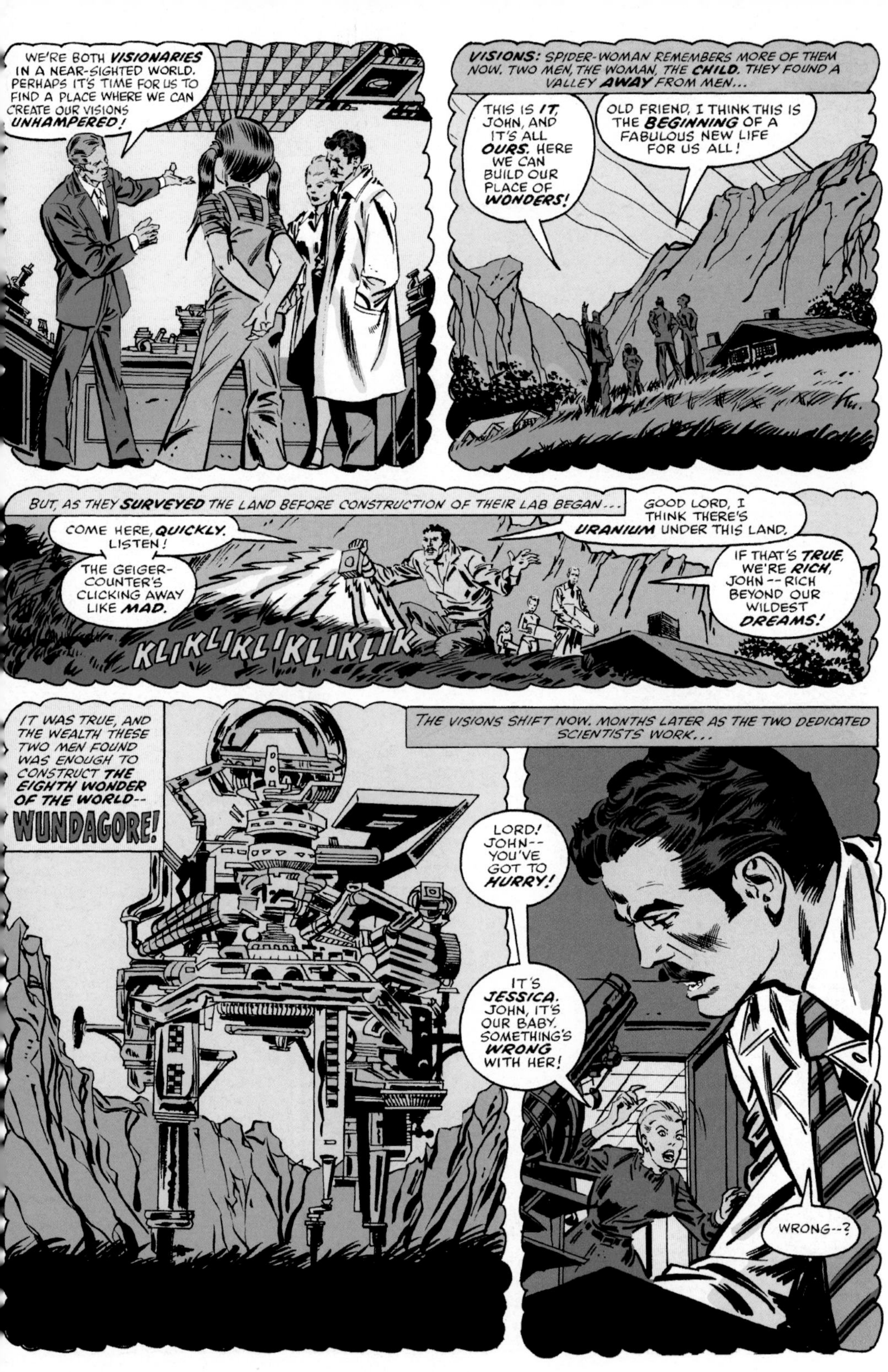
WE'RE BOTH VISIONARIES IN A NEAR-SIGHTED WORLD. PERHAPS IT'S TIME FOR US TO FIND A PLACE WHERE WE CAN CREATE OUR VISIONS UNHAMPERED!
VISIONS: SPIDER-WOMAN REMEMBERS MORE OF THEM NOW. TWO MEN, THE WOMAN, THE CHILD. THEY FOUND A VALLEY AWAY FROM MEN...
THIS IS IT, JOHN, AND IT'S ALL OURS. HERE WE CAN BUILD OUR PLACE OF WONDERS!
OLD FRIEND, I THINK THIS IS THE BEGINNING OF A FABULOUS NEW LIFE FOR US ALL!
BUT, AS THEY SURVEYED THE LAND BEFORE CONSTRUCTION OF THEIR LAB BEGAN...
COME HERE, QUICKLY. LISTEN!
THE GEIGER-COUNTER'S CLICKING AWAY LIKE MAD.
KLIKLIKLIKLIKLIK
GOOD LORD, I THINK THERE'S URANIUM UNDER THIS LAND.
IF THAT'S TRUE, WE'RE RICH, JOHN -- RICH BEYOND OUR WILDEST DREAMS!
IT WAS TRUE, AND THE WEALTH THESE TWO MEN FOUND WAS ENOUGH TO CONSTRUCT THE EIGHTH WONDER OF THE WORLD--
WUNDAGORE!
THE VISIONS SHIFT NOW. MONTHS LATER AS THE TWO DEDICATED SCIENTISTS WORK...
LORD! JOHN-- YOU'VE GOT TO HURRY!
IT'S JESSICA. JOHN, IT'S OUR BABY. SOMETHING'S WRONG WITH HER!
WRONG--?

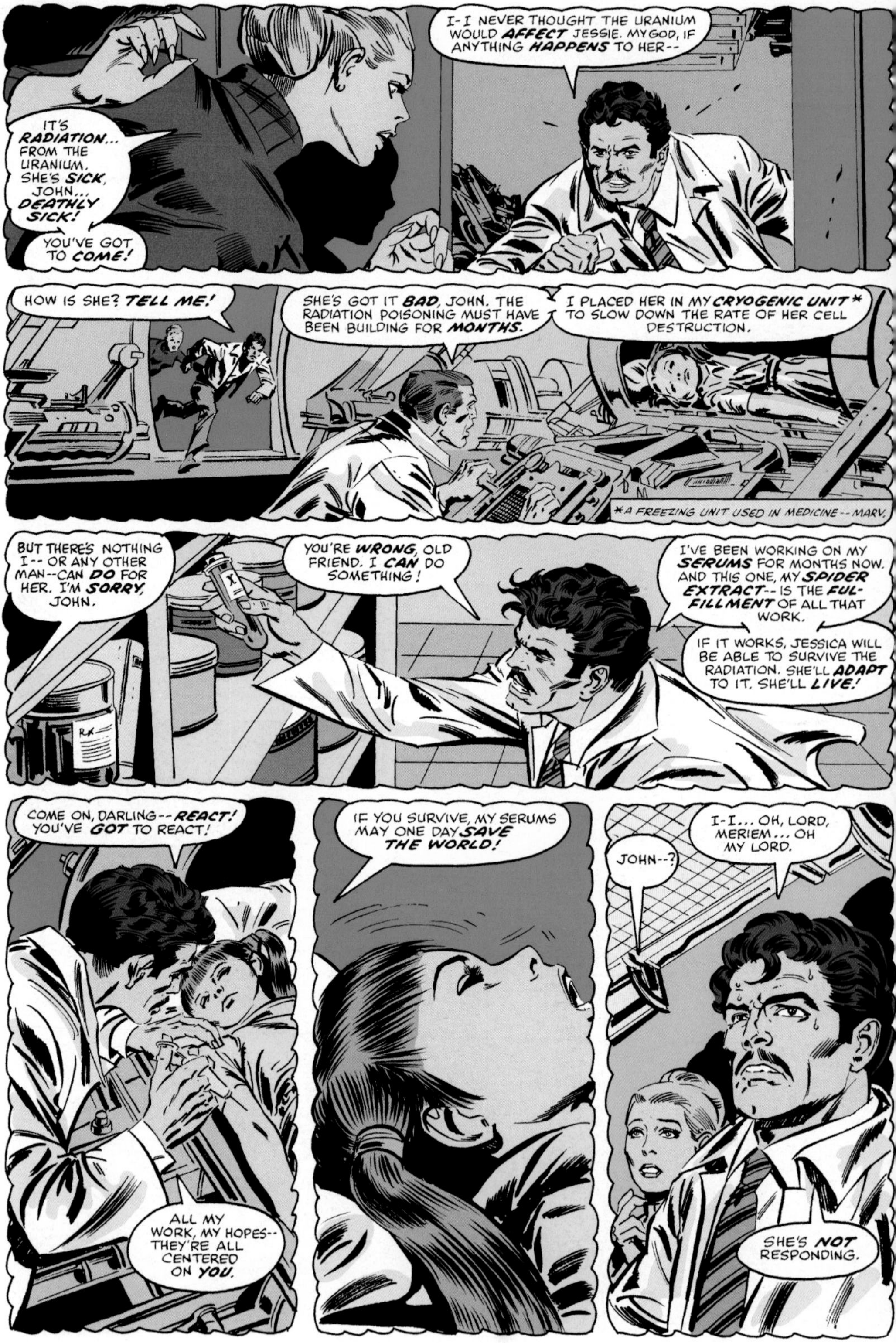
IT'S RADIATION... FROM THE URANIUM. SHE'S SICK, JOHN... DEATHLY SICK!
YOU'VE GOT TO COME!
I-I NEVER THOUGHT THE URANIUM WOULD AFFECT JESSIE. MY GOD, IF ANYTHING HAPPENS TO HER--
HOW IS SHE? TELL ME!
SHE'S GOT IT BAD, JOHN. THE RADIATION POISONING MUST HAVE BEEN BUILDING FOR MONTHS.
I PLACED HER IN MY CRYOGENIC UNIT* TO SLOW DOWN THE RATE OF HER CELL DESTRUCTION.
*A FREEZING UNIT USED IN MEDICINE--MARV.
BUT THERE'S NOTHING I-- OR ANY OTHER MAN--CAN DO FOR HER. I'M SORRY, JOHN.
YOU'RE WRONG, OLD FRIEND. I CAN DO SOMETHING!
I'VE BEEN WORKING ON MY SERUMS FOR MONTHS NOW. AND THIS ONE, MY SPIDER EXTRACT-- IS THE FULFILLMENT OF ALL THAT WORK.
IF IT WORKS, JESSICA WILL BE ABLE TO SURVIVE THE RADIATION. SHE'LL ADAPT TO IT. SHE'LL LIVE!
COME ON, DARLING--REACT! YOU'VE GOT TO REACT!
ALL MY WORK, MY HOPES-- THEY'RE ALL CENTERED ON YOU.
IF YOU SURVIVE, MY SERUMS MAY ONE DAY SAVE THE WORLD!
JOHN--?
I-I... OH, LORD, MERIEM... OH MY LORD.
SHE'S NOT RESPONDING.

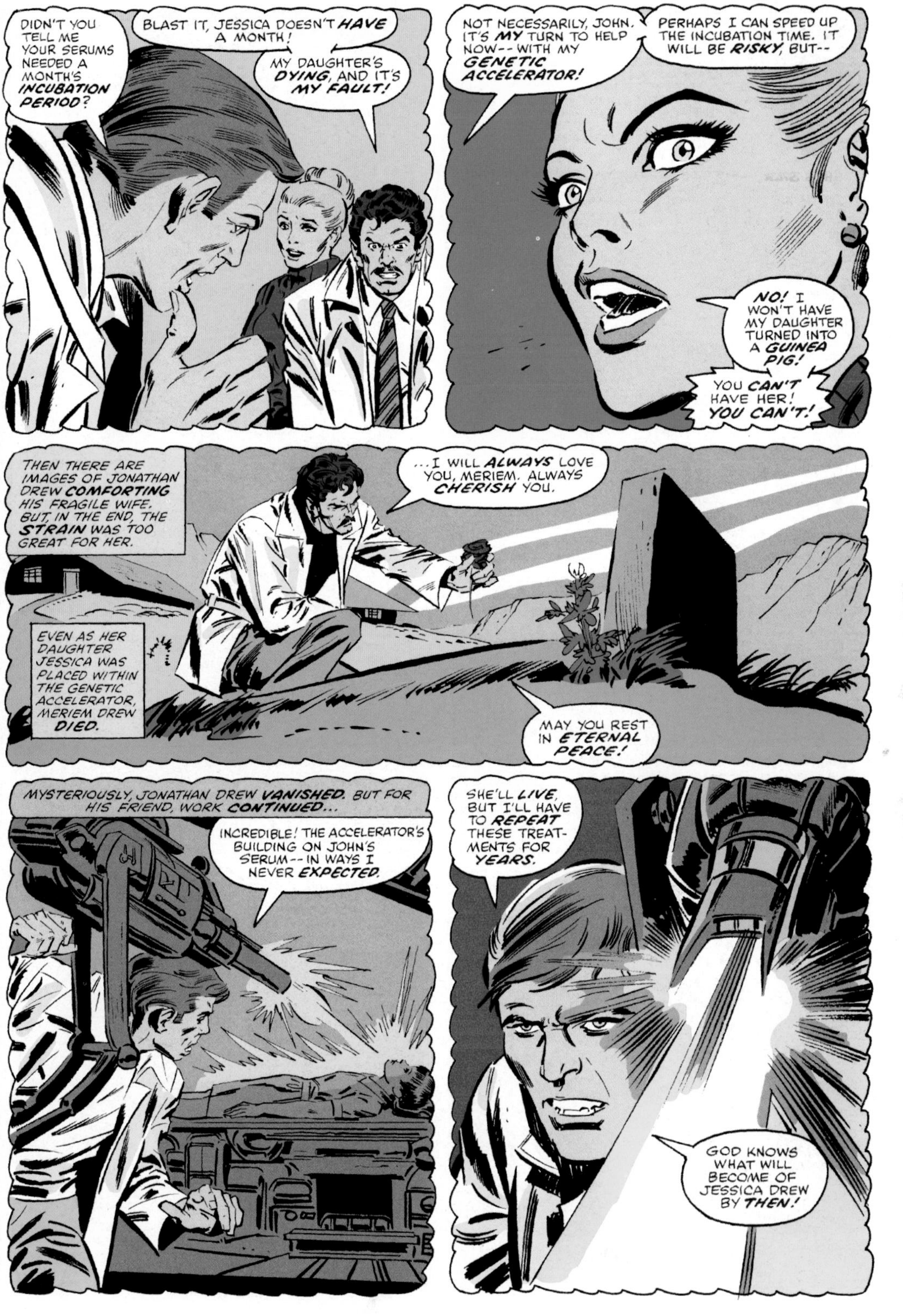
DIDN'T YOU TELL ME YOUR SERUMS NEEDED A MONTH'S INCUBATION PERIOD?
BLAST IT, JESSICA DOESN'T HAVE A MONTH!
MY DAUGHTER'S DYING, AND IT'S MY FAULT!
NOT NECESSARILY, JOHN. IT'S MY TURN TO HELP NOW-- WITH MY GENETIC ACCELERATOR!
PERHAPS I CAN SPEED UP THE INCUBATION TIME. IT WILL BE RISKY, BUT--
NO! I WON'T HAVE MY DAUGHTER TURNED INTO A GUINEA PIG!
YOU CAN'T HAVE HER! YOU CAN'T!
THEN THERE ARE IMAGES OF JONATHAN DREW COMFORTING HIS FRAGILE WIFE. BUT, IN THE END, THE STRAIN WAS TOO GREAT FOR HER.
...I WILL ALWAYS LOVE YOU, MERIEM. ALWAYS CHERISH YOU.
EVEN AS HER DAUGHTER JESSICA WAS PLACED WITHIN THE GENETIC ACCELERATOR, MERIEM DREW DIED.
MAY YOU REST IN ETERNAL PEACE!
MYSTERIOUSLY, JONATHAN DREW VANISHED. BUT FOR HIS FRIEND, WORK CONTINUED...
INCREDIBLE! THE ACCELERATOR'S BUILDING ON JOHN'S SERUM-- IN WAYS I NEVER EXPECTED.
SHE'LL LIVE, BUT I'LL HAVE TO REPEAT THESE TREATMENTS FOR YEARS.
GOD KNOWS WHAT WILL BECOME OF JESSICA DREW BY THEN!

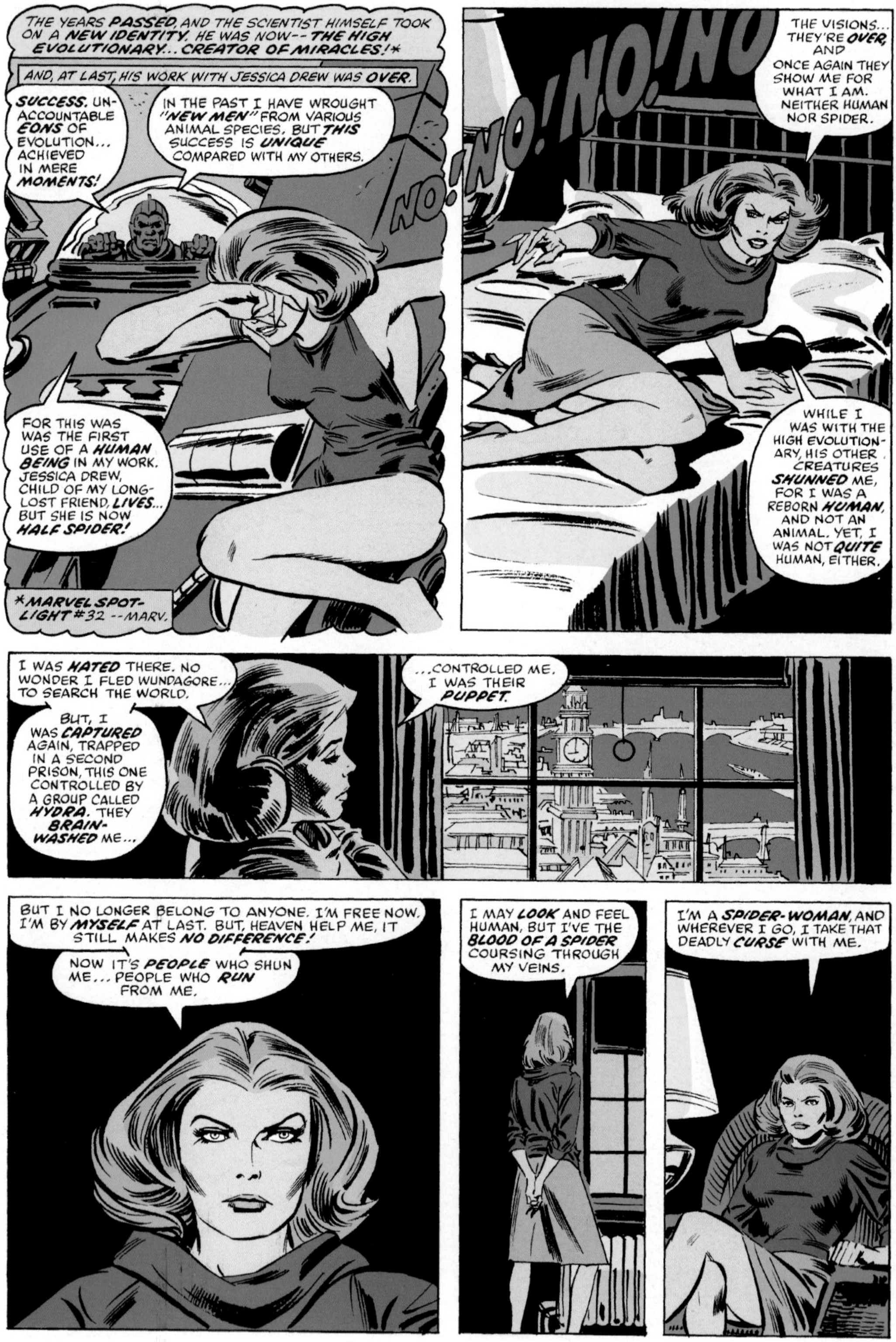
THE YEARS PASSED, AND THE SCIENTIST HIMSELF TOOK ON A NEW IDENTITY. HE WAS NOW-- THE HIGH EVOLUTIONARY... CREATOR OF MIRACLES!*
AND, AT LAST, HIS WORK WITH JESSICA DREW WAS OVER.
SUCCESS. UNACCOUNTABLE EONS OF EVOLUTION... ACHIEVED IN MERE MOMENTS!
IN THE PAST I HAVE WROUGHT "NEW MEN" FROM VARIOUS ANIMAL SPECIES. BUT THIS SUCCESS IS UNIQUE COMPARED WITH MY OTHERS.
FOR THIS WAS WAS THE FIRST USE OF A HUMAN BEING IN MY WORK. JESSICA DREW, CHILD OF MY LONG-LOST FRIEND, LIVES... BUT SHE IS NOW HALF SPIDER!
*MARVEL SPOTLIGHT #32 --MARV.
NO! NO! NO! NO
THE VISIONS... THEY'RE OVER, AND ONCE AGAIN THEY SHOW ME FOR WHAT I AM. NEITHER HUMAN NOR SPIDER.
WHILE I WAS WITH THE HIGH EVOLUTIONARY, HIS OTHER CREATURES SHUNNED ME, FOR I WAS A REBORN HUMAN, AND NOT AN ANIMAL. YET, I WAS NOT QUITE HUMAN, EITHER.
I WAS HATED THERE. NO WONDER I FLED WUNDAGORE... TO SEARCH THE WORLD.
BUT, I WAS CAPTURED AGAIN, TRAPPED IN A SECOND PRISON, THIS ONE CONTROLLED BY A GROUP CALLED HYDRA. THEY BRAINWASHED ME...
...CONTROLLED ME. I WAS THEIR PUPPET.
BUT I NO LONGER BELONG TO ANYONE. I'M FREE NOW. I'M BY MYSELF AT LAST. BUT, HEAVEN HELP ME, IT STILL MAKES NO DIFFERENCE!
NOW IT'S PEOPLE WHO SHUN ME... PEOPLE WHO RUN FROM ME.
I MAY LOOK AND FEEL HUMAN, BUT I'VE THE BLOOD OF A SPIDER COURSING THROUGH MY VEINS.
I'M A SPIDER-WOMAN, AND WHEREVER I GO, I TAKE THAT DEADLY CURSE WITH ME.

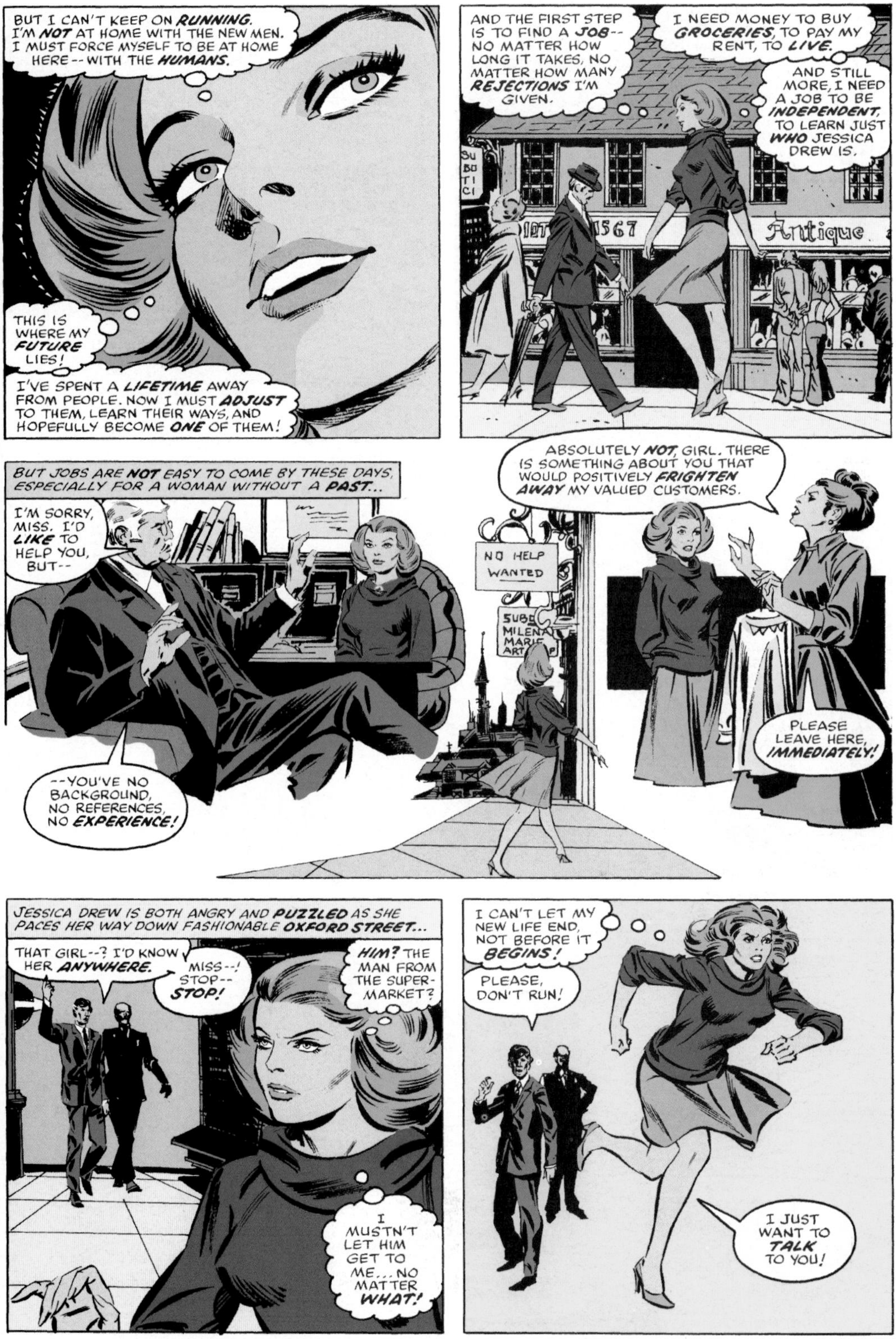

BUT I CAN'T KEEP ON RUNNING. I'M NOT AT HOME WITH THE NEW MEN. I MUST FORCE MYSELF TO BE AT HOME HERE -- WITH THE HUMANS.
THIS IS WHERE MY FUTURE LIES!
I'VE SPENT A LIFETIME AWAY FROM PEOPLE. NOW I MUST ADJUST TO THEM, LEARN THEIR WAYS, AND HOPEFULLY BECOME ONE OF THEM!
AND THE FIRST STEP IS TO FIND A JOB -- NO MATTER HOW LONG IT TAKES, NO MATTER HOW MANY REJECTIONS I'M GIVEN.
I NEED MONEY TO BUY GROCERIES, TO PAY MY RENT, TO LIVE.
AND STILL MORE, I NEED A JOB TO BE INDEPENDENT, TO LEARN JUST WHO JESSICA DREW IS.
Antique
BUT JOBS ARE NOT EASY TO COME BY THESE DAYS, ESPECIALLY FOR A WOMAN WITHOUT A PAST...
I'M SORRY, MISS. I'D LIKE TO HELP YOU, BUT--
--YOU'VE NO BACKGROUND, NO REFERENCES, NO EXPERIENCE!
NO HELP WANTED
ABSOLUTELY NOT, GIRL. THERE IS SOMETHING ABOUT YOU THAT WOULD POSITIVELY FRIGHTEN AWAY MY VALUED CUSTOMERS.
PLEASE LEAVE HERE, IMMEDIATELY!
JESSICA DREW IS BOTH ANGRY AND PUZZLED AS SHE PACES HER WAY DOWN FASHIONABLE OXFORD STREET...
THAT GIRL--? I'D KNOW HER ANYWHERE.
MISS--! STOP-- STOP!
HIM? THE MAN FROM THE SUPER-MARKET?
I MUSTN'T LET HIM GET TO ME... NO MATTER WHAT!
I CAN'T LET MY NEW LIFE END, NOT BEFORE IT BEGINS!
PLEASE, DON'T RUN!
I JUST WANT TO TALK TO YOU!

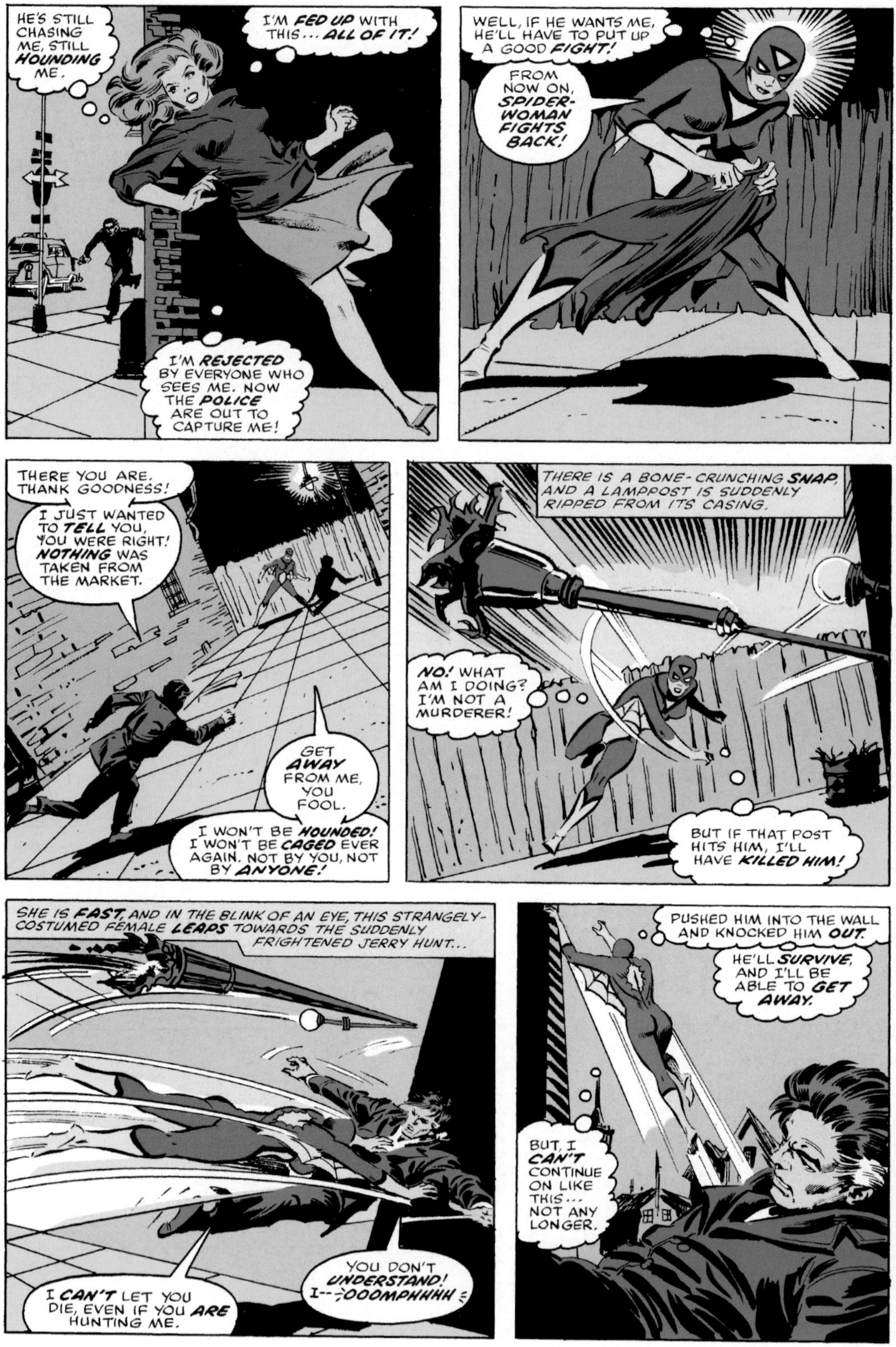
HE'S STILL CHASING ME, STILL HOUNDING ME.
I'M FED UP WITH THIS... ALL OF IT!
I'M REJECTED BY EVERYONE WHO SEES ME. NOW THE POLICE ARE OUT TO CAPTURE ME!
WELL, IF HE WANTS ME, HE'LL HAVE TO PUT UP A GOOD FIGHT!
FROM NOW ON, SPIDER-WOMAN FIGHTS BACK!
THERE YOU ARE. THANK GOODNESS!
I JUST WANTED TO TELL YOU, YOU WERE RIGHT! NOTHING WAS TAKEN FROM THE MARKET.
GET AWAY FROM ME, YOU FOOL.
I WON'T BE HOUNDED! I WON'T BE CAGED EVER AGAIN. NOT BY YOU, NOT BY ANYONE!
THERE IS A BONE-CRUNCHING SNAP, AND A LAMPPOST IS SUDDENLY RIPPED FROM ITS CASING.
NO! WHAT AM I DOING? I'M NOT A MURDERER!
BUT IF THAT POST HITS HIM, I'LL HAVE KILLED HIM!
SHE IS FAST, AND IN THE BLINK OF AN EYE, THIS STRANGELY-COSTUMED FEMALE LEAPS TOWARDS THE SUDDENLY FRIGHTENED JERRY HUNT...
I CAN'T LET YOU DIE, EVEN IF YOU ARE HUNTING ME.
YOU DON'T UNDERSTAND! I--OOOMPHHHH
PUSHED HIM INTO THE WALL AND KNOCKED HIM OUT.
HE'LL SURVIVE, AND I'LL BE ABLE TO GET AWAY.
BUT, I CAN'T CONTINUE ON LIKE THIS... NOT ANY LONGER.

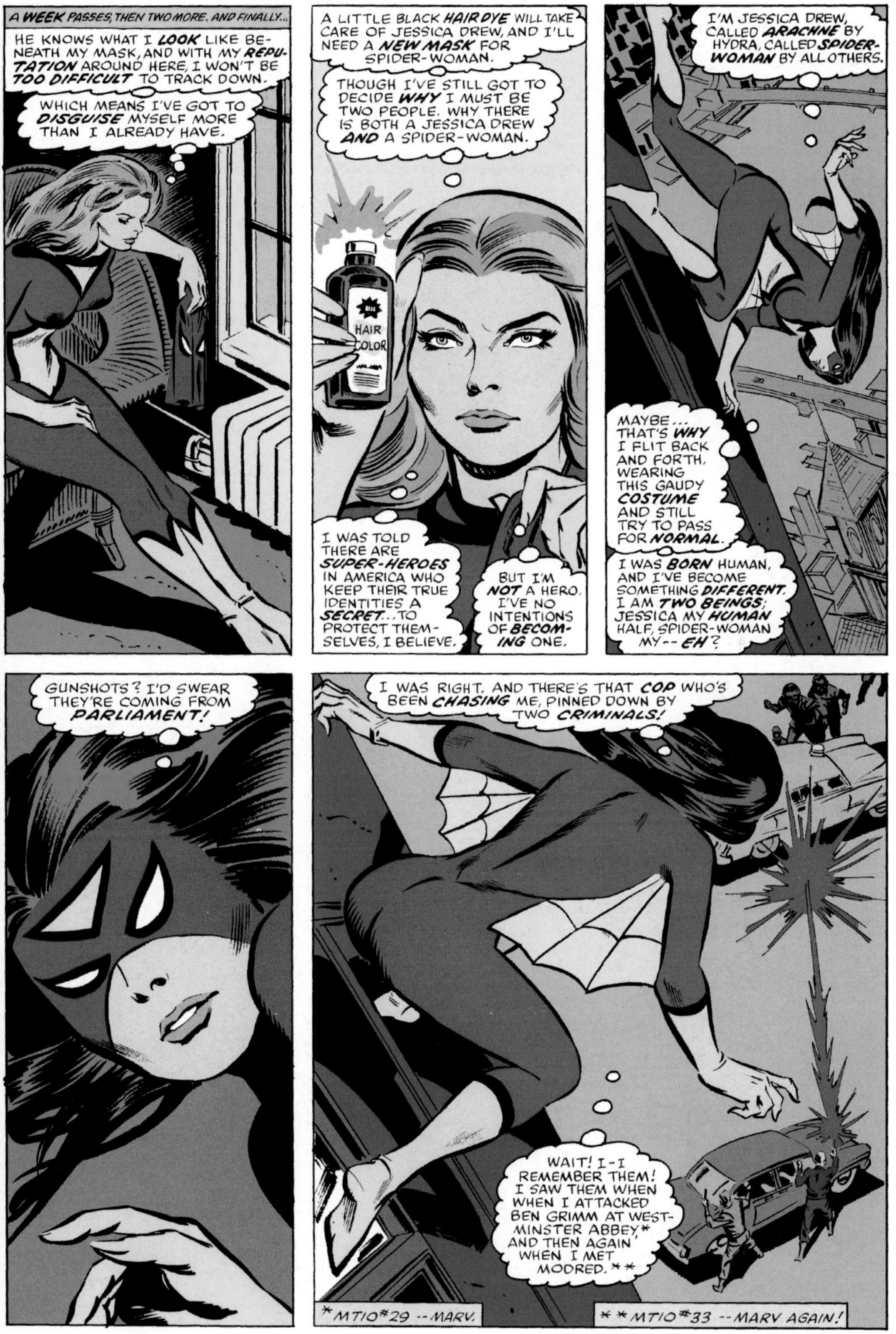
A WEEK PASSES, THEN TWO MORE. AND FINALLY...
HE KNOWS WHAT I LOOK LIKE BENEATH MY MASK, AND WITH MY REPUTATION AROUND HERE, I WON'T BE TOO DIFFICULT TO TRACK DOWN.
WHICH MEANS I'VE GOT TO DISGUISE MYSELF MORE THAN I ALREADY HAVE.
A LITTLE BLACK HAIR DYE WILL TAKE CARE OF JESSICA DREW, AND I'LL NEED A NEW MASK FOR SPIDER-WOMAN.
THOUGH I'VE STILL GOT TO DECIDE WHY I MUST BE TWO PEOPLE. WHY THERE IS BOTH A JESSICA DREW AND A SPIDER-WOMAN.
HAIR COLOR
I WAS TOLD THERE ARE SUPER-HEROES IN AMERICA WHO KEEP THEIR TRUE IDENTITIES A SECRET... TO PROTECT THEMSELVES, I BELIEVE.
BUT I'M NOT A HERO. I'VE NO INTENTIONS OF BECOMING ONE.
I'M JESSICA DREW, CALLED ARACHNE BY HYDRA, CALLED SPIDER-WOMAN BY ALL OTHERS.
MAYBE... THAT'S WHY I FLIT BACK AND FORTH, WEARING THIS GAUDY COSTUME AND STILL TRY TO PASS FOR NORMAL.
I WAS BORN HUMAN, AND I'VE BECOME SOMETHING DIFFERENT. I AM TWO BEINGS; JESSICA MY HUMAN HALF, SPIDER-WOMAN MY-- EH?
GUNSHOTS? I'D SWEAR THEY'RE COMING FROM PARLIAMENT!
I WAS RIGHT. AND THERE'S THAT COP WHO'S BEEN CHASING ME, PINNED DOWN BY TWO CRIMINALS!
WAIT! I-I REMEMBER THEM! I SAW THEM WHEN I ATTACKED BEN GRIMM AT WESTMINSTER ABBEY* AND THEN AGAIN WHEN I MET MODRED.**
*MTIO #29 --MARV.
**MTIO #33 --MARV AGAIN!

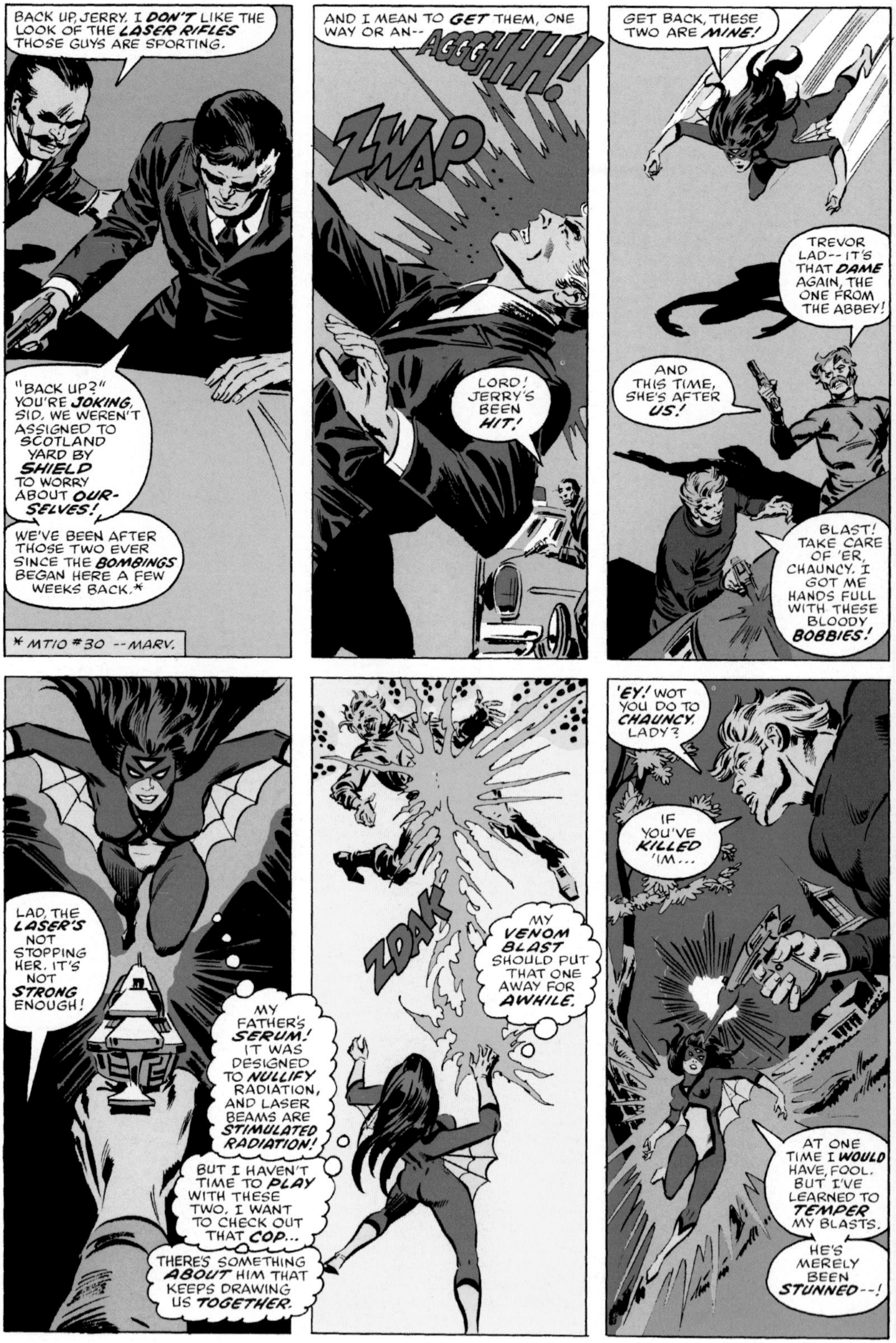

BACK UP, JERRY. I DON'T LIKE THE LOOK OF THE LASER RIFLES THOSE GUYS ARE SPORTING.
"BACK UP?" YOU'RE JOKING, SID. WE WEREN'T ASSIGNED TO SCOTLAND YARD BY SHIELD TO WORRY ABOUT OURSELVES!
WE'VE BEEN AFTER THOSE TWO EVER SINCE THE BOMBINGS BEGAN HERE A FEW WEEKS BACK.*
* MT10 #30 --MARV.
AND I MEAN TO GET THEM, ONE WAY OR AN--
AGGGHHH!
ZWAP
LORD! JERRY'S BEEN HIT!
GET BACK, THESE TWO ARE MINE!
TREVOR LAD-- IT'S THAT DAME AGAIN, THE ONE FROM THE ABBEY!
AND THIS TIME, SHE'S AFTER US!
BLAST! TAKE CARE OF 'ER, CHAUNCY. I GOT ME HANDS FULL WITH THESE BLOODY BOBBIES!
LAD, THE LASER'S NOT STOPPING HER. IT'S NOT STRONG ENOUGH!
MY FATHER'S SERUM! IT WAS DESIGNED TO NULLIFY RADIATION, AND LASER BEAMS ARE STIMULATED RADIATION!
BUT I HAVEN'T TIME TO PLAY WITH THESE TWO. I WANT TO CHECK OUT THAT COP...
THERE'S SOMETHING ABOUT HIM THAT KEEPS DRAWING US TOGETHER.
ZDAK
MY VENOM BLAST SHOULD PUT THAT ONE AWAY FOR AWHILE.
'EY! WOT YOU DO TO CHAUNCY, LADY?
IF YOU'VE KILLED 'IM...
AT ONE TIME I WOULD HAVE, FOOL. BUT I'VE LEARNED TO TEMPER MY BLASTS.
HE'S MERELY BEEN STUNNED--!

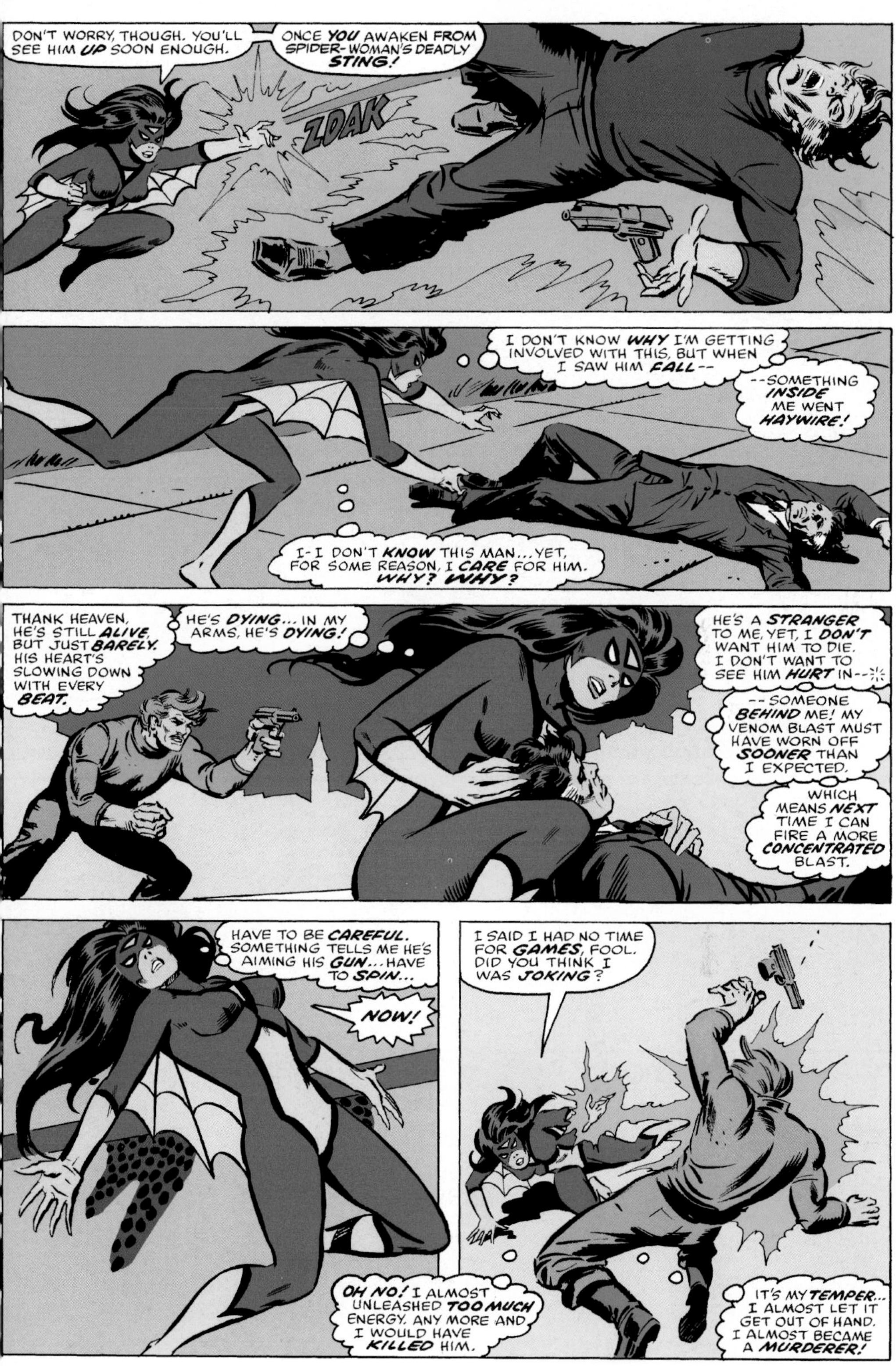
DON'T WORRY, THOUGH. YOU'LL SEE HIM UP SOON ENOUGH.
ONCE YOU AWAKEN FROM SPIDER-WOMAN'S DEADLY STING!
ZDAK
I DON'T KNOW WHY I'M GETTING INVOLVED WITH THIS, BUT WHEN I SAW HIM FALL--
--SOMETHING INSIDE ME WENT HAYWIRE!
I-I DON'T KNOW THIS MAN... YET, FOR SOME REASON, I CARE FOR HIM. WHY? WHY?
THANK HEAVEN, HE'S STILL ALIVE, BUT JUST BARELY. HIS HEART'S SLOWING DOWN WITH EVERY BEAT.
HE'S DYING... IN MY ARMS, HE'S DYING!
HE'S A STRANGER TO ME, YET, I DON'T WANT HIM TO DIE. I DON'T WANT TO SEE HIM HURT IN--
--SOMEONE BEHIND ME! MY VENOM BLAST MUST HAVE WORN OFF SOONER THAN I EXPECTED.
WHICH MEANS NEXT TIME I CAN FIRE A MORE CONCENTRATED BLAST.
HAVE TO BE CAREFUL. SOMETHING TELLS ME HE'S AIMING HIS GUN... HAVE TO SPIN...
NOW!
I SAID I HAD NO TIME FOR GAMES, FOOL. DID YOU THINK I WAS JOKING?
OH NO! I ALMOST UNLEASHED TOO MUCH ENERGY. ANY MORE AND I WOULD HAVE KILLED HIM.
IT'S MY TEMPER... I ALMOST LET IT GET OUT OF HAND. I ALMOST BECAME A MURDERER!

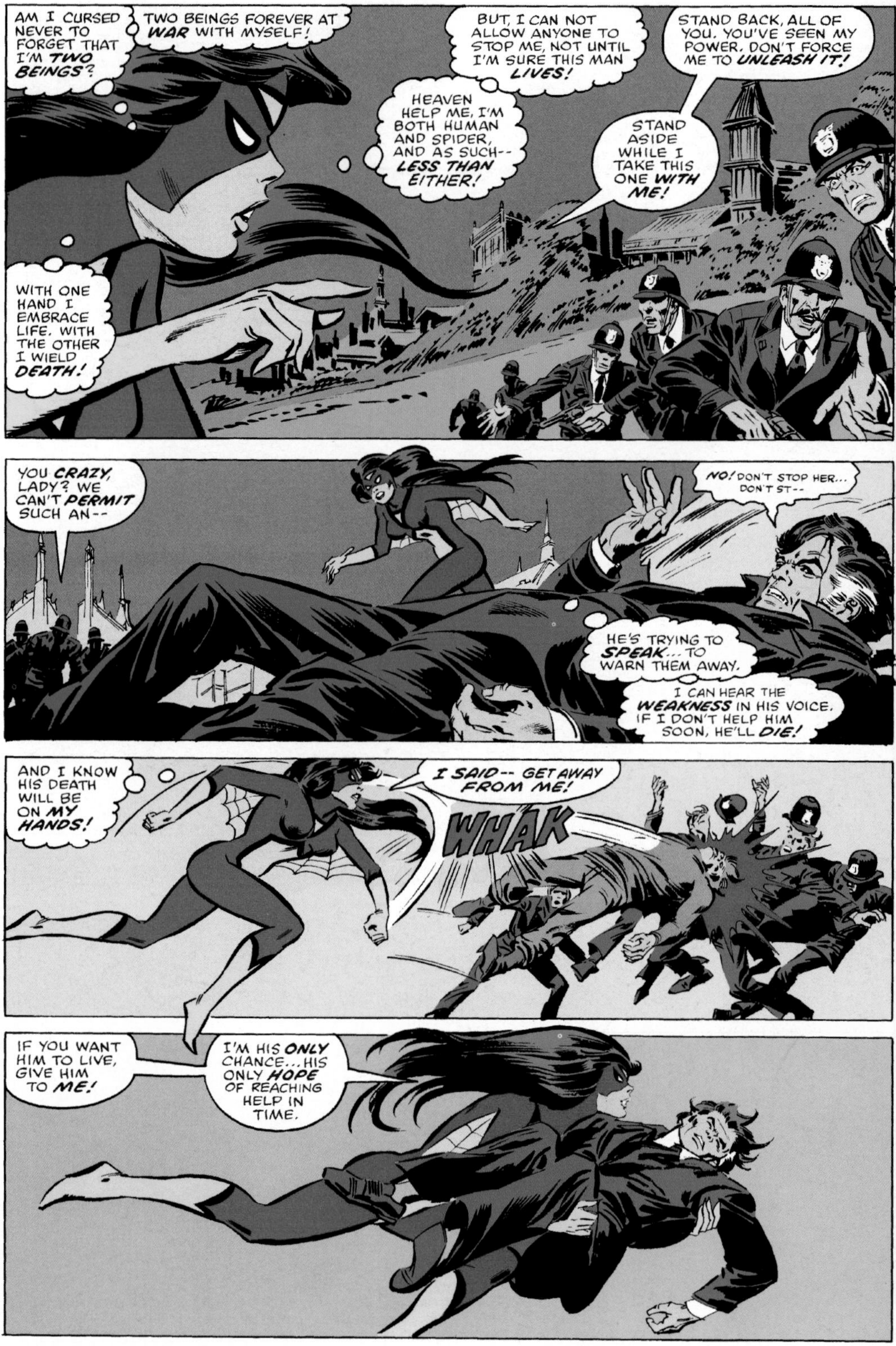
AM I CURSED NEVER TO FORGET THAT I'M TWO BEINGS?
TWO BEINGS FOREVER AT WAR WITH MYSELF!
HEAVEN HELP ME, I'M BOTH HUMAN AND SPIDER, AND AS SUCH-- LESS THAN EITHER!
BUT, I CAN NOT ALLOW ANYONE TO STOP ME, NOT UNTIL I'M SURE THIS MAN LIVES!
STAND BACK, ALL OF YOU. YOU'VE SEEN MY POWER. DON'T FORCE ME TO UNLEASH IT!
STAND ASIDE WHILE I TAKE THIS ONE WITH ME!
WITH ONE HAND I EMBRACE LIFE. WITH THE OTHER I WIELD DEATH!
YOU CRAZY, LADY? WE CAN'T PERMIT SUCH AN--
NO! DON'T STOP HER... DON'T ST--
HE'S TRYING TO SPEAK... TO WARN THEM AWAY.
I CAN HEAR THE WEAKNESS IN HIS VOICE. IF I DON'T HELP HIM SOON, HE'LL DIE!
AND I KNOW HIS DEATH WILL BE ON MY HANDS!
I SAID-- GET AWAY FROM ME!
WHAK
IF YOU WANT HIM TO LIVE, GIVE HIM TO ME!
I'M HIS ONLY CHANCE... HIS ONLY HOPE OF REACHING HELP IN TIME.

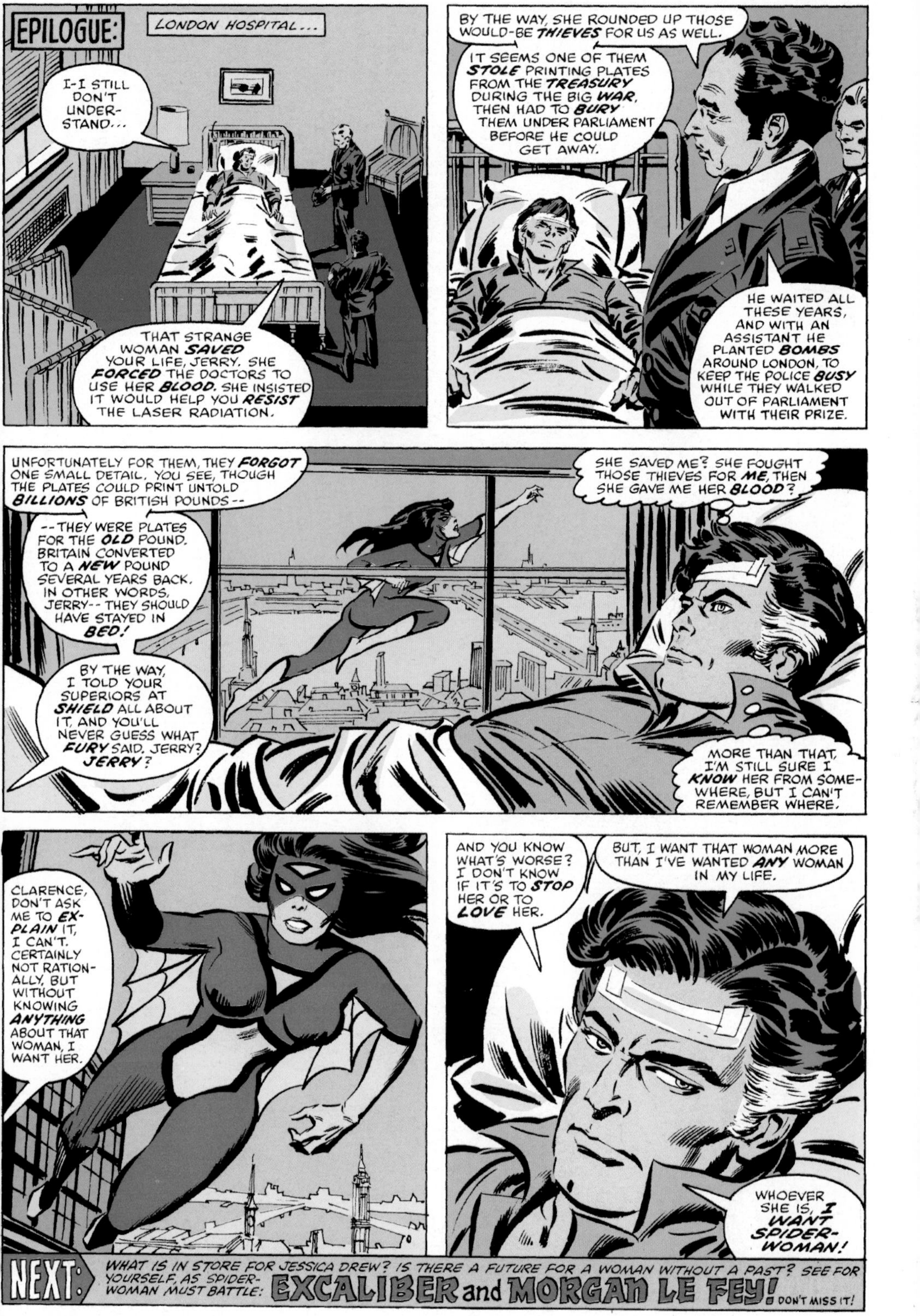
EPILOGUE:
LONDON HOSPITAL...
I-I STILL DON'T UNDER-STAND...
THAT STRANGE WOMAN SAVED YOUR LIFE, JERRY. SHE FORCED THE DOCTORS TO USE HER BLOOD. SHE INSISTED IT WOULD HELP YOU RESIST THE LASER RADIATION.
BY THE WAY, SHE ROUNDED UP THOSE WOULD-BE THIEVES FOR US AS WELL.
IT SEEMS ONE OF THEM STOLE PRINTING PLATES FROM THE TREASURY DURING THE BIG WAR, THEN HAD TO BURY THEM UNDER PARLIAMENT BEFORE HE COULD GET AWAY.
HE WAITED ALL THESE YEARS, AND WITH AN ASSISTANT HE PLANTED BOMBS AROUND LONDON, TO KEEP THE POLICE BUSY WHILE THEY WALKED OUT OF PARLIAMENT WITH THEIR PRIZE.
UNFORTUNATELY FOR THEM, THEY FORGOT ONE SMALL DETAIL, YOU SEE, THOUGH THE PLATES COULD PRINT UNTOLD BILLIONS OF BRITISH POUNDS--
--THEY WERE PLATES FOR THE OLD POUND. BRITAIN CONVERTED TO A NEW POUND SEVERAL YEARS BACK. IN OTHER WORDS, JERRY-- THEY SHOULD HAVE STAYED IN BED!
BY THE WAY, I TOLD YOUR SUPERIORS AT SHIELD ALL ABOUT IT, AND YOU'LL NEVER GUESS WHAT FURY SAID, JERRY? JERRY?
SHE SAVED ME? SHE FOUGHT THOSE THIEVES FOR ME, THEN SHE GAVE ME HER BLOOD?
MORE THAN THAT, I'M STILL SURE I KNOW HER FROM SOME-WHERE, BUT I CAN'T REMEMBER WHERE.
CLARENCE, DON'T ASK ME TO EX-PLAIN IT, I CAN'T. CERTAINLY NOT RATION-ALLY, BUT WITHOUT KNOWING ANYTHING ABOUT THAT WOMAN, I WANT HER.
AND YOU KNOW WHAT'S WORSE? I DON'T KNOW IF IT'S TO STOP HER OR TO LOVE HER.
BUT, I WANT THAT WOMAN MORE THAN I'VE WANTED ANY WOMAN IN MY LIFE.
WHOEVER SHE IS, I WANT SPIDER-WOMAN!
NEXT:
WHAT IS IN STORE FOR JESSICA DREW? IS THERE A FUTURE FOR A WOMAN WITHOUT A PAST? SEE FOR YOURSELF, AS SPIDER-WOMAN MUST BATTLE:
EXCALIBER and MORGAN LE FEY!
DON'T MISS IT!

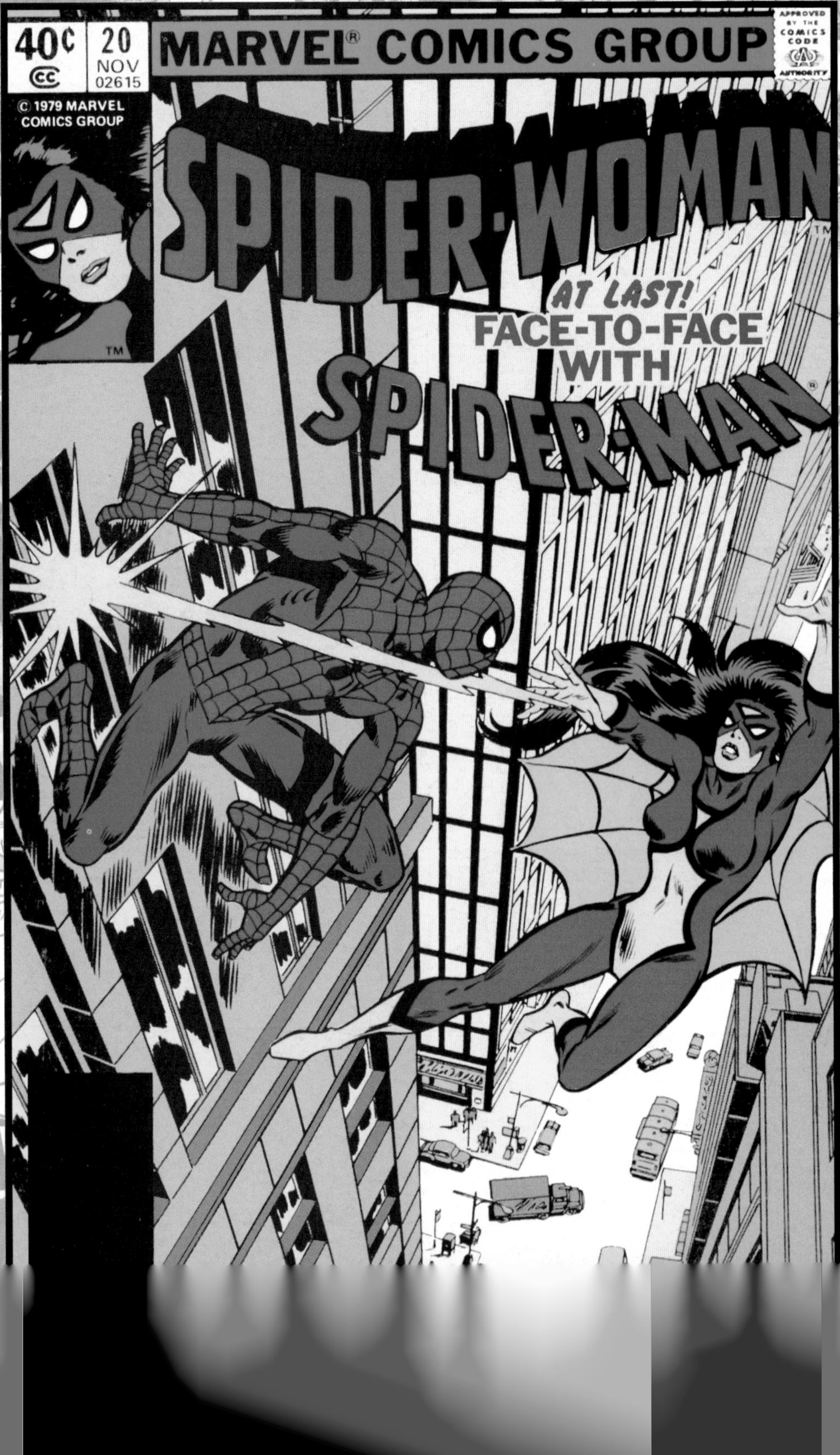
40¢
20
NOV
02615
MARVEL® COMICS GROUP
APPROVED BY THE COMICS CODE AUTHORITY
© 1979 MARVEL COMICS GROUP
SPIDER-WOMAN™
AT LAST!
FACE-TO-FACE WITH
SPIDER-MAN®

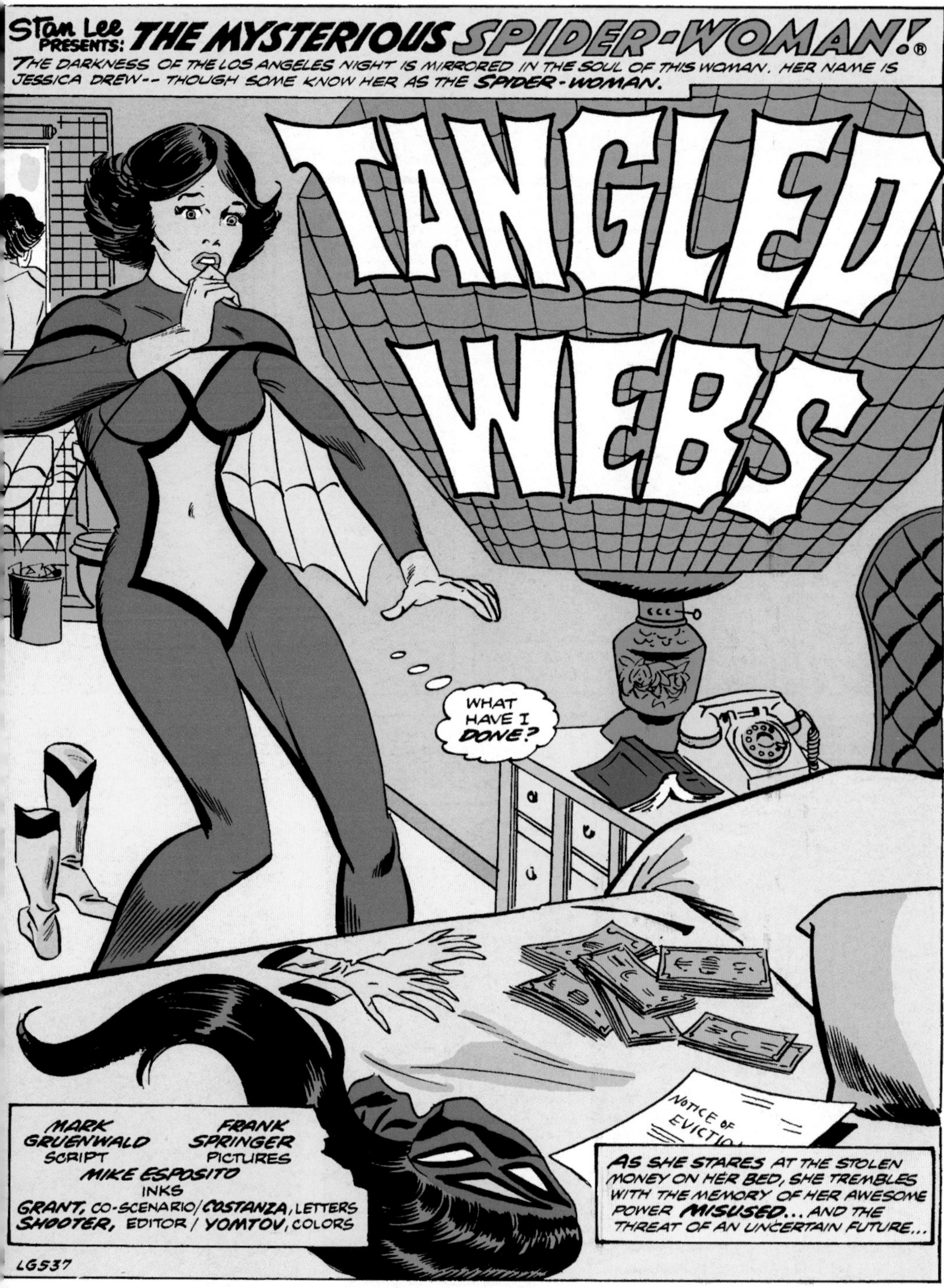
Stan Lee PRESENTS: THE MYSTERIOUS SPIDER-WOMAN!®
THE DARKNESS OF THE LOS ANGELES NIGHT IS MIRRORED IN THE SOUL OF THIS WOMAN. HER NAME IS JESSICA DREW-- THOUGH SOME KNOW HER AS THE SPIDER-WOMAN.
TANGLED WEBS
WHAT HAVE I DONE?
NOTICE OF EVICTIO
MARK GRUENWALD SCRIPT
FRANK SPRINGER PICTURES
MIKE ESPOSITO INKS
GRANT, CO-SCENARIO/COSTANZA, LETTERS
SHOOTER, EDITOR / YOMTOV, COLORS
AS SHE STARES AT THE STOLEN MONEY ON HER BED, SHE TREMBLES WITH THE MEMORY OF HER AWESOME POWER MISUSED... AND THE THREAT OF AN UNCERTAIN FUTURE...
LG537

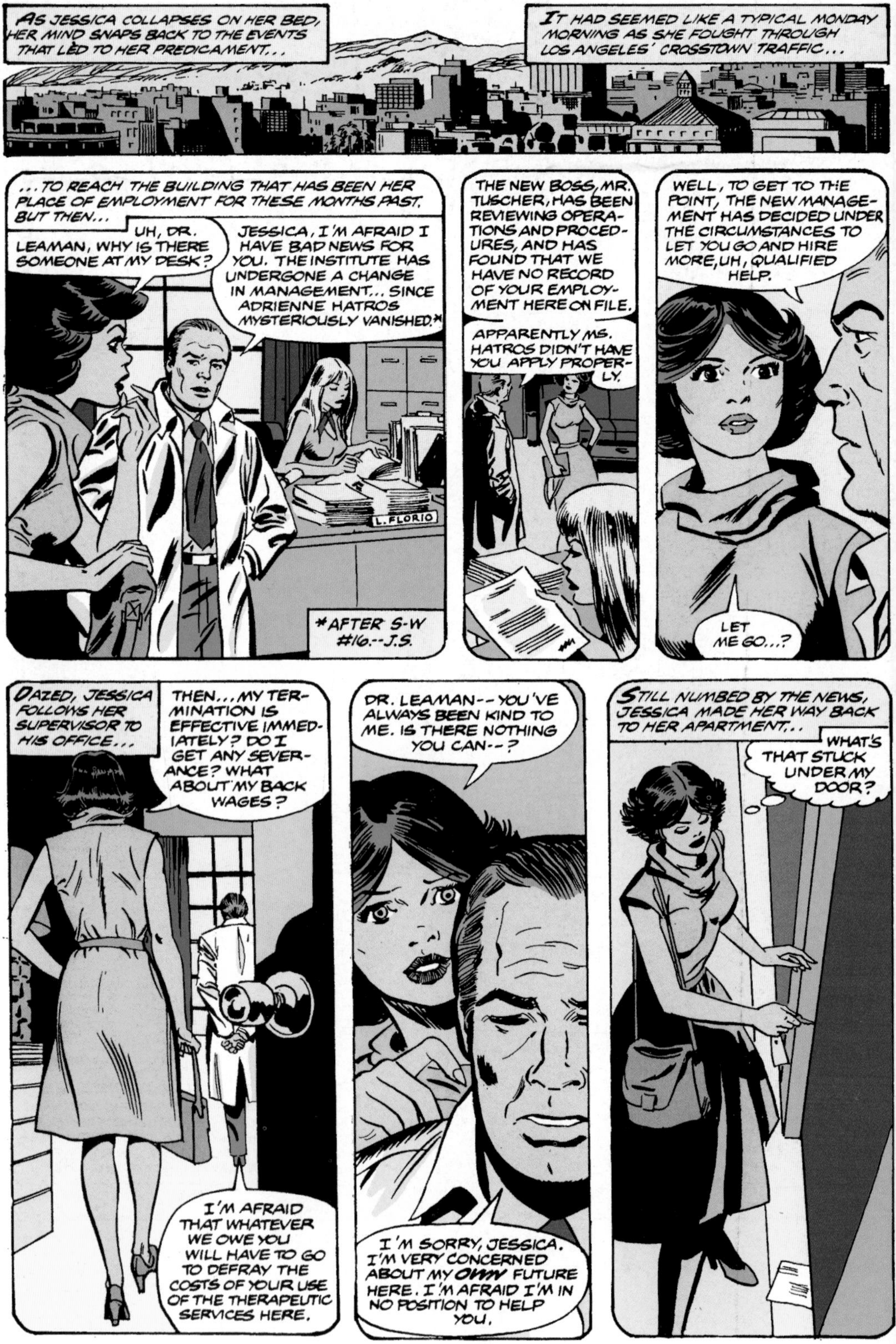
AS JESSICA COLLAPSES ON HER BED, HER MIND SNAPS BACK TO THE EVENTS THAT LED TO HER PREDICAMENT...
IT HAD SEEMED LIKE A TYPICAL MONDAY MORNING AS SHE FOUGHT THROUGH LOS ANGELES' CROSSTOWN TRAFFIC...
...TO REACH THE BUILDING THAT HAS BEEN HER PLACE OF EMPLOYMENT FOR THESE MONTHS PAST. BUT THEN...
UH, DR. LEAMAN, WHY IS THERE SOMEONE AT MY DESK?
JESSICA, I'M AFRAID I HAVE BAD NEWS FOR YOU. THE INSTITUTE HAS UNDERGONE A CHANGE IN MANAGEMENT... SINCE ADRIENNE HATROS MYSTERIOUSLY VANISHED.*
L. FLORIO
*AFTER S-W #16.--J.S.
THE NEW BOSS, MR. TUSCHER, HAS BEEN REVIEWING OPERATIONS AND PROCEDURES, AND HAS FOUND THAT WE HAVE NO RECORD OF YOUR EMPLOYMENT HERE ON FILE.
APPARENTLY MS. HATROS DIDN'T HAVE YOU APPLY PROPERLY.
WELL, TO GET TO THE POINT, THE NEW MANAGEMENT HAS DECIDED UNDER THE CIRCUMSTANCES TO LET YOU GO AND HIRE MORE, UH, QUALIFIED HELP.
LET ME GO...?
DAZED, JESSICA FOLLOWS HER SUPERVISOR TO HIS OFFICE...
THEN... MY TERMINATION IS EFFECTIVE IMMEDIATELY? DO I GET ANY SEVERANCE? WHAT ABOUT MY BACK WAGES?
I'M AFRAID THAT WHATEVER WE OWE YOU WILL HAVE TO GO TO DEFRAY THE COSTS OF YOUR USE OF THE THERAPEUTIC SERVICES HERE.
DR. LEAMAN--YOU'VE ALWAYS BEEN KIND TO ME. IS THERE NOTHING YOU CAN--?
I'M SORRY, JESSICA. I'M VERY CONCERNED ABOUT MY OWN FUTURE HERE. I'M AFRAID I'M IN NO POSITION TO HELP YOU.
STILL NUMBED BY THE NEWS, JESSICA MADE HER WAY BACK TO HER APARTMENT...
WHAT'S THAT STUCK UNDER MY DOOR?

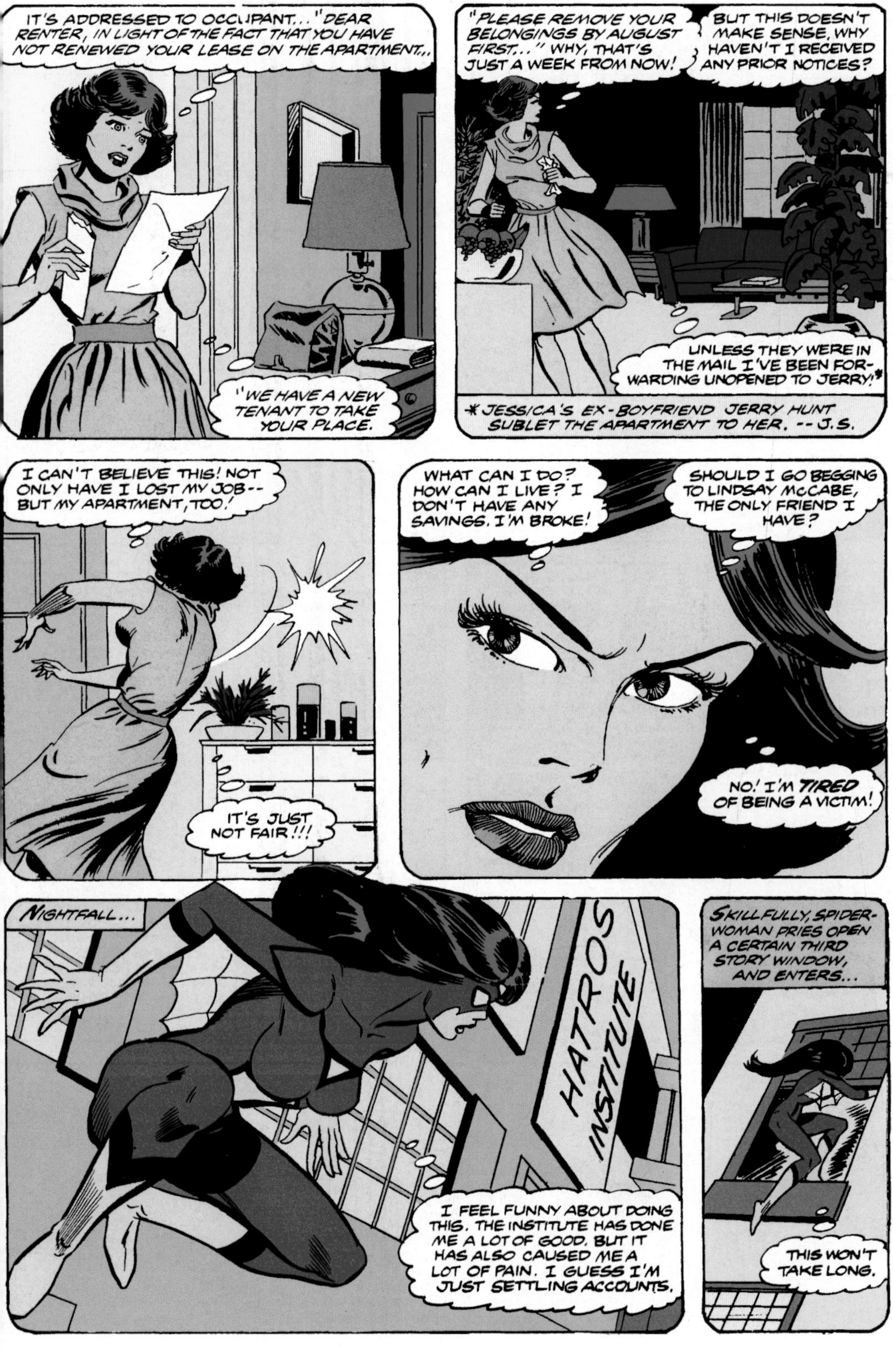
IT'S ADDRESSED TO OCCUPANT... "DEAR RENTER, IN LIGHT OF THE FACT THAT YOU HAVE NOT RENEWED YOUR LEASE ON THE APARTMENT...
"WE HAVE A NEW TENANT TO TAKE YOUR PLACE.
"PLEASE REMOVE YOUR BELONGINGS BY AUGUST FIRST..." WHY, THAT'S JUST A WEEK FROM NOW!
BUT THIS DOESN'T MAKE SENSE. WHY HAVEN'T I RECEIVED ANY PRIOR NOTICES?
UNLESS THEY WERE IN THE MAIL I'VE BEEN FORWARDING UNOPENED TO JERRY!*
*JESSICA'S EX-BOYFRIEND JERRY HUNT SUBLET THE APARTMENT TO HER. -- J.S.
I CAN'T BELIEVE THIS! NOT ONLY HAVE I LOST MY JOB-- BUT MY APARTMENT, TOO!
IT'S JUST NOT FAIR!!!
WHAT CAN I DO? HOW CAN I LIVE? I DON'T HAVE ANY SAVINGS. I'M BROKE!
SHOULD I GO BEGGING TO LINDSAY McCABE, THE ONLY FRIEND I HAVE?
NO! I'M TIRED OF BEING A VICTIM!
NIGHTFALL...
HATROS INSTITUTE
I FEEL FUNNY ABOUT DOING THIS. THE INSTITUTE HAS DONE ME A LOT OF GOOD. BUT IT HAS ALSO CAUSED ME A LOT OF PAIN. I GUESS I'M JUST SETTLING ACCOUNTS.
SKILLFULLY, SPIDER-WOMAN PRIES OPEN A CERTAIN THIRD STORY WINDOW, AND ENTERS...
THIS WON'T TAKE LONG.

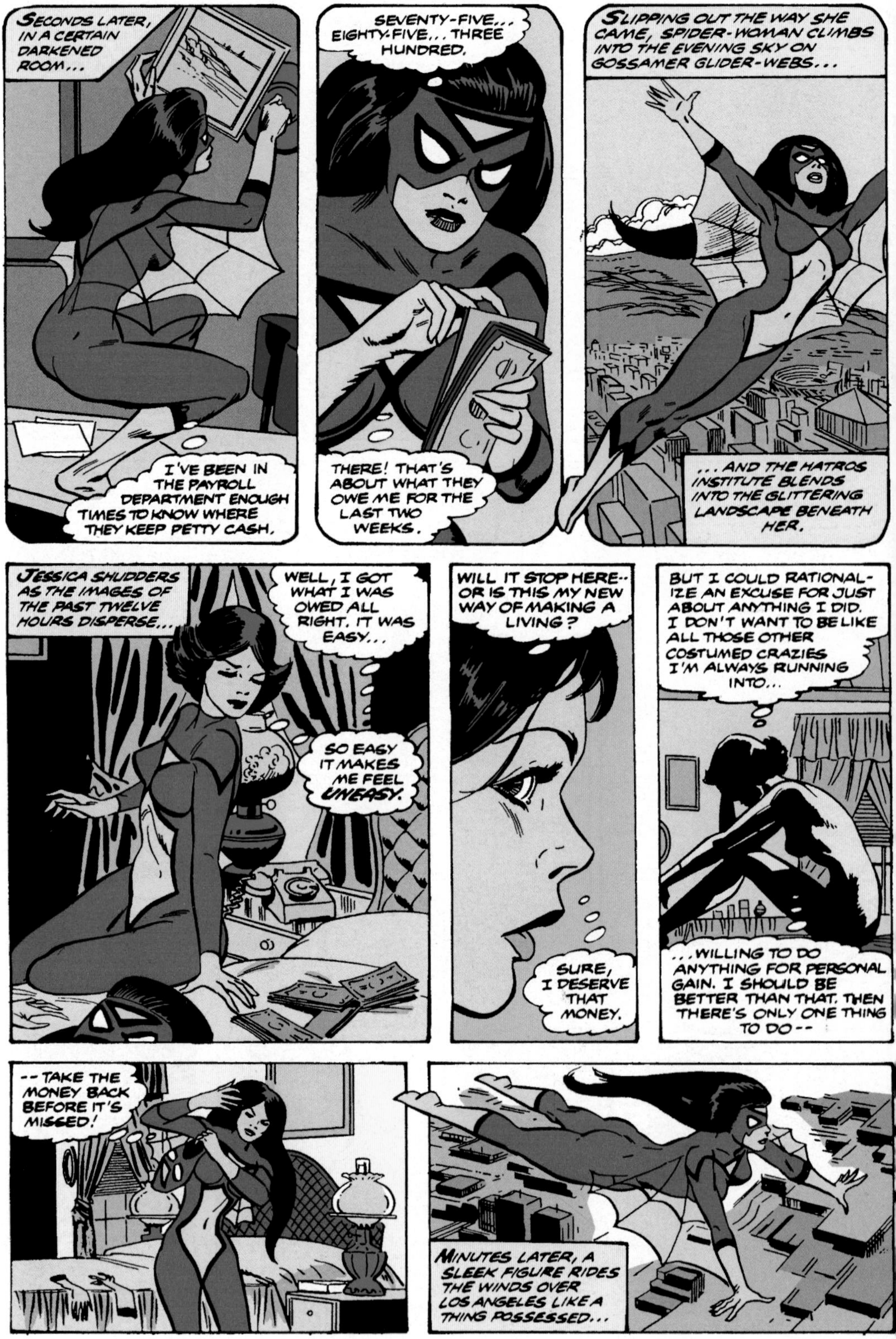
SECONDS LATER, IN A CERTAIN DARKENED ROOM...
I'VE BEEN IN THE PAYROLL DEPARTMENT ENOUGH TIMES TO KNOW WHERE THEY KEEP PETTY CASH.
SEVENTY-FIVE... EIGHTY-FIVE... THREE HUNDRED.
THERE! THAT'S ABOUT WHAT THEY OWE ME FOR THE LAST TWO WEEKS.
SLIPPING OUT THE WAY SHE CAME, SPIDER-WOMAN CLIMBS INTO THE EVENING SKY ON GOSSAMER GLIDER-WEBS...
...AND THE HATROS INSTITUTE BLENDS INTO THE GLITTERING LANDSCAPE BENEATH HER.
JESSICA SHUDDERS AS THE IMAGES OF THE PAST TWELVE HOURS DISPERSE...
WELL, I GOT WHAT I WAS OWED ALL RIGHT. IT WAS EASY...
SO EASY IT MAKES ME FEEL UNEASY.
WILL IT STOP HERE-- OR IS THIS MY NEW WAY OF MAKING A LIVING?
SURE, I DESERVE THAT MONEY.
BUT I COULD RATIONALIZE AN EXCUSE FOR JUST ABOUT ANYTHING I DID. I DON'T WANT TO BE LIKE ALL THOSE OTHER COSTUMED CRAZIES I'M ALWAYS RUNNING INTO...
...WILLING TO DO ANYTHING FOR PERSONAL GAIN. I SHOULD BE BETTER THAN THAT. THEN THERE'S ONLY ONE THING TO DO--
--TAKE THE MONEY BACK BEFORE IT'S MISSED!
MINUTES LATER, A SLEEK FIGURE RIDES THE WINDS OVER LOS ANGELES LIKE A THING POSSESSED...

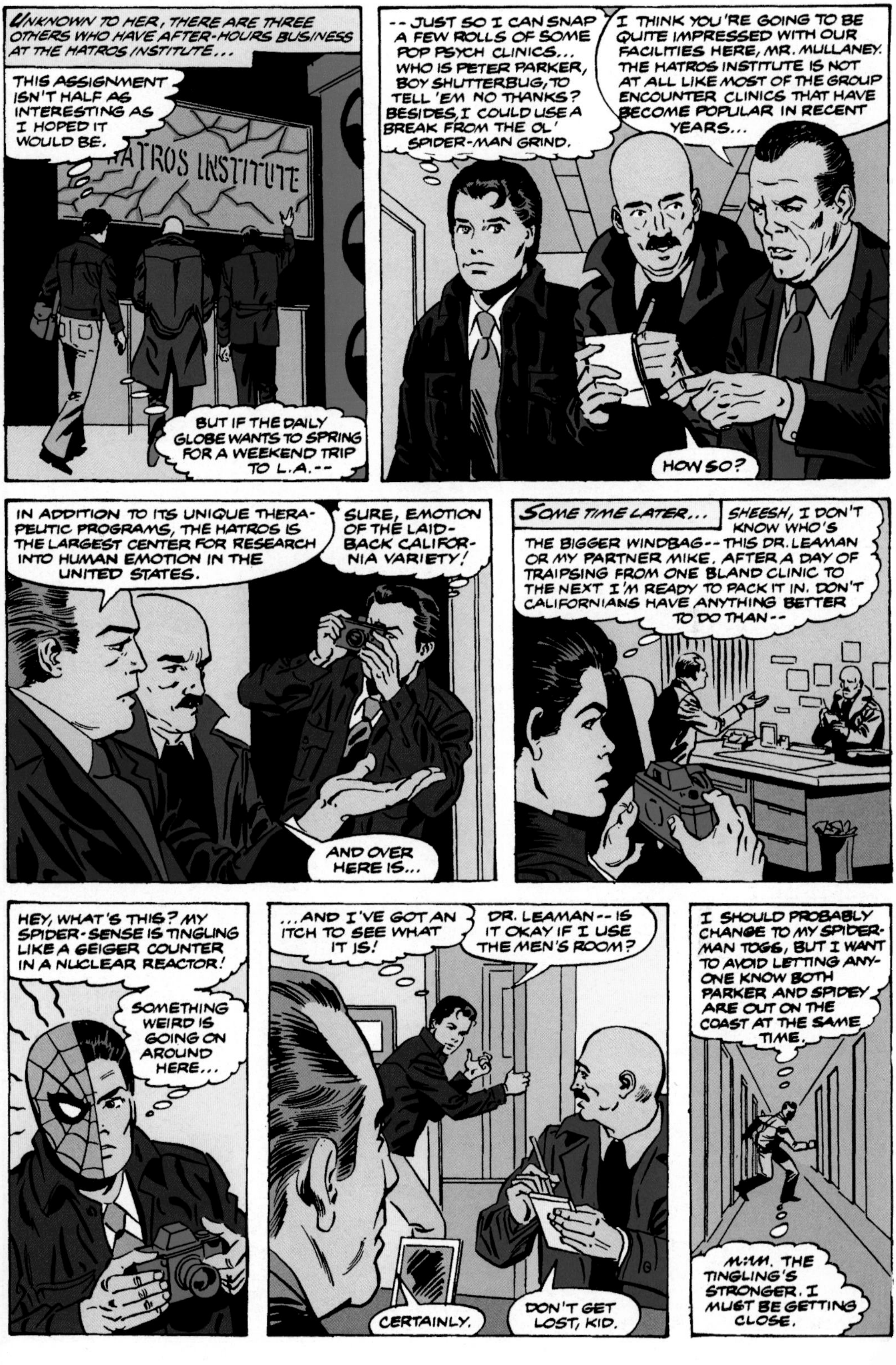
UNKNOWN TO HER, THERE ARE THREE OTHERS WHO HAVE AFTER-HOURS BUSINESS AT THE HATROS INSTITUTE...
THIS ASSIGNMENT ISN'T HALF AS INTERESTING AS I HOPED IT WOULD BE.
HATROS INSTITUTE
BUT IF THE DAILY GLOBE WANTS TO SPRING FOR A WEEKEND TRIP TO L.A.--
--JUST SO I CAN SNAP A FEW ROLLS OF SOME POP PSYCH CLINICS... WHO IS PETER PARKER, BOY SHUTTERBUG, TO TELL 'EM NO THANKS? BESIDES, I COULD USE A BREAK FROM THE OL' SPIDER-MAN GRIND.
I THINK YOU'RE GOING TO BE QUITE IMPRESSED WITH OUR FACILITIES HERE, MR. MULLANEY. THE HATROS INSTITUTE IS NOT AT ALL LIKE MOST OF THE GROUP ENCOUNTER CLINICS THAT HAVE BECOME POPULAR IN RECENT YEARS...
HOW SO?
IN ADDITION TO ITS UNIQUE THERAPEUTIC PROGRAMS, THE HATROS IS THE LARGEST CENTER FOR RESEARCH INTO HUMAN EMOTION IN THE UNITED STATES.
SURE, EMOTION OF THE LAID-BACK CALIFORNIA VARIETY!
AND OVER HERE IS...
SOME TIME LATER...
SHEESH, I DON'T KNOW WHO'S THE BIGGER WINDBAG--THIS DR. LEAMAN OR MY PARTNER MIKE. AFTER A DAY OF TRAIPSING FROM ONE BLAND CLINIC TO THE NEXT I'M READY TO PACK IT IN. DON'T CALIFORNIANS HAVE ANYTHING BETTER TO DO THAN--
HEY, WHAT'S THIS? MY SPIDER-SENSE IS TINGLING LIKE A GEIGER COUNTER IN A NUCLEAR REACTOR!
SOMETHING WEIRD IS GOING ON AROUND HERE...
...AND I'VE GOT AN ITCH TO SEE WHAT IT IS!
DR. LEAMAN--IS IT OKAY IF I USE THE MEN'S ROOM?
CERTAINLY.
DON'T GET LOST, KID.
I SHOULD PROBABLY CHANGE TO MY SPIDER-MAN TOGS, BUT I WANT TO AVOID LETTING ANYONE KNOW BOTH PARKER AND SPIDEY ARE OUT ON THE COAST AT THE SAME TIME.
MMM. THE TINGLING'S STRONGER. I MUST BE GETTING CLOSE.

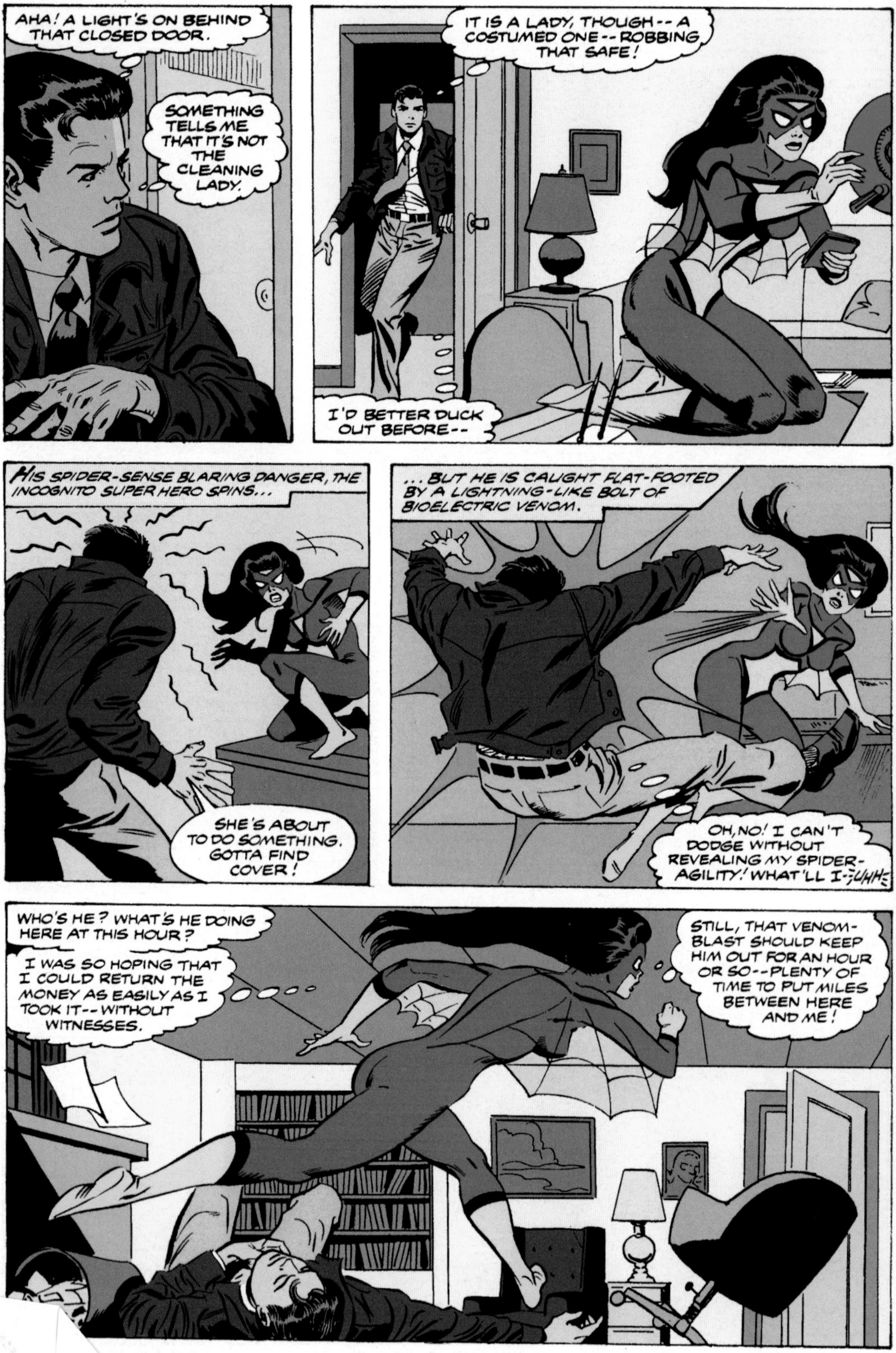
AHA! A LIGHT'S ON BEHIND THAT CLOSED DOOR.
SOMETHING TELLS ME THAT IT'S NOT THE CLEANING LADY.
IT IS A LADY, THOUGH -- A COSTUMED ONE -- ROBBING THAT SAFE!
I'D BETTER DUCK OUT BEFORE--
HIS SPIDER-SENSE BLARING DANGER, THE INCOGNITO SUPER HERO SPINS...
SHE'S ABOUT TO DO SOMETHING. GOTTA FIND COVER!
... BUT HE IS CAUGHT FLAT-FOOTED BY A LIGHTNING-LIKE BOLT OF BIOELECTRIC VENOM.
OH, NO! I CAN'T DODGE WITHOUT REVEALING MY SPIDER-AGILITY! WHAT'LL I-- UHH!
WHO'S HE? WHAT'S HE DOING HERE AT THIS HOUR?
I WAS SO HOPING THAT I COULD RETURN THE MONEY AS EASILY AS I TOOK IT -- WITHOUT WITNESSES.
STILL, THAT VENOM-BLAST SHOULD KEEP HIM OUT FOR AN HOUR OR SO -- PLENTY OF TIME TO PUT MILES BETWEEN HERE AND ME!

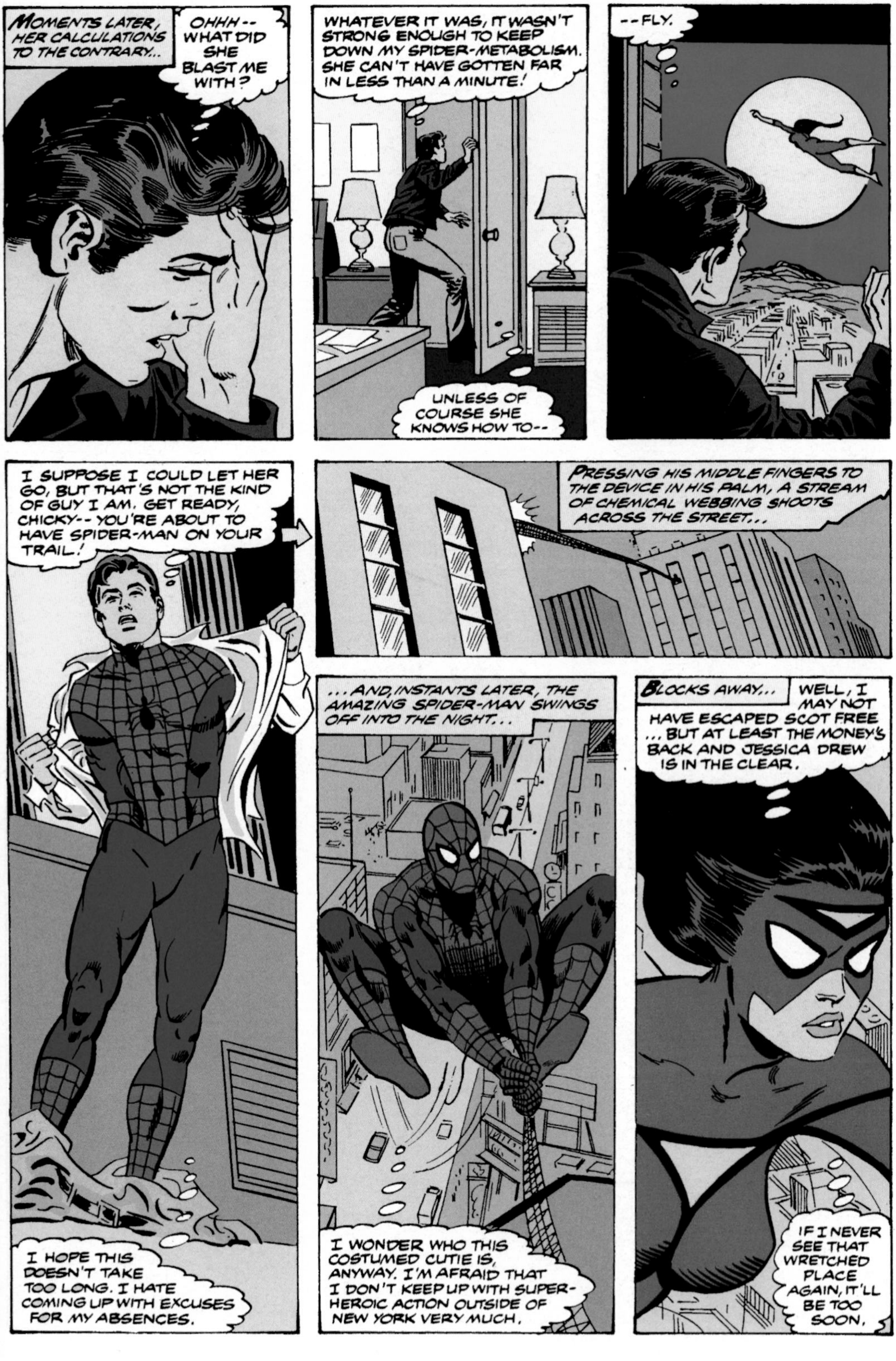
MOMENTS LATER, HER CALCULATIONS TO THE CONTRARY...
OHHH-- WHAT DID SHE BLAST ME WITH?
WHATEVER IT WAS, IT WASN'T STRONG ENOUGH TO KEEP DOWN MY SPIDER-METABOLISM. SHE CAN'T HAVE GOTTEN FAR IN LESS THAN A MINUTE!
UNLESS OF COURSE SHE KNOWS HOW TO--
--FLY.
I SUPPOSE I COULD LET HER GO, BUT THAT'S NOT THE KIND OF GUY I AM. GET READY, CHICKY-- YOU'RE ABOUT TO HAVE SPIDER-MAN ON YOUR TRAIL!
I HOPE THIS DOESN'T TAKE TOO LONG. I HATE COMING UP WITH EXCUSES FOR MY ABSENCES.
PRESSING HIS MIDDLE FINGERS TO THE DEVICE IN HIS PALM, A STREAM OF CHEMICAL WEBBING SHOOTS ACROSS THE STREET...
...AND, INSTANTS LATER, THE AMAZING SPIDER-MAN SWINGS OFF INTO THE NIGHT...
I WONDER WHO THIS COSTUMED CUTIE IS, ANYWAY. I'M AFRAID THAT I DON'T KEEP UP WITH SUPER-HEROIC ACTION OUTSIDE OF NEW YORK VERY MUCH.
BLOCKS AWAY...
WELL, I MAY NOT HAVE ESCAPED SCOT FREE ... BUT AT LEAST THE MONEY'S BACK AND JESSICA DREW IS IN THE CLEAR.
IF I NEVER SEE THAT WRETCHED PLACE AGAIN, IT'LL BE TOO SOON.

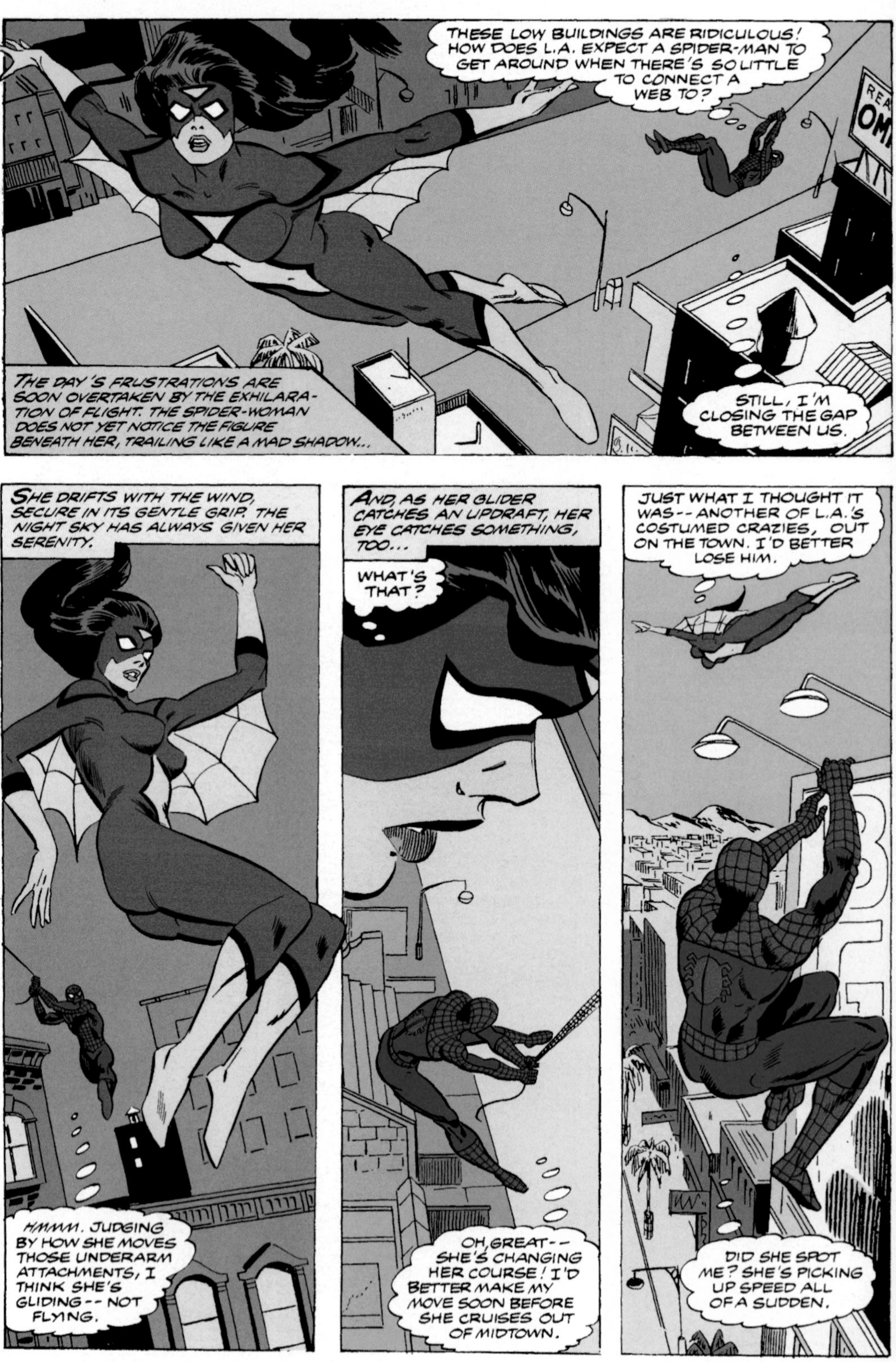
THESE LOW BUILDINGS ARE RIDICULOUS! HOW DOES L.A. EXPECT A SPIDER-MAN TO GET AROUND WHEN THERE'S SO LITTLE TO CONNECT A WEB TO?
THE DAY'S FRUSTRATIONS ARE SOON OVERTAKEN BY THE EXHILARATION OF FLIGHT. THE SPIDER-WOMAN DOES NOT YET NOTICE THE FIGURE BENEATH HER, TRAILING LIKE A MAD SHADOW...
STILL, I'M CLOSING THE GAP BETWEEN US.
SHE DRIFTS WITH THE WIND, SECURE IN ITS GENTLE GRIP. THE NIGHT SKY HAS ALWAYS GIVEN HER SERENITY.
HMMM. JUDGING BY HOW SHE MOVES THOSE UNDERARM ATTACHMENTS, I THINK SHE'S GLIDING -- NOT FLYING.
AND, AS HER GLIDER CATCHES AN UPDRAFT, HER EYE CATCHES SOMETHING, TOO...
WHAT'S THAT?
OH, GREAT-- SHE'S CHANGING HER COURSE! I'D BETTER MAKE MY MOVE SOON BEFORE SHE CRUISES OUT OF MIDTOWN.
JUST WHAT I THOUGHT IT WAS-- ANOTHER OF L.A.'S COSTUMED CRAZIES, OUT ON THE TOWN. I'D BETTER LOSE HIM.
DID SHE SPOT ME? SHE'S PICKING UP SPEED ALL OF A SUDDEN.

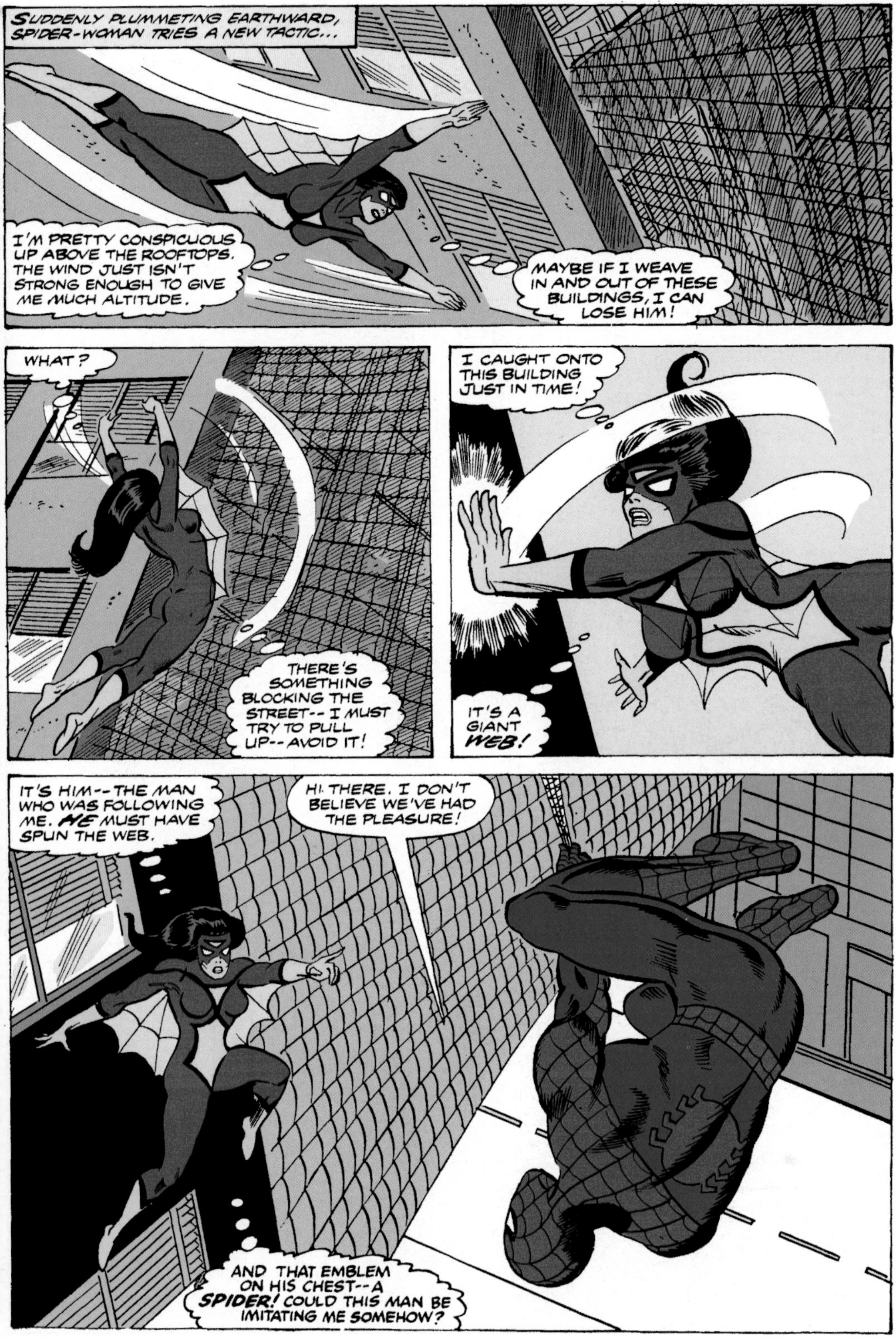
SUDDENLY PLUMMETING EARTHWARD, SPIDER-WOMAN TRIES A NEW TACTIC...
I'M PRETTY CONSPICUOUS UP ABOVE THE ROOFTOPS. THE WIND JUST ISN'T STRONG ENOUGH TO GIVE ME MUCH ALTITUDE.
MAYBE IF I WEAVE IN AND OUT OF THESE BUILDINGS, I CAN LOSE HIM!
WHAT?
THERE'S SOMETHING BLOCKING THE STREET-- I MUST TRY TO PULL UP-- AVOID IT!
I CAUGHT ONTO THIS BUILDING JUST IN TIME!
IT'S A GIANT WEB!
IT'S HIM-- THE MAN WHO WAS FOLLOWING ME. HE MUST HAVE SPUN THE WEB.
HI. THERE. I DON'T BELIEVE WE'VE HAD THE PLEASURE!
AND THAT EMBLEM ON HIS CHEST-- A SPIDER! COULD THIS MAN BE IMITATING ME SOMEHOW?

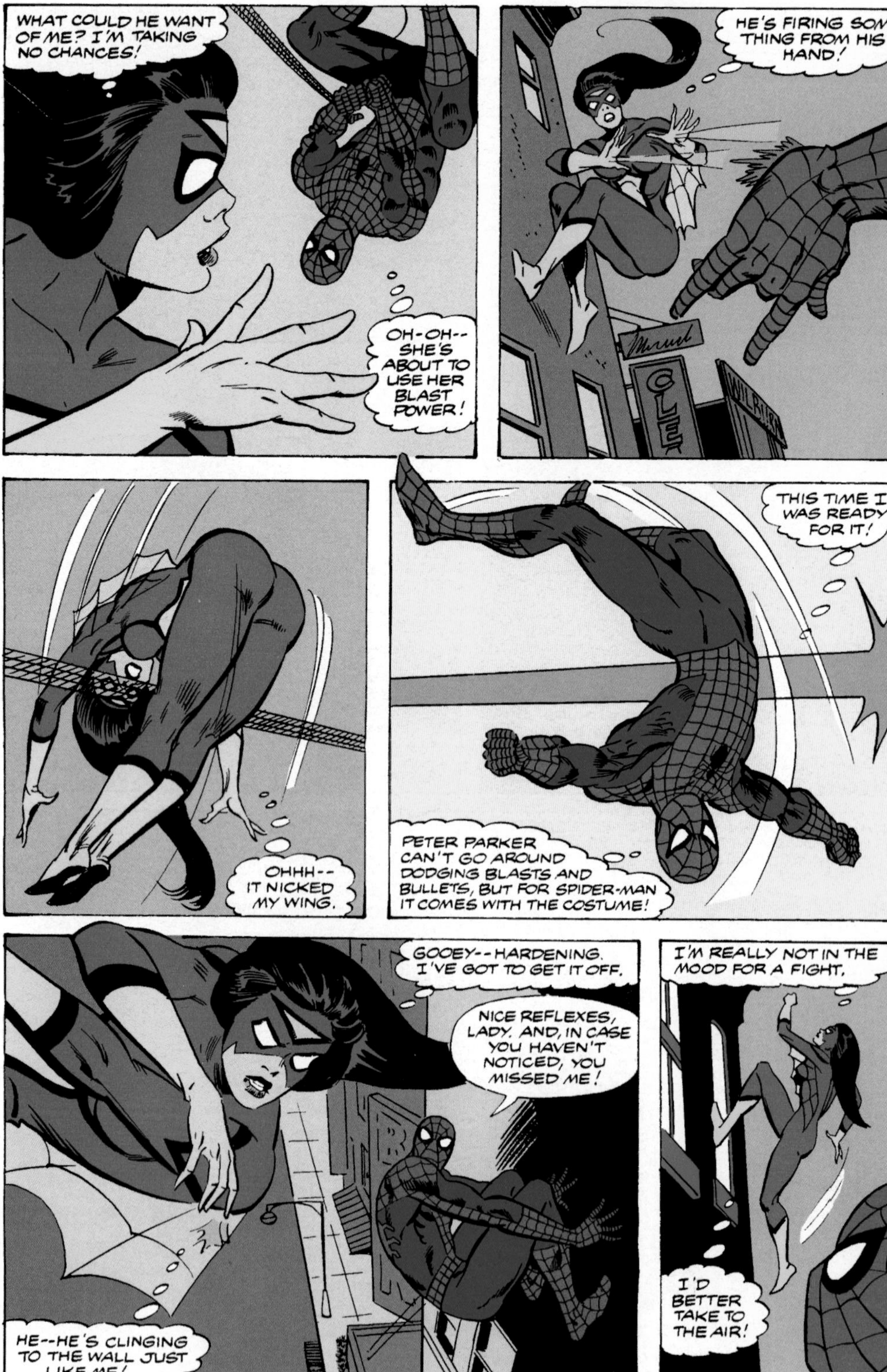
WHAT COULD HE WANT OF ME? I'M TAKING NO CHANCES!
OH-OH-- SHE'S ABOUT TO USE HER BLAST POWER!
HE'S FIRING SOMETHING FROM HIS HAND!
OHHH-- IT NICKED MY WING.
THIS TIME I WAS READY FOR IT!
PETER PARKER CAN'T GO AROUND DODGING BLASTS AND BULLETS, BUT FOR SPIDER-MAN IT COMES WITH THE COSTUME!
GOOEY--HARDENING. I'VE GOT TO GET IT OFF.
NICE REFLEXES, LADY. AND, IN CASE YOU HAVEN'T NOTICED, YOU MISSED ME!
HE--HE'S CLINGING TO THE WALL JUST LIKE ME!
I'M REALLY NOT IN THE MOOD FOR A FIGHT.
I'D BETTER TAKE TO THE AIR!

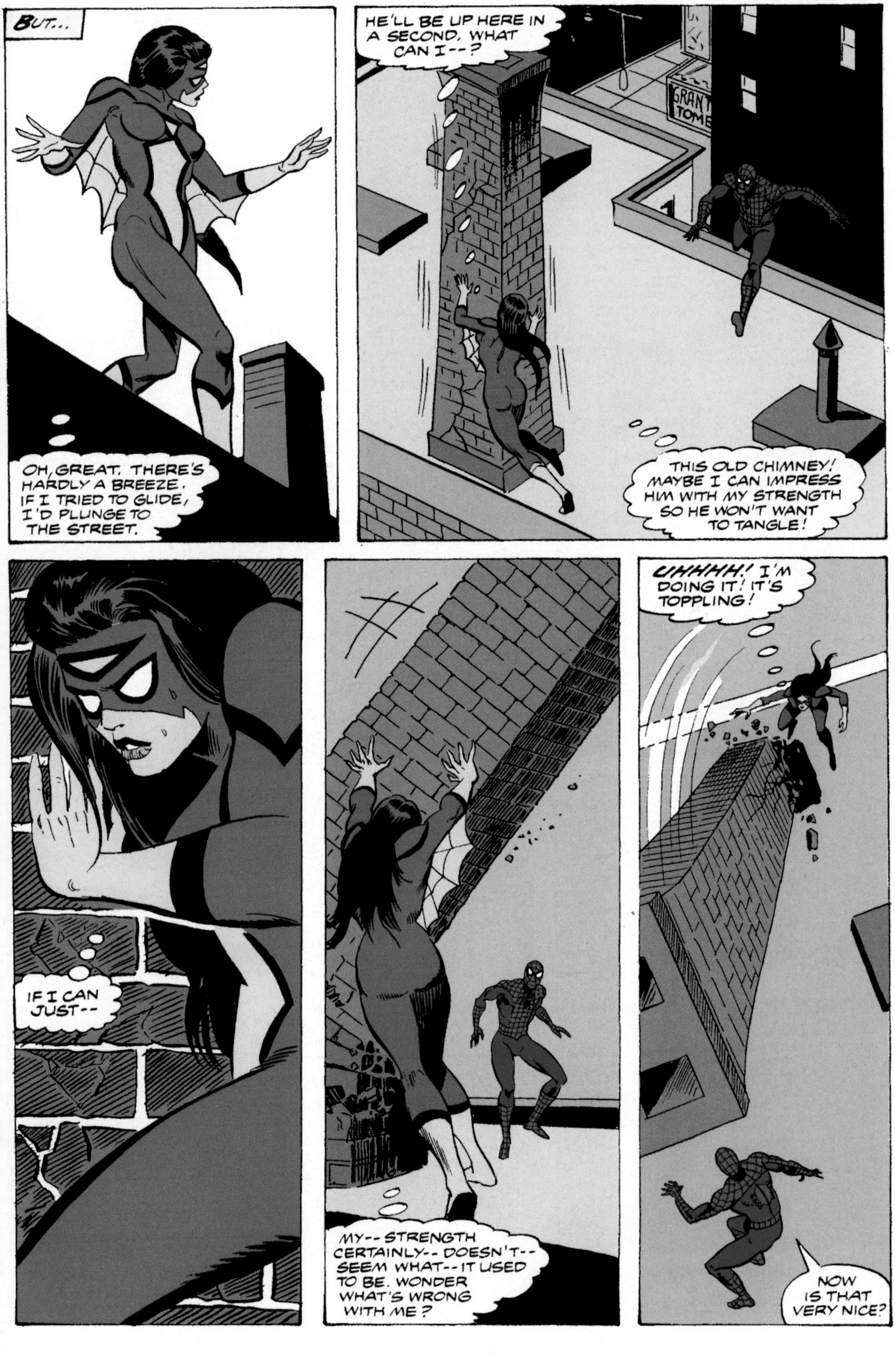
BUT...
OH, GREAT. THERE'S HARDLY A BREEZE. IF I TRIED TO GLIDE, I'D PLUNGE TO THE STREET.
HE'LL BE UP HERE IN A SECOND. WHAT CAN I--?
GRANT'S TOMB
THIS OLD CHIMNEY! MAYBE I CAN IMPRESS HIM WITH MY STRENGTH SO HE WON'T WANT TO TANGLE!
IF I CAN JUST--
MY-- STRENGTH CERTAINLY-- DOESN'T-- SEEM WHAT-- IT USED TO BE. WONDER WHAT'S WRONG WITH ME?
UHHHH! I'M DOING IT! IT'S TOPPLING!
NOW IS THAT VERY NICE?

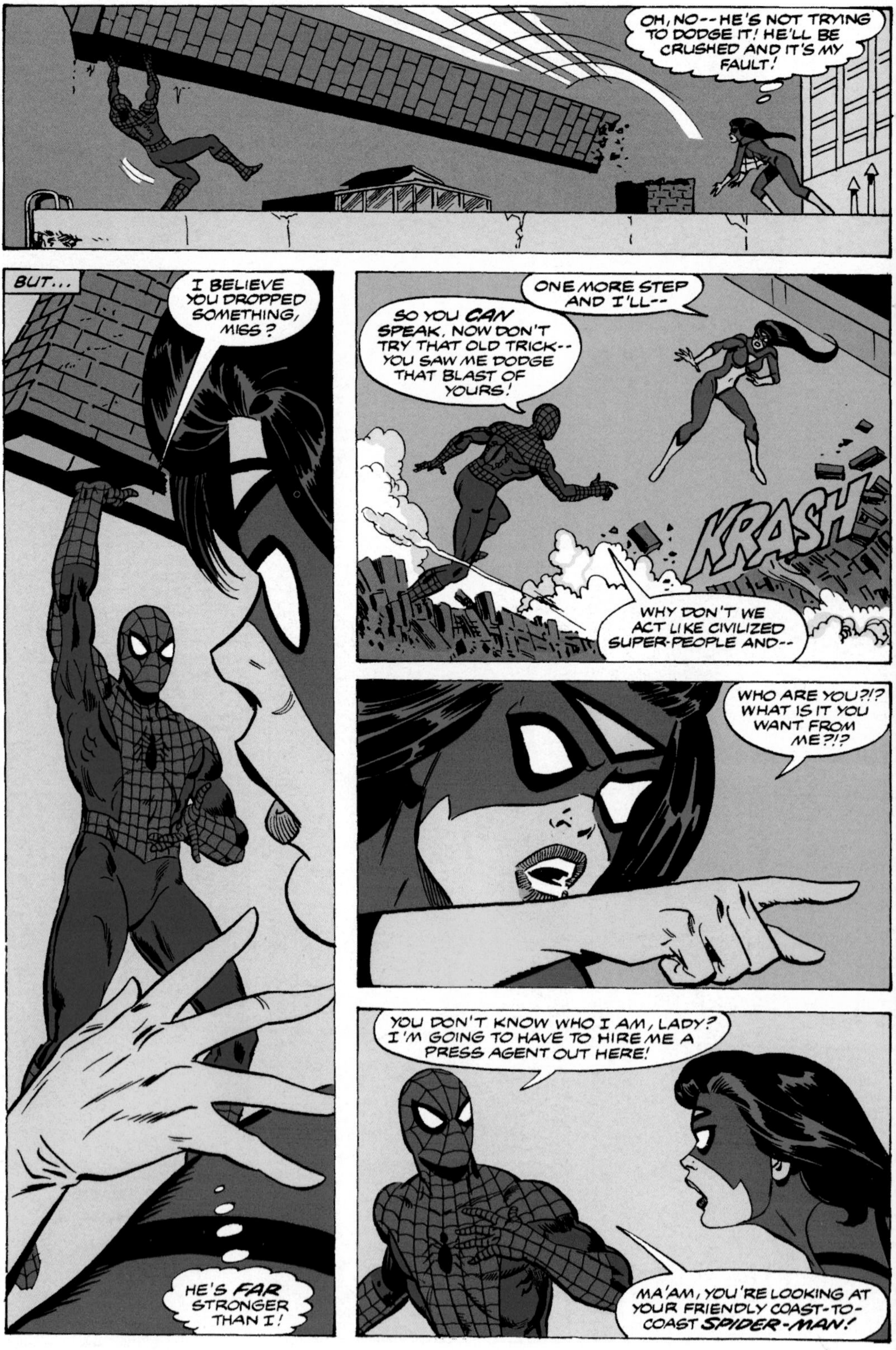
OH, NO--HE'S NOT TRYING TO DODGE IT! HE'LL BE CRUSHED AND IT'S MY FAULT!
BUT...
I BELIEVE YOU DROPPED SOMETHING, MISS?
HE'S FAR STRONGER THAN I!
ONE MORE STEP AND I'LL--
SO YOU CAN SPEAK. NOW DON'T TRY THAT OLD TRICK--YOU SAW ME DODGE THAT BLAST OF YOURS!
KRASH
WHY DON'T WE ACT LIKE CIVILIZED SUPER-PEOPLE AND--
WHO ARE YOU?!? WHAT IS IT YOU WANT FROM ME?!?
YOU DON'T KNOW WHO I AM, LADY? I'M GOING TO HAVE TO HIRE ME A PRESS AGENT OUT HERE!
MA'AM, YOU'RE LOOKING AT YOUR FRIENDLY COAST-TO-COAST SPIDER-MAN!

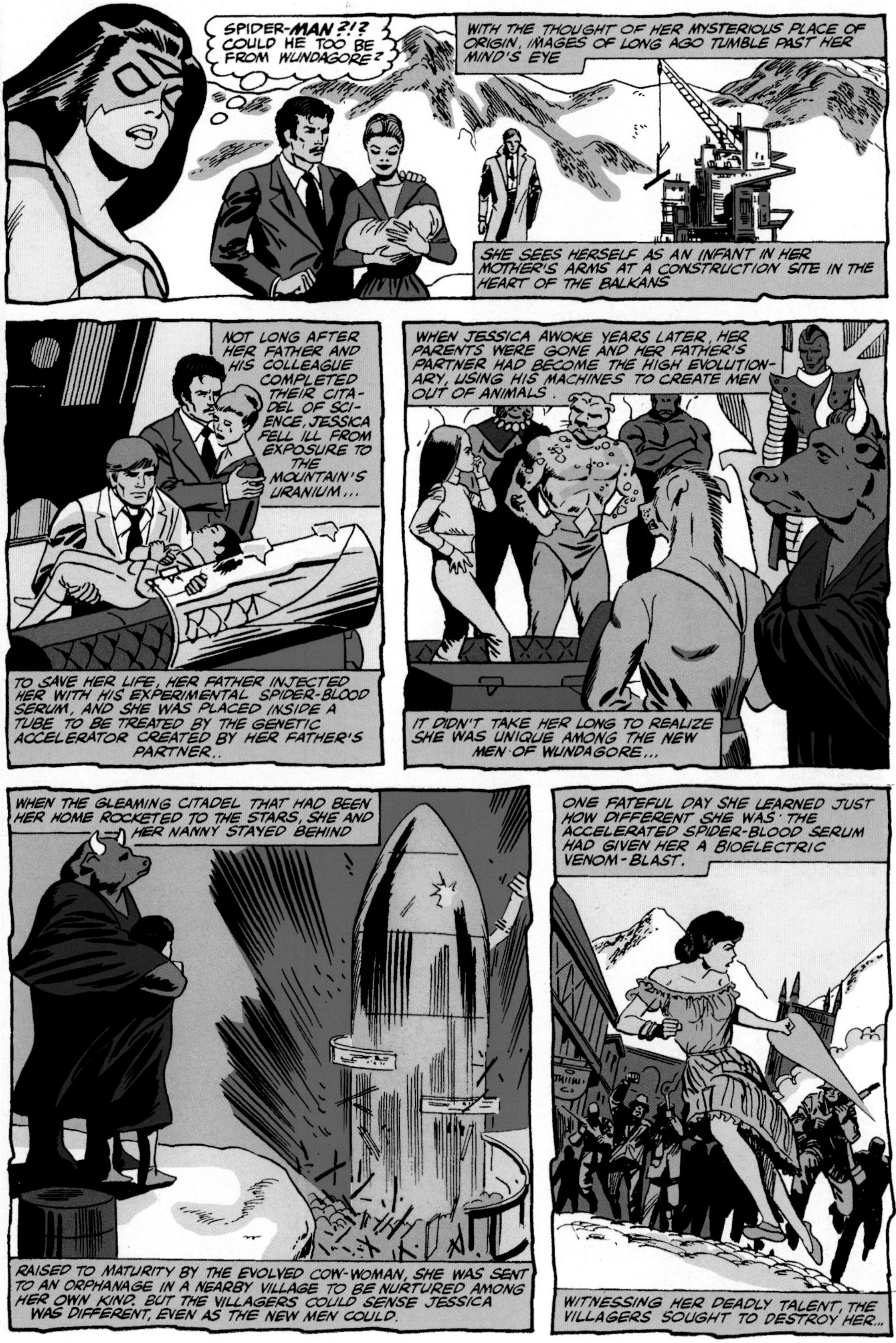
SPIDER-MAN?!? COULD HE TOO BE FROM WUNDAGORE?
WITH THE THOUGHT OF HER MYSTERIOUS PLACE OF ORIGIN, IMAGES OF LONG AGO TUMBLE PAST HER MIND'S EYE
SHE SEES HERSELF AS AN INFANT IN HER MOTHER'S ARMS AT A CONSTRUCTION SITE IN THE HEART OF THE BALKANS
NOT LONG AFTER HER FATHER AND HIS COLLEAGUE COMPLETED THEIR CITADEL OF SCIENCE, JESSICA FELL ILL FROM EXPOSURE TO THE MOUNTAIN'S URANIUM...
TO SAVE HER LIFE, HER FATHER INJECTED HER WITH HIS EXPERIMENTAL SPIDER-BLOOD SERUM, AND SHE WAS PLACED INSIDE A TUBE TO BE TREATED BY THE GENETIC ACCELERATOR CREATED BY HER FATHER'S PARTNER..
WHEN JESSICA AWOKE YEARS LATER, HER PARENTS WERE GONE AND HER FATHER'S PARTNER HAD BECOME THE HIGH EVOLUTIONARY, USING HIS MACHINES TO CREATE MEN OUT OF ANIMALS.
IT DIDN'T TAKE HER LONG TO REALIZE SHE WAS UNIQUE AMONG THE NEW MEN OF WUNDAGORE...
WHEN THE GLEAMING CITADEL THAT HAD BEEN HER HOME ROCKETED TO THE STARS, SHE AND HER NANNY STAYED BEHIND
RAISED TO MATURITY BY THE EVOLVED COW-WOMAN, SHE WAS SENT TO AN ORPHANAGE IN A NEARBY VILLAGE TO BE NURTURED AMONG HER OWN KIND. BUT THE VILLAGERS COULD SENSE JESSICA WAS DIFFERENT, EVEN AS THE NEW MEN COULD.
ONE FATEFUL DAY SHE LEARNED JUST HOW DIFFERENT SHE WAS: THE ACCELERATED SPIDER-BLOOD SERUM HAD GIVEN HER A BIOELECTRIC VENOM-BLAST.
WITNESSING HER DEADLY TALENT, THE VILLAGERS SOUGHT TO DESTROY HER...

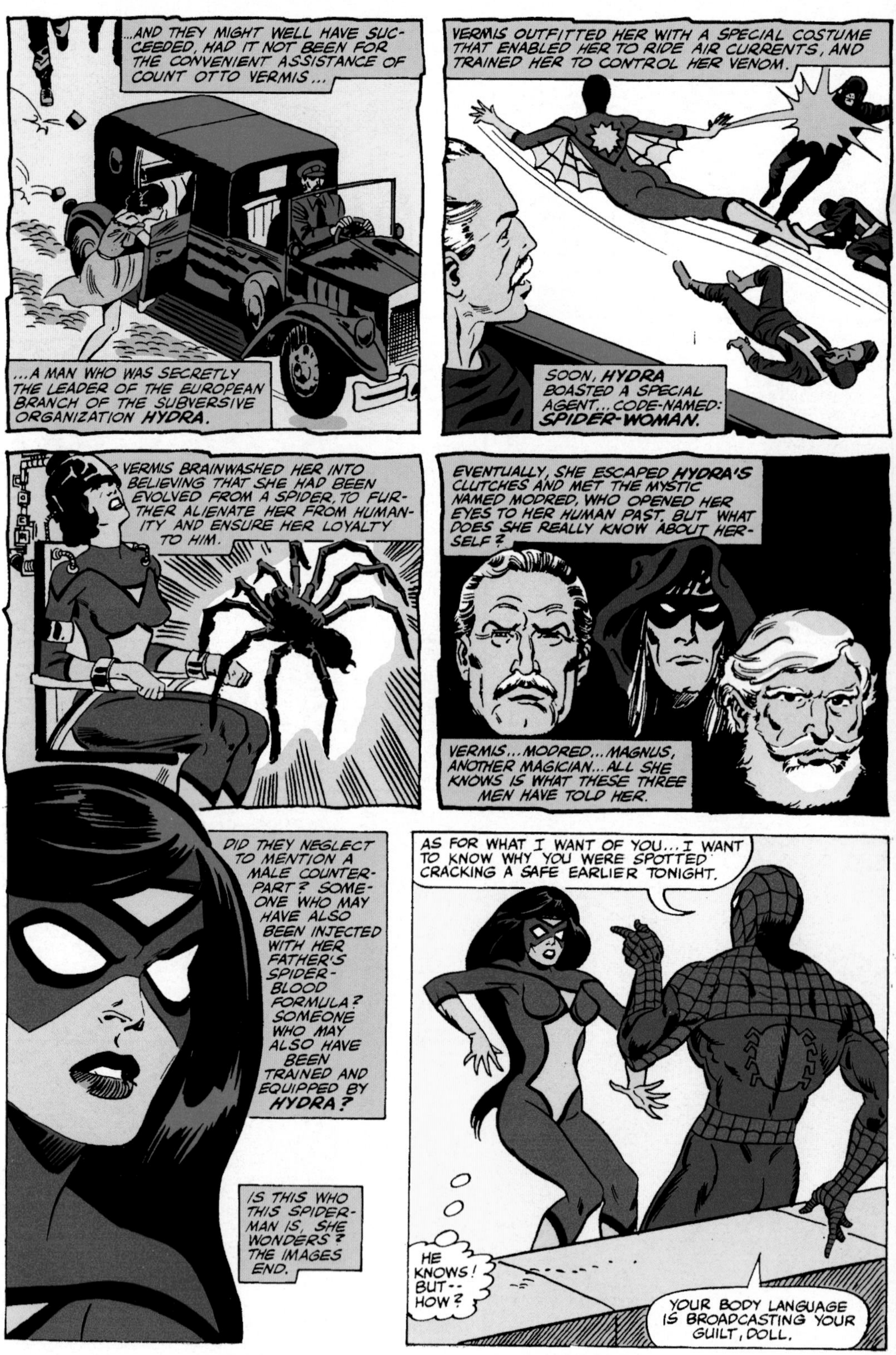
...AND THEY MIGHT WELL HAVE SUCCEEDED, HAD IT NOT BEEN FOR THE CONVENIENT ASSISTANCE OF COUNT OTTO VERMIS...
...A MAN WHO WAS SECRETLY THE LEADER OF THE EUROPEAN BRANCH OF THE SUBVERSIVE ORGANIZATION HYDRA.
VERMIS OUTFITTED HER WITH A SPECIAL COSTUME THAT ENABLED HER TO RIDE AIR CURRENTS, AND TRAINED HER TO CONTROL HER VENOM.
SOON, HYDRA BOASTED A SPECIAL AGENT... CODE-NAMED: SPIDER-WOMAN.
VERMIS BRAINWASHED HER INTO BELIEVING THAT SHE HAD BEEN EVOLVED FROM A SPIDER, TO FURTHER ALIENATE HER FROM HUMANITY AND ENSURE HER LOYALTY TO HIM.
EVENTUALLY, SHE ESCAPED HYDRA'S CLUTCHES AND MET THE MYSTIC NAMED MODRED, WHO OPENED HER EYES TO HER HUMAN PAST, BUT WHAT DOES SHE REALLY KNOW ABOUT HERSELF?
VERMIS... MODRED... MAGNUS, ANOTHER MAGICIAN... ALL SHE KNOWS IS WHAT THESE THREE MEN HAVE TOLD HER.
DID THEY NEGLECT TO MENTION A MALE COUNTERPART? SOMEONE WHO MAY HAVE ALSO BEEN INJECTED WITH HER FATHER'S SPIDER-BLOOD FORMULA? SOMEONE WHO MAY ALSO HAVE BEEN TRAINED AND EQUIPPED BY HYDRA?
IS THIS WHO THIS SPIDER-MAN IS, SHE WONDERS? THE IMAGES END.
AS FOR WHAT I WANT OF YOU... I WANT TO KNOW WHY YOU WERE SPOTTED CRACKING A SAFE EARLIER TONIGHT.
HE KNOWS! BUT--HOW?
YOUR BODY LANGUAGE IS BROADCASTING YOUR GUILT, DOLL.

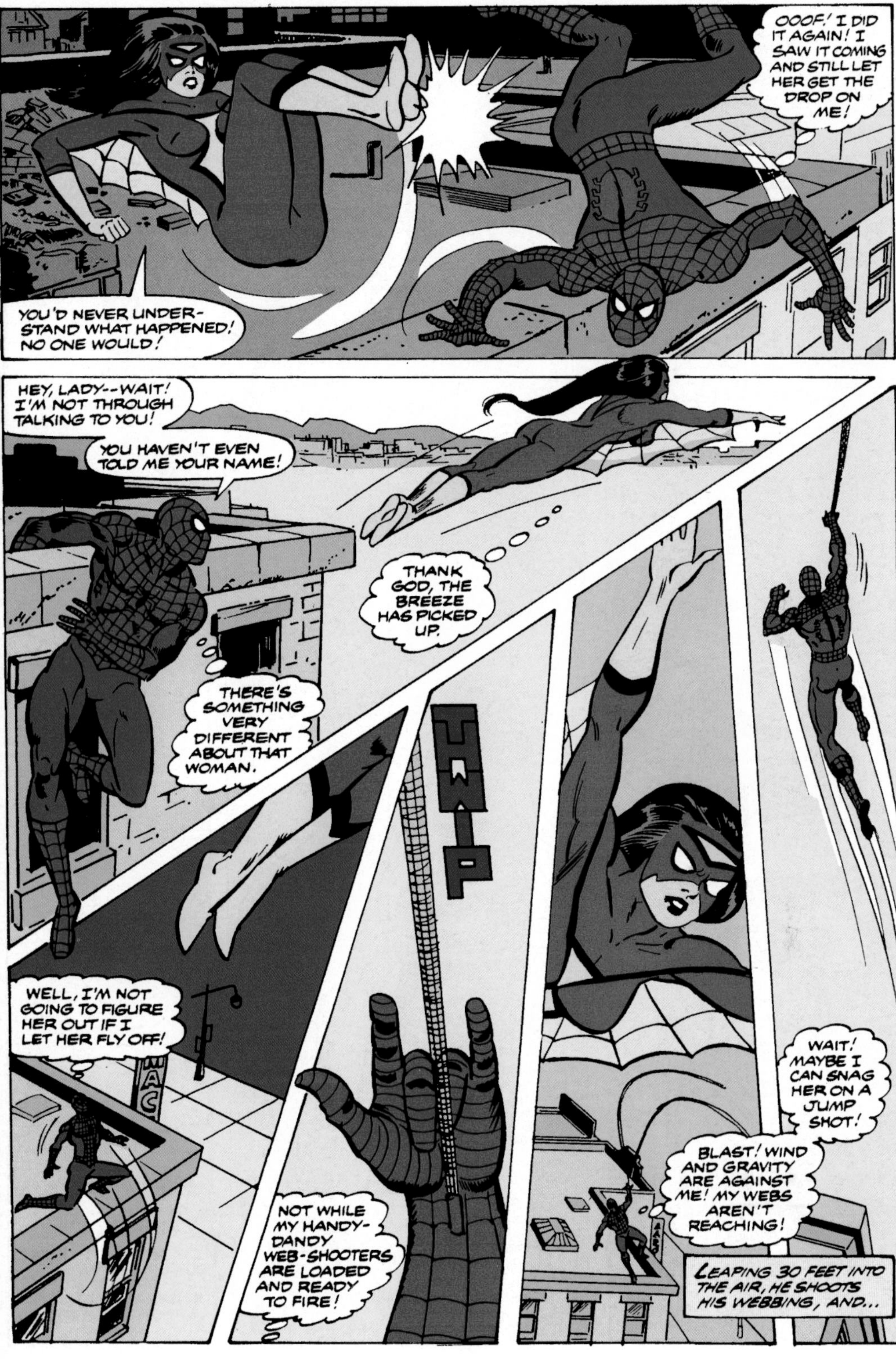
OOOF! I DID IT AGAIN! I SAW IT COMING AND STILL LET HER GET THE DROP ON ME!
YOU'D NEVER UNDERSTAND WHAT HAPPENED! NO ONE WOULD!
HEY, LADY--WAIT! I'M NOT THROUGH TALKING TO YOU!
YOU HAVEN'T EVEN TOLD ME YOUR NAME!
THANK GOD, THE BREEZE HAS PICKED UP.
THERE'S SOMETHING VERY DIFFERENT ABOUT THAT WOMAN.
THWIP
WELL, I'M NOT GOING TO FIGURE HER OUT IF I LET HER FLY OFF!
NOT WHILE MY HANDY-DANDY WEB-SHOOTERS ARE LOADED AND READY TO FIRE!
WAIT! MAYBE I CAN SNAG HER ON A JUMP SHOT!
BLAST! WIND AND GRAVITY ARE AGAINST ME! MY WEBS AREN'T REACHING!
LEAPING 30 FEET INTO THE AIR, HE SHOOTS HIS WEBBING, AND...

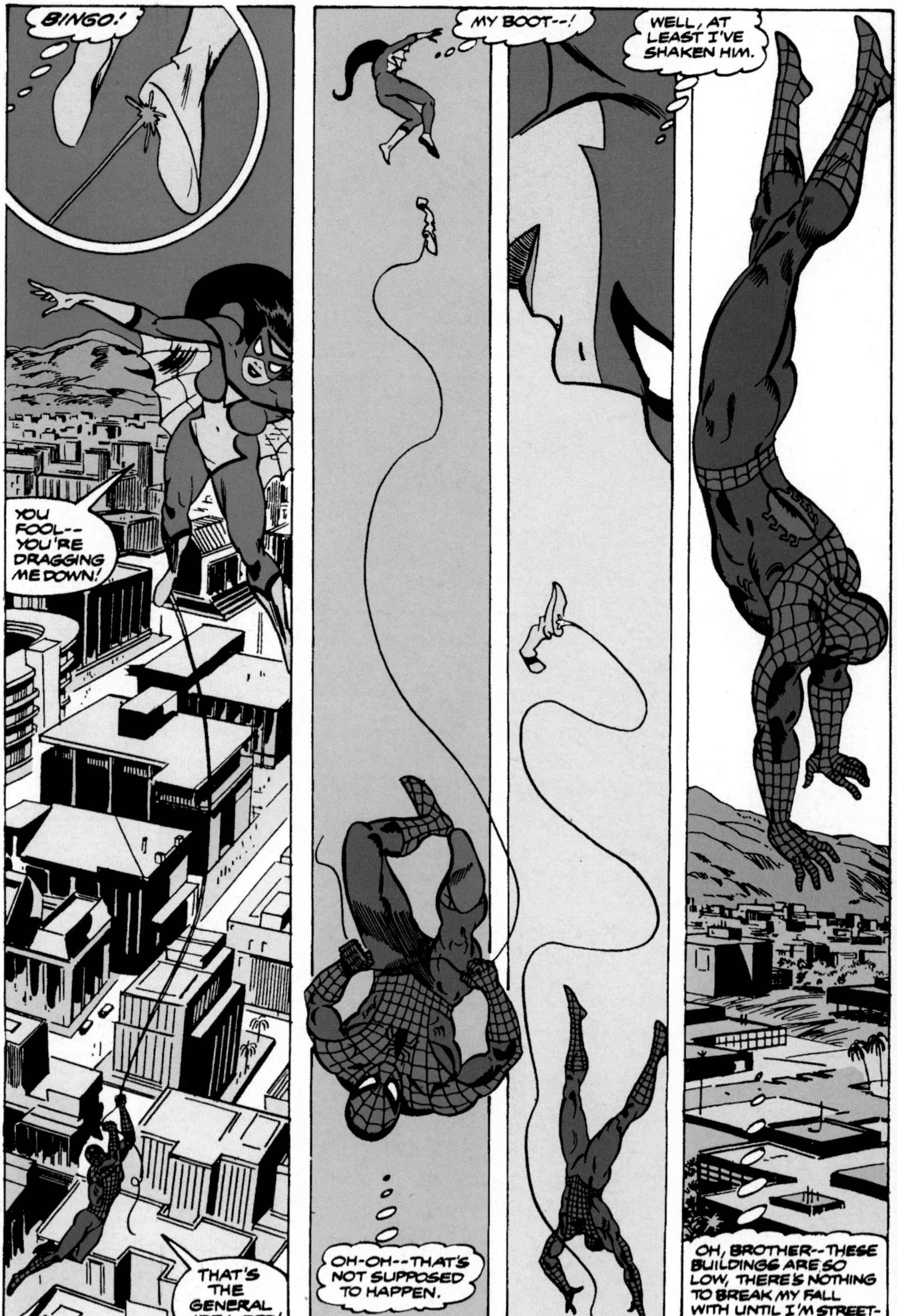
BINGO!
YOU FOOL-- YOU'RE DRAGGING ME DOWN!
THAT'S THE GENERAL IDEA, RED!
MY BOOT--!
OH-OH--THAT'S NOT SUPPOSED TO HAPPEN.
WELL, AT LEAST I'VE SHAKEN HIM.
OH, BROTHER--THESE BUILDINGS ARE SO LOW, THERE'S NOTHING TO BREAK MY FALL WITH UNTIL I'M STREET-LEVEL!

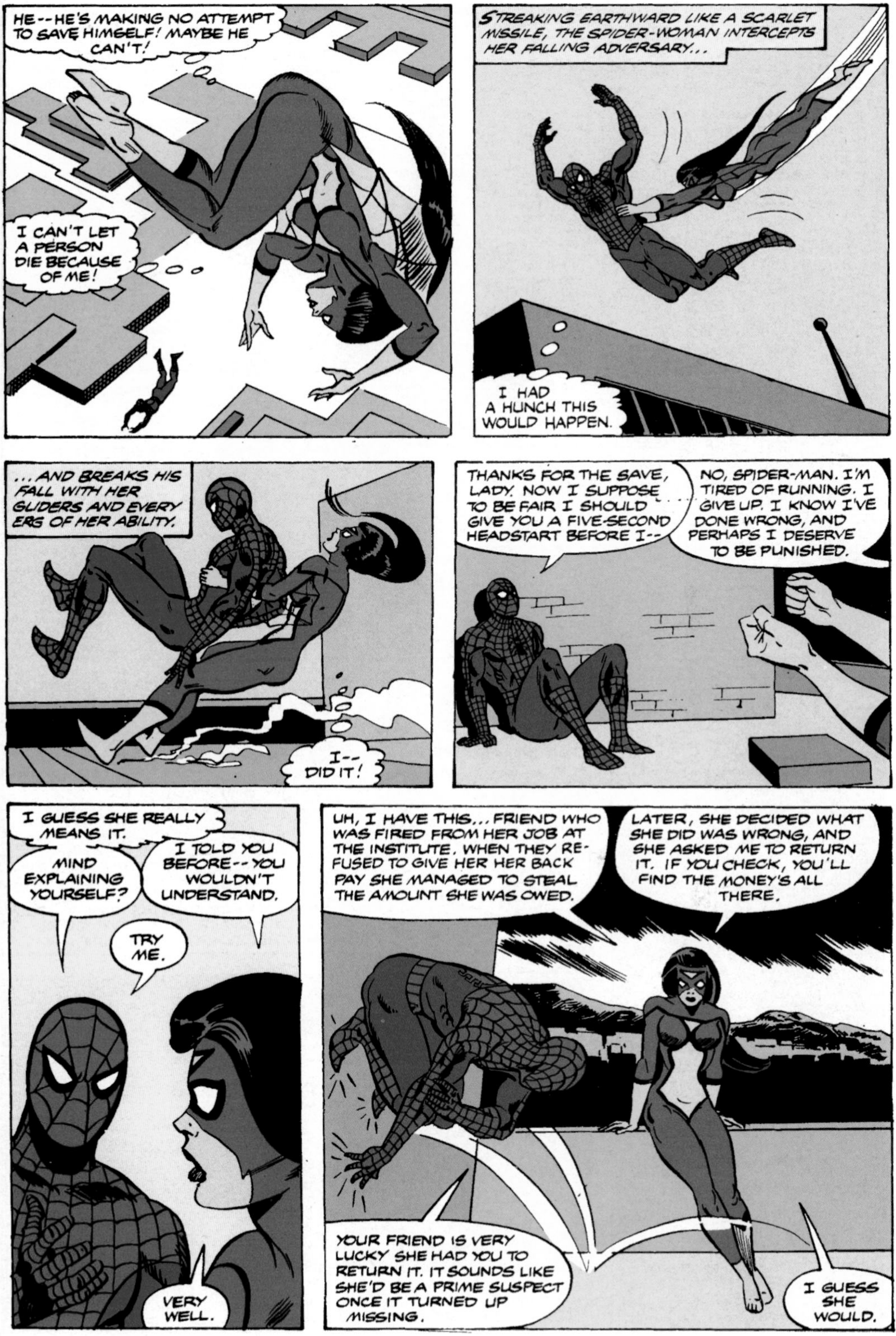
HE--HE'S MAKING NO ATTEMPT TO SAVE HIMSELF! MAYBE HE CAN'T!
I CAN'T LET A PERSON DIE BECAUSE OF ME!
STREAKING EARTHWARD LIKE A SCARLET MISSILE, THE SPIDER-WOMAN INTERCEPTS HER FALLING ADVERSARY...
I HAD A HUNCH THIS WOULD HAPPEN.
...AND BREAKS HIS FALL WITH HER GLIDERS AND EVERY ERG OF HER ABILITY.
I-- DID IT!
THANKS FOR THE SAVE, LADY. NOW I SUPPOSE TO BE FAIR I SHOULD GIVE YOU A FIVE-SECOND HEADSTART BEFORE I--
NO, SPIDER-MAN. I'M TIRED OF RUNNING. I GIVE UP. I KNOW I'VE DONE WRONG, AND PERHAPS I DESERVE TO BE PUNISHED.
I GUESS SHE REALLY MEANS IT.
MIND EXPLAINING YOURSELF?
I TOLD YOU BEFORE--YOU WOULDN'T UNDERSTAND.
TRY ME.
VERY WELL.
UH, I HAVE THIS... FRIEND WHO WAS FIRED FROM HER JOB AT THE INSTITUTE. WHEN THEY REFUSED TO GIVE HER HER BACK PAY SHE MANAGED TO STEAL THE AMOUNT SHE WAS OWED.
LATER, SHE DECIDED WHAT SHE DID WAS WRONG, AND SHE ASKED ME TO RETURN IT. IF YOU CHECK, YOU'LL FIND THE MONEY'S ALL THERE.
YOUR FRIEND IS VERY LUCKY SHE HAD YOU TO RETURN IT. IT SOUNDS LIKE SHE'D BE A PRIME SUSPECT ONCE IT TURNED UP MISSING.
I GUESS SHE WOULD.

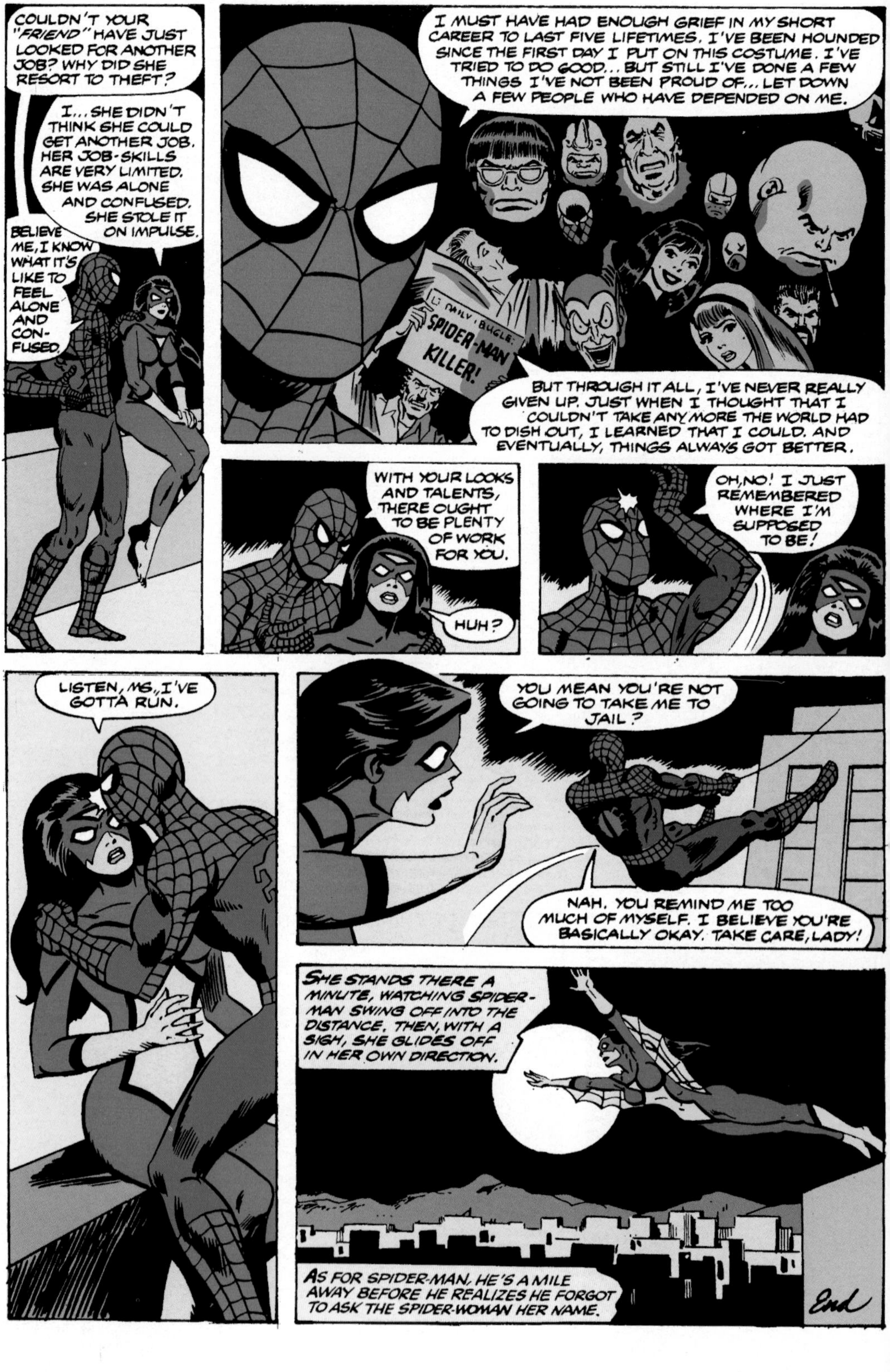
COULDN'T YOUR "FRIEND" HAVE JUST LOOKED FOR ANOTHER JOB? WHY DID SHE RESORT TO THEFT?
I... SHE DIDN'T THINK SHE COULD GET ANOTHER JOB. HER JOB-SKILLS ARE VERY LIMITED. SHE WAS ALONE AND CONFUSED. SHE STOLE IT ON IMPULSE.
BELIEVE ME, I KNOW WHAT IT'S LIKE TO FEEL ALONE AND CON-FUSED.
I MUST HAVE HAD ENOUGH GRIEF IN MY SHORT CAREER TO LAST FIVE LIFETIMES. I'VE BEEN HOUNDED SINCE THE FIRST DAY I PUT ON THIS COSTUME. I'VE TRIED TO DO GOOD... BUT STILL I'VE DONE A FEW THINGS I'VE NOT BEEN PROUD OF... LET DOWN A FEW PEOPLE WHO HAVE DEPENDED ON ME.
DAILY BUGLE
SPIDER-MAN KILLER!
BUT THROUGH IT ALL, I'VE NEVER REALLY GIVEN UP. JUST WHEN I THOUGHT THAT I COULDN'T TAKE ANY MORE THE WORLD HAD TO DISH OUT, I LEARNED THAT I COULD. AND EVENTUALLY, THINGS ALWAYS GOT BETTER.
WITH YOUR LOOKS AND TALENTS, THERE OUGHT TO BE PLENTY OF WORK FOR YOU.
HUH?
OH, NO! I JUST REMEMBERED WHERE I'M SUPPOSED TO BE!
LISTEN, MS., I'VE GOTTA RUN.
YOU MEAN YOU'RE NOT GOING TO TAKE ME TO JAIL?
NAH. YOU REMIND ME TOO MUCH OF MYSELF. I BELIEVE YOU'RE BASICALLY OKAY. TAKE CARE, LADY!
SHE STANDS THERE A MINUTE, WATCHING SPIDER-MAN SWING OFF INTO THE DISTANCE. THEN, WITH A SIGH, SHE GLIDES OFF IN HER OWN DIRECTION.
AS FOR SPIDER-MAN, HE'S A MILE AWAY BEFORE HE REALIZES HE FORGOT TO ASK THE SPIDER-WOMAN HER NAME.
End

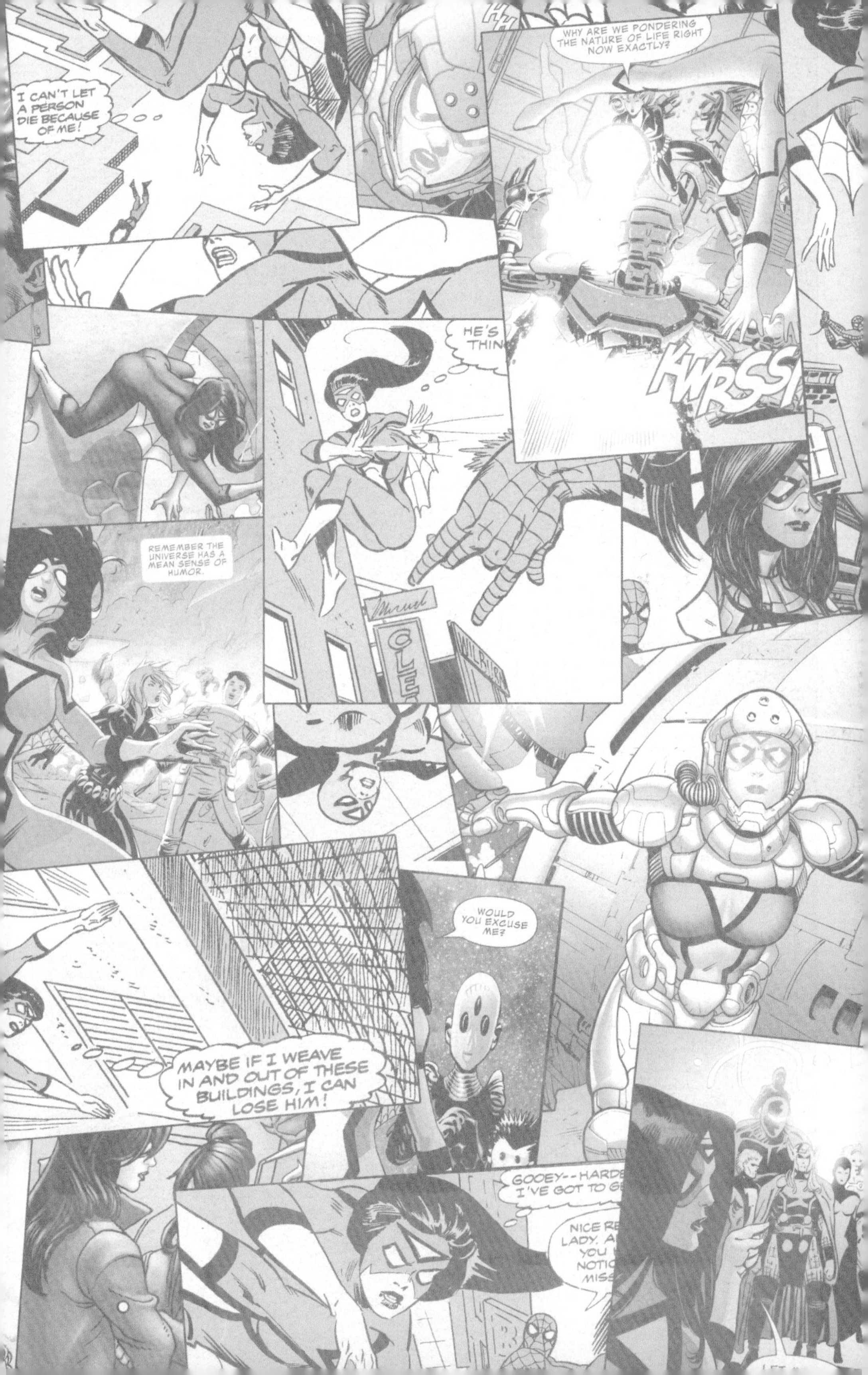

I CAN'T LET A PERSON DIE BECAUSE OF ME!
WHY ARE WE PONDERING THE NATURE OF LIFE RIGHT NOW EXACTLY?
REMEMBER THE UNIVERSE HAS A MEAN SENSE OF HUMOR.
WOULD YOU EXCUSE ME?
MAYBE IF I WEAVE IN AND OUT OF THESE BUILDINGS, I CAN LOSE HIM!

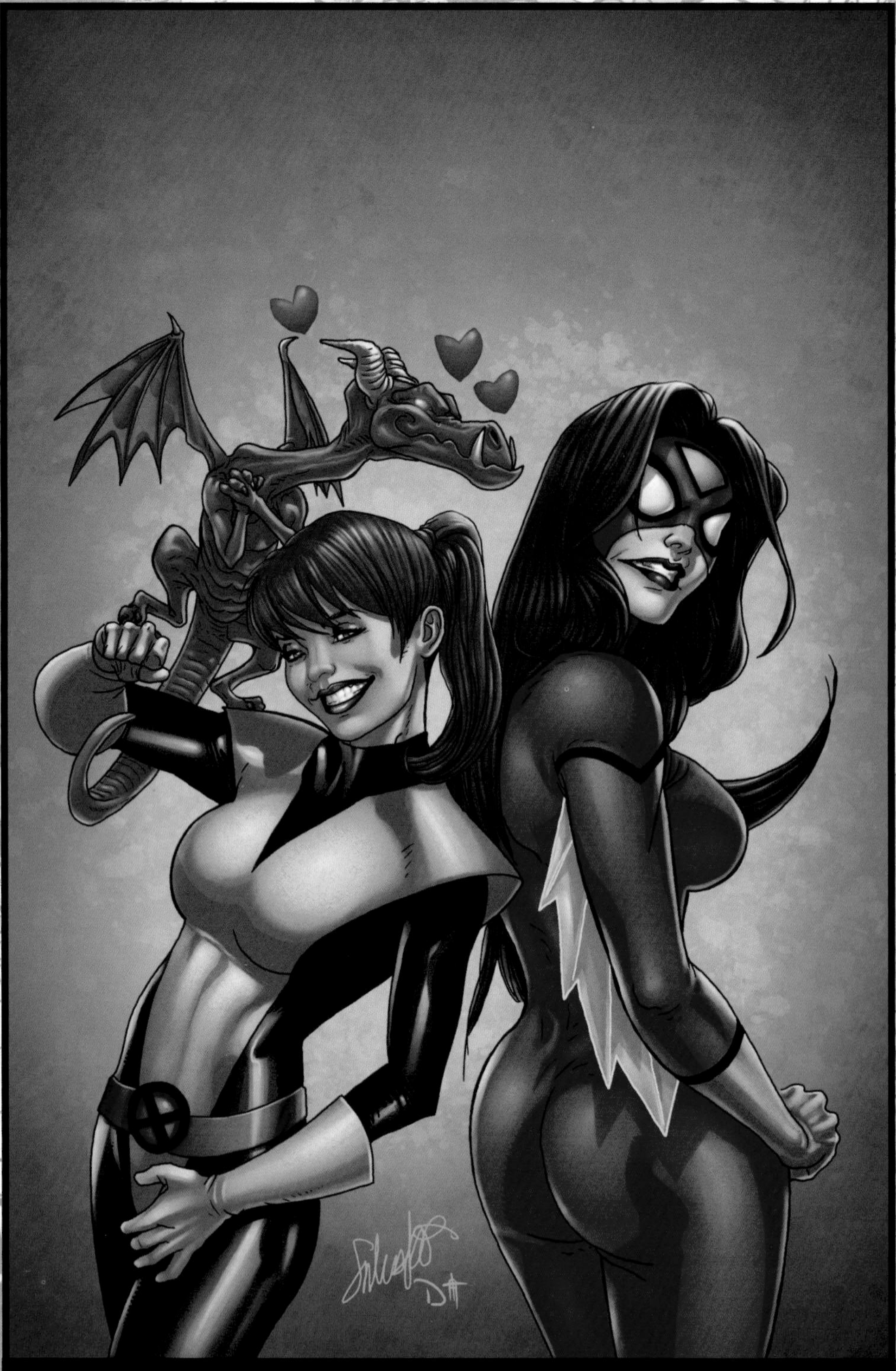

A+X #8

SPIDER-WOMAN IS JOINED BY KITTY PRYDE AND LOCKHEED TO TRACK DOWN A MYSTERIOUS METEORITE BEFORE IT FALLS INTO THE WRONG HANDS!

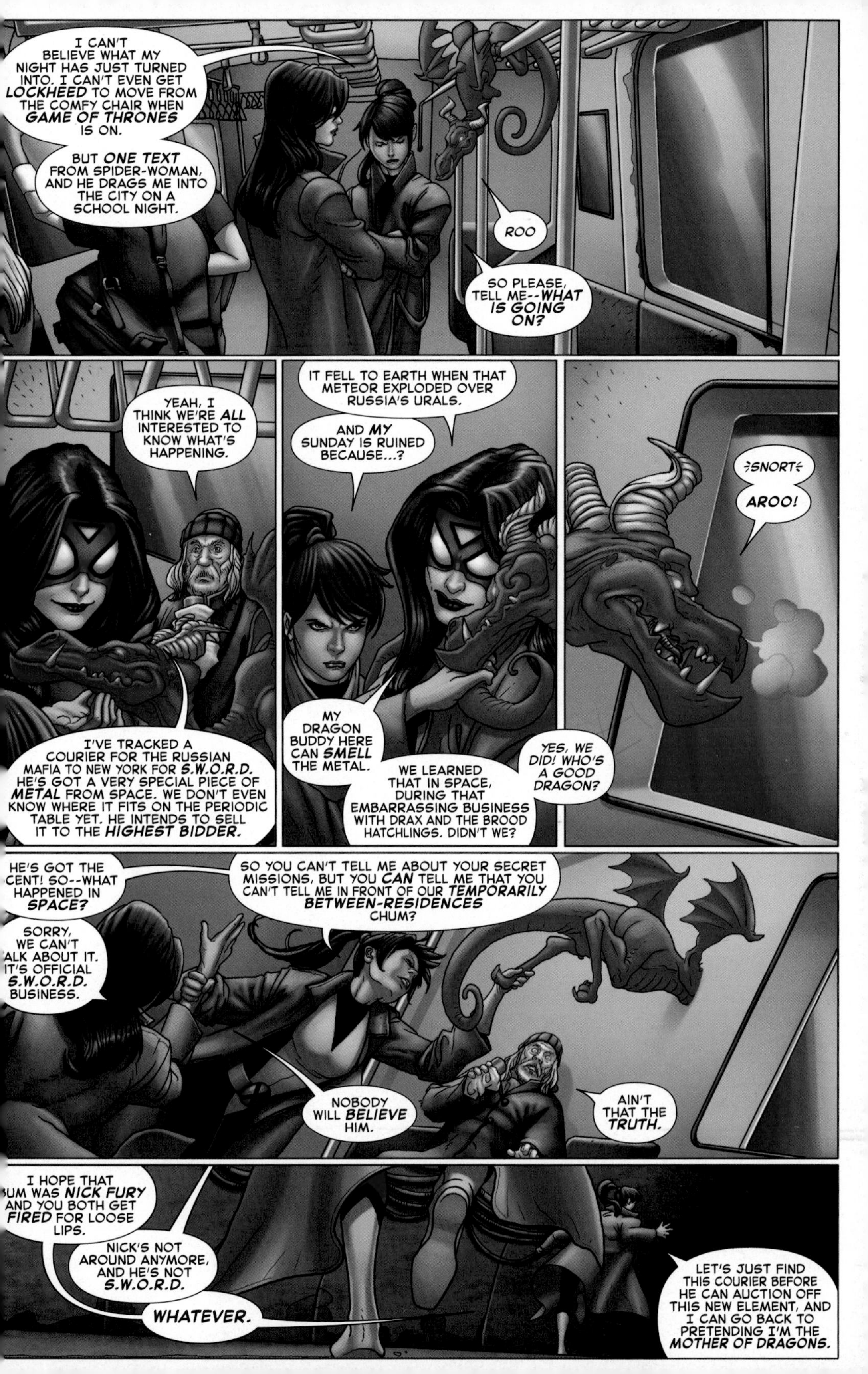

I CAN'T BELIEVE WHAT MY NIGHT HAS JUST TURNED INTO. I CAN'T EVEN GET LOCKHEED TO MOVE FROM THE COMFY CHAIR WHEN GAME OF THRONES IS ON.
BUT ONE TEXT FROM SPIDER-WOMAN, AND HE DRAGS ME INTO THE CITY ON A SCHOOL NIGHT.
ROO
SO PLEASE, TELL ME--WHAT IS GOING ON?
YEAH, I THINK WE'RE ALL INTERESTED TO KNOW WHAT'S HAPPENING.
I'VE TRACKED A COURIER FOR THE RUSSIAN MAFIA TO NEW YORK FOR S.W.O.R.D. HE'S GOT A VERY SPECIAL PIECE OF METAL FROM SPACE. WE DON'T EVEN KNOW WHERE IT FITS ON THE PERIODIC TABLE YET. HE INTENDS TO SELL IT TO THE HIGHEST BIDDER.
IT FELL TO EARTH WHEN THAT METEOR EXPLODED OVER RUSSIA'S URALS.
AND MY SUNDAY IS RUINED BECAUSE...?
MY DRAGON BUDDY HERE CAN SMELL THE METAL.
WE LEARNED THAT IN SPACE, DURING THAT EMBARRASSING BUSINESS WITH DRAX AND THE BROOD HATCHLINGS. DIDN'T WE?
YES, WE DID! WHO'S A GOOD DRAGON?
SNORT
AROO!
HE'S GOT THE CENT! SO--WHAT HAPPENED IN SPACE?
SORRY, WE CAN'T ALK ABOUT IT. IT'S OFFICIAL S.W.O.R.D. BUSINESS.
SO YOU CAN'T TELL ME ABOUT YOUR SECRET MISSIONS, BUT YOU CAN TELL ME THAT YOU CAN'T TELL ME IN FRONT OF OUR TEMPORARILY BETWEEN-RESIDENCES CHUM?
NOBODY WILL BELIEVE HIM.
AIN'T THAT THE TRUTH.
I HOPE THAT UM WAS NICK FURY AND YOU BOTH GET FIRED FOR LOOSE LIPS.
NICK'S NOT AROUND ANYMORE, AND HE'S NOT S.W.O.R.D.
WHATEVER.
LET'S JUST FIND THIS COURIER BEFORE HE CAN AUCTION OFF THIS NEW ELEMENT, AND I CAN GO BACK TO PRETENDING I'M THE MOTHER OF DRAGONS.

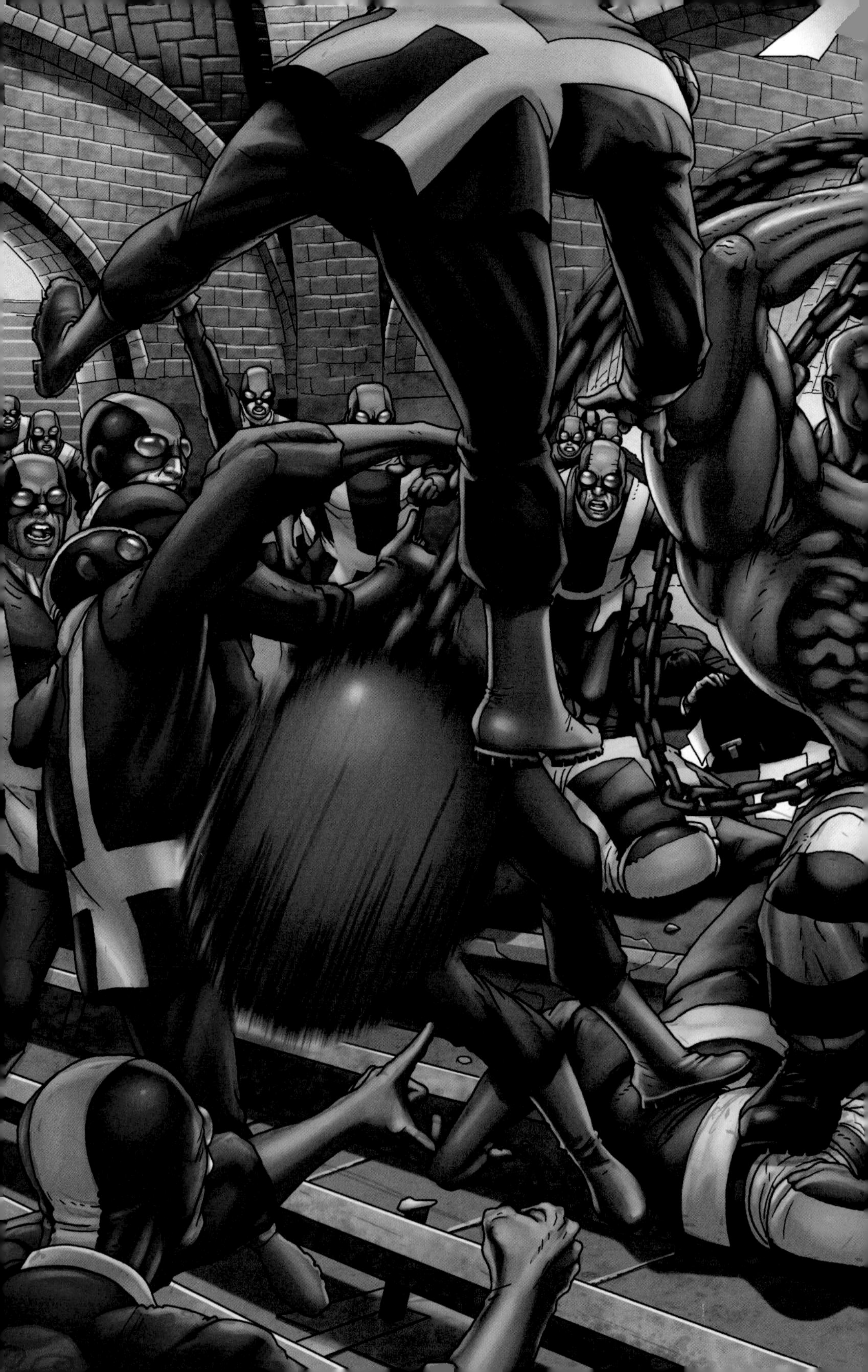

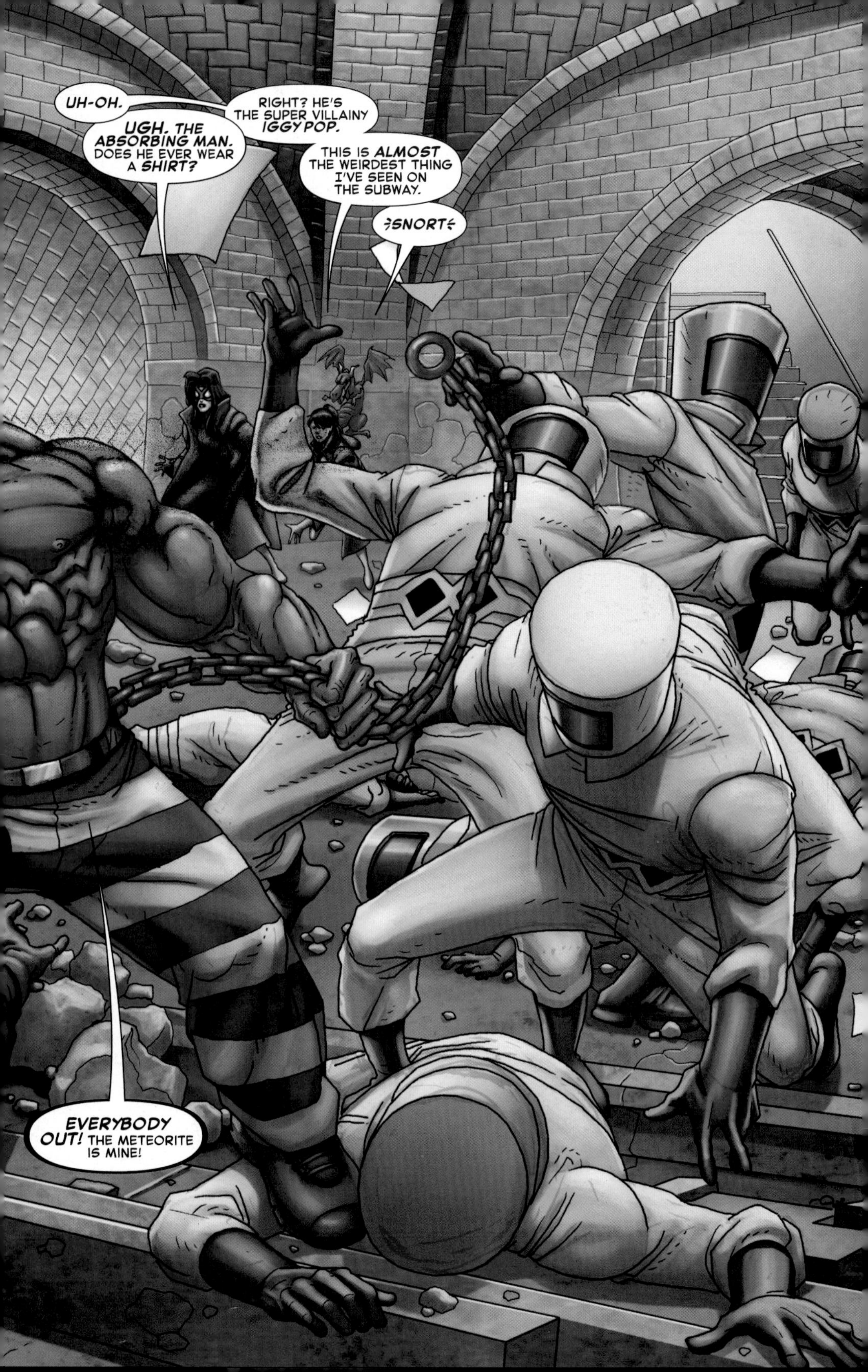
UH-OH.
RIGHT? HE'S THE SUPER VILLAINY IGGY POP.
UGH. THE ABSORBING MAN. DOES HE EVER WEAR A SHIRT?
THIS IS ALMOST THE WEIRDEST THING I'VE SEEN ON THE SUBWAY.
SNORT
EVERYBODY OUT! THE METEORITE IS MINE!

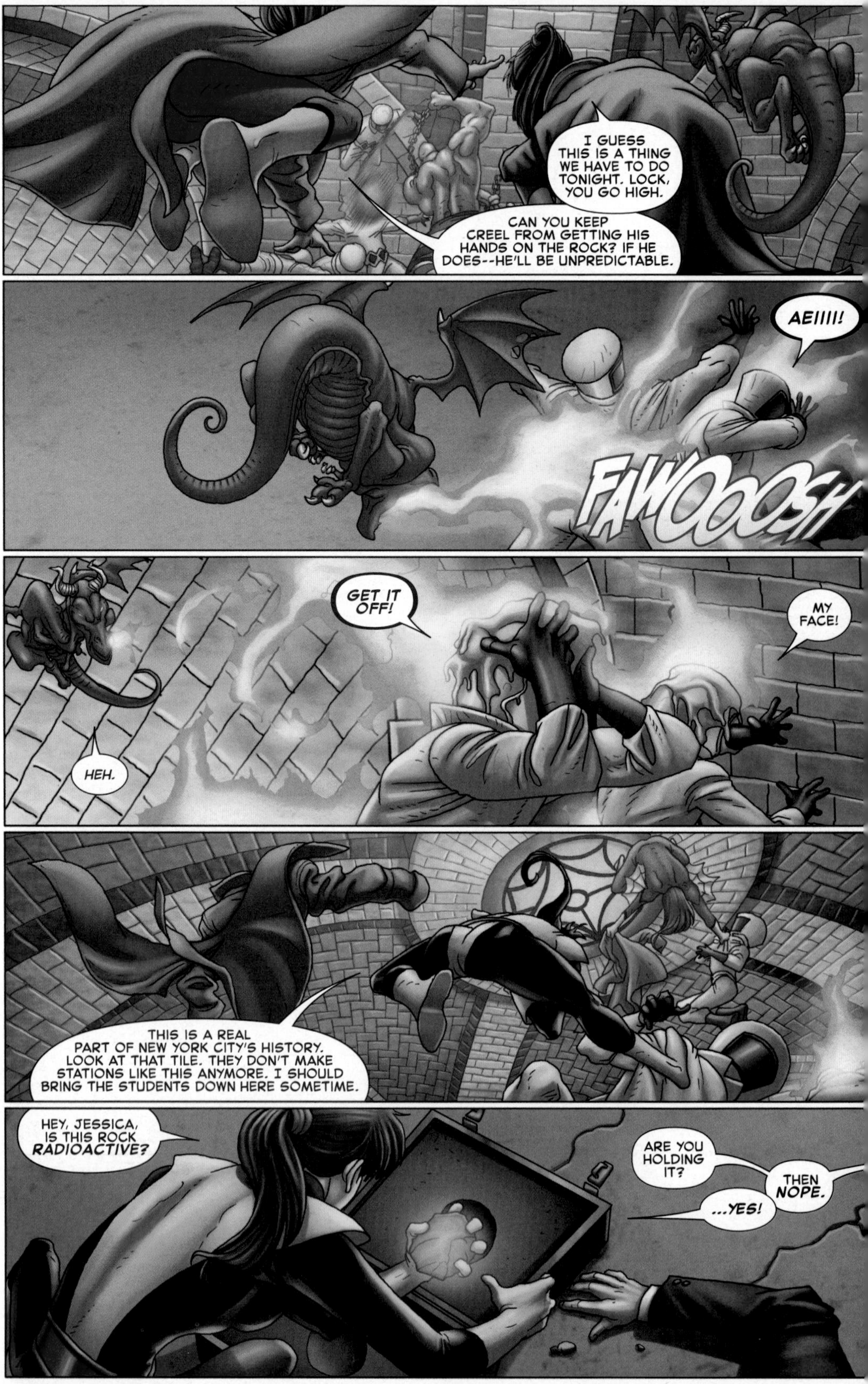
I GUESS THIS IS A THING WE HAVE TO DO TONIGHT. LOCK, YOU GO HIGH.
CAN YOU KEEP CREEL FROM GETTING HIS HANDS ON THE ROCK? IF HE DOES--HE'LL BE UNPREDICTABLE.
AEIIII!
FAWOOOSH
GET IT OFF!
MY FACE!
HEH.
THIS IS A REAL PART OF NEW YORK CITY'S HISTORY. LOOK AT THAT TILE. THEY DON'T MAKE STATIONS LIKE THIS ANYMORE. I SHOULD BRING THE STUDENTS DOWN HERE SOMETIME.
HEY, JESSICA, IS THIS ROCK *RADIOACTIVE?*
ARE YOU HOLDING IT?
...YES!
THEN *NOPE.*

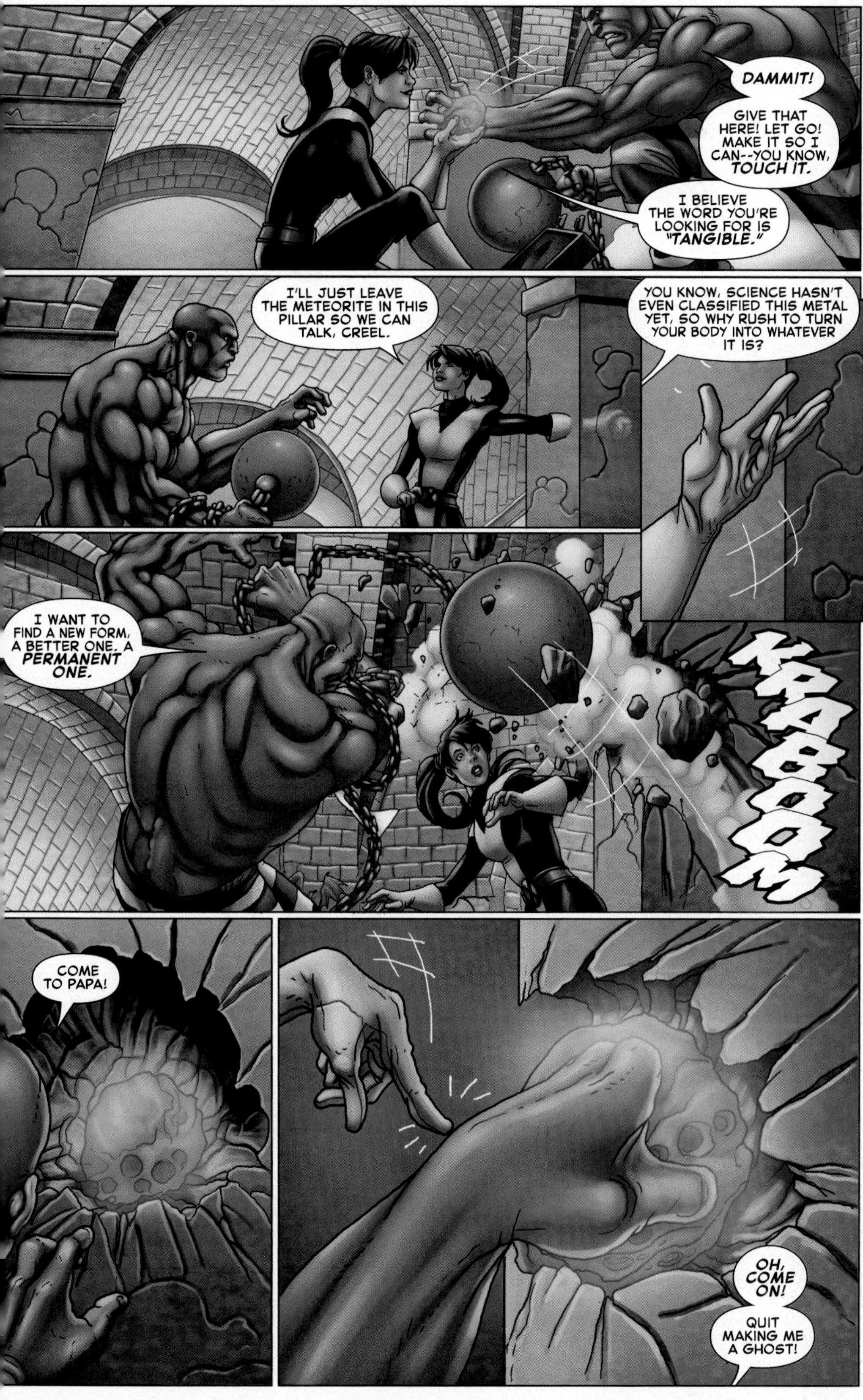
DAMMIT!
GIVE THAT HERE! LET GO! MAKE IT SO I CAN--YOU KNOW, *TOUCH IT.*
I BELIEVE THE WORD YOU'RE LOOKING FOR IS "*TANGIBLE.*"
I'LL JUST LEAVE THE METEORITE IN THIS PILLAR SO WE CAN TALK, CREEL.
YOU KNOW, SCIENCE HASN'T EVEN CLASSIFIED THIS METAL YET, SO WHY RUSH TO TURN YOUR BODY INTO WHATEVER IT IS?
I WANT TO FIND A NEW FORM, A BETTER ONE. A *PERMANENT ONE.*
KRABOOOM
COME TO PAPA!
OH, COME ON!
QUIT MAKING ME A GHOST!

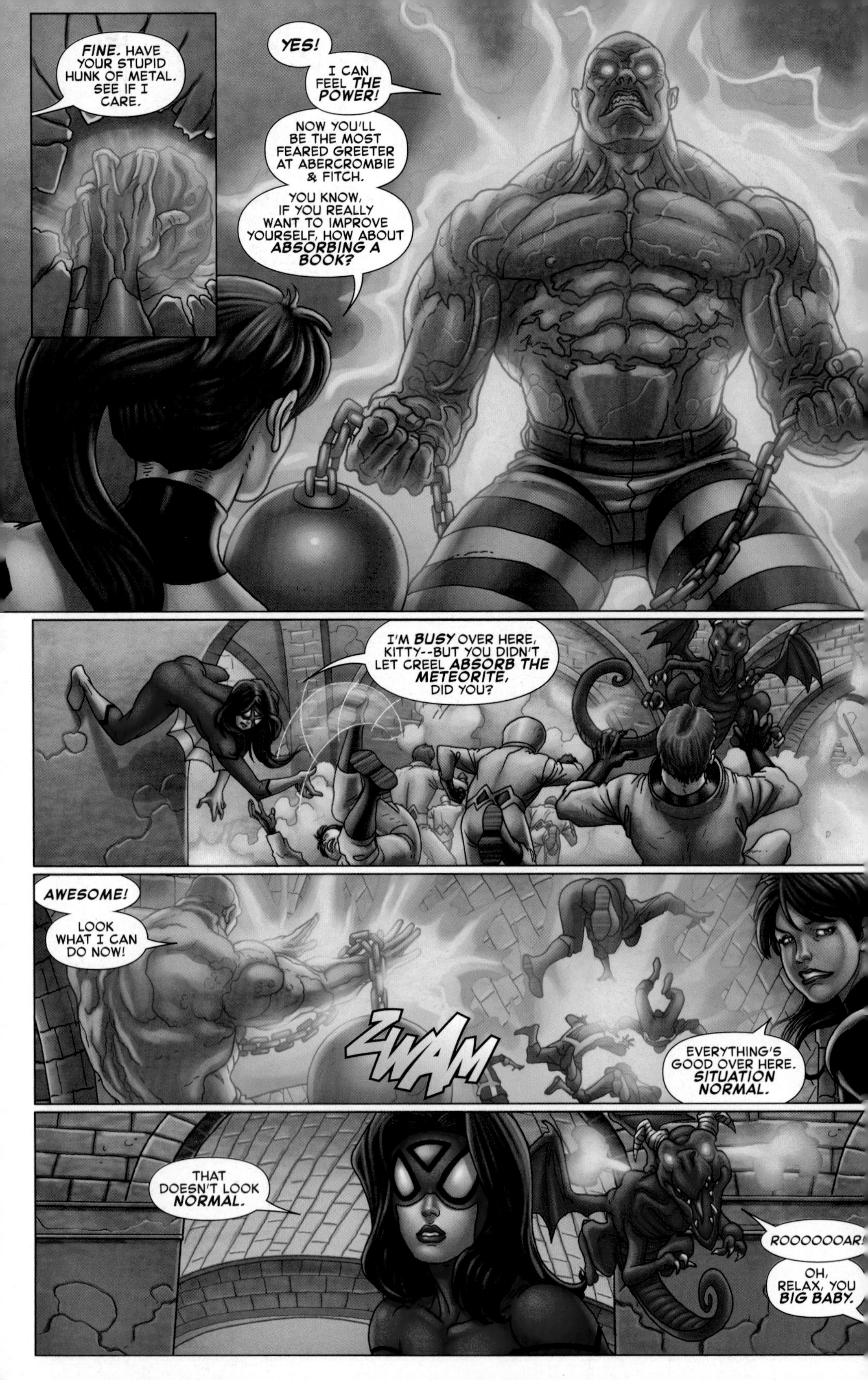
FINE. HAVE YOUR STUPID HUNK OF METAL. SEE IF I CARE.
YES!
I CAN FEEL THE POWER!
NOW YOU'LL BE THE MOST FEARED GREETER AT ABERCROMBIE & FITCH.
YOU KNOW, IF YOU REALLY WANT TO IMPROVE YOURSELF, HOW ABOUT ABSORBING A BOOK?
I'M BUSY OVER HERE, KITTY--BUT YOU DIDN'T LET CREEL ABSORB THE METEORITE, DID YOU?
AWESOME!
LOOK WHAT I CAN DO NOW!
ZWAM
EVERYTHING'S GOOD OVER HERE. SITUATION NORMAL.
THAT DOESN'T LOOK NORMAL.
ROOOOOOAR!
OH, RELAX, YOU BIG BABY.

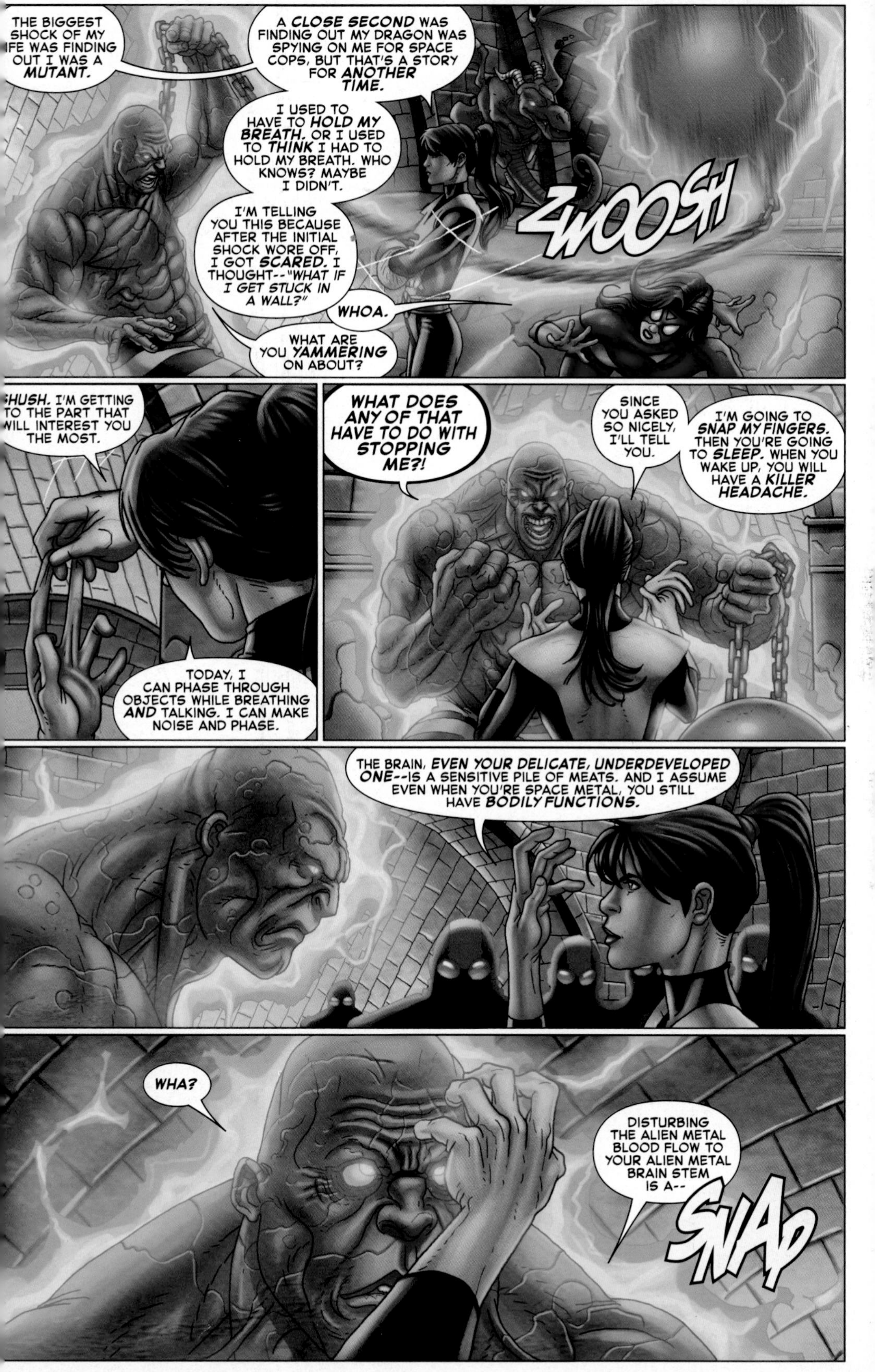

THE BIGGEST SHOCK OF MY LIFE WAS FINDING OUT I WAS A MUTANT.
A CLOSE SECOND WAS FINDING OUT MY DRAGON WAS SPYING ON ME FOR SPACE COPS, BUT THAT'S A STORY FOR ANOTHER TIME.
I USED TO HAVE TO HOLD MY BREATH. OR I USED TO THINK I HAD TO HOLD MY BREATH. WHO KNOWS? MAYBE I DIDN'T.
I'M TELLING YOU THIS BECAUSE AFTER THE INITIAL SHOCK WORE OFF, I GOT SCARED. I THOUGHT--"WHAT IF I GET STUCK IN A WALL?"
ZWOOSH
WHOA.
WHAT ARE YOU YAMMERING ON ABOUT?
SHUSH. I'M GETTING TO THE PART THAT WILL INTEREST YOU THE MOST.
TODAY, I CAN PHASE THROUGH OBJECTS WHILE BREATHING AND TALKING. I CAN MAKE NOISE AND PHASE.
WHAT DOES ANY OF THAT HAVE TO DO WITH STOPPING ME?!
SINCE YOU ASKED SO NICELY, I'LL TELL YOU.
I'M GOING TO SNAP MY FINGERS. THEN YOU'RE GOING TO SLEEP. WHEN YOU WAKE UP, YOU WILL HAVE A KILLER HEADACHE.
THE BRAIN, EVEN YOUR DELICATE, UNDERDEVELOPED ONE--IS A SENSITIVE PILE OF MEATS. AND I ASSUME EVEN WHEN YOU'RE SPACE METAL, YOU STILL HAVE BODILY FUNCTIONS.
WHA?
DISTURBING THE ALIEN METAL BLOOD FLOW TO YOUR ALIEN METAL BRAIN STEM IS A--
SNAP

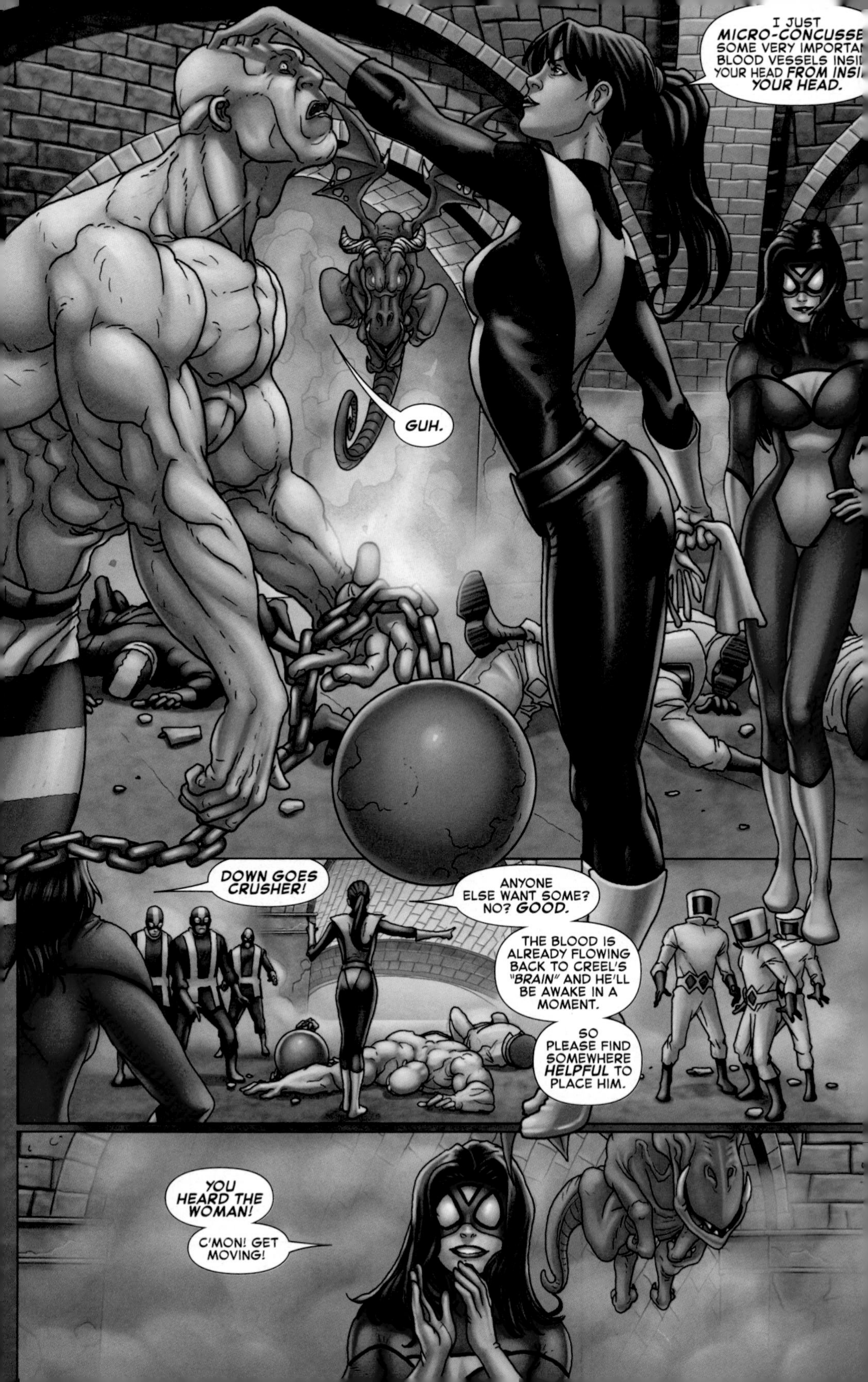
I JUST MICRO-CONCUSSE SOME VERY IMPORTAN BLOOD VESSELS INSID YOUR HEAD FROM INSI YOUR HEAD.
GUH.
DOWN GOES CRUSHER!
ANYONE ELSE WANT SOME? NO? GOOD.
THE BLOOD IS ALREADY FLOWING BACK TO CREEL'S "BRAIN" AND HE'LL BE AWAKE IN A MOMENT.
SO PLEASE FIND SOMEWHERE HELPFUL TO PLACE HIM.
YOU HEARD THE WOMAN!
C'MON! GET MOVING!

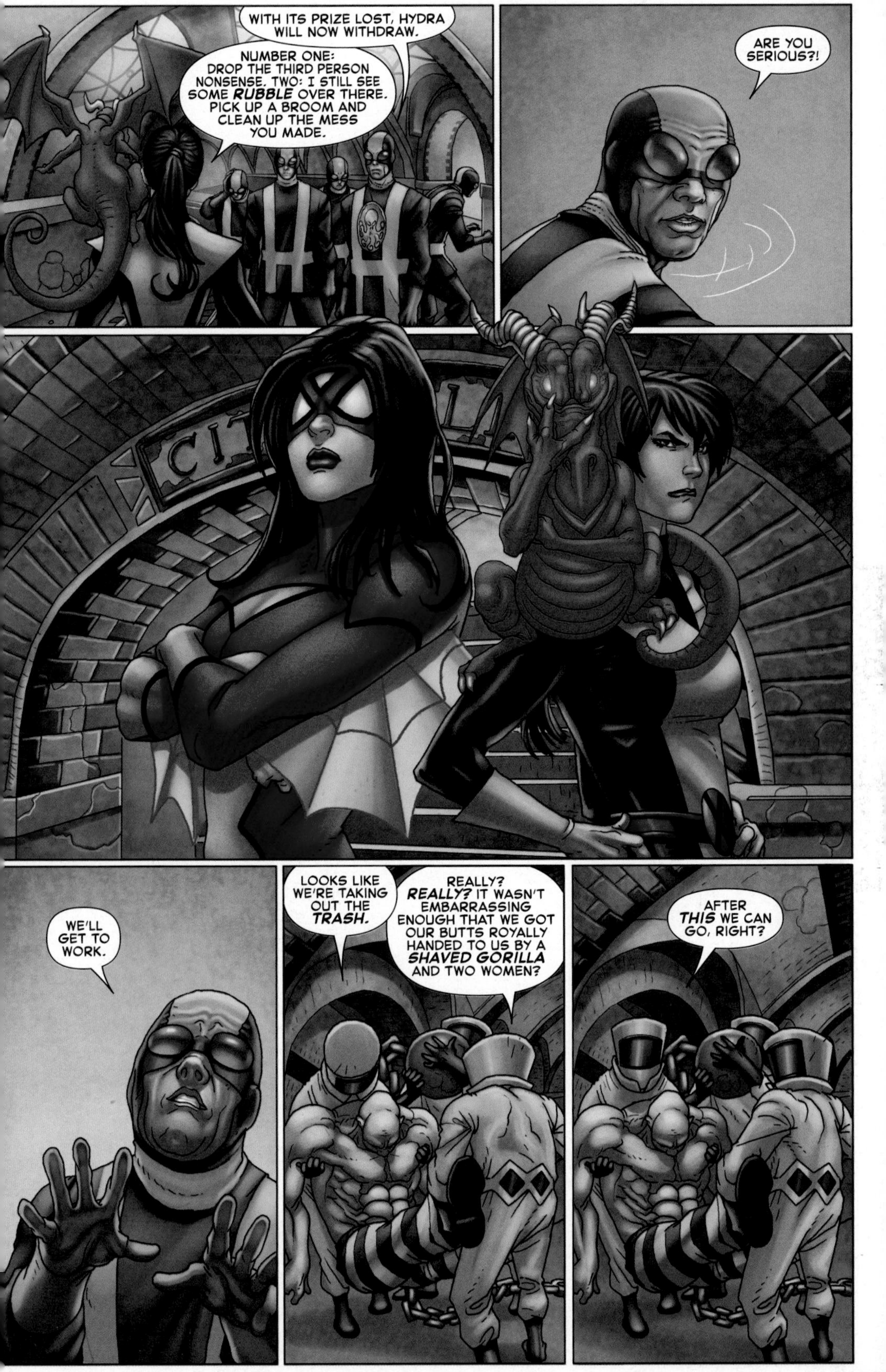
WITH ITS PRIZE LOST, HYDRA WILL NOW WITHDRAW.
NUMBER ONE: DROP THE THIRD PERSON NONSENSE. TWO: I STILL SEE SOME *RUBBLE* OVER THERE. PICK UP A BROOM AND CLEAN UP THE MESS YOU MADE.
ARE YOU SERIOUS?!
WE'LL GET TO WORK.
LOOKS LIKE WE'RE TAKING OUT THE *TRASH.*
REALLY? *REALLY?* IT WASN'T EMBARRASSING ENOUGH THAT WE GOT OUR BUTTS ROYALLY HANDED TO US BY A *SHAVED GORILLA* AND TWO WOMEN?
AFTER *THIS* WE CAN GO, RIGHT?

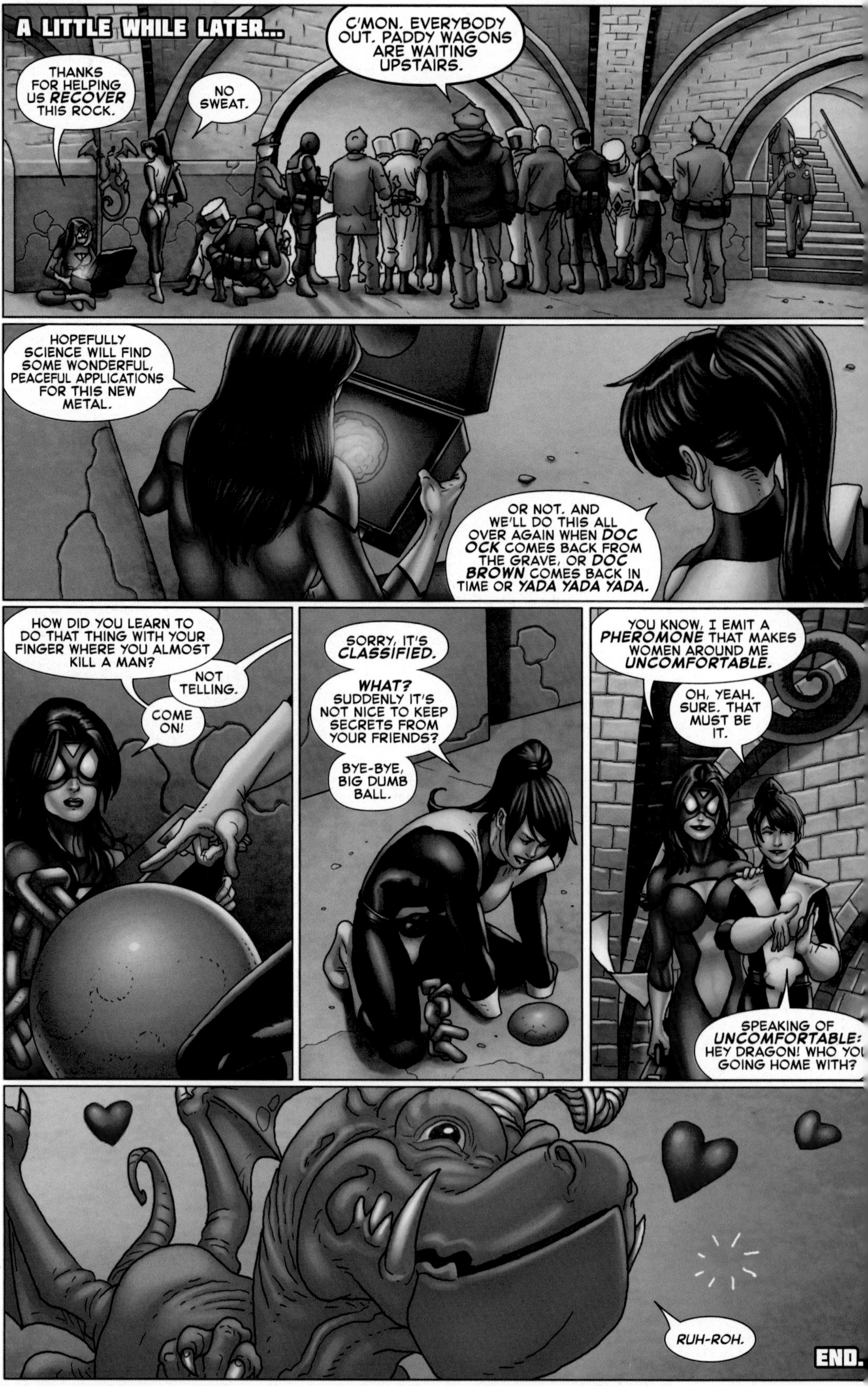
A LITTLE WHILE LATER...
THANKS FOR HELPING US RECOVER THIS ROCK.
NO SWEAT.
C'MON. EVERYBODY OUT. PADDY WAGONS ARE WAITING UPSTAIRS.
HOPEFULLY SCIENCE WILL FIND SOME WONDERFUL, PEACEFUL APPLICATIONS FOR THIS NEW METAL.
OR NOT. AND WE'LL DO THIS ALL OVER AGAIN WHEN DOC OCK COMES BACK FROM THE GRAVE, OR DOC BROWN COMES BACK IN TIME OR YADA YADA YADA.
HOW DID YOU LEARN TO DO THAT THING WITH YOUR FINGER WHERE YOU ALMOST KILL A MAN?
NOT TELLING.
COME ON!
SORRY, IT'S CLASSIFIED.
WHAT? SUDDENLY IT'S NOT NICE TO KEEP SECRETS FROM YOUR FRIENDS?
BYE-BYE, BIG DUMB BALL.
YOU KNOW, I EMIT A PHEROMONE THAT MAKES WOMEN AROUND ME UNCOMFORTABLE.
OH, YEAH. SURE. THAT MUST BE IT.
SPEAKING OF UNCOMFORTABLE: HEY DRAGON! WHO YOU GOING HOME WITH?
RUH-ROH.
END.

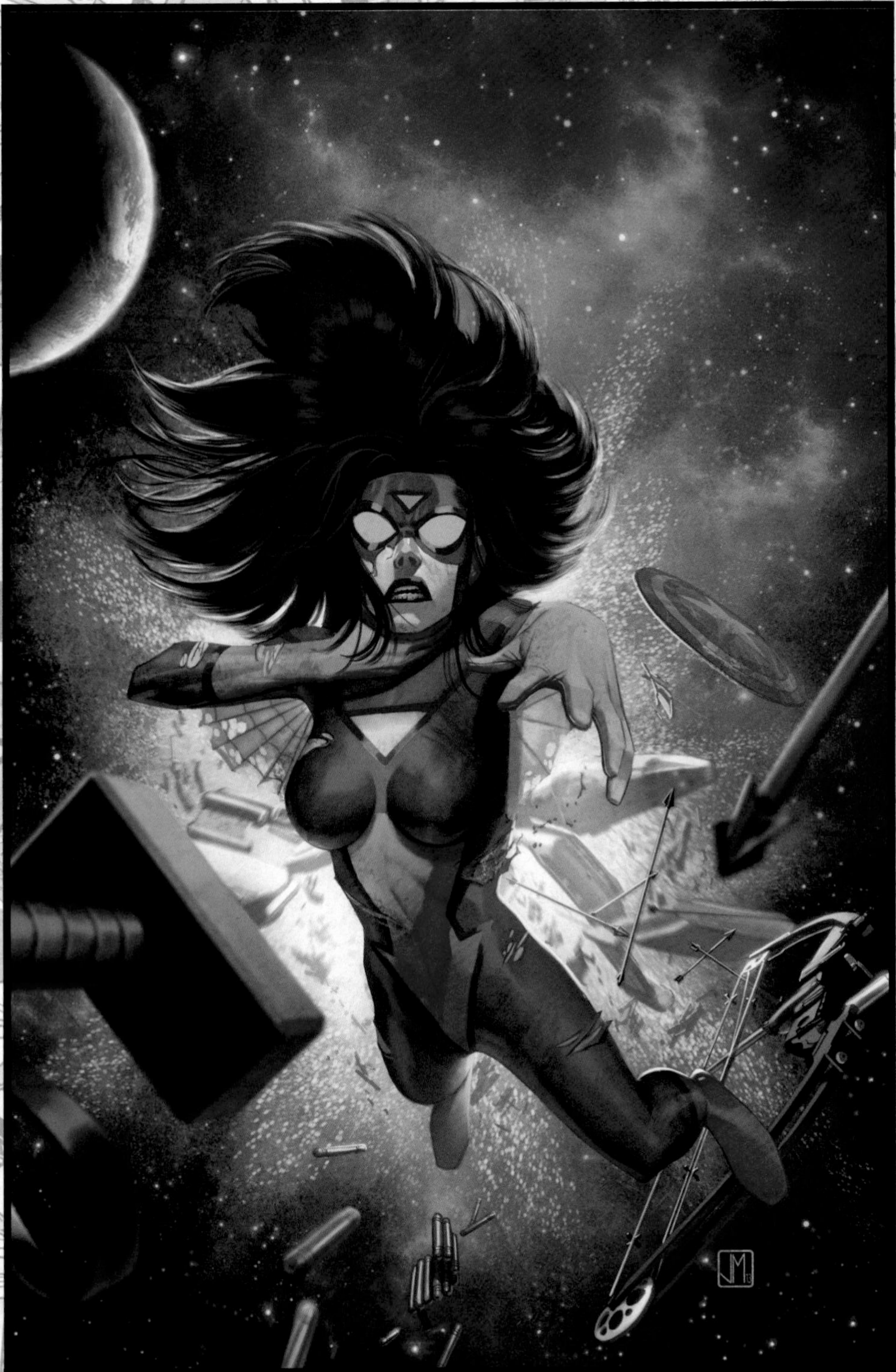

AVENGERS ASSEMBLE (2012) #18

THE ALIEN RACE KNOWN AS THE BUILDERS HAS TORN A DESTRUCTIVE PATH THROUGH THE GALAXY, AND IT'S UP TO SPIDER-WOMAN AND THE AVENGERS TO STOP THEM FROM REACHING EARTH!

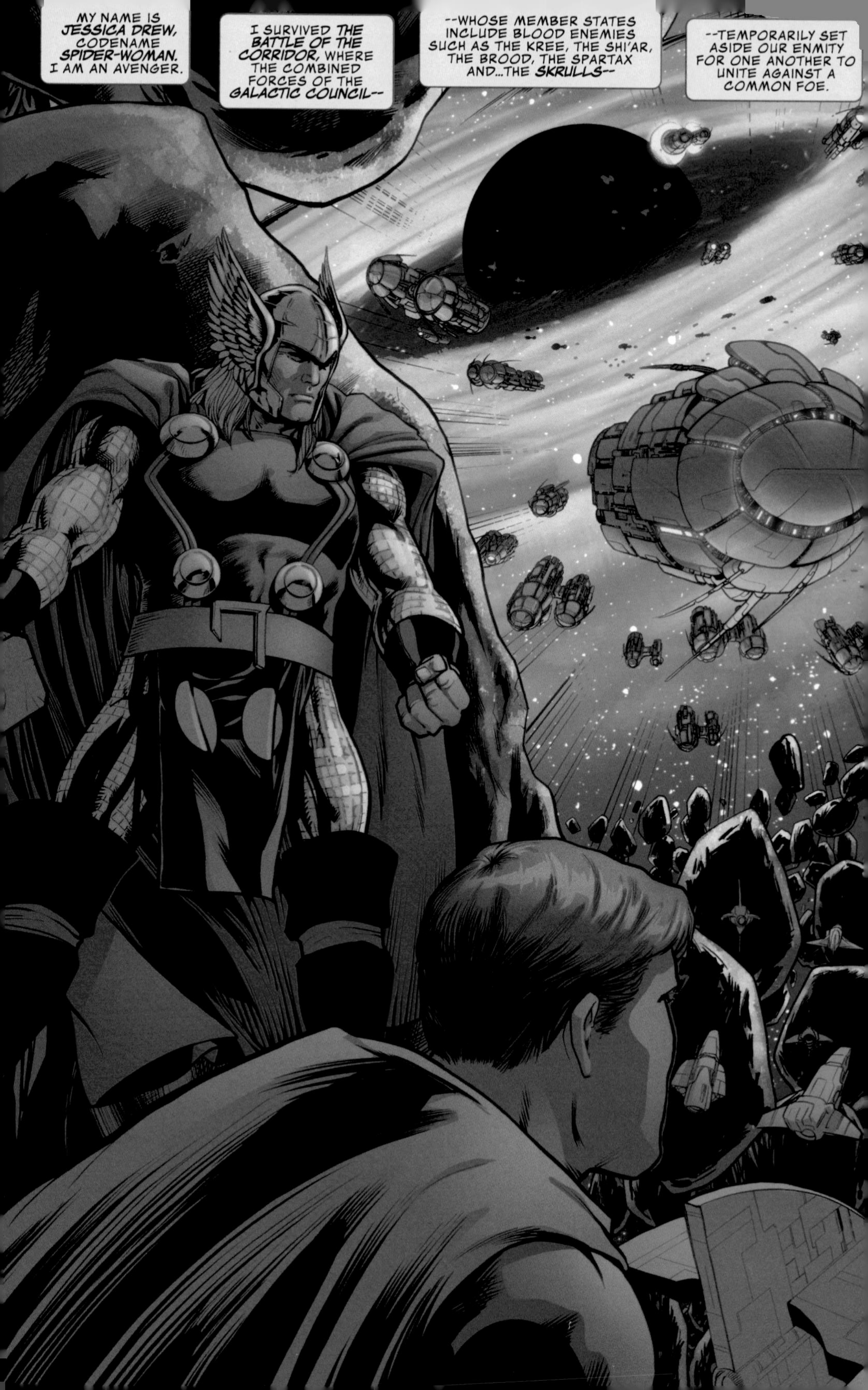
MY NAME IS JESSICA DREW, CODENAME SPIDER-WOMAN. I AM AN AVENGER.
I SURVIVED THE BATTLE OF THE CORRIDOR, WHERE THE COMBINED FORCES OF THE GALACTIC COUNCIL--
--WHOSE MEMBER STATES INCLUDE BLOOD ENEMIES SUCH AS THE KREE, THE SHI'AR, THE BROOD, THE SPARTAX AND...THE SKRULLS--
--TEMPORARILY SET ASIDE OUR ENMITY FOR ONE ANOTHER TO UNITE AGAINST A COMMON FOE.

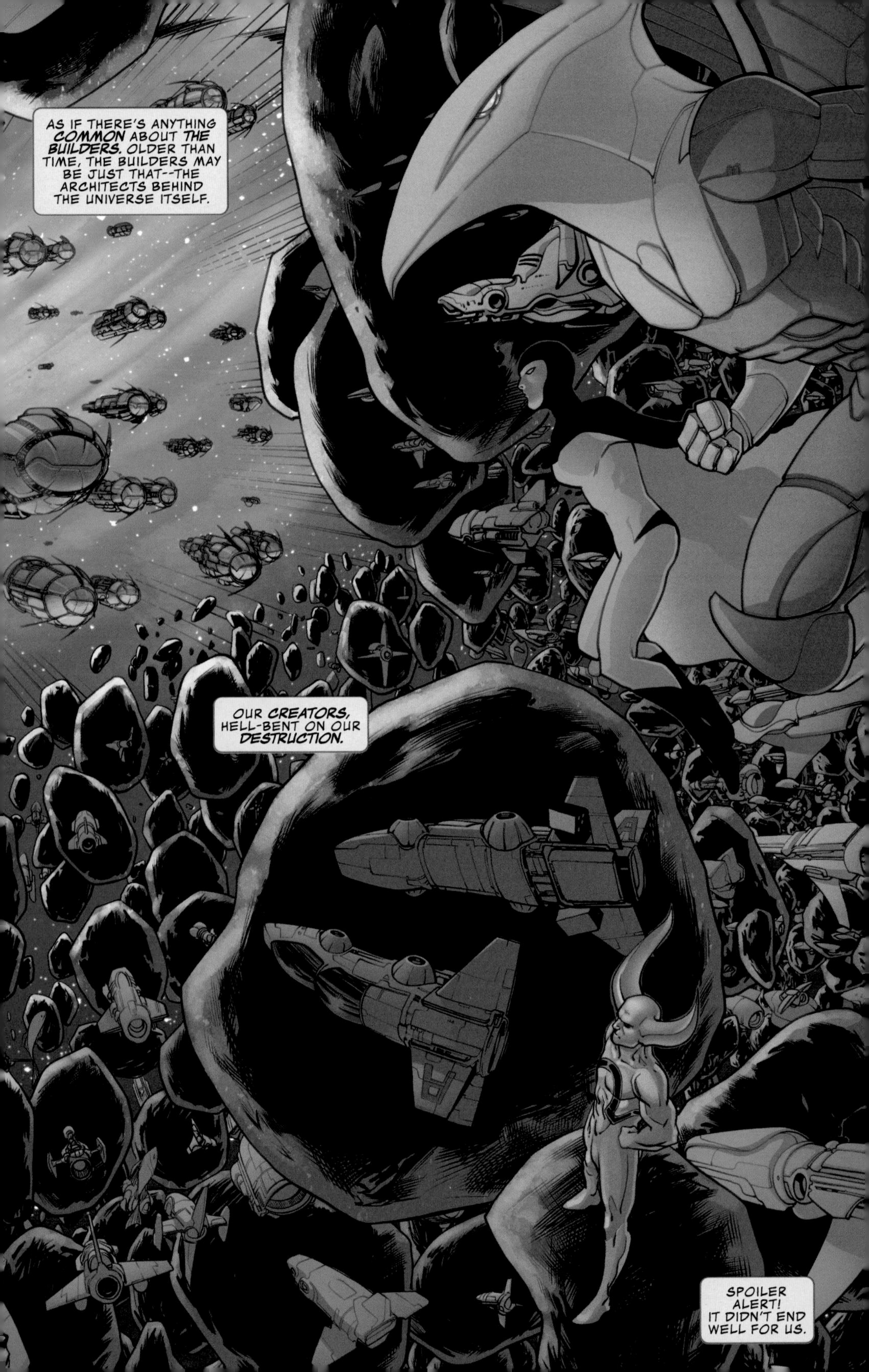
AS IF THERE'S ANYTHING COMMON ABOUT THE BUILDERS. OLDER THAN TIME, THE BUILDERS MAY BE JUST THAT--THE ARCHITECTS BEHIND THE UNIVERSE ITSELF.
OUR CREATORS, HELL-BENT ON OUR DESTRUCTION.
SPOILER ALERT! IT DIDN'T END WELL FOR US.

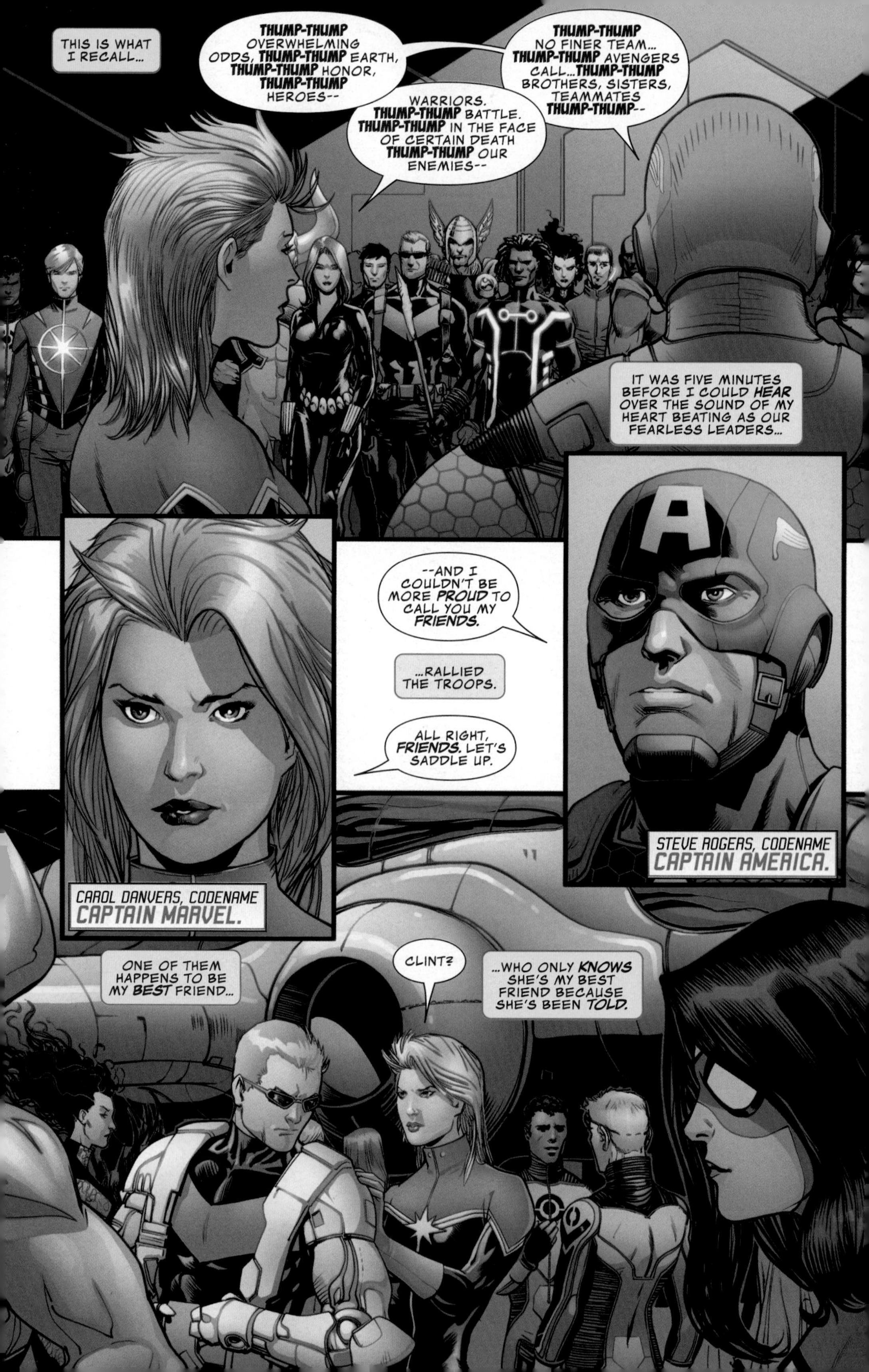
THIS IS WHAT I RECALL...
THUMP-THUMP OVERWHELMING ODDS, THUMP-THUMP EARTH, THUMP-THUMP HONOR, THUMP-THUMP HEROES--
WARRIORS. THUMP-THUMP BATTLE. THUMP-THUMP IN THE FACE OF CERTAIN DEATH THUMP-THUMP OUR ENEMIES--
THUMP-THUMP NO FINER TEAM... THUMP-THUMP AVENGERS CALL...THUMP-THUMP BROTHERS, SISTERS, TEAMMATES THUMP-THUMP--
IT WAS FIVE MINUTES BEFORE I COULD HEAR OVER THE SOUND OF MY HEART BEATING AS OUR FEARLESS LEADERS...
--AND I COULDN'T BE MORE PROUD TO CALL YOU MY FRIENDS.
...RALLIED THE TROOPS.
ALL RIGHT, FRIENDS. LET'S SADDLE UP.
CAROL DANVERS, CODENAME CAPTAIN MARVEL.
STEVE ROGERS, CODENAME CAPTAIN AMERICA.
ONE OF THEM HAPPENS TO BE MY BEST FRIEND...
CLINT?
...WHO ONLY KNOWS SHE'S MY BEST FRIEND BECAUSE SHE'S BEEN TOLD.

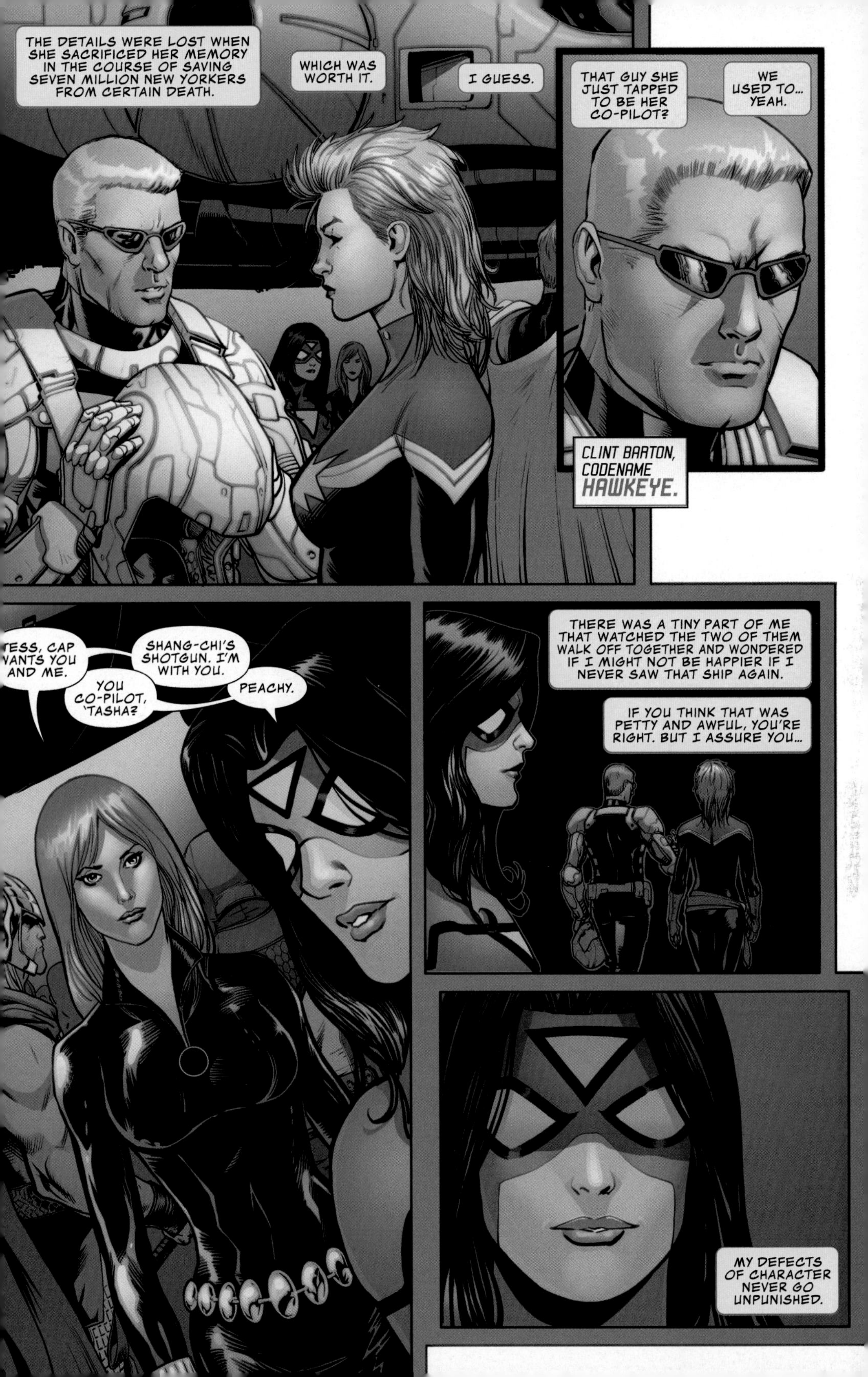

THE DETAILS WERE LOST WHEN SHE SACRIFICED HER MEMORY IN THE COURSE OF SAVING SEVEN MILLION NEW YORKERS FROM CERTAIN DEATH.
WHICH WAS WORTH IT.
I GUESS.
THAT GUY SHE JUST TAPPED TO BE HER CO-PILOT?
WE USED TO... YEAH.
CLINT BARTON, CODENAME HAWKEYE.
TESS, CAP WANTS YOU AND ME.
SHANG-CHI'S SHOTGUN. I'M WITH YOU.
YOU CO-PILOT, 'TASHA?
PEACHY.
THERE WAS A TINY PART OF ME THAT WATCHED THE TWO OF THEM WALK OFF TOGETHER AND WONDERED IF I MIGHT NOT BE HAPPIER IF I NEVER SAW THAT SHIP AGAIN.
IF YOU THINK THAT WAS PETTY AND AWFUL, YOU'RE RIGHT. BUT I ASSURE YOU...
MY DEFECTS OF CHARACTER NEVER GO UNPUNISHED.

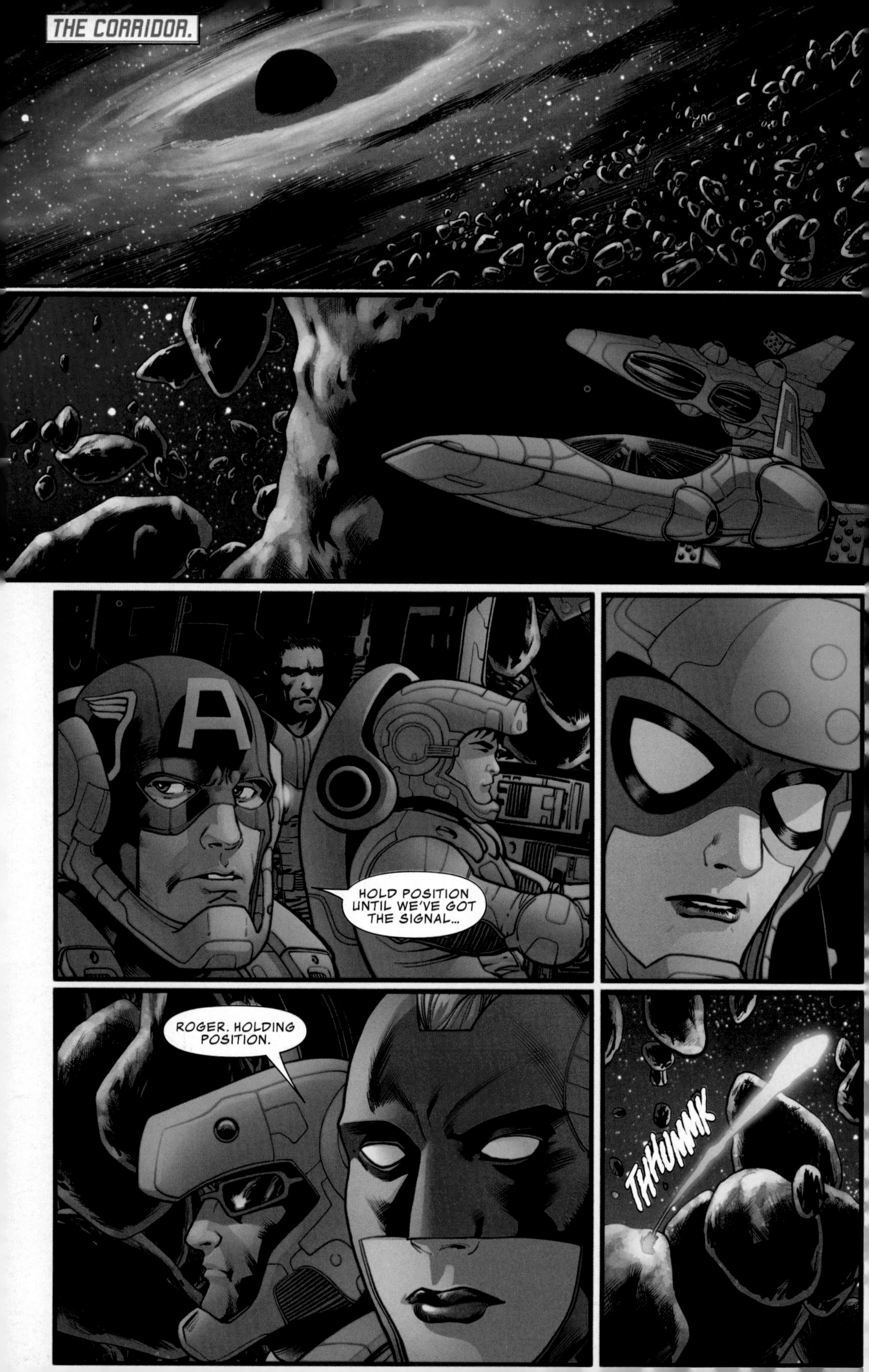
THE CORRIDOR.
HOLD POSITION UNTIL WE'VE GOT THE SIGNAL...
ROGER. HOLDING POSITION.
THHUMMK

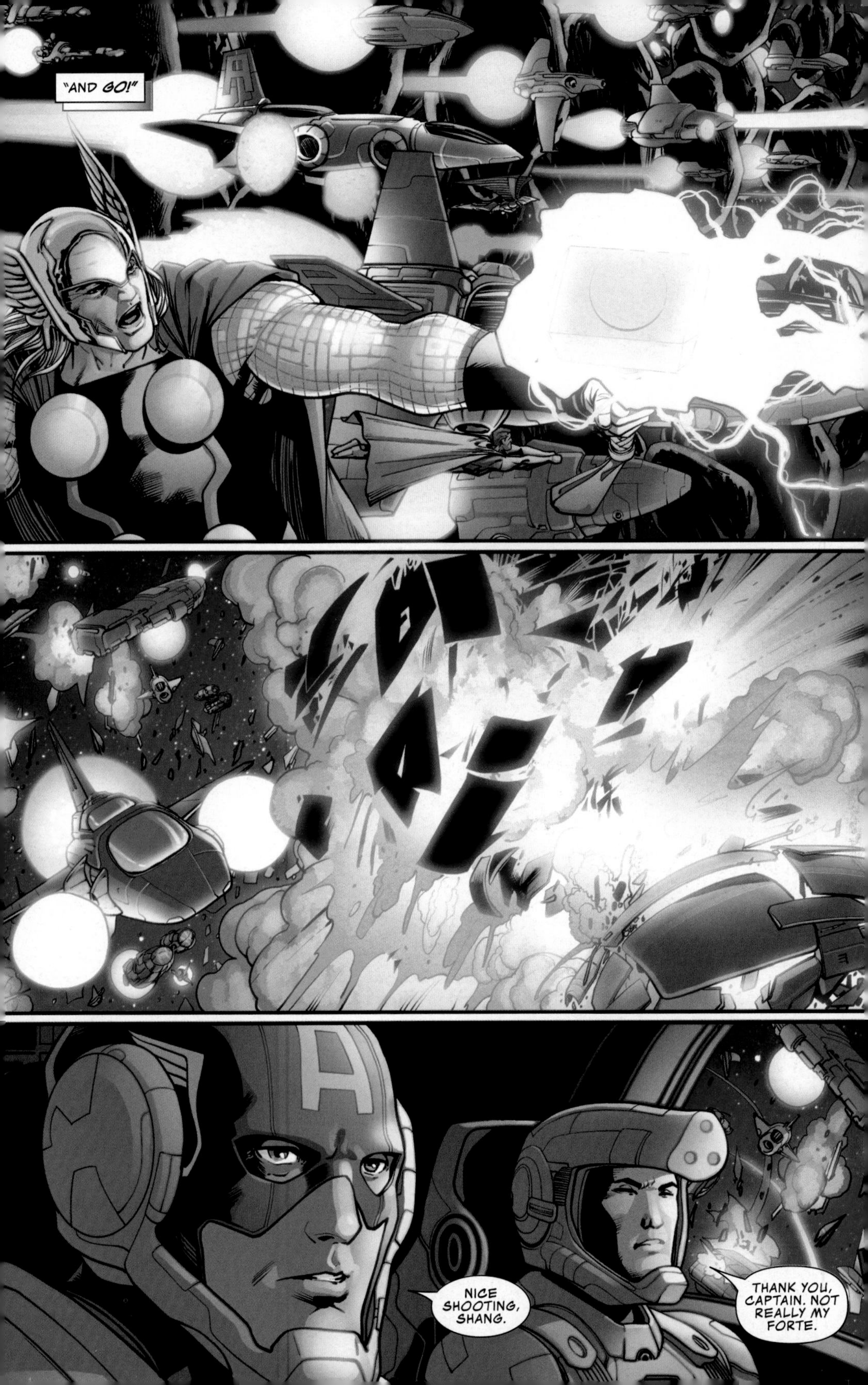
"AND GO!"
NICE SHOOTING, SHANG.
THANK YOU, CAPTAIN. NOT REALLY MY FORTE.

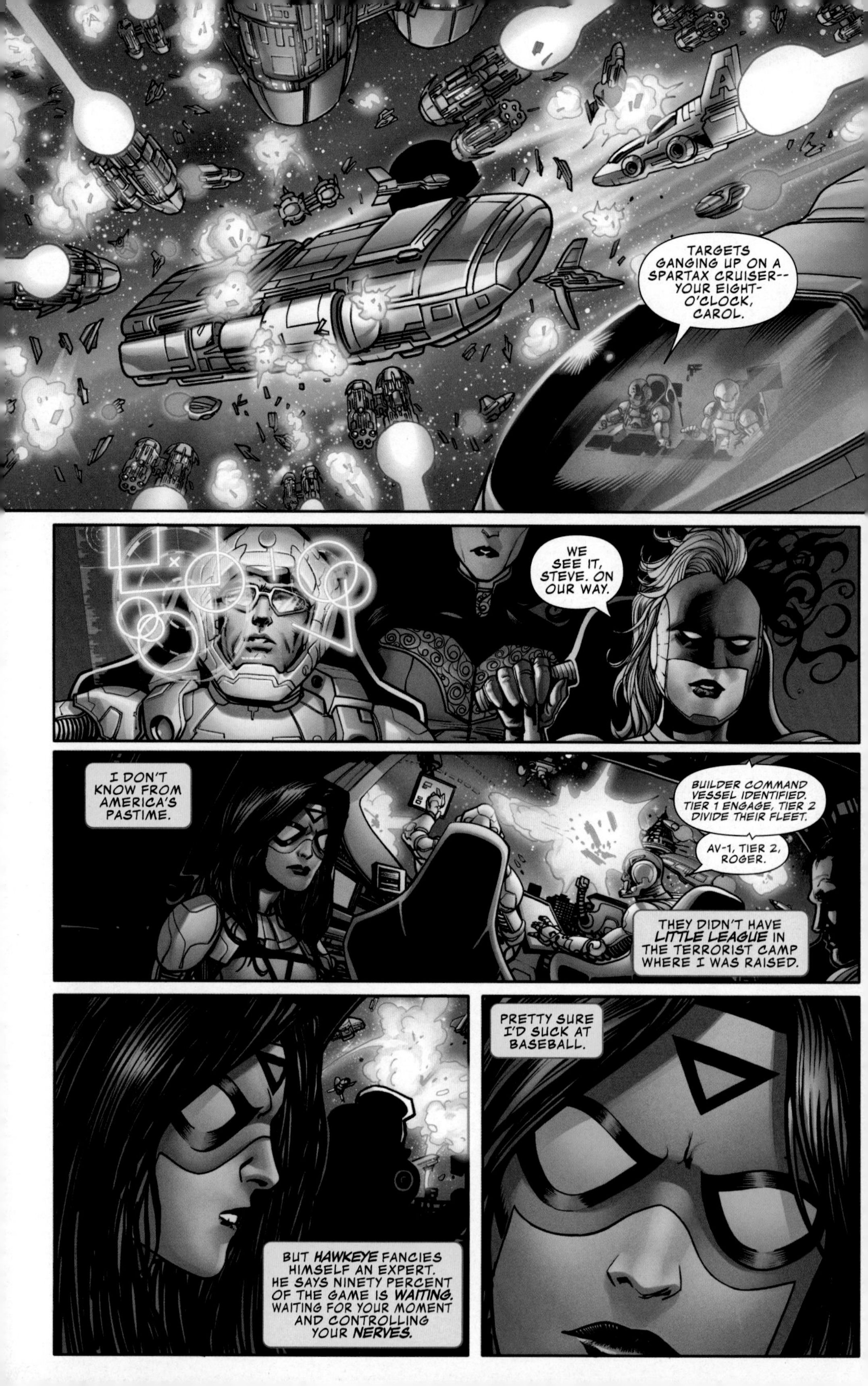
TARGETS GANGING UP ON A SPARTAX CRUISER-- YOUR EIGHT-O'CLOCK, CAROL.
WE SEE IT, STEVE. ON OUR WAY.
I DON'T KNOW FROM AMERICA'S PASTIME.
BUILDER COMMAND VESSEL IDENTIFIED. TIER 1 ENGAGE, TIER 2 DIVIDE THEIR FLEET.
AV-1, TIER 2, ROGER.
THEY DIDN'T HAVE LITTLE LEAGUE IN THE TERRORIST CAMP WHERE I WAS RAISED.
BUT HAWKEYE FANCIES HIMSELF AN EXPERT. HE SAYS NINETY PERCENT OF THE GAME IS WAITING. WAITING FOR YOUR MOMENT AND CONTROLLING YOUR NERVES.
PRETTY SURE I'D SUCK AT BASEBALL.

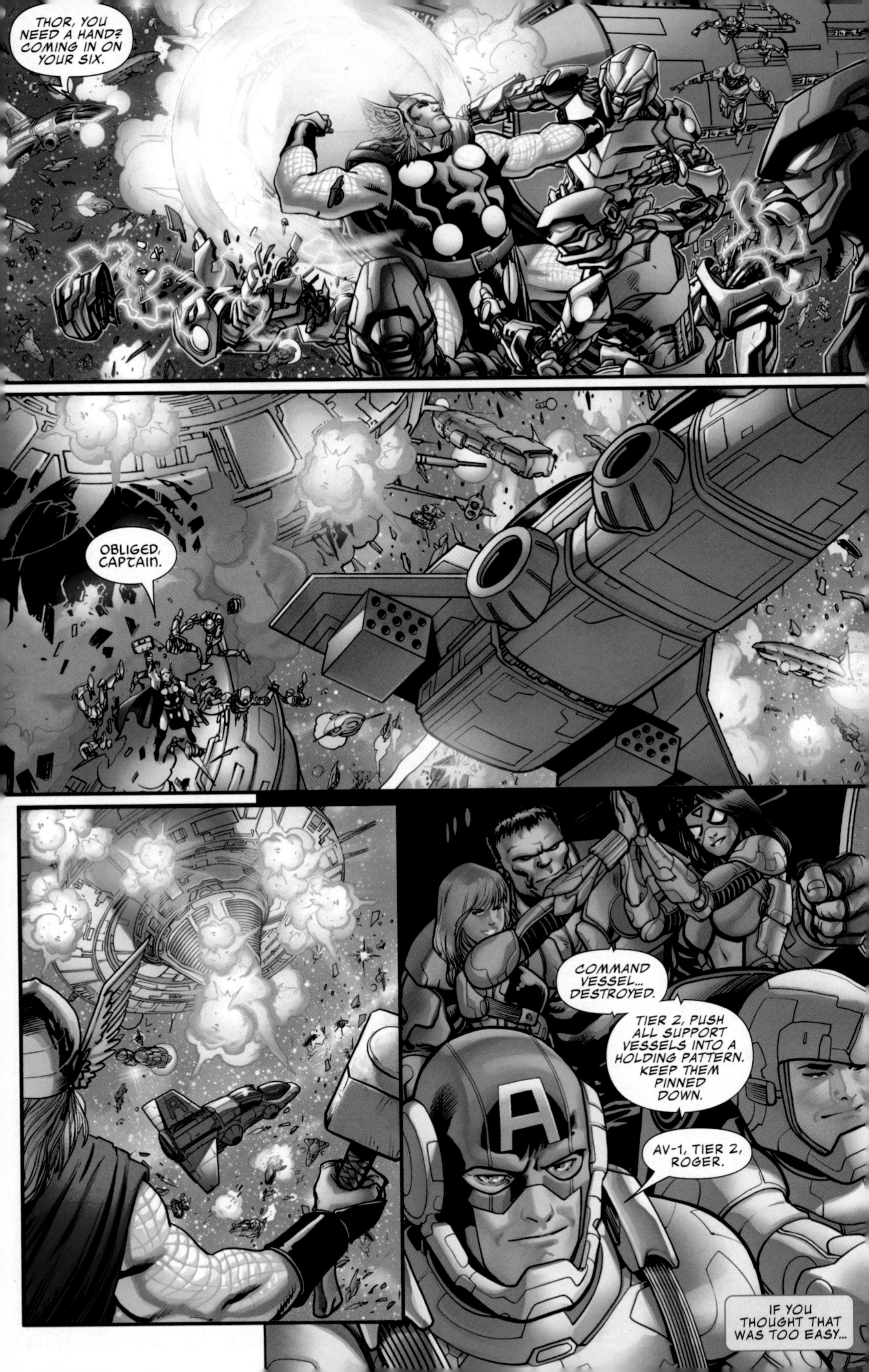
THOR, YOU NEED A HAND? COMING IN ON YOUR SIX.
OBLIGED, CAPTAIN.
COMMAND VESSEL... DESTROYED.
TIER 2, PUSH ALL SUPPORT VESSELS INTO A HOLDING PATTERN. KEEP THEM PINNED DOWN.
AV-1, TIER 2, ROGER.
IF YOU THOUGHT THAT WAS TOO EASY...

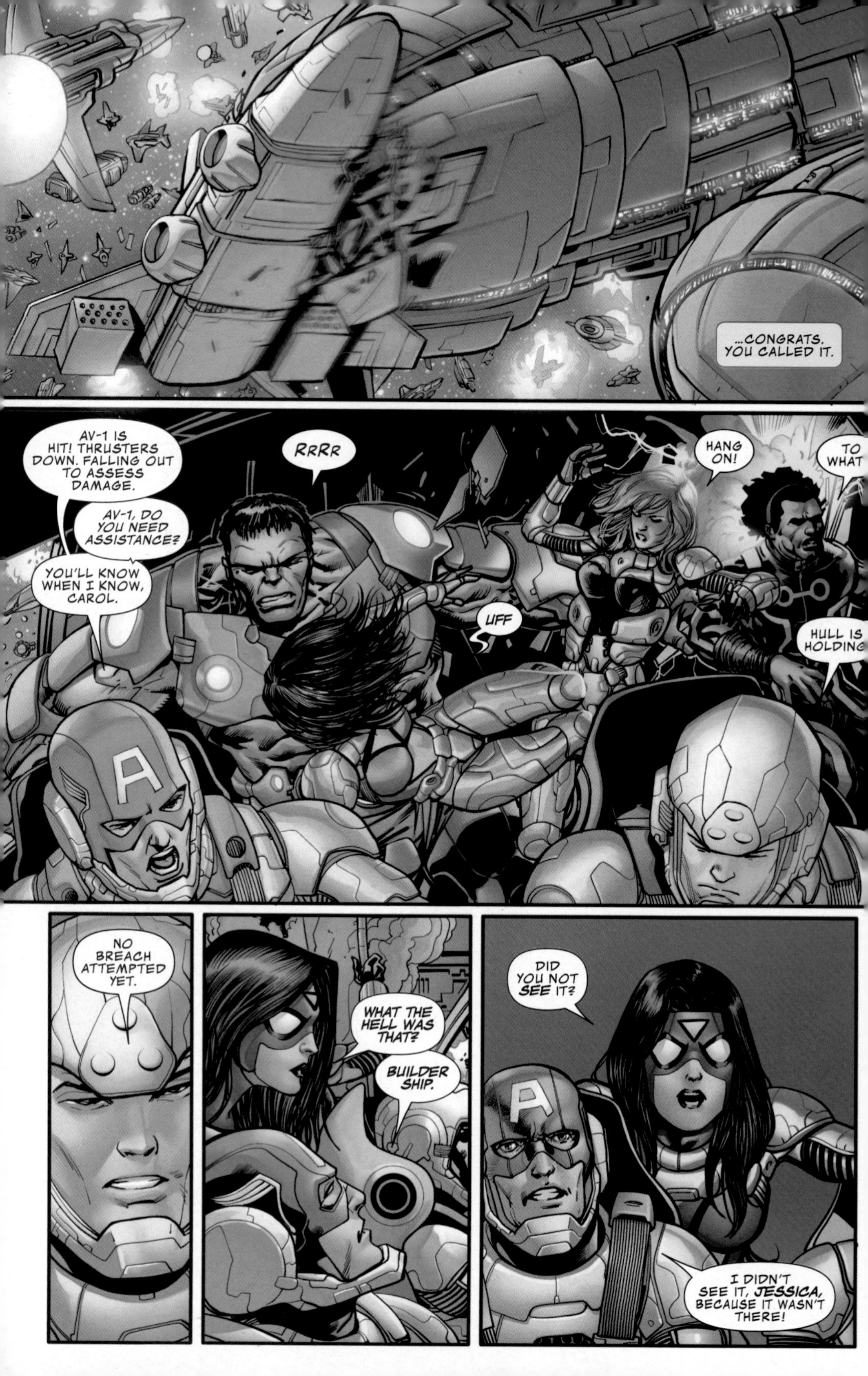
...CONGRATS. YOU CALLED IT.
AV-1 IS HIT! THRUSTERS DOWN. FALLING OUT TO ASSESS DAMAGE.
AV-1, DO YOU NEED ASSISTANCE?
YOU'LL KNOW WHEN I KNOW, CAROL.
RRRR
UFF
HANG ON!
TO WHAT
HULL IS HOLDING
NO BREACH ATTEMPTED YET.
WHAT THE HELL WAS THAT?
BUILDER SHIP.
DID YOU NOT SEE IT?
I DIDN'T SEE IT, JESSICA, BECAUSE IT WASN'T THERE!

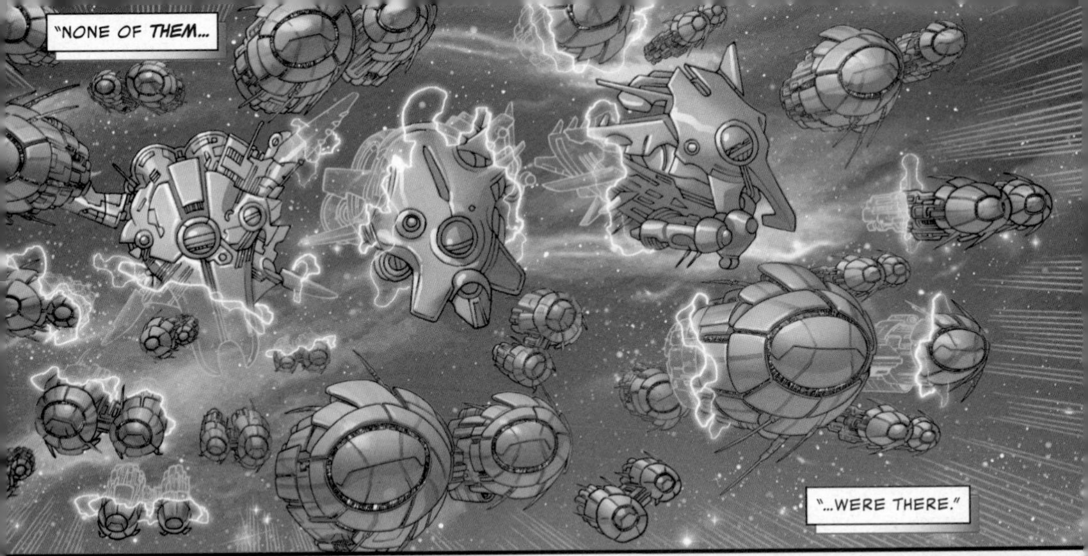
"NONE OF THEM...
"...WERE THERE."

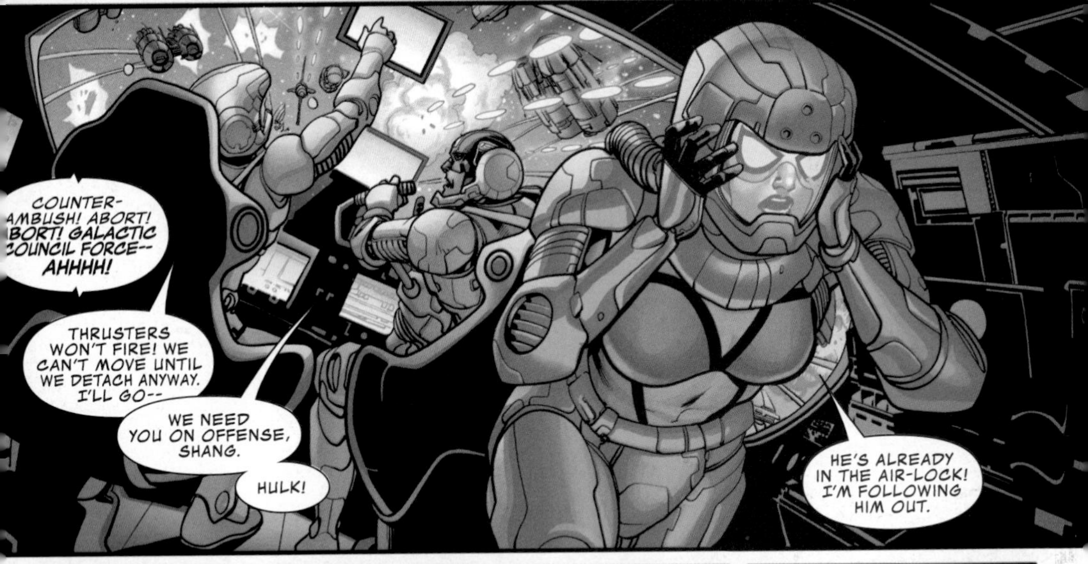
COUNTER-AMBUSH! ABORT! ABORT! GALACTIC COUNCIL FORCE-- AHHHH!
THRUSTERS WON'T FIRE! WE CAN'T MOVE UNTIL WE DETACH ANYWAY. I'LL GO--
WE NEED YOU ON OFFENSE, SHANG.
HULK!
HE'S ALREADY IN THE AIR-LOCK! I'M FOLLOWING HIM OUT.

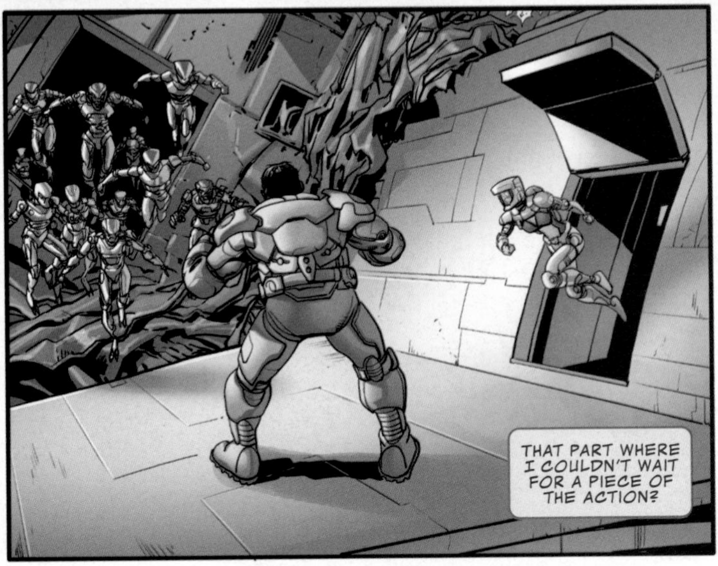
THAT PART WHERE I COULDN'T WAIT FOR A PIECE OF THE ACTION?

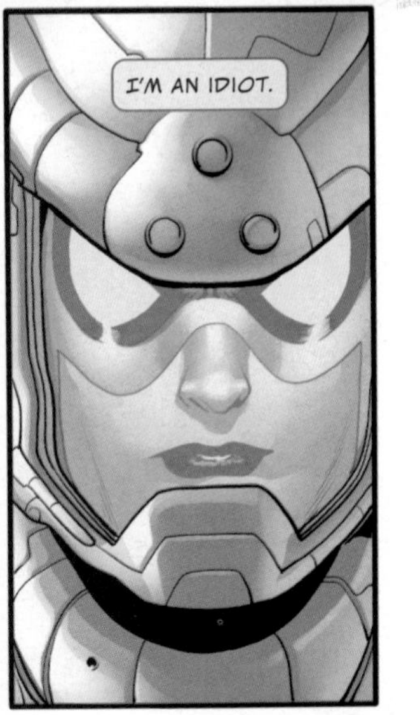
I'M AN IDIOT.

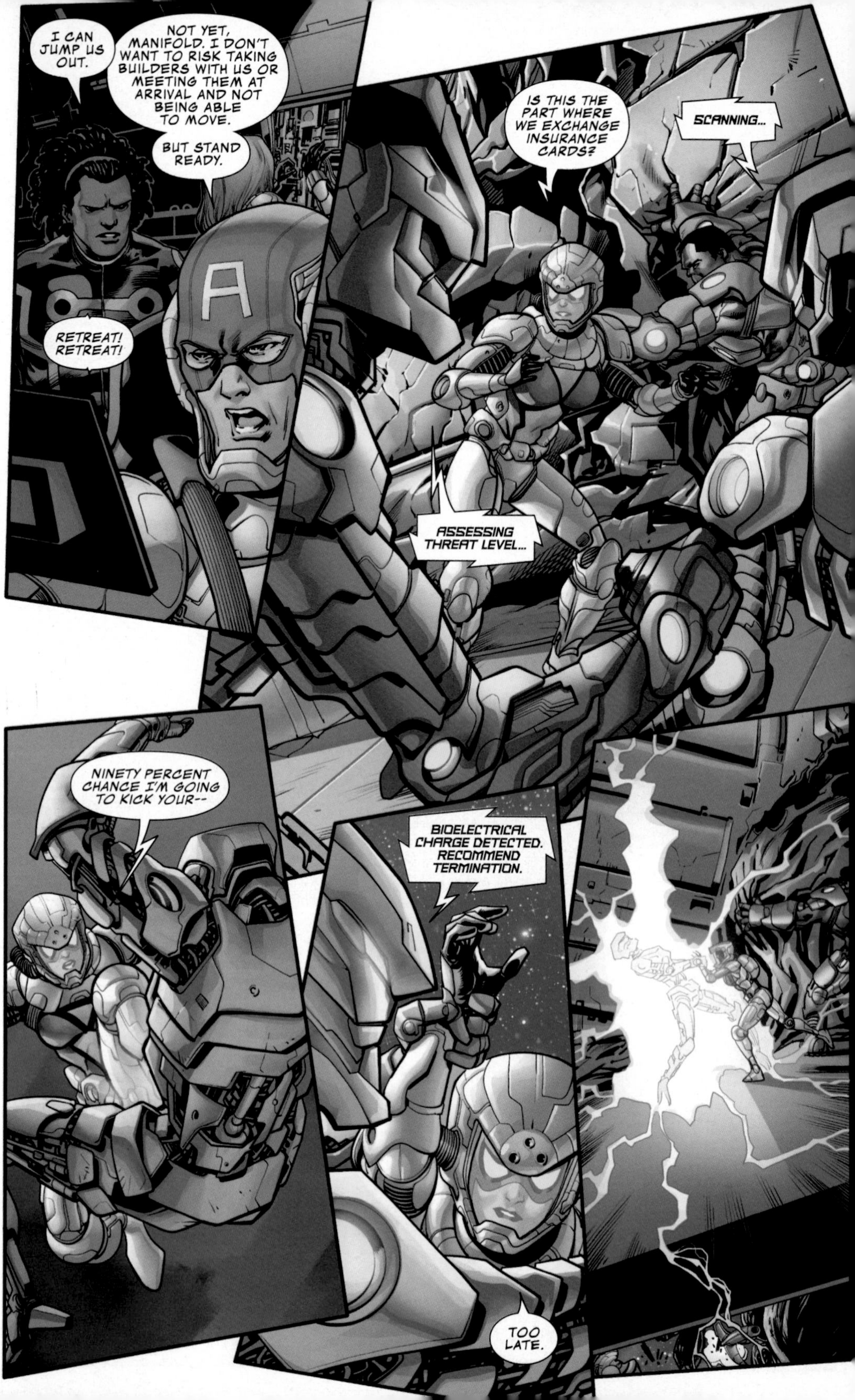
I CAN JUMP US OUT.
NOT YET, MANIFOLD. I DON'T WANT TO RISK TAKING BUILDERS WITH US OR MEETING THEM AT ARRIVAL AND NOT BEING ABLE TO MOVE.
BUT STAND READY.
RETREAT! RETREAT!
IS THIS THE PART WHERE WE EXCHANGE INSURANCE CARDS?
SCANNING...
ASSESSING THREAT LEVEL...
NINETY PERCENT CHANCE I'M GOING TO KICK YOUR--
BIOELECTRICAL CHARGE DETECTED. RECOMMEND TERMINATION.
TOO LATE.

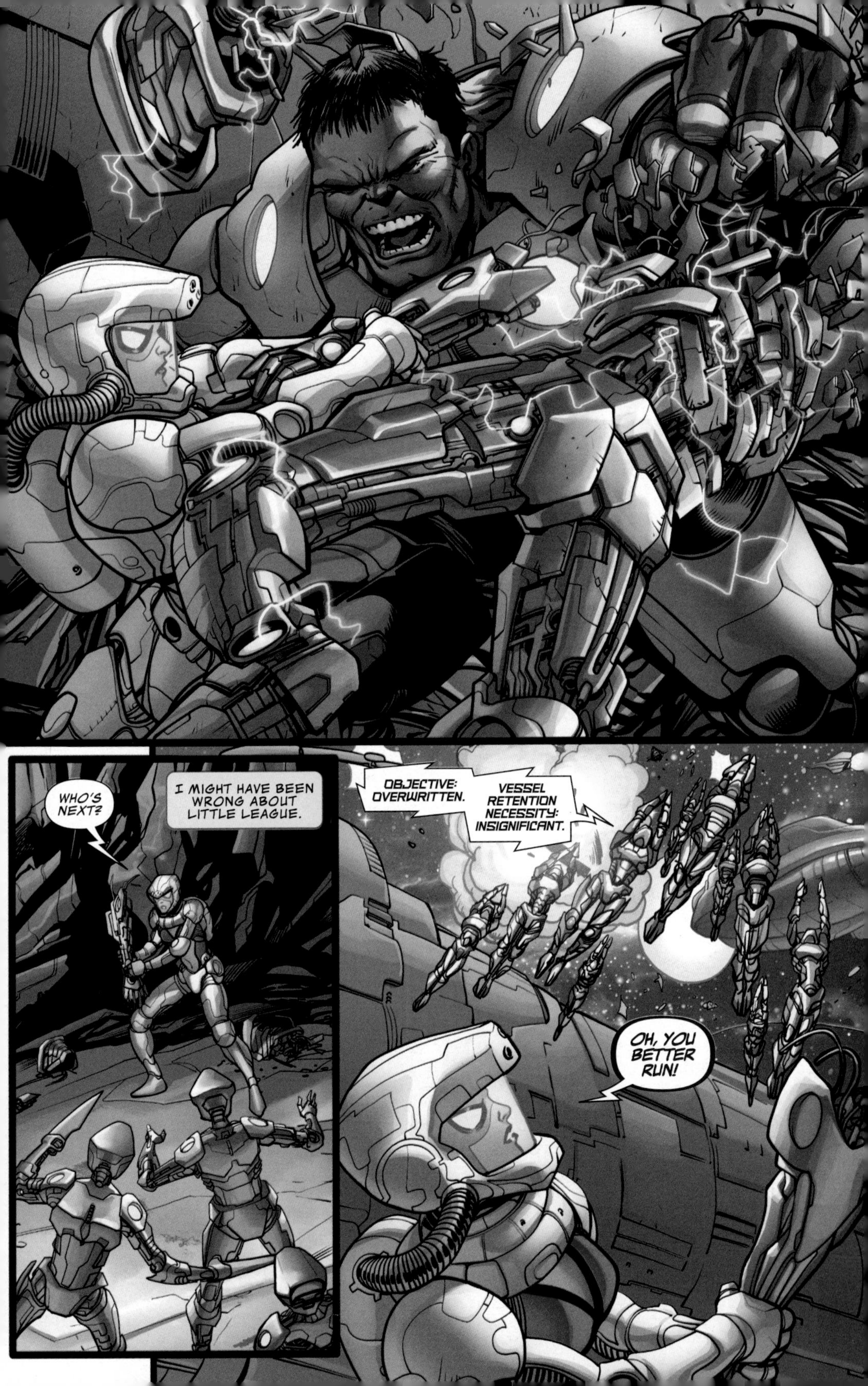
WHO'S NEXT?
I MIGHT HAVE BEEN WRONG ABOUT LITTLE LEAGUE.
OBJECTIVE: OVERWRITTEN.
VESSEL RETENTION NECESSITY: INSIGNIFICANT.
OH, YOU BETTER RUN!

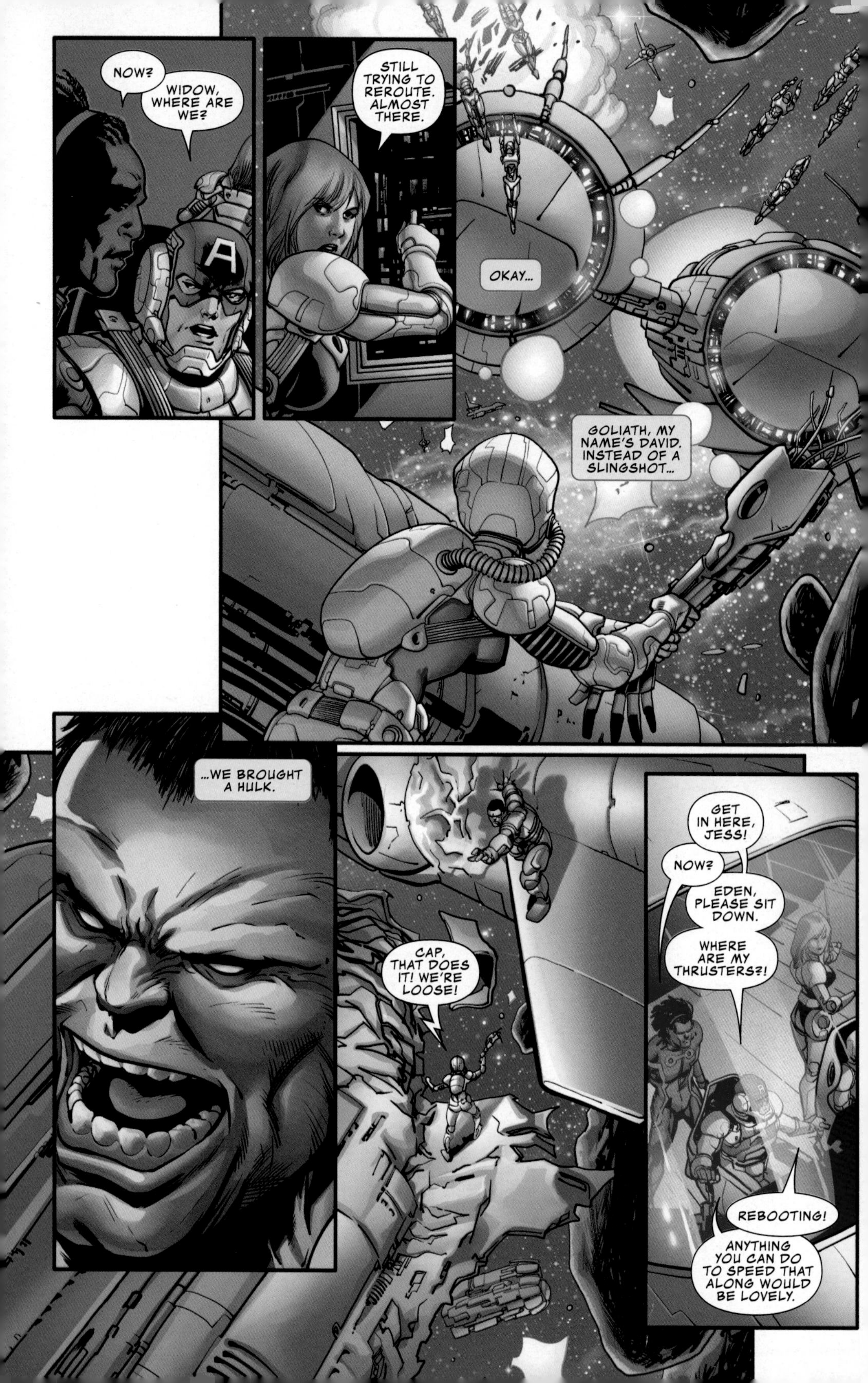
NOW?
WIDOW, WHERE ARE WE?
STILL TRYING TO REROUTE. ALMOST THERE.
OKAY...
GOLIATH, MY NAME'S DAVID. INSTEAD OF A SLINGSHOT...
...WE BROUGHT A HULK.
CAP, THAT DOES IT! WE'RE LOOSE!
GET IN HERE, JESS!
NOW?
EDEN, PLEASE SIT DOWN.
WHERE ARE MY THRUSTERS?!
REBOOTING!
ANYTHING YOU CAN DO TO SPEED THAT ALONG WOULD BE LOVELY.

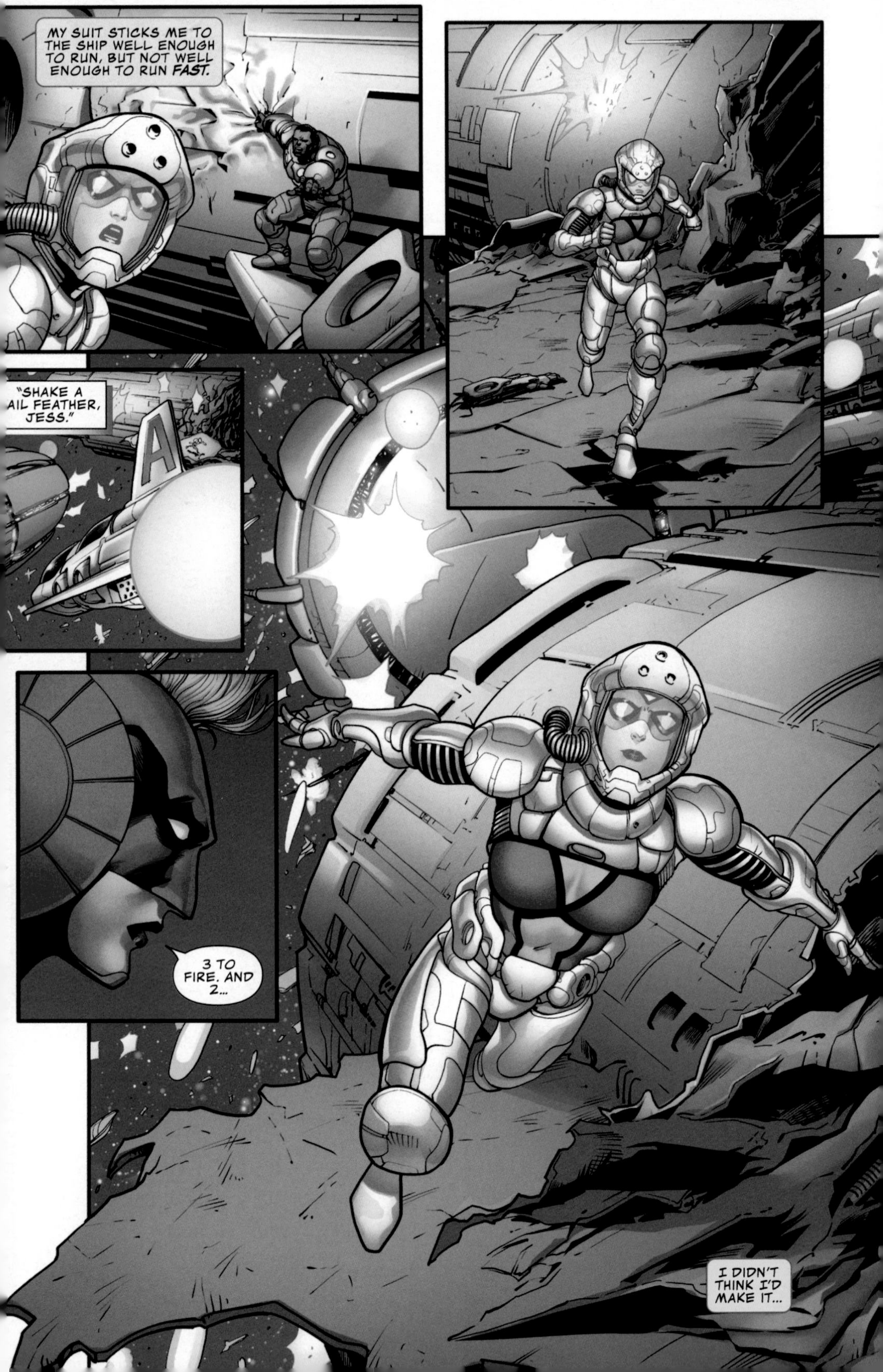
MY SUIT STICKS ME TO THE SHIP WELL ENOUGH TO RUN, BUT NOT WELL ENOUGH TO RUN *FAST.*
"SHAKE A AIL FEATHER, JESS."
3 TO FIRE. AND 2...
I DIDN'T THINK I'D MAKE IT...

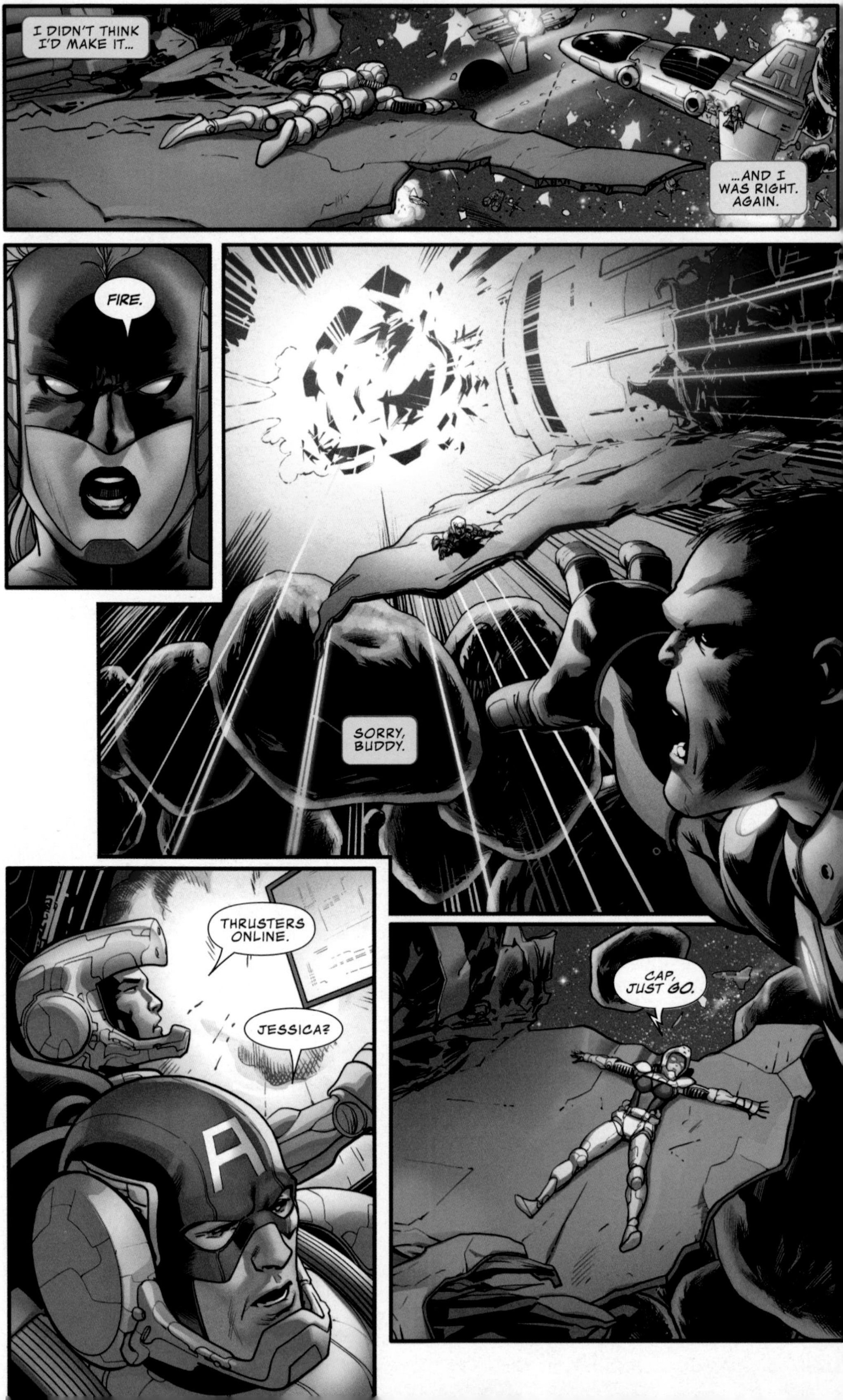
I DIDN'T THINK I'D MAKE IT...
...AND I WAS RIGHT. AGAIN.
FIRE.
SORRY, BUDDY.
THRUSTERS ONLINE.
JESSICA?
CAP, JUST GO.

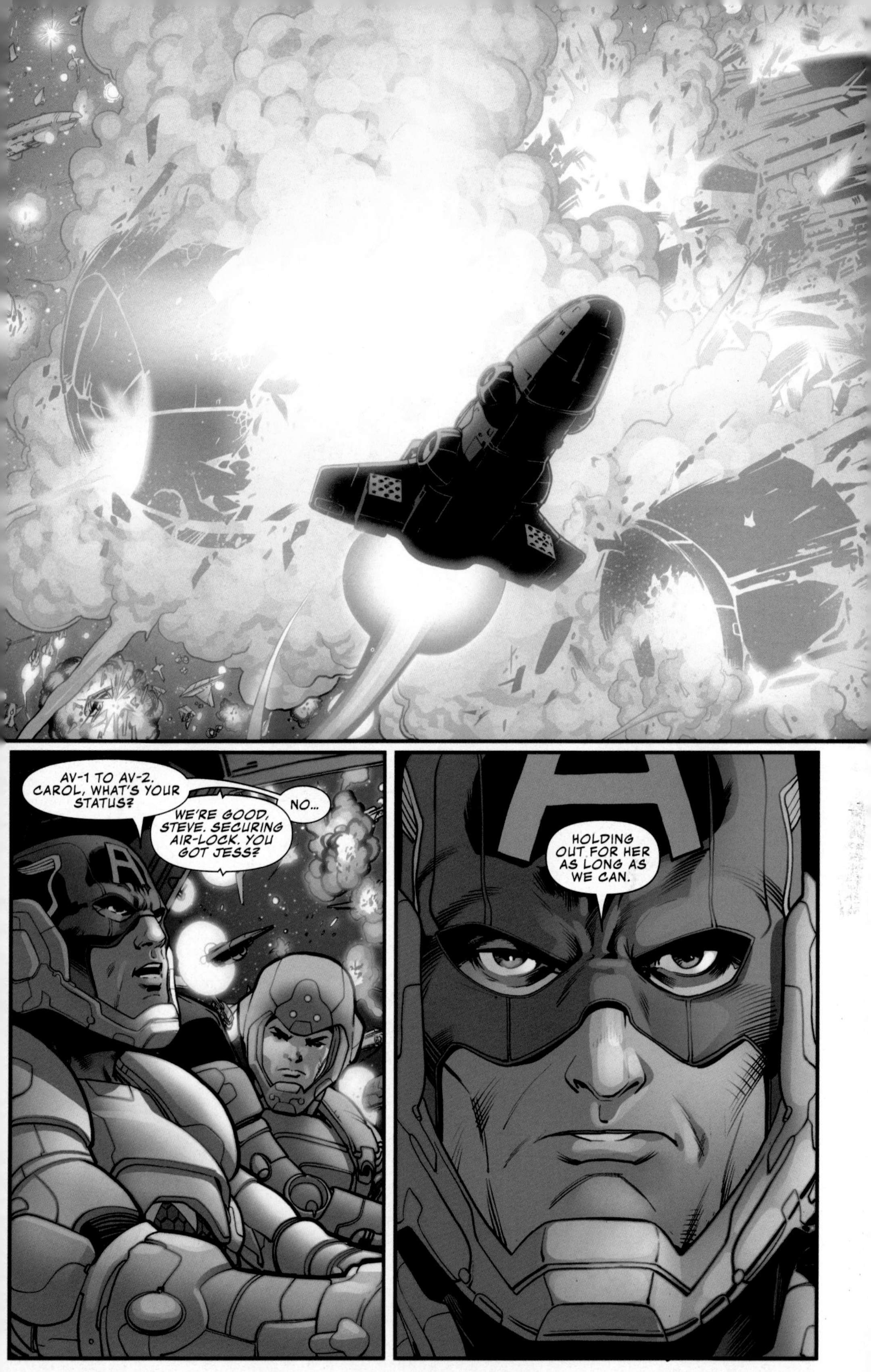
AV-1 TO AV-2. CAROL, WHAT'S YOUR STATUS?
WE'RE GOOD, STEVE. SECURING AIR-LOCK. YOU GOT JESS?
NO...
HOLDING OUT FOR HER AS LONG AS WE CAN.

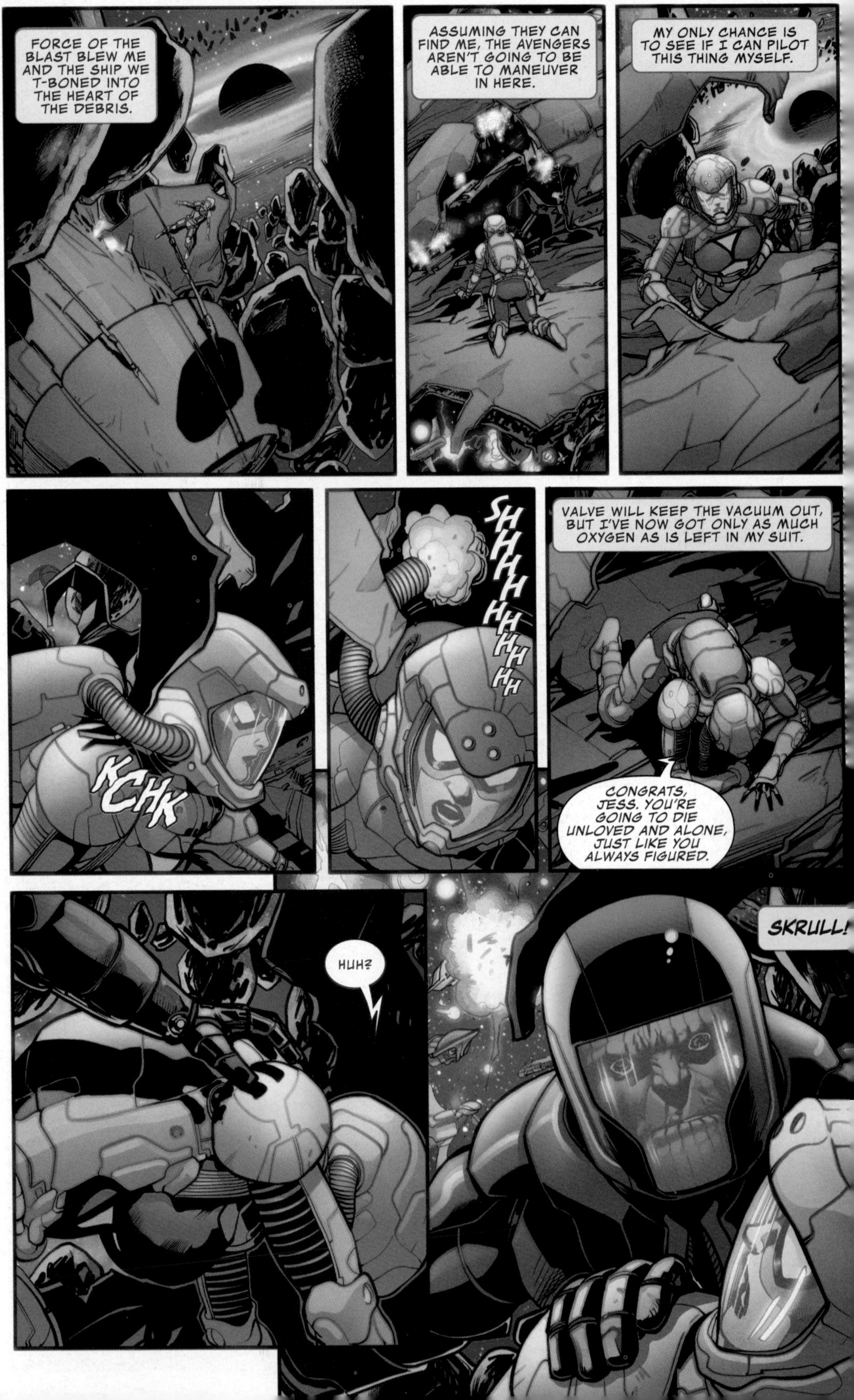
FORCE OF THE BLAST BLEW ME AND THE SHIP WE T-BONED INTO THE HEART OF THE DEBRIS.
ASSUMING THEY CAN FIND ME, THE AVENGERS AREN'T GOING TO BE ABLE TO MANEUVER IN HERE.
MY ONLY CHANCE IS TO SEE IF I CAN PILOT THIS THING MYSELF.
KCHK
SHHHHHHHHH
VALVE WILL KEEP THE VACUUM OUT, BUT I'VE NOW GOT ONLY AS MUCH OXYGEN AS IS LEFT IN MY SUIT.
CONGRATS, JESS. YOU'RE GOING TO DIE UNLOVED AND ALONE, JUST LIKE YOU ALWAYS FIGURED.
HUH?
SKRULL!

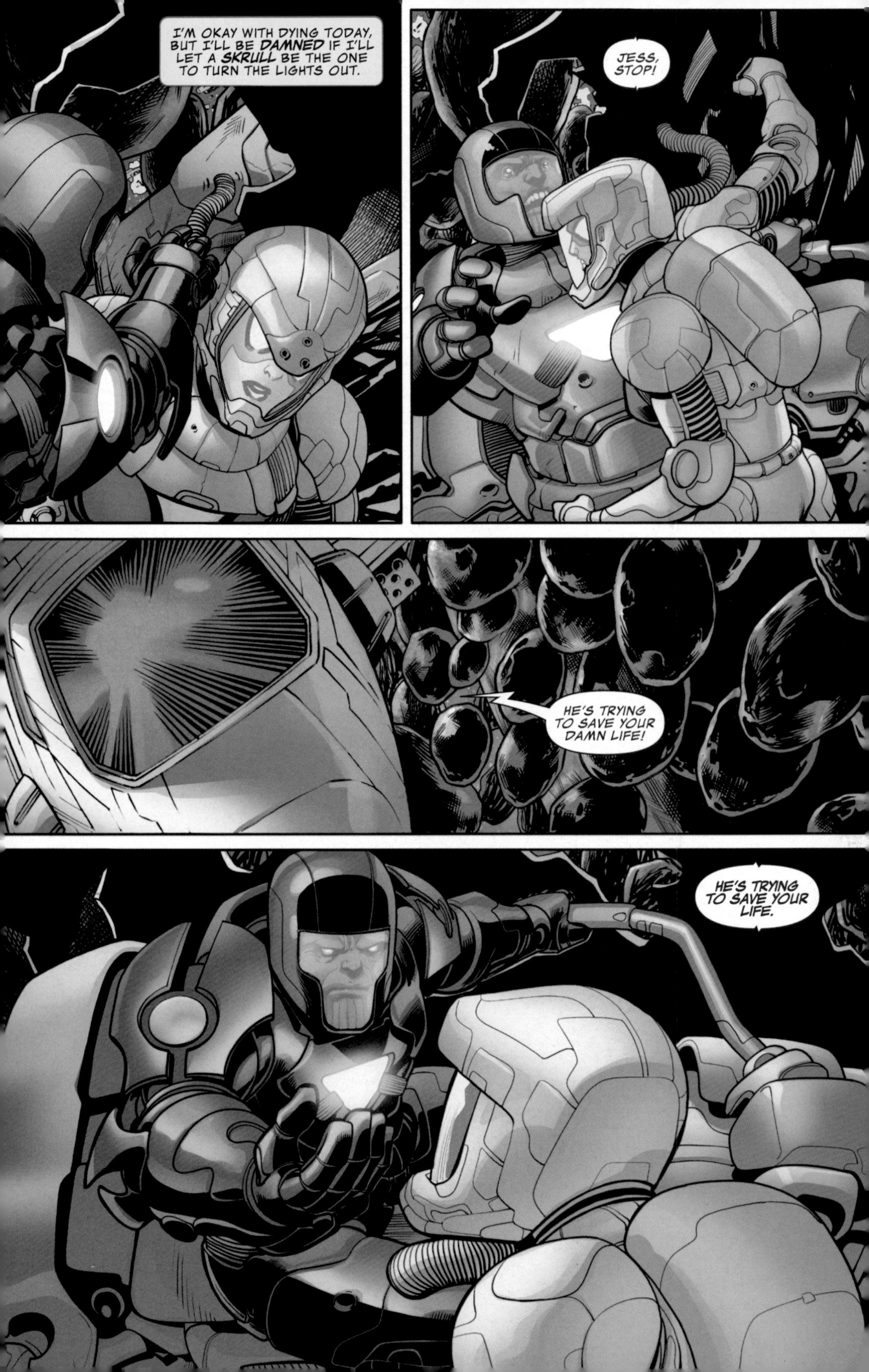
I'M OKAY WITH DYING TODAY, BUT I'LL BE DAMNED IF I'LL LET A SKRULL BE THE ONE TO TURN THE LIGHTS OUT.
JESS, STOP!
HE'S TRYING TO SAVE YOUR DAMN LIFE!
HE'S TRYING TO SAVE YOUR LIFE.

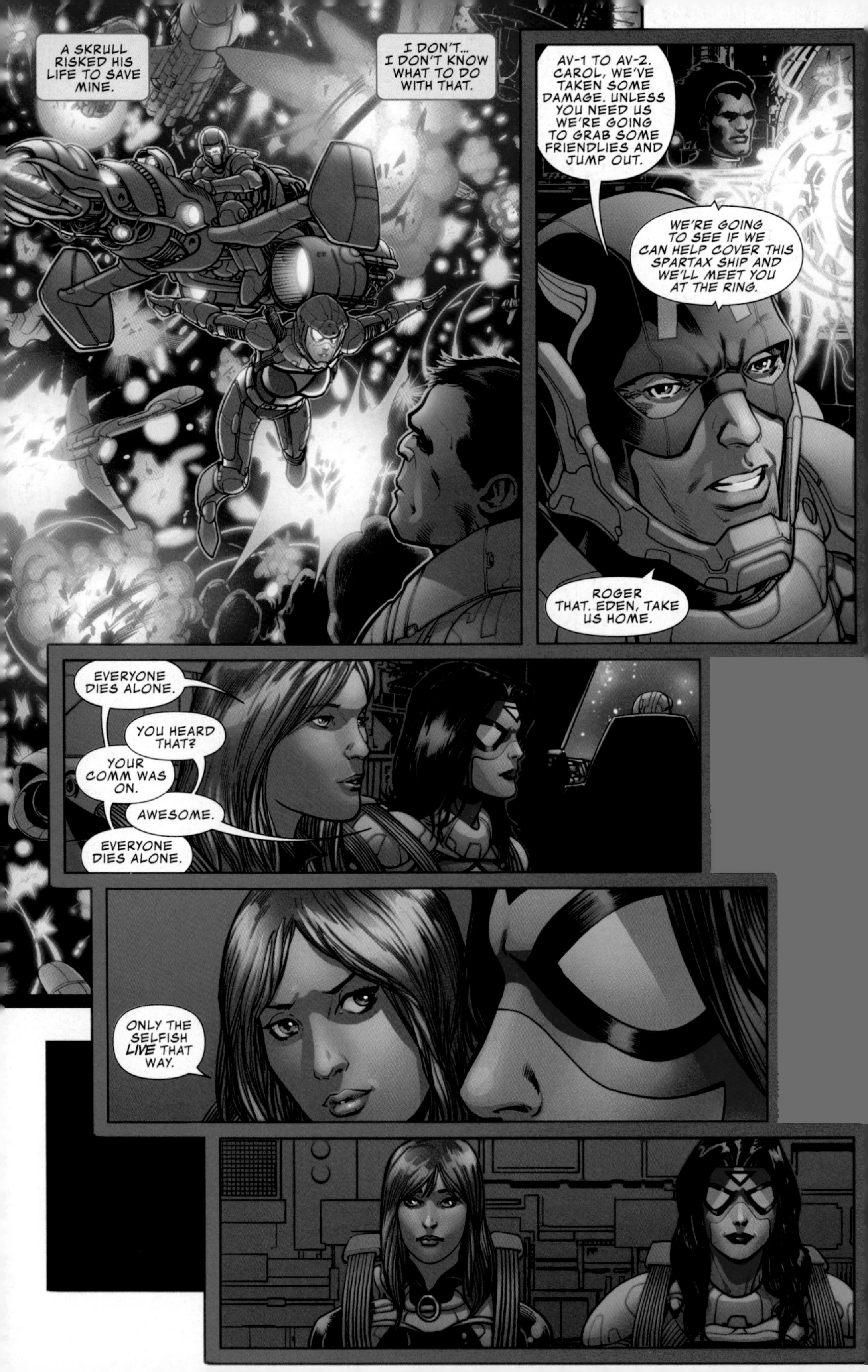
A SKRULL RISKED HIS LIFE TO SAVE MINE.
I DON'T... I DON'T KNOW WHAT TO DO WITH THAT.
AV-1 TO AV-2. CAROL, WE'VE TAKEN SOME DAMAGE. UNLESS YOU NEED US WE'RE GOING TO GRAB SOME FRIENDLIES AND JUMP OUT.
WE'RE GOING TO SEE IF WE CAN HELP COVER THIS SPARTAX SHIP AND WE'LL MEET YOU AT THE RING.
ROGER THAT. EDEN, TAKE US HOME.
EVERYONE DIES ALONE.
YOU HEARD THAT?
YOUR COMM WAS ON.
AWESOME.
EVERYONE DIES ALONE.
ONLY THE SELFISH *LIVE* THAT WAY.

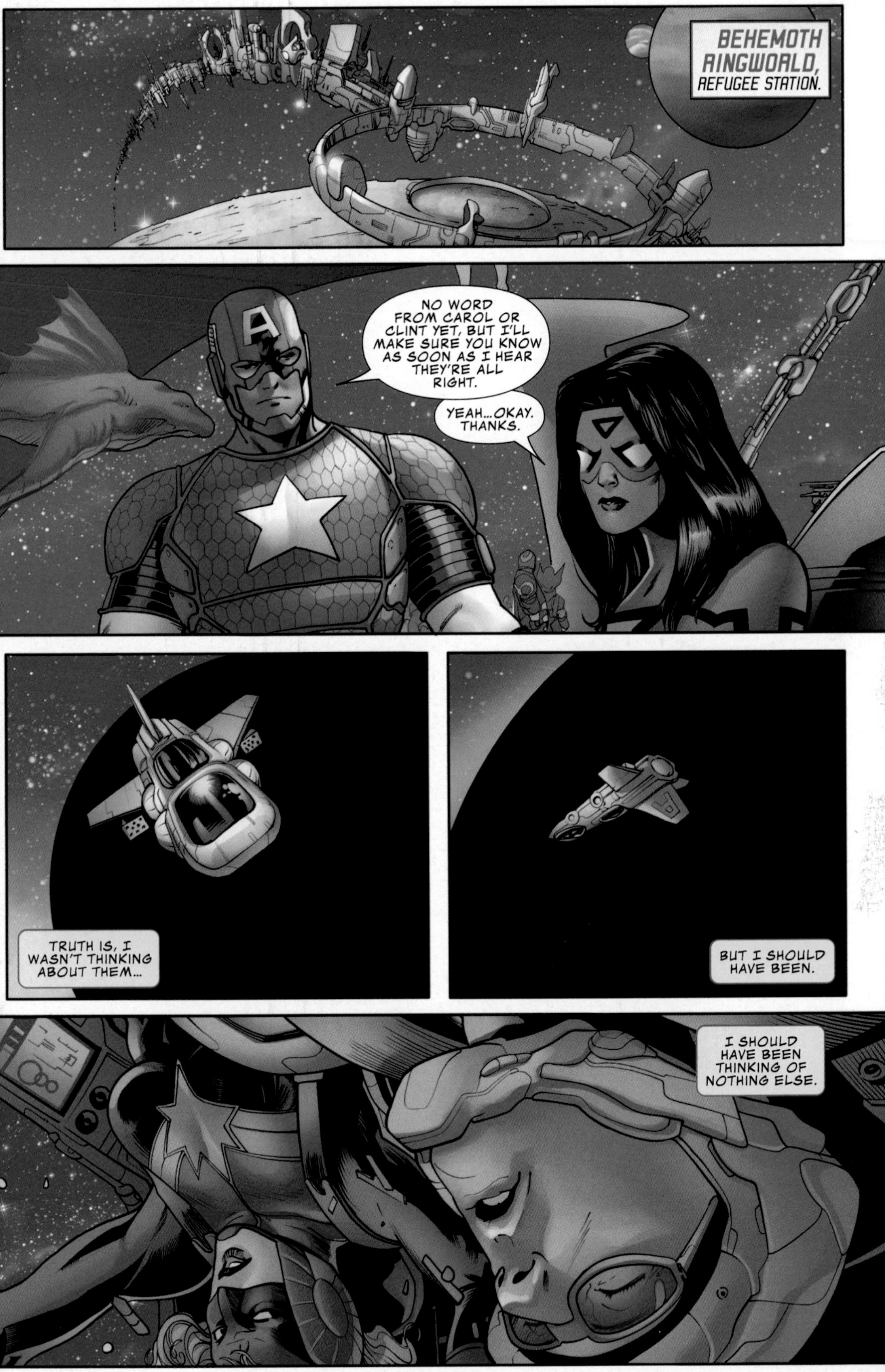
BEHEMOTH RINGWORLD, REFUGEE STATION.
NO WORD FROM CAROL OR CLINT YET, BUT I'LL MAKE SURE YOU KNOW AS SOON AS I HEAR THEY'RE ALL RIGHT.
YEAH...OKAY. THANKS.
TRUTH IS, I WASN'T THINKING ABOUT THEM...
BUT I SHOULD HAVE BEEN.
I SHOULD HAVE BEEN THINKING OF NOTHING ELSE.

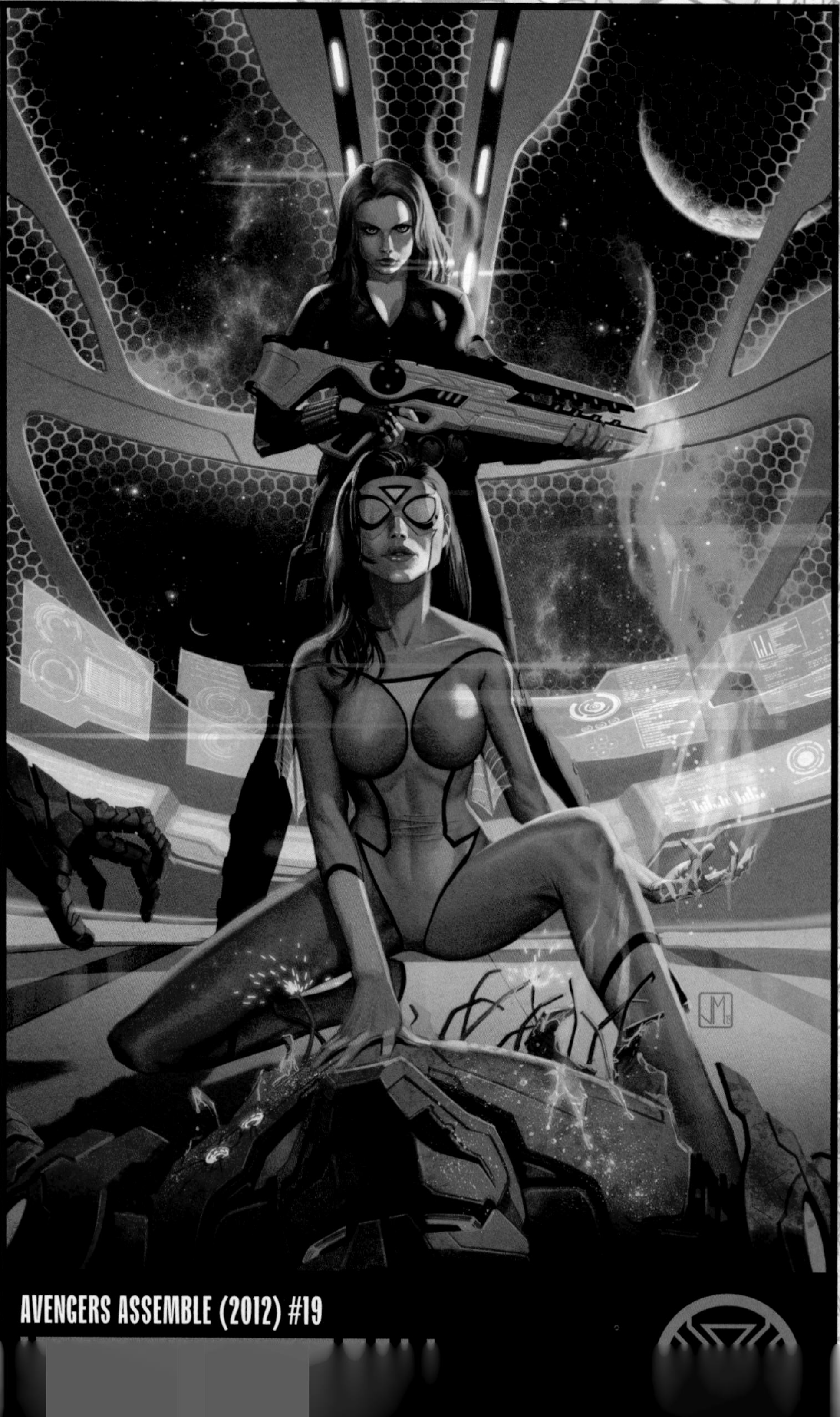

AVENGERS ASSEMBLE (2012) #19

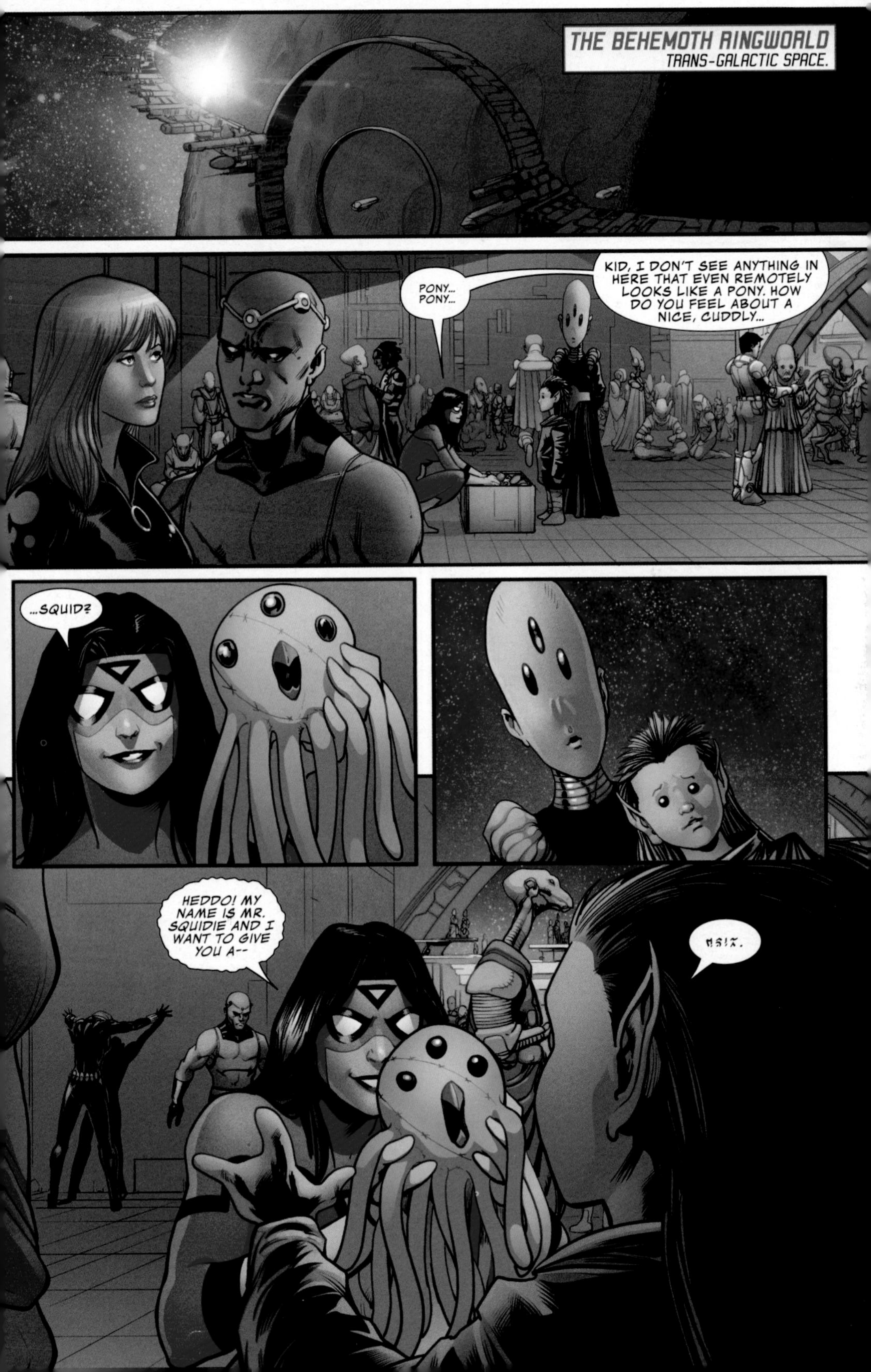
THE BEHEMOTH RINGWORLD
TRANS-GALACTIC SPACE.
PONY... PONY...
KID, I DON'T SEE ANYTHING IN HERE THAT EVEN REMOTELY LOOKS LIKE A PONY. HOW DO YOU FEEL ABOUT A NICE, CUDDLY...
...SQUID?
HEDDO! MY NAME IS MR. SQUIDIE AND I WANT TO GIVE YOU A--

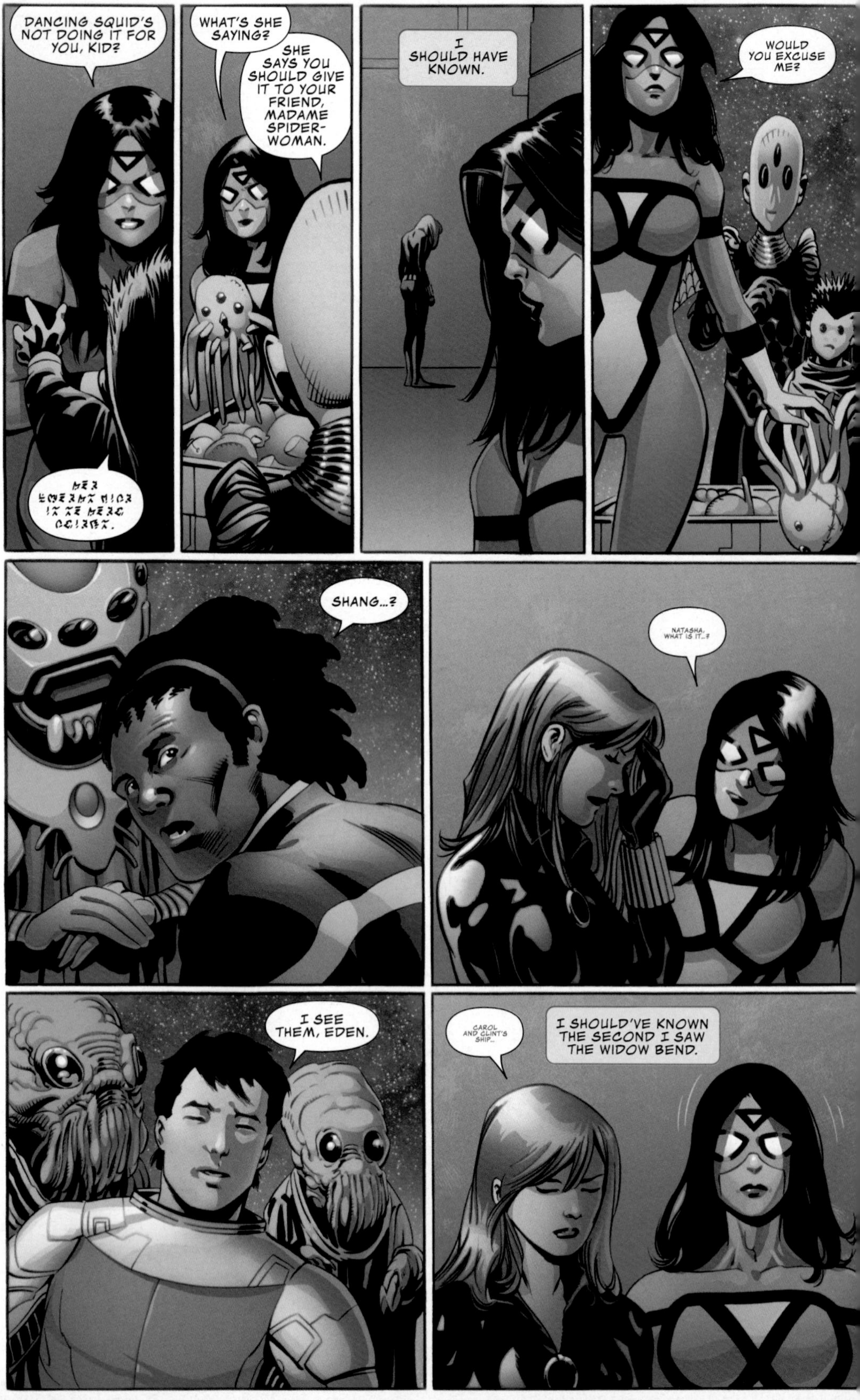
DANCING SQUID'S NOT DOING IT FOR YOU, KID?
WHAT'S SHE SAYING?
SHE SAYS YOU SHOULD GIVE IT TO YOUR FRIEND, MADAME SPIDER-WOMAN.
I SHOULD HAVE KNOWN.
WOULD YOU EXCUSE ME?
SHANG...?
NATASHA, WHAT IS IT...?
I SEE THEM, EDEN.
I SHOULD'VE KNOWN THE SECOND I SAW THE WIDOW BEND.
CAROL AND CLINT'S SHIP...

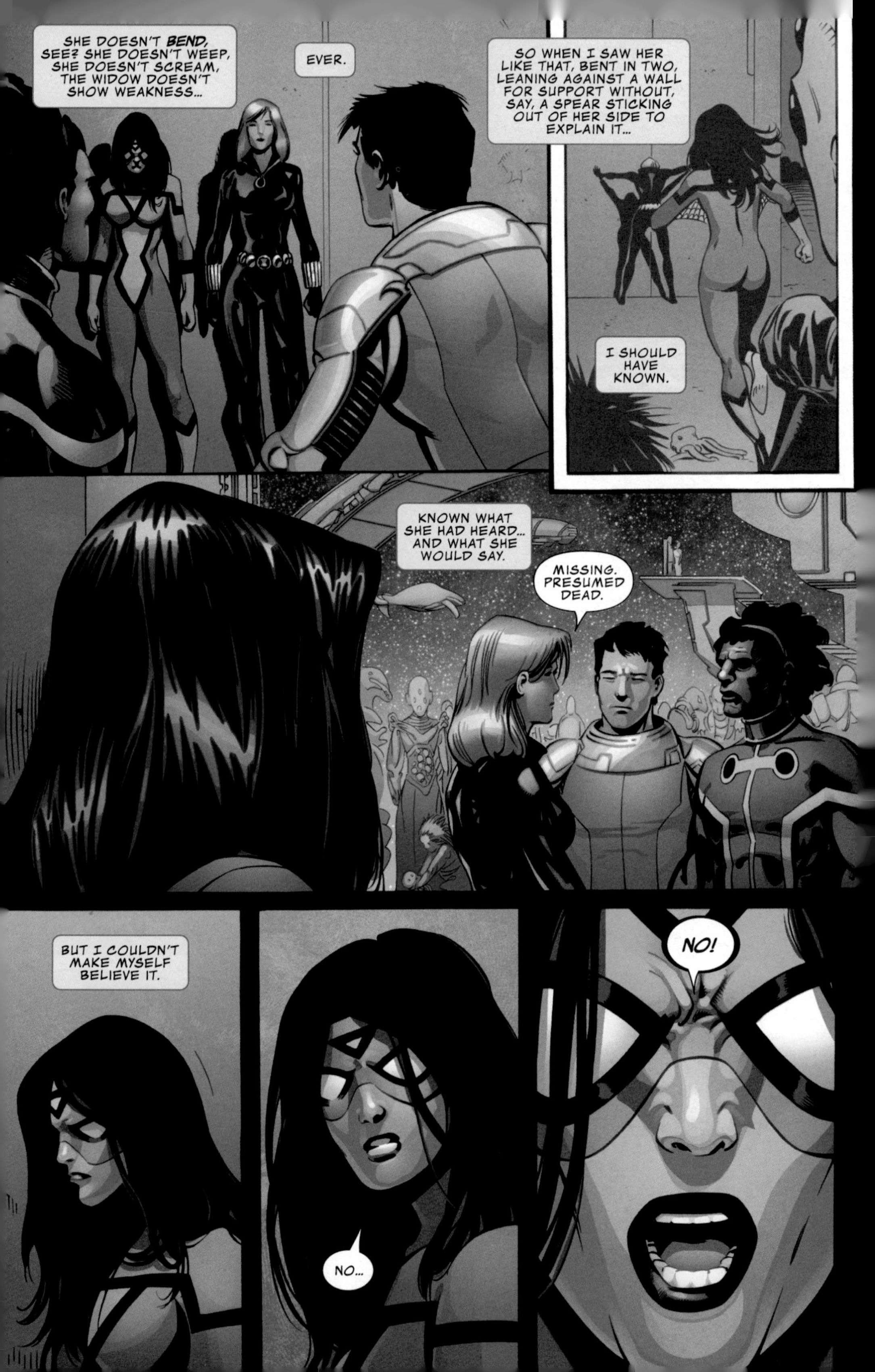
SHE DOESN'T BEND, SEE? SHE DOESN'T WEEP, SHE DOESN'T SCREAM, THE WIDOW DOESN'T SHOW WEAKNESS...
EVER.
SO WHEN I SAW HER LIKE THAT, BENT IN TWO, LEANING AGAINST A WALL FOR SUPPORT WITHOUT, SAY, A SPEAR STICKING OUT OF HER SIDE TO EXPLAIN IT...
I SHOULD HAVE KNOWN.
KNOWN WHAT SHE HAD HEARD... AND WHAT SHE WOULD SAY.
MISSING. PRESUMED DEAD.
BUT I COULDN'T MAKE MYSELF BELIEVE IT.
NO...
NO!

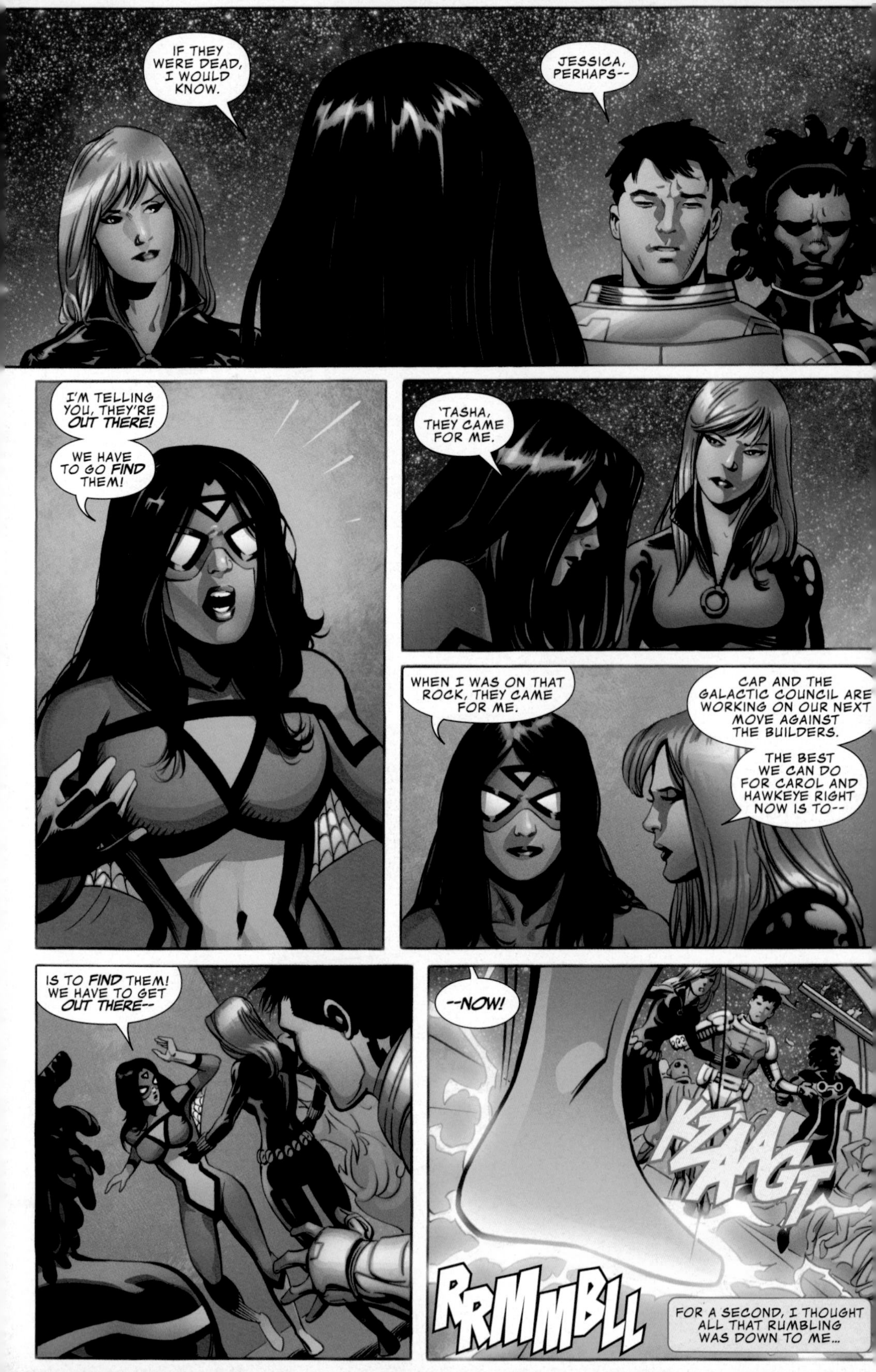
IF THEY WERE DEAD, I WOULD KNOW.
JESSICA, PERHAPS--
I'M TELLING YOU, THEY'RE OUT THERE!
WE HAVE TO GO FIND THEM!
'TASHA, THEY CAME FOR ME.
WHEN I WAS ON THAT ROCK, THEY CAME FOR ME.
CAP AND THE GALACTIC COUNCIL ARE WORKING ON OUR NEXT MOVE AGAINST THE BUILDERS.
THE BEST WE CAN DO FOR CAROL AND HAWKEYE RIGHT NOW IS TO--
IS TO FIND THEM! WE HAVE TO GET OUT THERE--
--NOW!
KZAAGT
RRMMBLL
FOR A SECOND, I THOUGHT ALL THAT RUMBLING WAS DOWN TO ME...

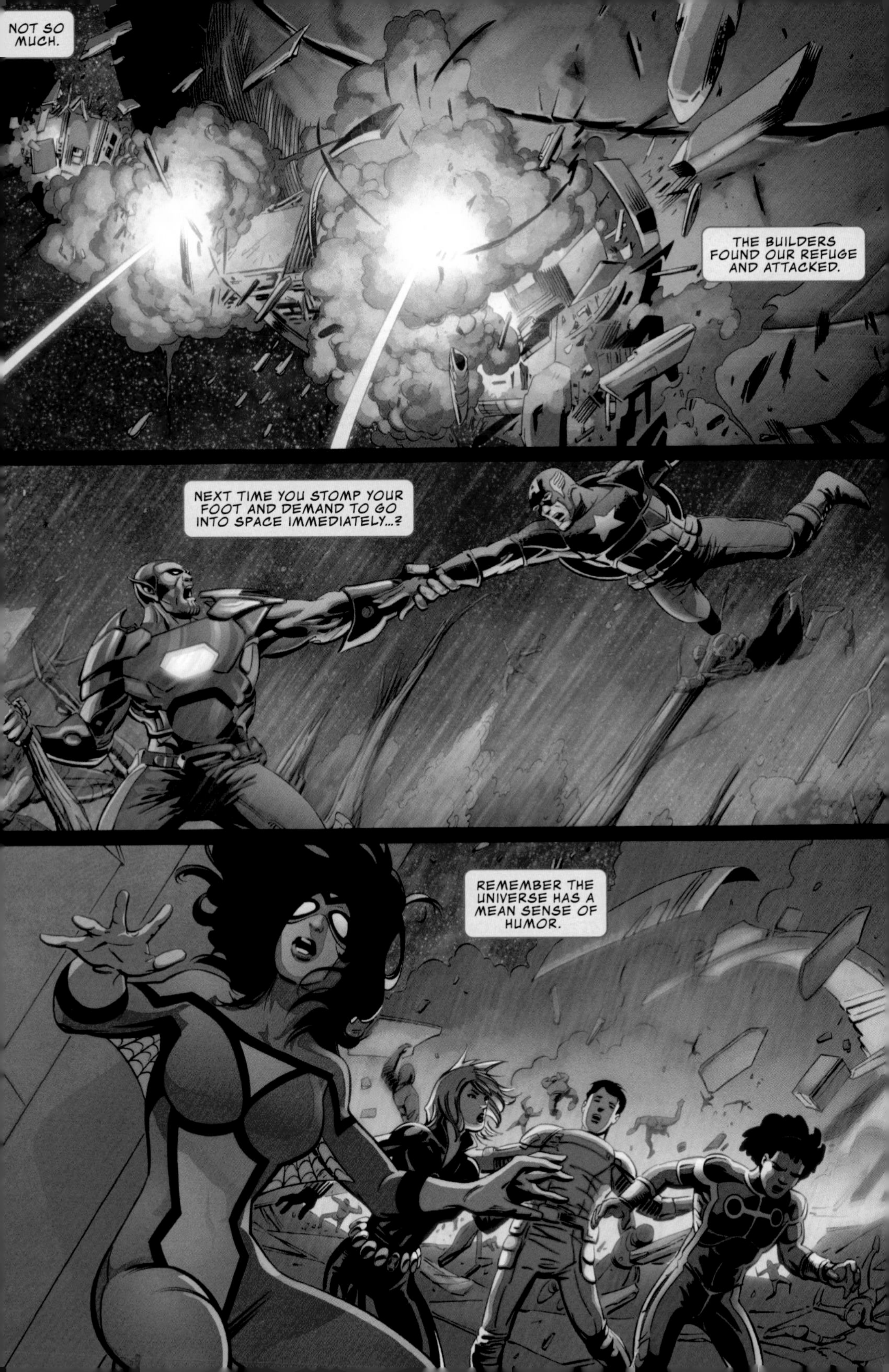
NOT SO MUCH.
THE BUILDERS FOUND OUR REFUGE AND ATTACKED.
NEXT TIME YOU STOMP YOUR FOOT AND DEMAND TO GO INTO SPACE IMMEDIATELY...?
REMEMBER THE UNIVERSE HAS A MEAN SENSE OF HUMOR.

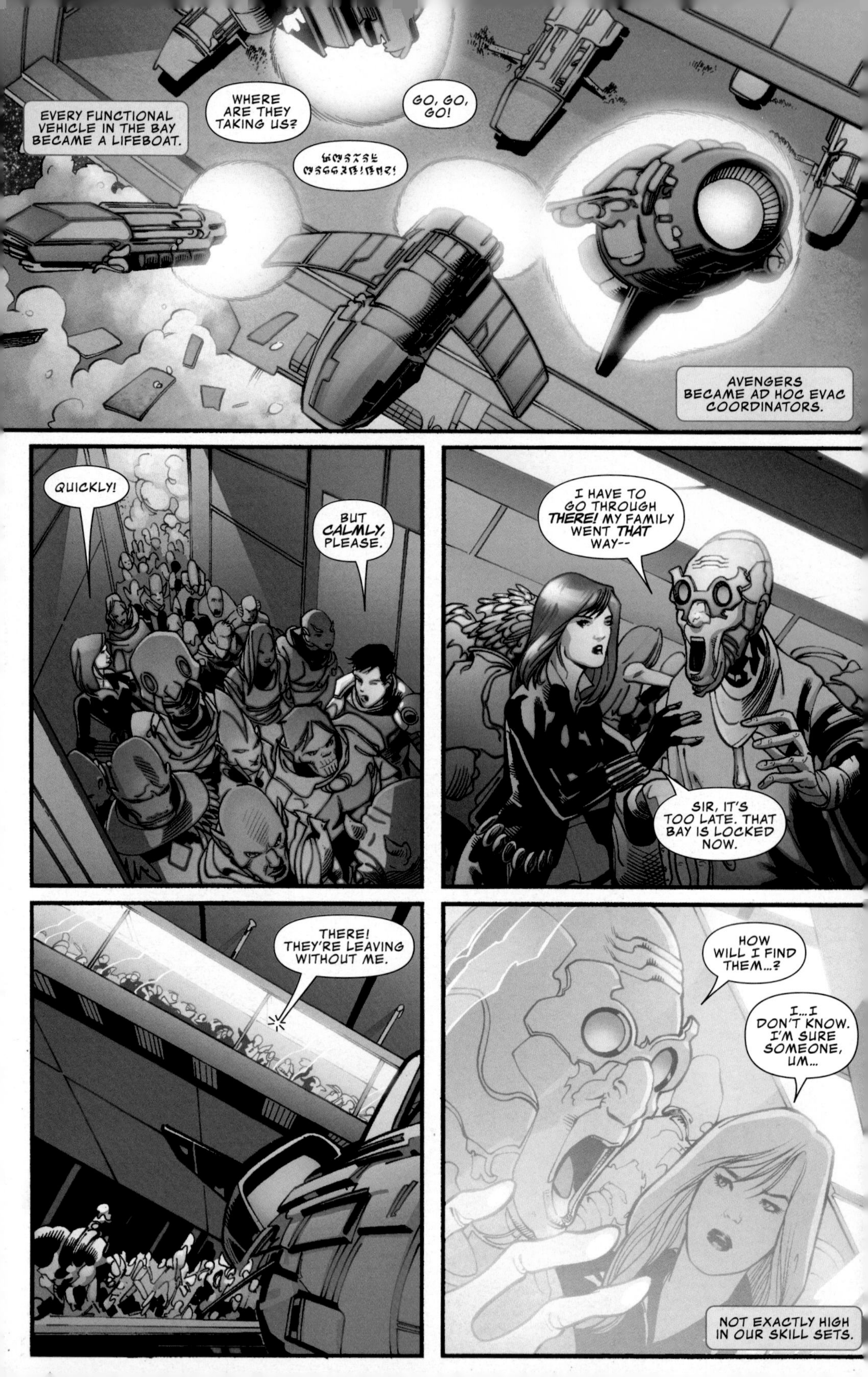
EVERY FUNCTIONAL VEHICLE IN THE BAY BECAME A LIFEBOAT.
WHERE ARE THEY TAKING US?
GO, GO, GO!
AVENGERS BECAME AD HOC EVAC COORDINATORS.
QUICKLY!
BUT CALMLY, PLEASE.
I HAVE TO GO THROUGH THERE! MY FAMILY WENT THAT WAY--
SIR, IT'S TOO LATE. THAT BAY IS LOCKED NOW.
THERE! THEY'RE LEAVING WITHOUT ME.
HOW WILL I FIND THEM...?
I... I DON'T KNOW. I'M SURE SOMEONE, UM...
NOT EXACTLY HIGH IN OUR SKILL SETS.

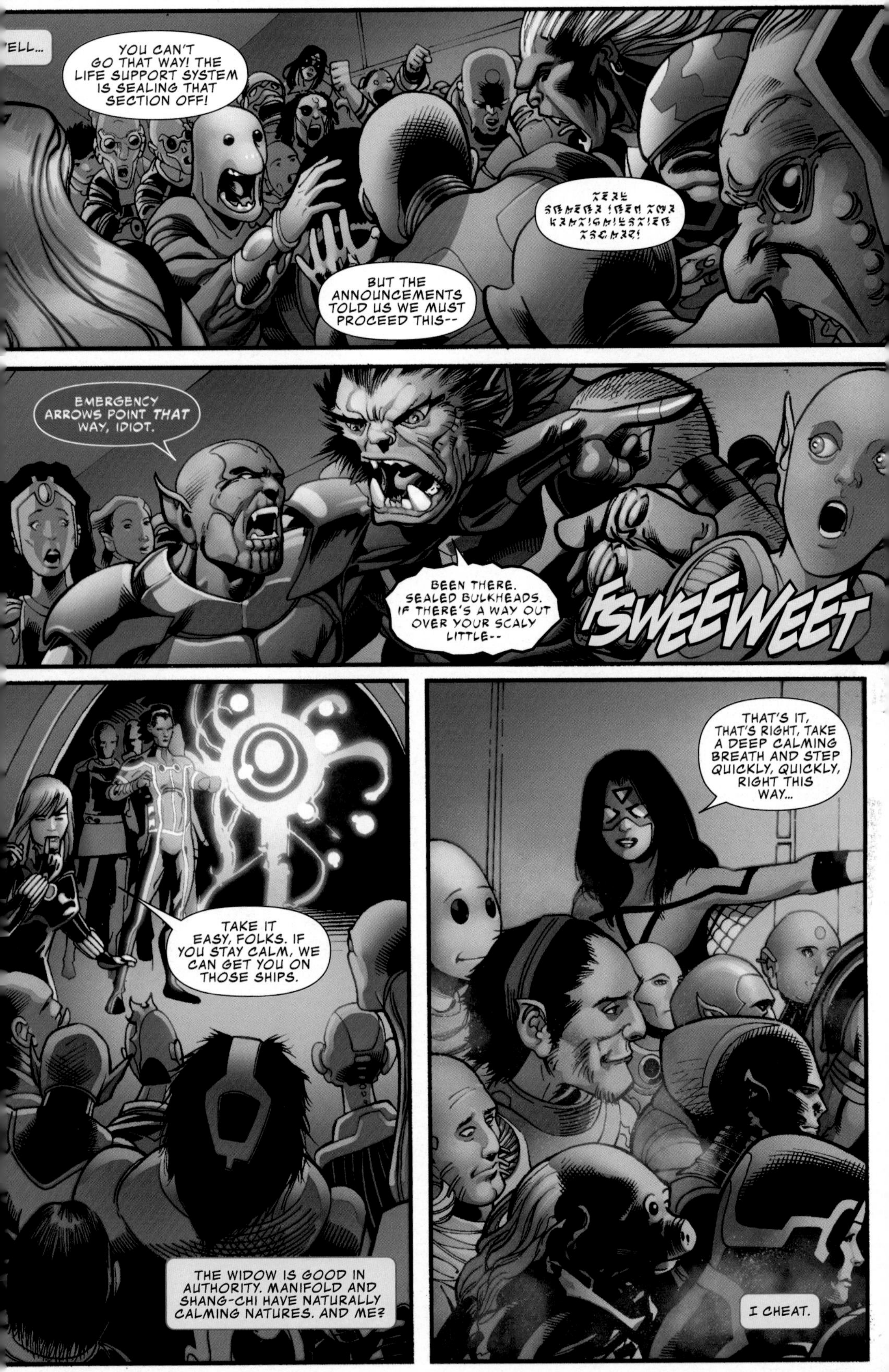

WELL...
YOU CAN'T GO THAT WAY! THE LIFE SUPPORT SYSTEM IS SEALING THAT SECTION OFF!
BUT THE ANNOUNCEMENTS TOLD US WE MUST PROCEED THIS--
EMERGENCY ARROWS POINT THAT WAY, IDIOT.
BEEN THERE. SEALED BULKHEADS. IF THERE'S A WAY OUT OVER YOUR SCALY LITTLE--
FSWEEWEET
TAKE IT EASY, FOLKS. IF YOU STAY CALM, WE CAN GET YOU ON THOSE SHIPS.
THE WIDOW IS GOOD IN AUTHORITY. MANIFOLD AND SHANG-CHI HAVE NATURALLY CALMING NATURES. AND ME?
THAT'S IT, THAT'S RIGHT, TAKE A DEEP CALMING BREATH AND STEP QUICKLY, QUICKLY, RIGHT THIS WAY...
I CHEAT.

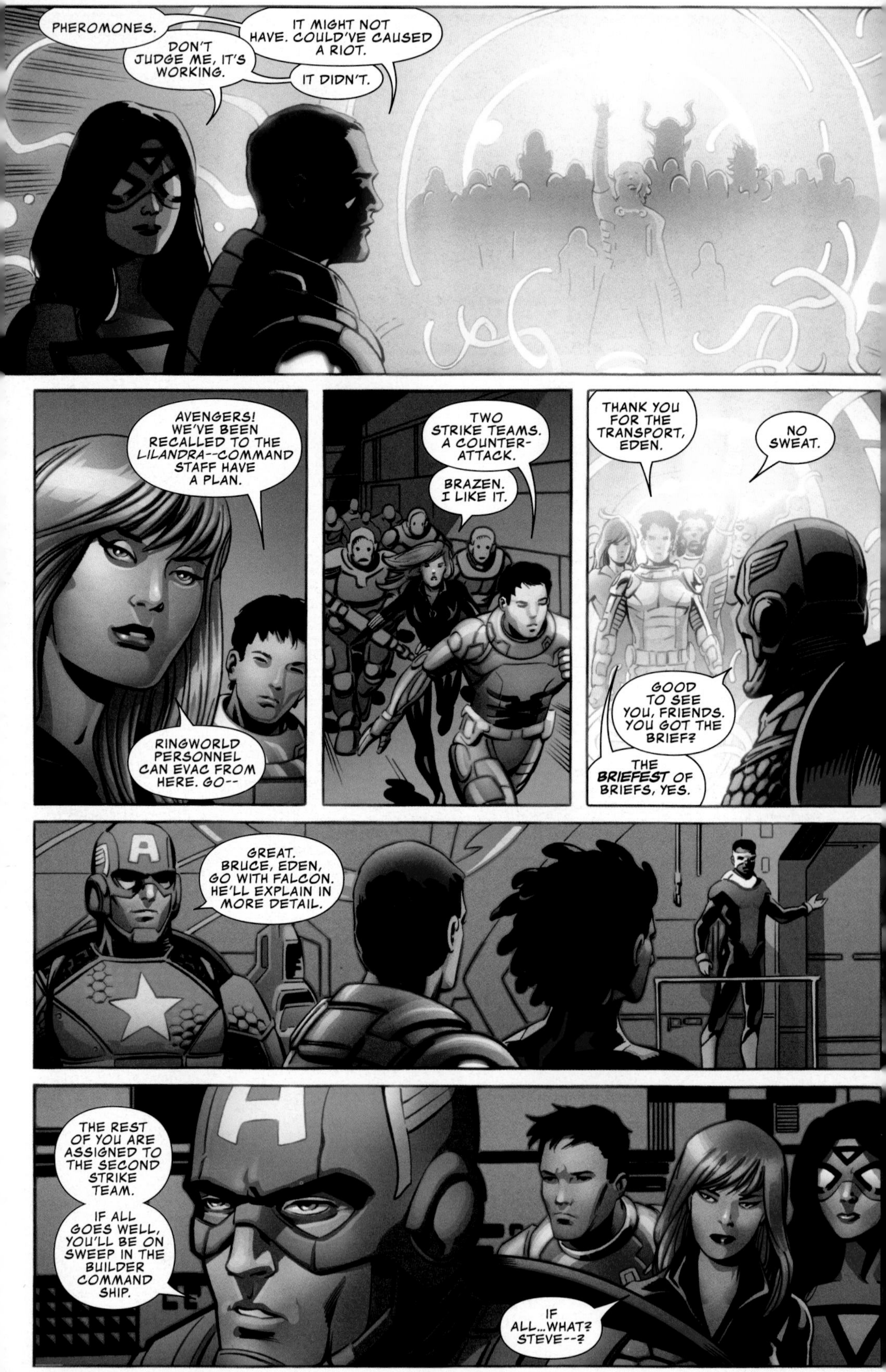
PHEROMONES.
IT MIGHT NOT HAVE. COULD'VE CAUSED A RIOT.
DON'T JUDGE ME, IT'S WORKING.
IT DIDN'T.
AVENGERS! WE'VE BEEN RECALLED TO THE *LILANDRA*--COMMAND STAFF HAVE A PLAN.
RINGWORLD PERSONNEL CAN EVAC FROM HERE. GO--
TWO STRIKE TEAMS. A COUNTER-ATTACK.
BRAZEN. I LIKE IT.
THANK YOU FOR THE TRANSPORT, EDEN.
NO SWEAT.
GOOD TO SEE YOU, FRIENDS. YOU GOT THE BRIEF?
THE ***BRIEFEST*** OF BRIEFS, YES.
GREAT. BRUCE, EDEN, GO WITH FALCON. HE'LL EXPLAIN IN MORE DETAIL.
THE REST OF YOU ARE ASSIGNED TO THE SECOND STRIKE TEAM.
IF ALL GOES WELL, YOU'LL BE ON SWEEP IN THE BUILDER COMMAND SHIP.
IF ALL...WHAT? STEVE--?

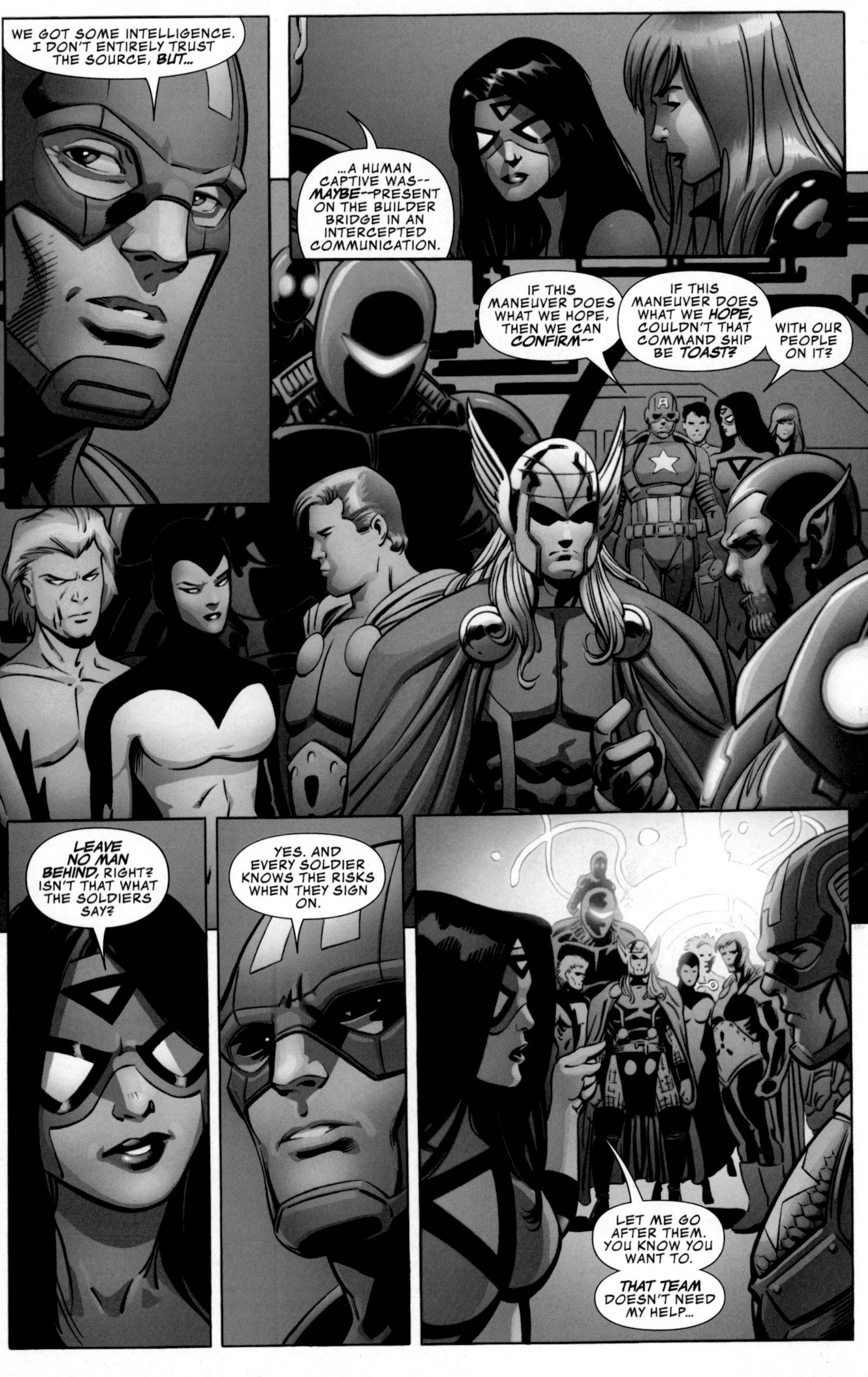
WE GOT SOME INTELLIGENCE. I DON'T ENTIRELY TRUST THE SOURCE, BUT...
...A HUMAN CAPTIVE WAS--MAYBE--PRESENT ON THE BUILDER BRIDGE IN AN INTERCEPTED COMMUNICATION.
IF THIS MANEUVER DOES WHAT WE HOPE, THEN WE CAN CONFIRM--
IF THIS MANEUVER DOES WHAT WE HOPE, COULDN'T THAT COMMAND SHIP BE TOAST?
WITH OUR PEOPLE ON IT?
LEAVE NO MAN BEHIND, RIGHT? ISN'T THAT WHAT THE SOLDIERS SAY?
YES. AND EVERY SOLDIER KNOWS THE RISKS WHEN THEY SIGN ON.
LET ME GO AFTER THEM. YOU KNOW YOU WANT TO.
THAT TEAM DOESN'T NEED MY HELP...

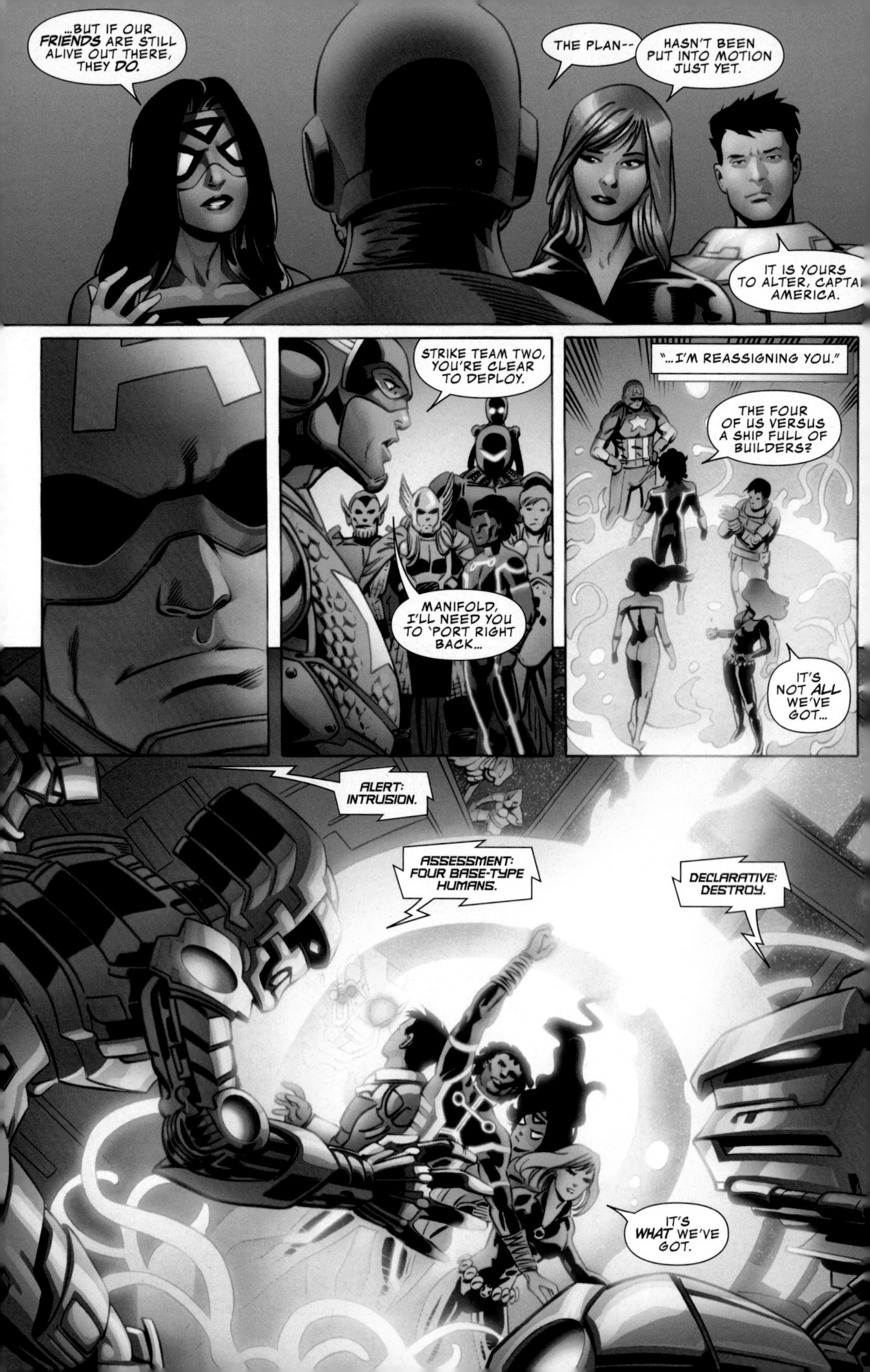
...BUT IF OUR FRIENDS ARE STILL ALIVE OUT THERE, THEY DO.
THE PLAN--
HASN'T BEEN PUT INTO MOTION JUST YET.
IT IS YOURS TO ALTER, CAPTAIN AMERICA.
STRIKE TEAM TWO, YOU'RE CLEAR TO DEPLOY.
MANIFOLD, I'LL NEED YOU TO 'PORT RIGHT BACK...
"...I'M REASSIGNING YOU."
THE FOUR OF US VERSUS A SHIP FULL OF BUILDERS?
IT'S NOT ALL WE'VE GOT...
ALERT: INTRUSION.
ASSESSMENT: FOUR BASE-TYPE HUMANS.
DECLARATIVE: DESTROY.
IT'S WHAT WE'VE GOT.

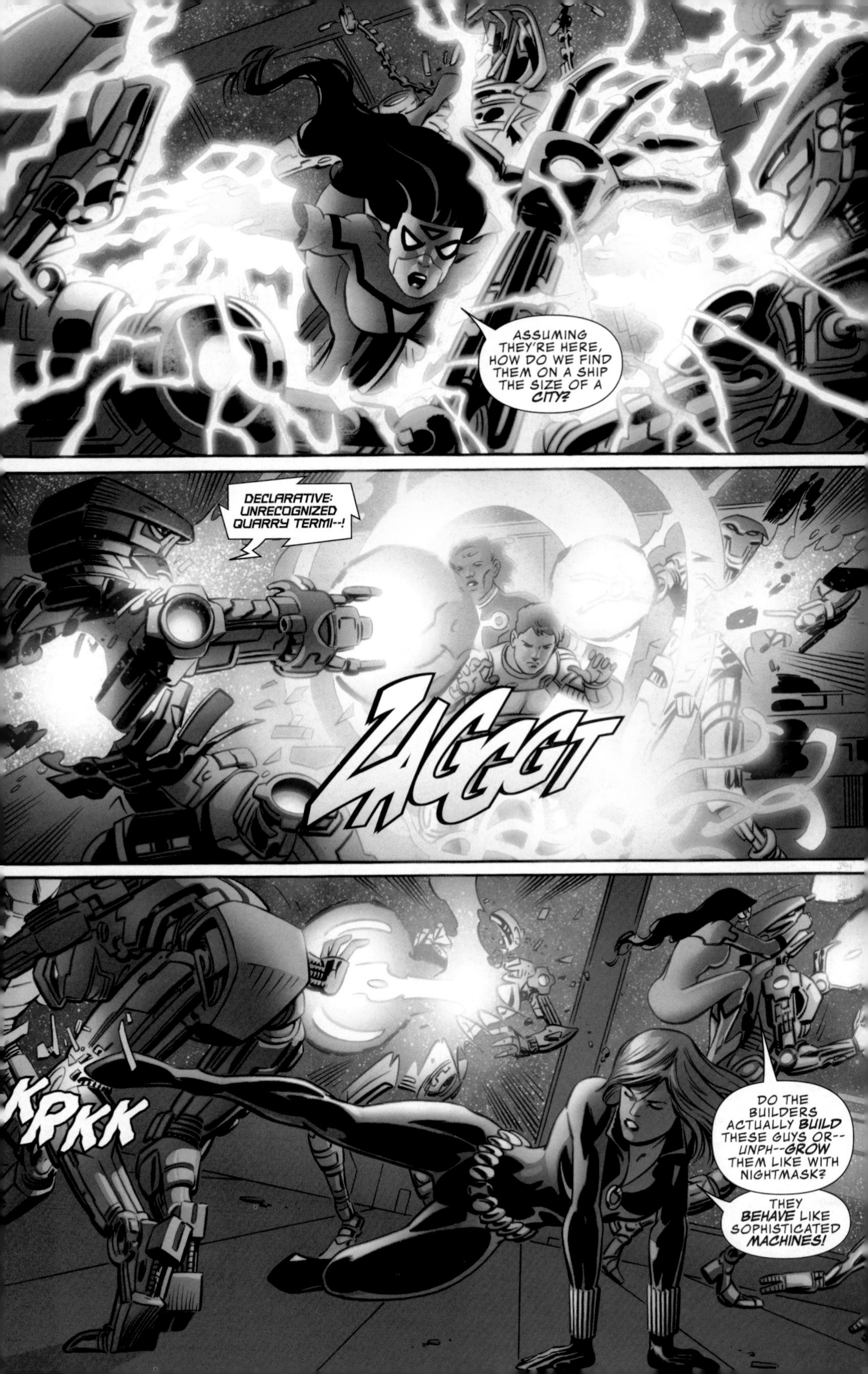
ASSUMING THEY'RE HERE, HOW DO WE FIND THEM ON A SHIP THE SIZE OF A CITY?
DECLARATIVE: UNRECOGNIZED QUARRY TERMI--!
ZAGGT
KRKK
DO THE BUILDERS ACTUALLY BUILD THESE GUYS OR-- UNPH--GROW THEM LIKE WITH NIGHTMASK?
THEY BEHAVE LIKE SOPHISTICATED MACHINES!

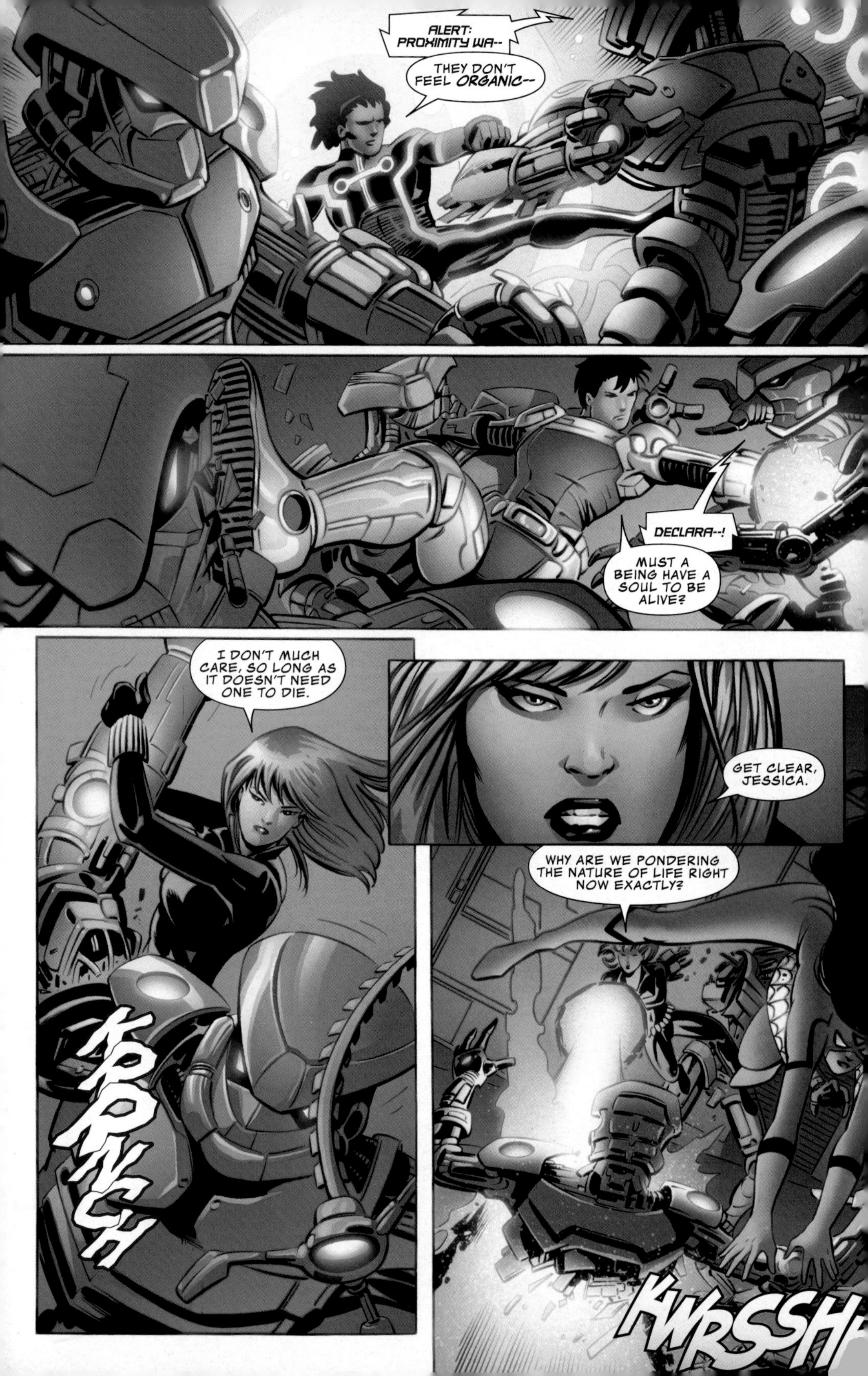

ALERT: PROXIMITY WA--
THEY DON'T FEEL ORGANIC--
DECLARA--!
MUST A BEING HAVE A SOUL TO BE ALIVE?
I DON'T MUCH CARE, SO LONG AS IT DOESN'T NEED ONE TO DIE.
KRNCH
GET CLEAR, JESSICA.
WHY ARE WE PONDERING THE NATURE OF LIFE RIGHT NOW EXACTLY?
KWRSSH

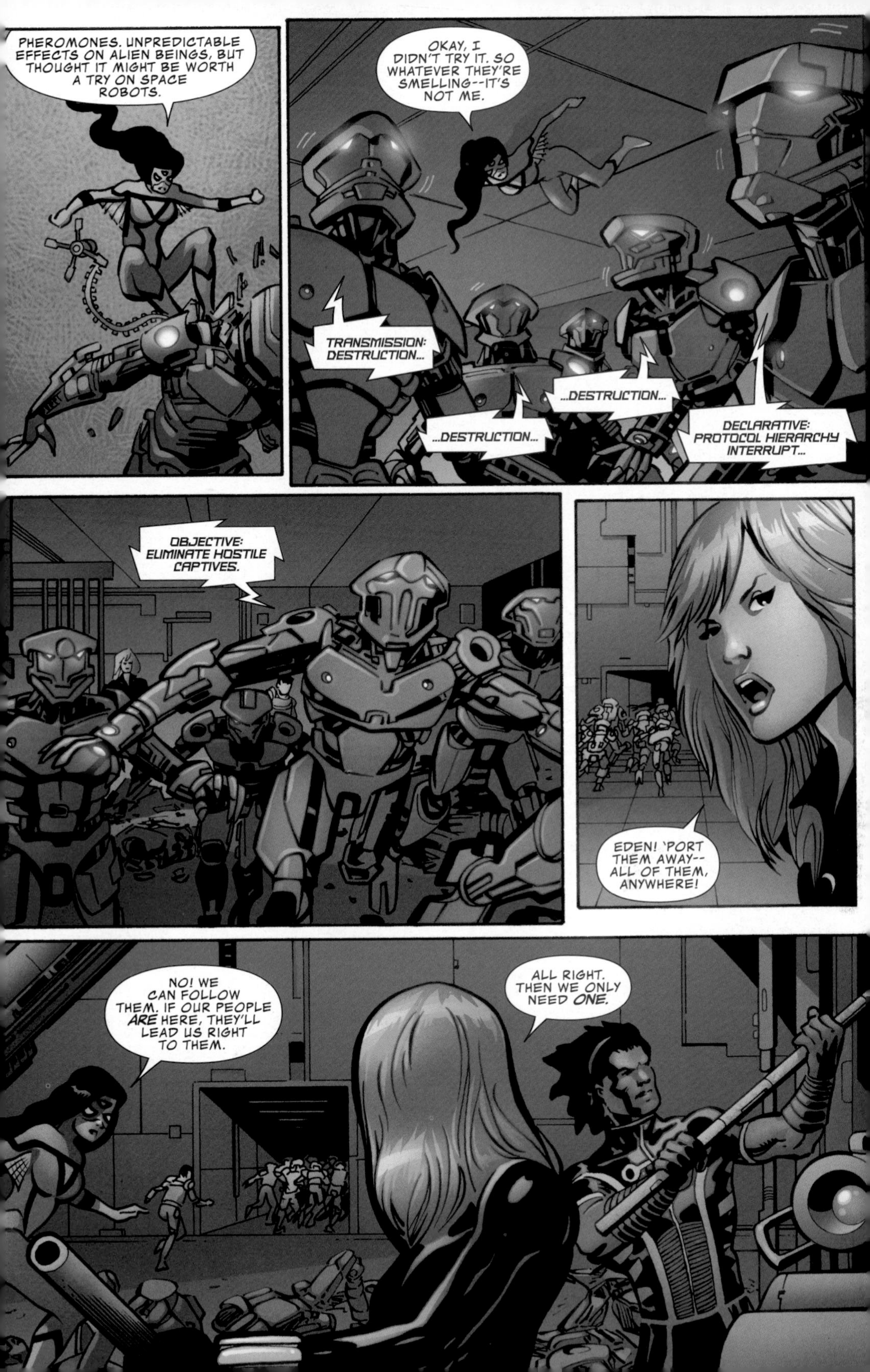
PHEROMONES. UNPREDICTABLE EFFECTS ON ALIEN BEINGS, BUT THOUGHT IT MIGHT BE WORTH A TRY ON SPACE ROBOTS.
OKAY, I DIDN'T TRY IT. SO WHATEVER THEY'RE SMELLING--IT'S NOT ME.
TRANSMISSION: DESTRUCTION...
...DESTRUCTION...
...DESTRUCTION...
DECLARATIVE: PROTOCOL HIERARCHY INTERRUPT...
OBJECTIVE: ELIMINATE HOSTILE CAPTIVES.
EDEN! 'PORT THEM AWAY--ALL OF THEM, ANYWHERE!
NO! WE CAN FOLLOW THEM. IF OUR PEOPLE ARE HERE, THEY'LL LEAD US RIGHT TO THEM.
ALL RIGHT. THEN WE ONLY NEED ONE.

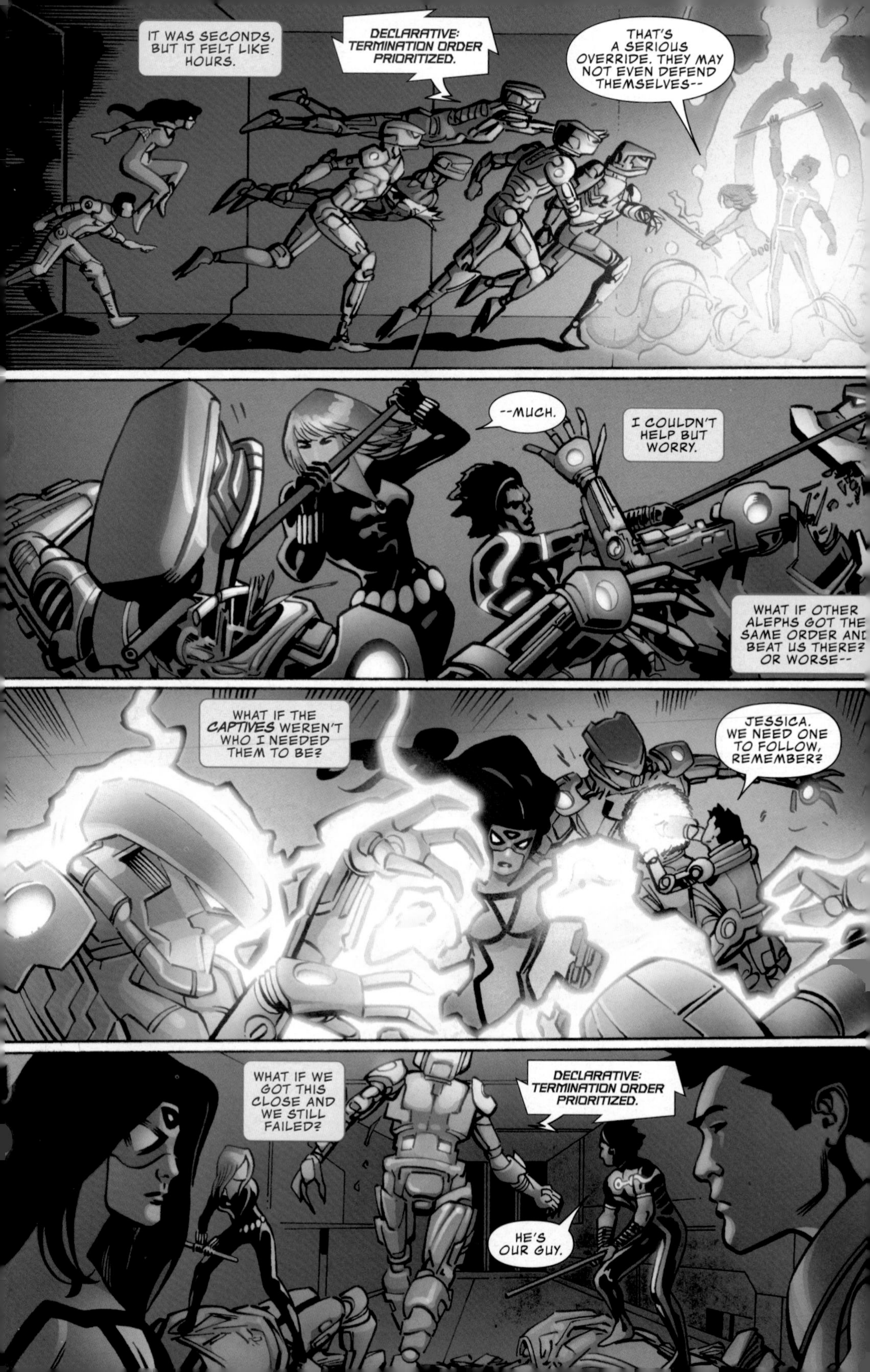
IT WAS SECONDS, BUT IT FELT LIKE HOURS.
DECLARATIVE: TERMINATION ORDER PRIORITIZED.
THAT'S A SERIOUS OVERRIDE. THEY MAY NOT EVEN DEFEND THEMSELVES--
--MUCH.
I COULDN'T HELP BUT WORRY.
WHAT IF OTHER ALEPHS GOT THE SAME ORDER AND BEAT US THERE? OR WORSE--
WHAT IF THE CAPTIVES WEREN'T WHO I NEEDED THEM TO BE?
JESSICA. WE NEED ONE TO FOLLOW, REMEMBER?
WHAT IF WE GOT THIS CLOSE AND WE STILL FAILED?
DECLARATIVE: TERMINATION ORDER PRIORITIZED.
HE'S OUR GUY.

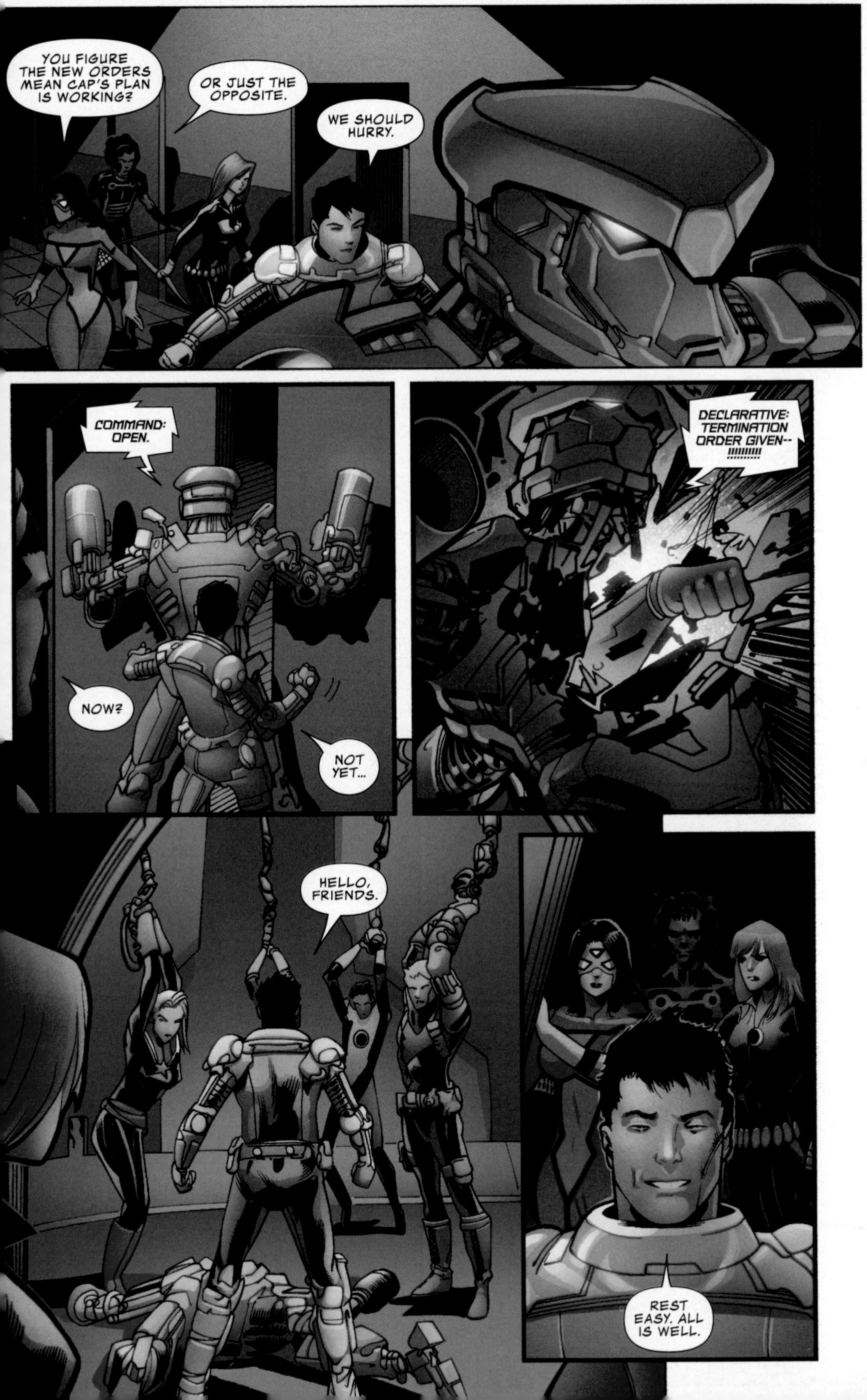
YOU FIGURE THE NEW ORDERS MEAN CAP'S PLAN IS WORKING?
OR JUST THE OPPOSITE.
WE SHOULD HURRY.
COMMAND: OPEN.
NOW?
NOT YET...
DECLARATIVE: TERMINATION ORDER GIVEN-- !!!!!!!!!!
HELLO, FRIENDS.
REST EASY. ALL IS WELL.

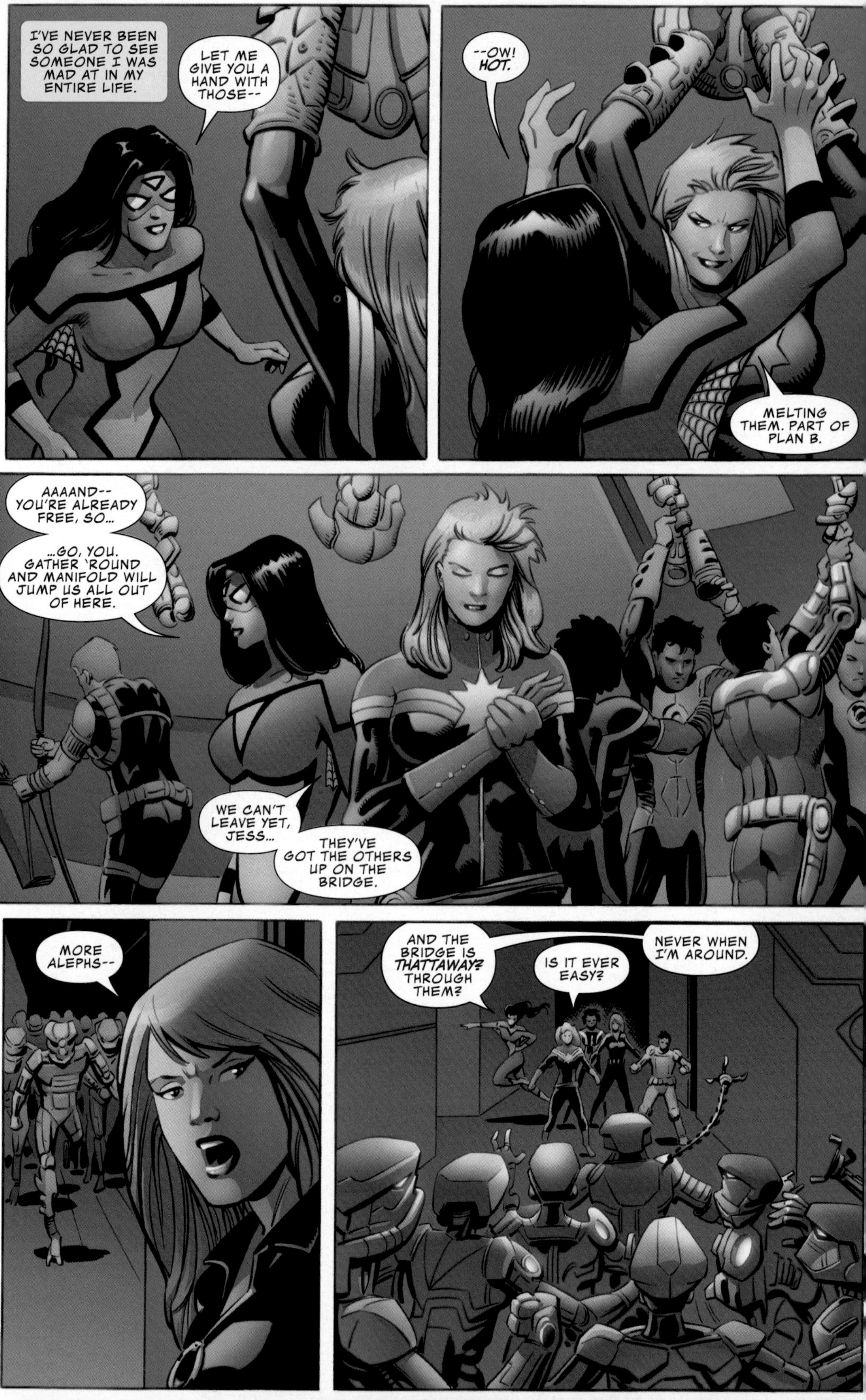
I'VE NEVER BEEN SO GLAD TO SEE SOMEONE I WAS MAD AT IN MY ENTIRE LIFE.
LET ME GIVE YOU A HAND WITH THOSE--
--OW! HOT.
MELTING THEM. PART OF PLAN B.
AAAAND-- YOU'RE ALREADY FREE, SO...
...GO, YOU. GATHER 'ROUND AND MANIFOLD WILL JUMP US ALL OUT OF HERE.
WE CAN'T LEAVE YET, JESS...
THEY'VE GOT THE OTHERS UP ON THE BRIDGE.
MORE ALEPHS--
AND THE BRIDGE IS THATTAWAY? THROUGH THEM?
IS IT EVER EASY?
NEVER WHEN I'M AROUND.

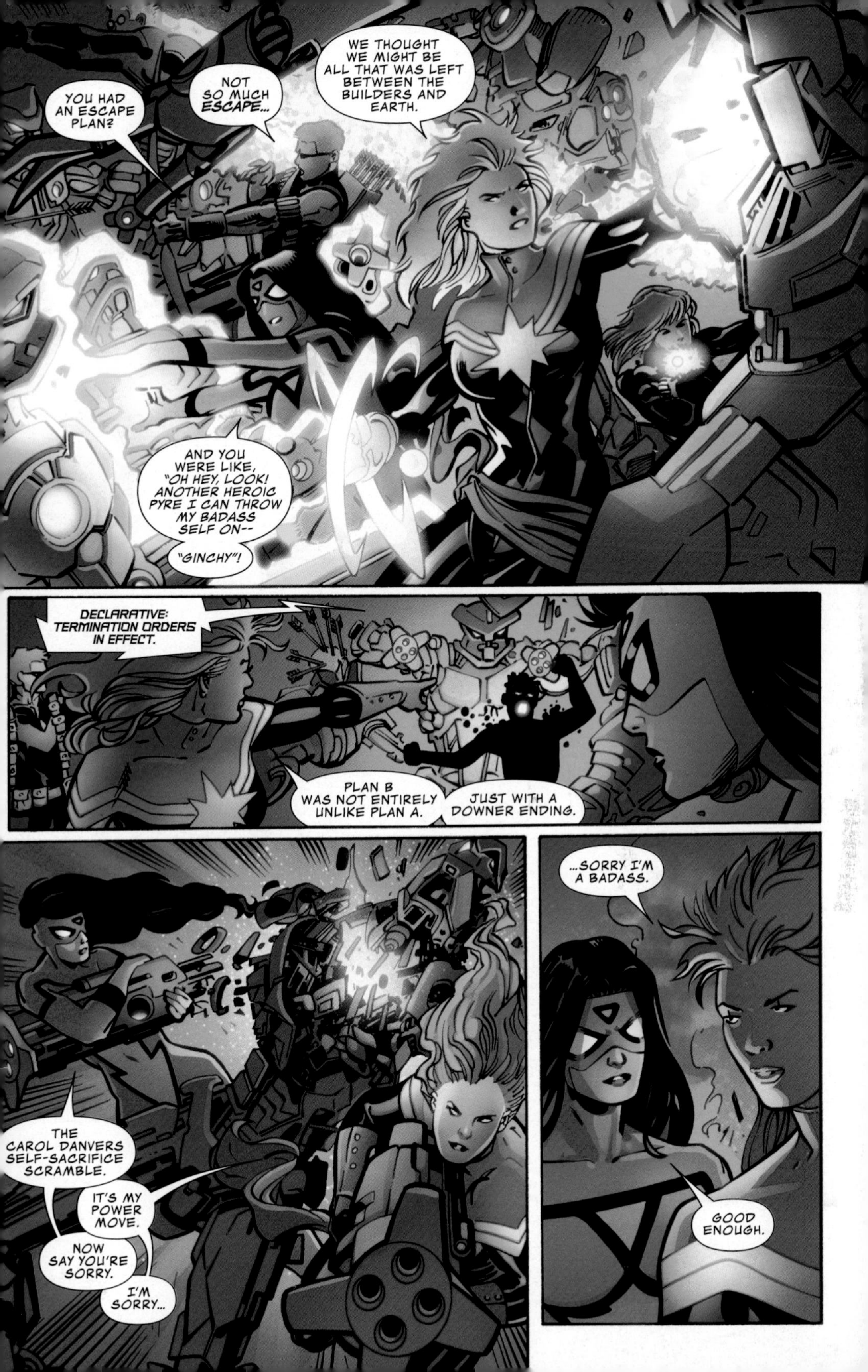
YOU HAD AN ESCAPE PLAN?
NOT SO MUCH ESCAPE...
WE THOUGHT WE MIGHT BE ALL THAT WAS LEFT BETWEEN THE BUILDERS AND EARTH.
AND YOU WERE LIKE, "OH HEY, LOOK! ANOTHER HEROIC PYRE I CAN THROW MY BADASS SELF ON--
"GINCHY"!
DECLARATIVE: TERMINATION ORDERS IN EFFECT.
PLAN B WAS NOT ENTIRELY UNLIKE PLAN A.
JUST WITH A DOWNER ENDING.
THE CAROL DANVERS SELF-SACRIFICE SCRAMBLE.
IT'S MY POWER MOVE.
NOW SAY YOU'RE SORRY.
I'M SORRY...
...SORRY I'M A BADASS.
GOOD ENOUGH.

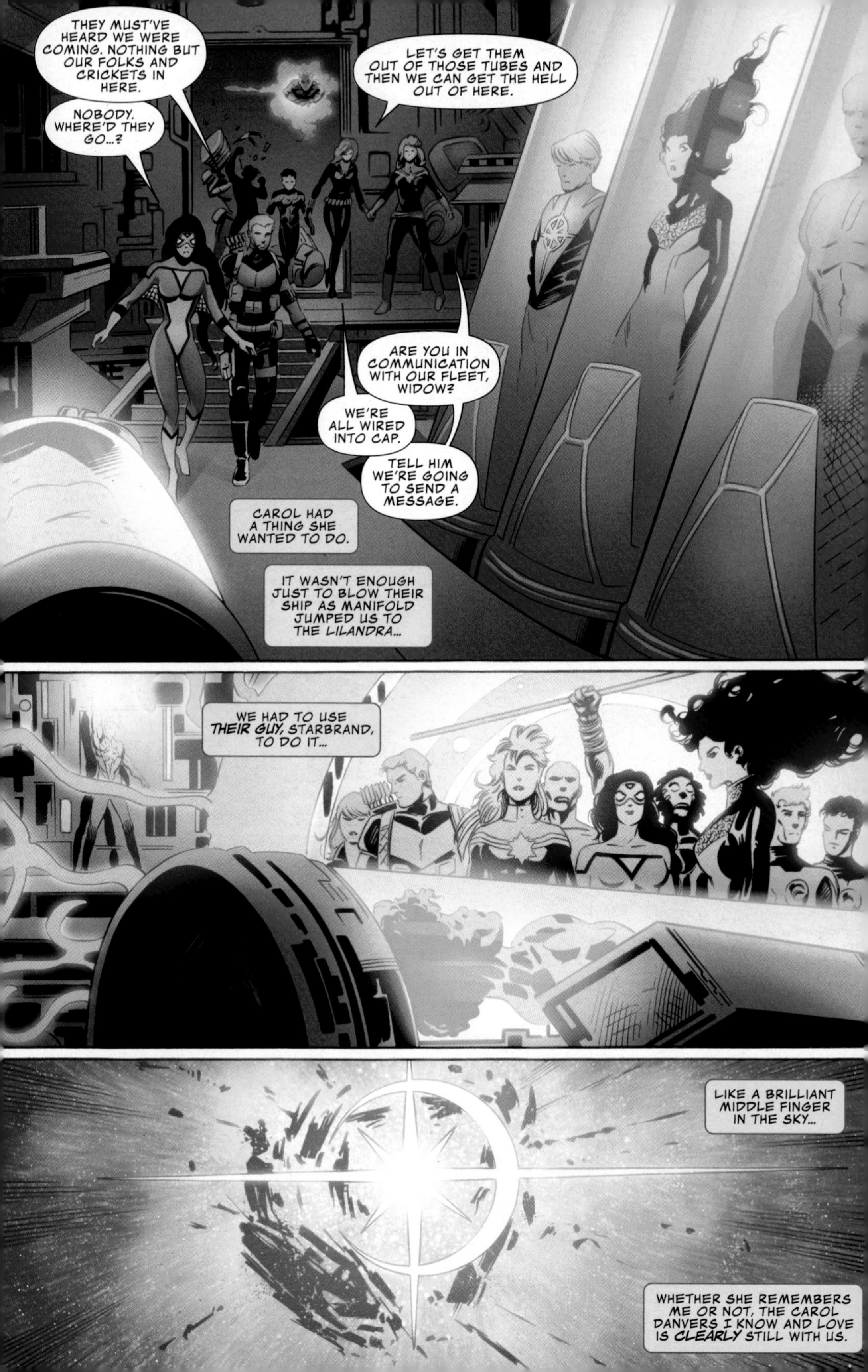
THEY MUST'VE HEARD WE WERE COMING. NOTHING BUT OUR FOLKS AND CRICKETS IN HERE.
NOBODY. WHERE'D THEY GO...?
LET'S GET THEM OUT OF THOSE TUBES AND THEN WE CAN GET THE HELL OUT OF HERE.
ARE YOU IN COMMUNICATION WITH OUR FLEET, WIDOW?
WE'RE ALL WIRED INTO CAP.
TELL HIM WE'RE GOING TO SEND A MESSAGE.
CAROL HAD A THING SHE WANTED TO DO.
IT WASN'T ENOUGH JUST TO BLOW THEIR SHIP AS MANIFOLD JUMPED US TO THE *LILANDRA*...
WE HAD TO USE ***THEIR GUY,*** STARBRAND, TO DO IT...
LIKE A BRILLIANT MIDDLE FINGER IN THE SKY...
WHETHER SHE REMEMBERS ME OR NOT, THE CAROL DANVERS I KNOW AND LOVE IS ***CLEARLY*** STILL WITH US.

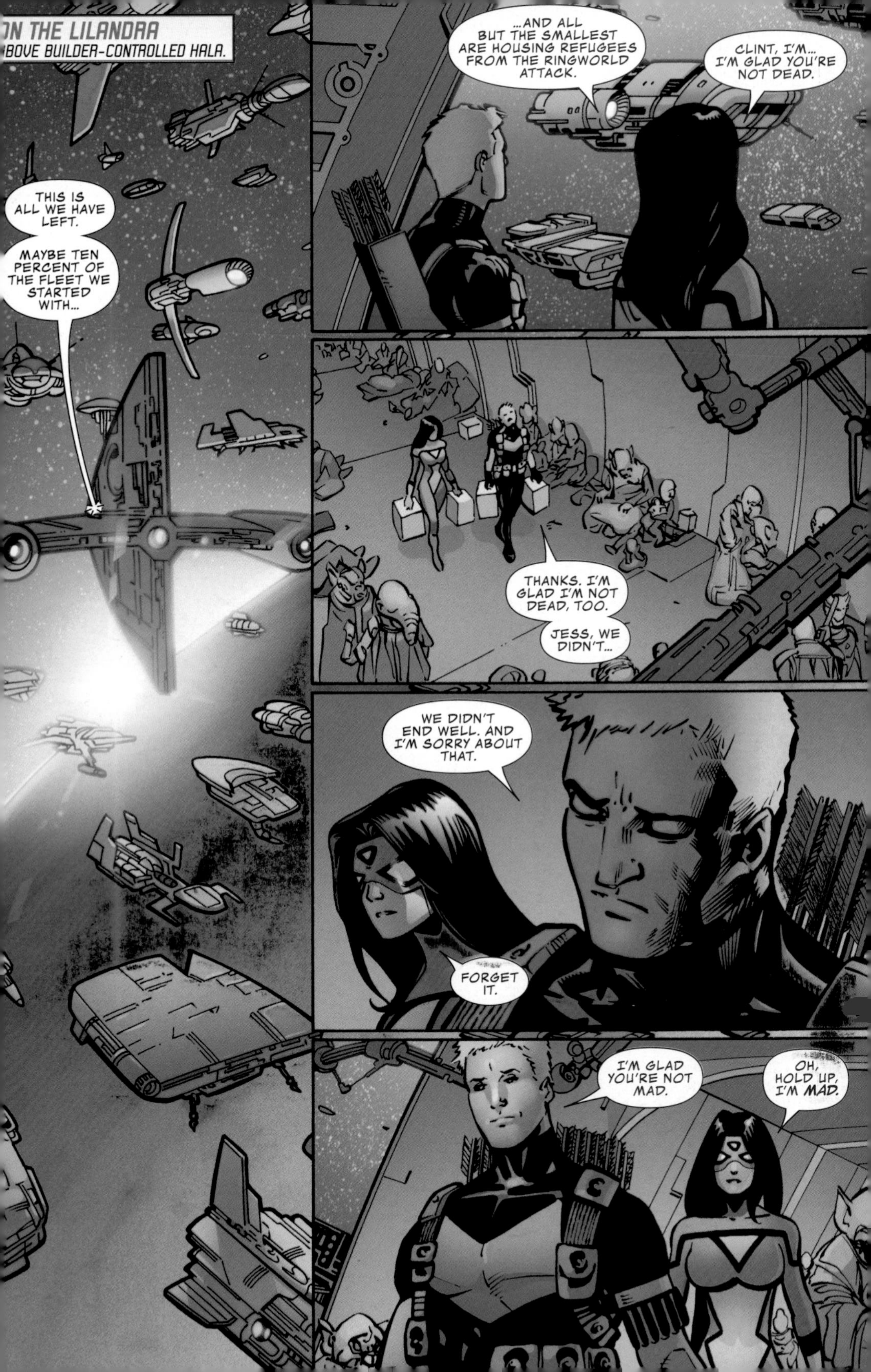
ON THE LILANDRA
ABOVE BUILDER-CONTROLLED HALA.
THIS IS ALL WE HAVE LEFT.
MAYBE TEN PERCENT OF THE FLEET WE STARTED WITH...
...AND ALL BUT THE SMALLEST ARE HOUSING REFUGEES FROM THE RINGWORLD ATTACK.
CLINT, I'M... I'M GLAD YOU'RE NOT DEAD.
THANKS. I'M GLAD I'M NOT DEAD, TOO.
JESS, WE DIDN'T...
WE DIDN'T END WELL. AND I'M SORRY ABOUT THAT.
FORGET IT.
I'M GLAD YOU'RE NOT MAD.
OH, HOLD UP, I'M *MAD*.

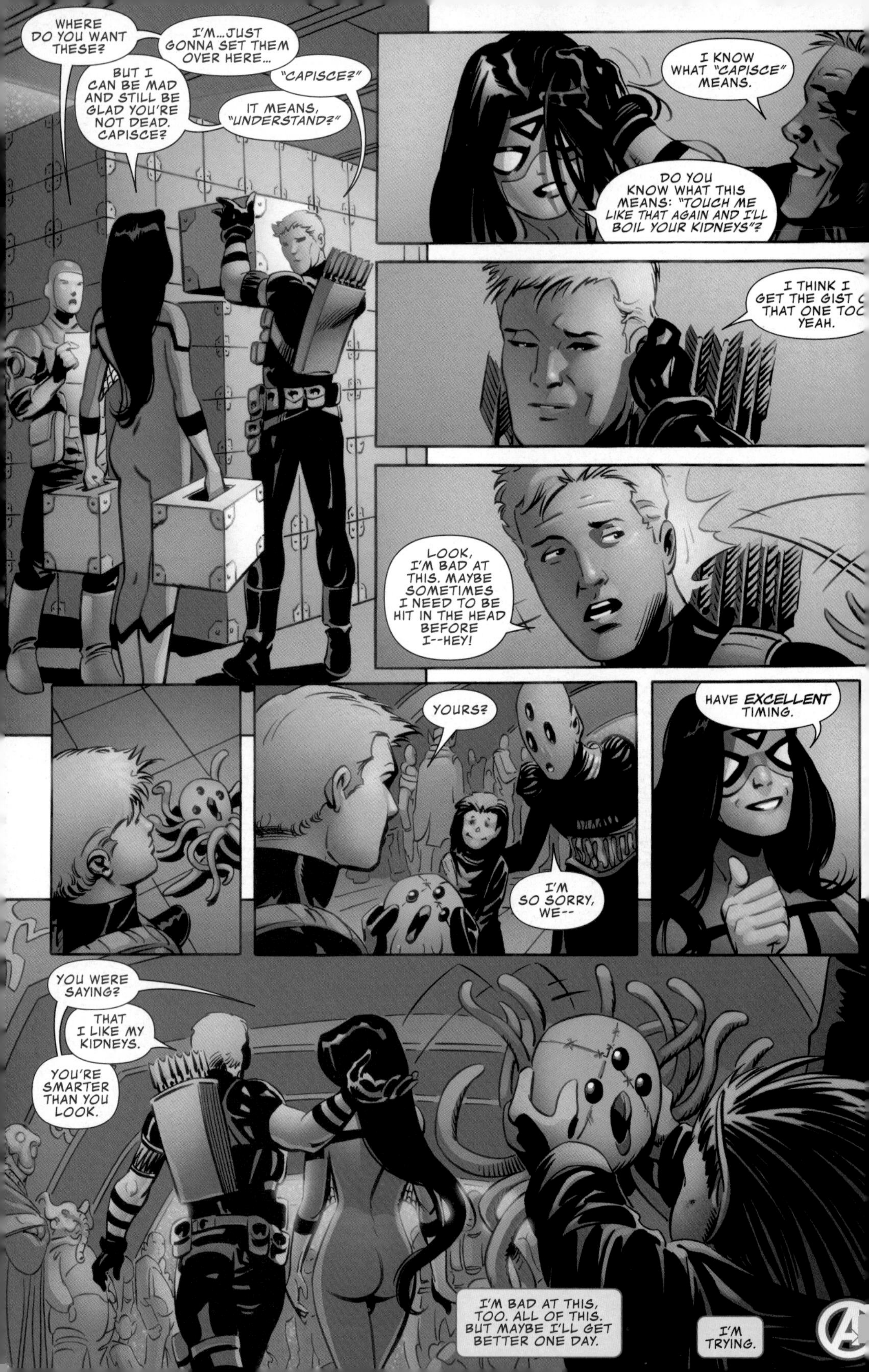
WHERE DO YOU WANT THESE?
I'M...JUST GONNA SET THEM OVER HERE...
BUT I CAN BE MAD AND STILL BE GLAD YOU'RE NOT DEAD. CAPISCE?
"CAPISCE?"
IT MEANS, "UNDERSTAND?"
I KNOW WHAT "CAPISCE" MEANS.
DO YOU KNOW WHAT THIS MEANS: "TOUCH ME LIKE THAT AGAIN AND I'LL BOIL YOUR KIDNEYS"?
I THINK I GET THE GIST OF THAT ONE TOO, YEAH.
LOOK, I'M BAD AT THIS. MAYBE SOMETIMES I NEED TO BE HIT IN THE HEAD BEFORE I--HEY!
YOURS?
I'M SO SORRY, WE--
HAVE EXCELLENT TIMING.
YOU WERE SAYING?
THAT I LIKE MY KIDNEYS.
YOU'RE SMARTER THAN YOU LOOK.
I'M BAD AT THIS, TOO. ALL OF THIS. BUT MAYBE I'LL GET BETTER ONE DAY.
I'M TRYING.

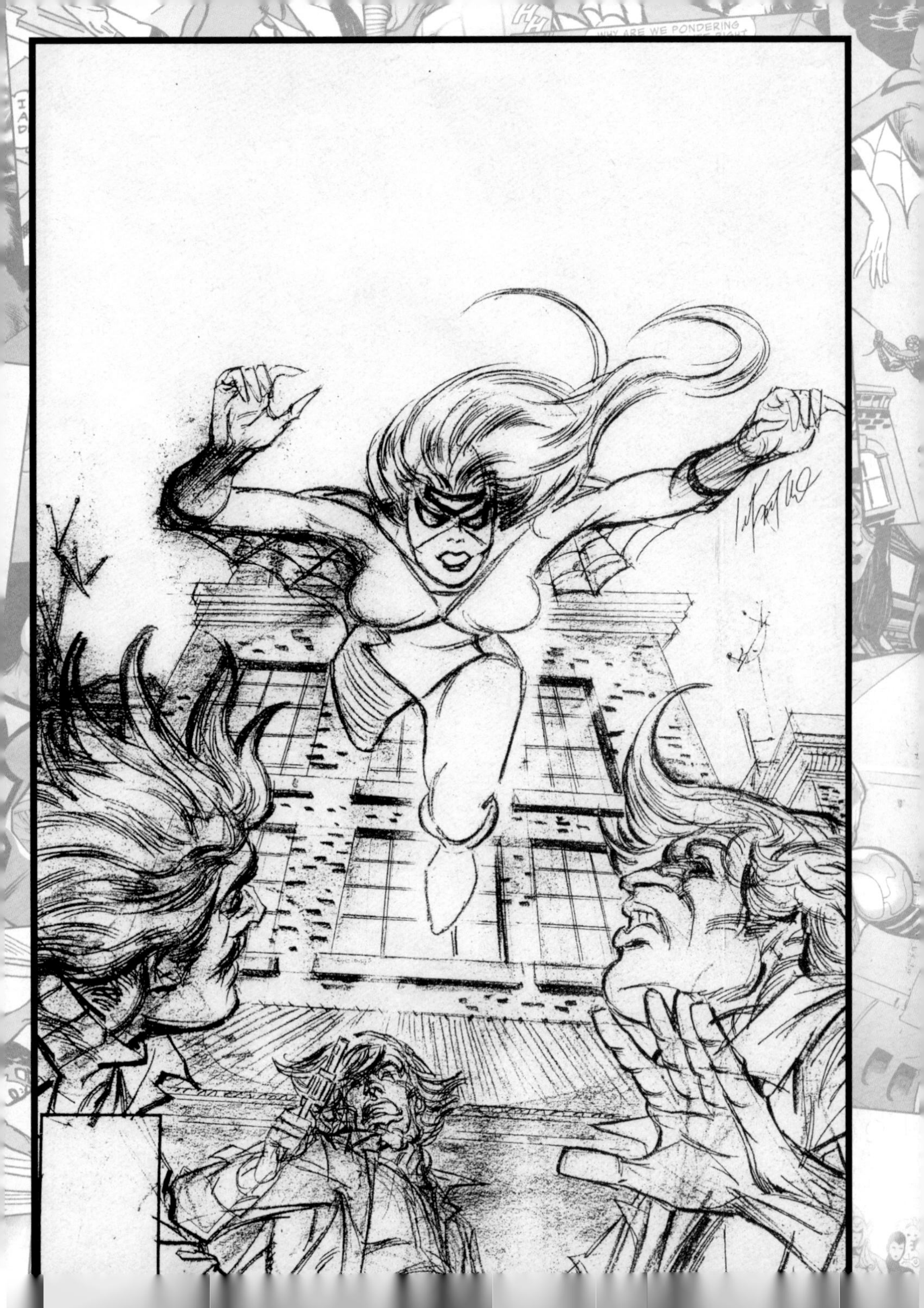
WHY ARE WE PONDERING

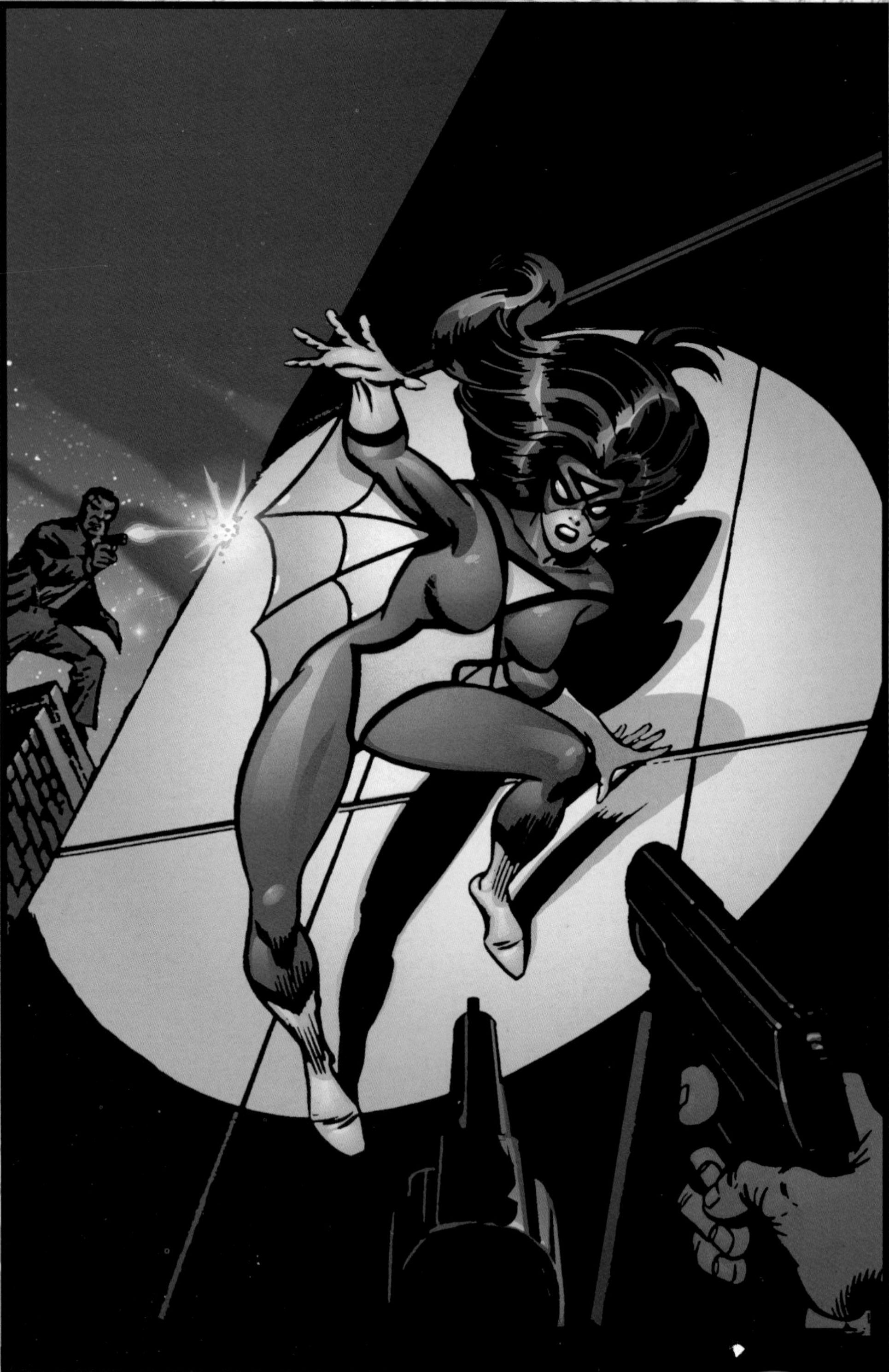

ESSENTIAL SPIDER-WOMAN VOL. 1 TPB

COVER BY JOE SINNOTT & AVALON'S IAN HANNIN